Sugar's Twice as Sweet

A Sugar, Georgia, Novel

By

Marina Adair

FOREVER

NEW YORK   BOSTON

Copyright © 2014 by Marina Chappie

Excerpt from *Sugar on Top* copyright © 2014 by Marina Chappie

Forever
Hachette Book Group
1290 Avenue of the Americas
New York, NY 10104

www.HachetteBookGroup.com

Printed in the United States of America

First Edition: November 2014
10 9 8 7 6 5 4 3 2 1

OPM

Forever is an imprint of Grand Central Publishing.
The Forever name and logo are trademarks of Hachette Book Group, Inc.

The Hachette Speakers Bureau provides a wide range of authors for speaking events. To find out more, go to www.hachettespeakersbureau.com or call (866) 376-6591.

The publisher is not responsible for websites (or their content) that are not owned by the publisher.

ATTENTION CORPORATIONS AND ORGANIZATIONS:

Most Hachette Book Group books are available at quantity discounts with bulk purchase for educational, business, or sales promotional use. For information, please call or write:

Special Markets Department, Hachette Book Group
237 Park Avenue, New York, NY 10017
Telephone: 1-800-222-6747 Fax: 1-800-477-5925

To my husband, Rocco,
with you everything is sweeter.

Acknowledgments

I would like to thank my fabulous agent, Jill Marsal, for guiding me through my first year of being a published author. And what a year! You are a fairy godmother, savvy agent, and dear friend all wrapped up in one.

A special thanks to my editor Michele Bidelspach for taking a chance on my work and pushing me to make this story the best it could be, and to the rest of the team at Grand Central for all of the amazing work and support.

I am forever grateful for the amazing women whom I am lucky enough to call friends: Hannah Jayne, Kori David, Diana Orgain, Marni Bates, Barbara Halliday, and, of course, you, Boo.

Finally, and most important, to my fabulous daughter and husband, for understanding that this is more than just my dream and believing in me no matter how crazy things got.

Sugar's Twice as Sweet

Chapter 1

⌒

Josephina Harrington had barely pulled on her pink lace panties and already she knew it was a mistake.

It wasn't the nearly naked part that had her worried. Or the pair of strappy stilettos, which had her teetering in the confined space. What had her sweating was how the hell she was going to stand back up.

Who knew joining the mile-high club could be so dangerous? Okay, so the jet was on the tarmac, but still.

Between her fiancé's high-profile life and orchestrating a Manhattan social front to ensure that Wilson's "career-making moment" went off with flawless perfection, Josephina and Wilson had hardly seen each other, let alone found time to talk about the wedding. So if engineering a totally out of the ordinary sexcapade got Wilson out of his business briefs and into hers, Josephina was more than willing. Especially since lately, "kinky" had consisted of her on top.

Grabbing a pink negligee from her bag, she tugged it

over her head, braced her hands on either wall of the minuscule bathroom, and slowly walked her way back up. A fluff here, a swipe there, and a few seductive kissy-faces in the mirror later, the normally professional Josephina was ready for Mission Get-the-Sizzle-Back.

Cracking open the door, she whispered in her steamiest come-hither voice, "Wilson, can you help me a minute?"

She pulled the door closed and smothered a nervous giggle. Wilson was going to flip, she was sure of it. One look at her in *this* and he would forget the contract, forget his conference call with the senator from New York, forget his pressing emails. Forget everything but them.

Muffled footsteps sounded outside the door and Josephina sucked in a breath. For the first time in—God she couldn't even remember—she felt hope swell.

The jet suddenly shifted as if someone had slammed a door in the underbelly. Had she been in sensible shoes, she wouldn't have been flung backward, wedging her butt between the toilet and the sink. Nor would she have, upon freeing herself, crashed through the bathroom door and flopped into the aisle.

Josephina froze on all fours, fanny up, and swallowed down embarrassment. All of the blood rushed to her cheeks as she took in the five surprised faces staring down at her.

She didn't remember getting up or the distinguished-looking businessmen quickly exiting onto the tarmac. But the look on Wilson's face would forever be seared into her memory.

"Jesus." His eyes raked over her and Josephina no longer felt sexy or seductive. She was no longer a woman claiming her destiny. She felt stupid and silly.

"Surprise," she choked out, resisting the urge to grab an in-flight blanket and toss it over her head. This was bad, she told herself. But not the end of the world. At least she hoped not.

"What the hell were you thinking?" Before Josephina could answer, Wilson held up an exasperated hand. "Never mind. Because that's the problem, you weren't thinking. You never think, you just do." He shook his head in a manner that she knew all too well. She had disappointed him—again.

"You're right." She took his hand. "And I'm sorry. I wanted to take your mind off work for a bit and maybe have a little fun. Besides, I bet those men have been in similar situations."

"*That* was a U.S. state senator." Oh, boy, this was worse than she thought. "*And* the man who will determine if I get the support I need for the new West Side resort. Not to mention a good chunk of the Japanese investors. And *this* . . ." Wilson's gaze raked over her guaranteed-to-make-him-flip blush-colored lace. And he had flipped. Just not in the way Josephina had been hoping. "You know what? I can't do this anymore. I'm done."

"What?"

He jerked his hand back and Josephina felt something inside hollow out.

"I was going to wait, but I think it's better that we do this now."

She wasn't sure if it was her poor choice in footwear or the finality in his voice, but the plane suddenly began to tilt. She gripped the headrest of a leather seatback.

"I can't do this anymore, Josephina. I can't marry you."

Josephina tilted her head, trying to clear her ears. Even though the jet hadn't left the runway, she determined it must be the cabin's pressure distorting his words. Because he couldn't be dumping her. They were perfect for each other.

Everyone thought so. Her friends loved him. Her parents loved him.

Sure, she could be impulsive, even flighty at times. But he said her creative side was cute. He had even said so in the wedding section of the *New York Times*.

"Damn it, don't cry." He handed her his handkerchief.

"I'm not." But she took it anyway, surprised to find she was crying. She never cried. Wilson said it made her skin blotchy.

"We both know that this hasn't been working for a while."

They did?

"Oh, God," she gasped, clutching the handkerchief, which was now a rumpled, snotty ball, to her chest. Everything was suddenly clear. "You said you didn't want to do this now. As in you were going to do this later? Were you just going to wait until we got to Paris and then dump me?"

He ran a hand through his hair before meeting her gaze. "We thought it would be best if they were there. We all agreed that you'd need the support."

"*We?*" The word caught in her throat, choking so bad it hurt to breathe. She'd thought this engagement was her first step in creating something of her own, something she could be proud of.

"Your parents agreed that—"

"My parents?" She stepped forward, jabbing a finger into his chest. "You talked to my parents before talking to me?" She poked him again—only harder, sending him backing away until he collided with an open tray table. "You broke up with my parents?"

"Calm down."

She grabbed him by his shirt collar and pulled him close. "This is calm."

A bitter taste filled her mouth. The only person she'd ever confided in had sold her out. Placed her in the position to look as if she, once again, couldn't successfully manage anything through to completion. Her engagement—as her parents would immediately point out—was another failure in a long list of Josephina missteps.

"This is exactly why we thought to do it around the table," he said. "You just feel and then act. You never take into consideration how it will affect anyone but yourself. I wanted to make this work. Our families get along, we have the same circle of friends. Every time you come with me I think, is today the day she does something that ruins what I've worked so hard to create?"

"I didn't know love could be such a liability." Her voice was small and pitiful. She winced at the sound.

Wilson swallowed and shifted his gaze. *Oh, my God.*

"Did you ever even love me?"

"I tried." His voice was gruff. "But with you, everything is hard, even love." Even if she had been able to form some kind of coherent sound, she never got the chance.

"Mr. Schmitt? I hate to interrupt, but if you want to make it to Paris in time for the meeting the pilot says we need to take off now."

Josephina turned and there standing in the doorway, dressed in pressed barracuda blue and illuminated by a golden halo, stood Wilson's head of business development, Babette Roberts. It was as if the heavens themselves had opened up to shine down on perfection. She was successful, polished, spoke five languages, and glided effortlessly down the aisle in her pencil skirt and Ivy League entitlement. Josephina looked down at herself and seriously considered jumping into a garment bag. And quite possibly zipping it up.

Babette smoothed her perfectly coifed hair and Josephina felt the room swallow her whole. She took a step back, then another, grabbing her purse and slowly making her way to freedom. When she hit the metal boarding plank she turned and bolted as fast as her wobbly legs would allow.

As the jet's engines roared to a start, drowning out the slapping of her heels on the tarmac, Josephina wondered, for the millionth time in as many seconds, why she had grabbed only her purse and not her clothes. And how it took a seven-carat Cartier bracelet, with its couture, diamond-encrusted-hook-and-eye latch—the one she'd spied in Wilson's briefcase last week—winking at her from Babette's wrist to realize that she was a fool.

* * *

Brett McGraw gaped at the screen on the opposite side of the bar, unable to believe his eyes. There, playing in fifty-five inches of HD glory, right below some antlers and next to the neon John Deere sign, were he and a Texas bombshell, twisted like a couple of pretzels. She was partially hidden by a wave of sweat-tangled hair but he was unmistakable, wearing only a black FCC censored tag and a Stetson. She was giving him the ride of his life, panting his name and swinging a distinctively green jacket over her head like a lasso.

Brett squinted at the screen. He remembered the night, remembered the hotel room, remembered winning his first PGA Masters. But he had a hell of a time remembering the girl's name. Until he read the ticker tape running across the bottom of the screen.

And damn near spit out his beer.

Brett leaned in for a second read: *Bethany Stone, daugh-*

*ter of Dirk Stone and heiress to the Stone Golf fortune, was
par for the course when she decided to take her family's endorsement of PGA's bad-boy cowboy, Brett McGraw, from
corporate to private with a single hole in one.*

Dirk Stone and Brett's older brother Cal were golf buddies, which was how Brett landed Stone Golf as his official
sponsor. If he lost Stone, he'd lose a good quarter of his rev-
enue and, he was afraid, Cal's respect. The last thought sent
a bunch of shitty emotions rushing over him.

"I'm fucked."

"In every way that counts," Jace McGraw, Brett's kid
brother and as of late roommate, said sparing a glance at the
television before sliding onto the bar stool next to him.

Jace waved over the bartender, a sexy redhead who was
all legs and cleavage in a tissue-thin tank, red bra, and golf-
bunny tattoo that peeked out when she leaned over the bar,
gifting him with an impressive view.

She looked at the screen, back to Brett, and gave a welcoming smile. "My, my, my, mister Brett, that's a mighty
large censored tag you got there."

Mister Brett flashed his million-dollar spokesman grin
and Jace groaned.

"Two beers and a hundred bucks if we get out of here
without being noticed," Jace said, waving her off.

"You got it." The pretty redhead tucked the bills in
her bra and walked away, hips swaying as if she knew he
was watching. And he was. So was Jace. Although Brett
was looking more out of habit than interest, which was
something he'd had a hard time mustering up lately. Being
wanted for his drive, on *and* off the course, was starting to
get old.

"I was hoping to get here before it hit the networks,"
Jace said.

Brett looked around the bar, noticing all eyes were on him. Especially the fluttering ones.

Resisting the urge to pull his Stone Golf hat lower, he turned to Jace, tilting his head back slightly to meet his dark gaze. His kid brother was built like a bull, had more tattoos than fingers, and with his buzzed head and bad-ass attitude people often mistook him for an ex-con instead of ex-military with one of the best mechanical minds in professional racing. Rather, *had* been in racing, until some journalist, looking for dirt on Brett, exposed Jace's past.

"You could have at least given me a heads up."

"You're lucky I didn't just give them your location myself. Hell, Brett, I haven't even been able to piss without some dill-rod shoving a camera in my face."

"My place is about as bad," a voice said from behind. Brett didn't have to turn to see who it was.

Cal sank down onto a stool on the other side of Brett, his shoulders shoving and his elbows jabbing, pressing all his older-brother bullshit into Brett's space. His brothers were range-tough, bad-ass, and overprotective as hell. And Brett couldn't help but grin because, man, he was glad to see them. Cal and Jace were the only two people in the world who had his back, no matter what.

"Any idea how bad this will get?" Jace asked.

"Not sure what the fallout will be yet," Cal said, picking up Brett's beer as though he wasn't sitting right there. "He needs to lie low and disappear for a couple of months."

The media had been hounding Brett for years, ever since he won his first Masters at twenty-three. This story, Brett's gut screamed, felt different.

"What about Illinois?" Jace asked.

Cal drained the beer. "I think he should skip Illinois."

"The John Deere Classic? They're one of my biggest

sponsors. I'm already on the roster. Hell, my face is on the fucking ad. It doesn't get more southern than a tractor, Cal. And McGraws don't hide."

Jace went on as if Brett hadn't even spoken. "What about the playoffs?"

"He's done well enough in the first part of the year. Even if he skips June and July he should still have enough points to make it into the FedEx Cup," Cal said, looking disappointed as hell.

"Wait! You want me to lie low until the end of August? That's ten weeks!"

Not gonna happen. The last few months Brett's focus had been shit and he didn't know why. There wasn't any one thing he could point to, he just felt indifferent—about everything. Not a good place to be. But if he stood a chance at taking the FedEx Cup this year, he needed to be on top of his game. He needed a win in Illinois.

"Yeah, ten weeks, playboy," Jace said. "Time for the sponsors to settle down and the news to move on to someone or something else."

"Hold up. You are all acting like you've never had a wild one-nighter. She was ready, I was horny, and the rest of it is none of your damn business."

"Actually, when Grandma Hattie started playing the video for her Bible group, in my living room, it became my business." Cal's mouth turned up a little at the edge.

Brett tugged his hat down this time, wishing he could crawl right into it. He hadn't done anything wrong, but Grandma Hattie had been like a mama to him and his brothers. After his parents had died, she'd stepped in and single-handedly raised all three of them. Not an easy task, since Brett and his brothers were a handful.

"Ah, hell." Who wanted their grandma to see them getting it on? Plus, Hattie had the biggest mouth in Sugar, possibly the entire South. "Knowing her, she's set up a paying peep show, complete with popped corn and sweet tea."

"Since it has over a million downloads on YouTube, I'm guessing that's the least of your troubles," Jace said, looking amused enough for the entire bar.

"Again, two consenting, *single* adults blowing off steam. Not five o'clock news material."

"It is when you sleep with Dirk Stone's daughter. His *only* daughter."

Yeah, he got that part.

"First off, that video was taken two years ago," Brett defended. "And before you ask, no, I didn't know she was taping it. And no, I had no idea who she was."

"Yeah, too bad none of that matters. All the press will see is your play-it-loose reputation," Jace pointed out, knowing full well how a reputation can be more convincing than actual evidence.

Brett swore, because Jace was right. Even though Brett didn't talk, women usually did. And he'd never bothered to deny the rumors.

"Damn it, Brett," Cal said. "You'll be lucky if all you lose is Stone's endorsement. If he jumps it won't be long before others follow suit."

"He can't dump me, we have a contract. And as long as I keep winning the others will stick."

"According to Stone, he can and says he will," Cal confirmed. "Your contract is up for renewal after this season. Plus, any sponsor can pull their endorsement if they can prove you acted in a way that could adversely affect their image."

"The man made his fortune selling golf balls. How much morality can there be in golf balls?"

"This is Georgia," Jace pointed out. "A God-fearing,

Bible-thumping state. What the hell did you think would happen?"

"Not this." Brett was always so careful. He might look as if he played life fast and loose, but persona and reality didn't always mesh. He took into account every action, knowing his life was made up of perception and percentages. It was never just his career on the line. A lot of families were dependent on his swing and ability to sell ad space.

Even the residents of Sugar, Georgia, weren't above cashing in on his name, and that income source would dry up real quick if his sponsors bailed. Which was exactly why he took his responsibility seriously. The people of Sugar might live for gossip but they took strong exception to outsiders butting in on their business. They also protected their own—and that meant he had to do whatever it took to ride out the scandal.

He just wished like hell he were enjoying this ride half as much as the girl still gyrating on the screen.

The bartender came back, carrying a tray of beers and swinging her hips in the universal sign for *I'm game*. "Figured your friends would be thirsty, too." She offered up three beers, a bowl of peanuts, and a seductive wink. "If you need me, you just let me know. I'm always available to whet your thirst, Mr. Brett."

"Thank you, ma'am. Seems like you have some thirsty customers over there," Cal said shoving his beer to the side and giving the waitress a polite kiss-off.

She puckered her lips up in a pout and mouthed for Brett to call her before heading off to the other side of the bar.

Cal glared and Brett didn't see the big deal. He was upfront with women, always made sure they knew it was a no-strings situation, always left them more than satisfied, and always acted like a gentleman.

Bottom line—he loved women. And they loved him right back.

"Wipe that smug-ass grin off your face," Jace said, sounding equally amused and pissed.

"The only reason you're still standing is because Payton made me promise to bring you home in one piece." Cal ran a hand through his hair and looked every bit the stressed, single dad of a teen girl.

Shit.

"Payton saw it?"

"No, I got her out of the room before it got good, but she's already asking questions."

"What did you tell her?"

"Nothing yet, but I have to come up with something. She's twelve. *Twelve*, Brett. Do you think she won't hear about it at school? Or from Hattie and her Bible group?" Cal leveled him with a glare. "Hattie's already saying she's going to tan your bare hide. Right below and to the right of that tattoo of yours."

"Wait? Did you say home? As in Sugar?"

"Yup." Now it was Cal's turn to smile.

He'd rather face a whole course of pissed-off sponsors than that town. When Brett left for college it was on a scholarship set up by the good people of Sugar. When he made the PGA they threw a parade in his honor. After his first Masters win they'd named a highway after him.

At the thought of going home with this scandal surrounding him, Brett felt that familiar churning in his gut. It happened whenever he thought about letting people down. Which was why he'd kept his visits home short and sweet.

"Sorry, guys. I can't go home." Even the word felt wrong. It no longer referred to the aged farmhouse they'd been raised in. With his first Masters purse, Brett had built Hattie her dream home on the back side of the family property, which butted up to Sugar Lake. The ridiculous McMansion, with is marble floors and sweeping staircase, was situated right off the newly named Brett McGraw Highway and served as a painful reminder of all that had been lost. "I've got the John Deere Classic."

"We already decided, you're skipping Illinois," Jace reminded him.

Cal put his hands up, effectively cutting off any argument Brett could have made. "What you need to be worrying about is Stone's daughter, especially since she is getting married in a few weeks and tensions in the family are now probably running high. Let's give Stone a chance to lie low. Cool down. Forget about you and his precious baby girl. And give your agent a chance to fix this without having you screw it up by parading around town with a herd of horny golf-bunnies in your wake."

"Cal's right. Giving it a few months to let the media frenzy die down wouldn't hurt," Jace added, and Brett felt like an ass. The earlier stress Brett was picking up wasn't just for him, the stations were probably playing all the footage from Jace's arrest. Every time his kid brother moved on with his life—new job, new town, new girl—his past always seemed to resurface and fuck it up. Brett's career was a big reason it kept resurfacing. That Jace was crashing at Brett's place in Atlanta only made it worse.

If he went home the hype would fizzle. No photos, no story. And in Sugar *no one* would make it easy on the press. Last time the media had come to town sniffing out a story the locals had, with a southern smile and a *Bless your heart*, rolled up the welcome mats.

"You were thinking about helping Cletus host the Sugar

summer golf program for the kids this year anyway," Jace offered, trying to polish the obvious turd that was Brett's predicament. Brett had been one of those kids. Actually he was the flagship student. As far as Brett was concerned, Cletus Boyle was one of the reasons he was a professional golfer and not in jail.

"So basically you two came here to tell me it would be a great place to *lie low* for the next few months?" Beyond a better grip, Brett doubted he had anything positive to offer these kids other than how to fuck up your life in one night.

"I came down here to kick your ass. Cletus came up with the idea of you helping out for the summer," Cal said, piling on the guilt. "Full time."

Full time? "Crap, he saw the video?"

"Called a few minutes after it broke. Thought you could use some time dredging the lake for golf balls and figuring shit out. I happen to agree," Cal said.

Great, Cletus wasn't looking for a mentor for the kids. He was looking for a way to save Brett from himself. Again.

"And Hattie said you promised to MC the Sugar Ladies' summer concert in July."

"I said I'd *try* to make it." Which in Hattie terms meant she was free to leverage his name for a good cause. This time it was the Sugar Medical Center's new pediatric ward. The town had spent the better part of the year trying to raise funds to finish the project—and Brett was their secret weapon.

He squeezed the bridge of his nose, not seeing any way around this. He was already here, in the great state of Georgia, with apparently nowhere pressing to be until the playoffs. Which meant that he had to go back to the one place that made him feel like that scared fourteen-year-old kid who'd just lost his parents, looking like a coward with his tail between his legs.

"Fine, ten weeks," Brett groaned.

* * *

"Aren't you even curious about what Wilson is up to?" Russell, the delivery boy for Big Wang's, asked, leaning against the door frame of Josephina's New York high-rise, a bag of takeout dangling from his finger.

"Nope." Curiosity had faded the second Wilson's jet had pulled away, leaving her half naked and stranded on a corporate tarmac. She was curious, though, about how long a woman, who was clearly wearing the same wrinkled slacks and chocolate-stained blouse from three days ago when she tried to leave the house, could live on Chinese food before she began to look pathetic.

"Because his Facebook status says engaged."

"It's said engaged for the past two years." *Two years, seven months, and eleven days.* Josephina dug through her wallet and pulled out two bills.

"To Babette Roberts," Russell threw out.

Josephina froze. Her eyes flew to Russell's.

"How do you know?" she whispered, hating the way her voice shook.

"Sherman told me when he let me up."

Sherman was the doorman. He took his job seriously, and his gossip to the bank. If he was telling the delivery boy about her disaster of a life, the entire co-op had been informed days ago.

Great. Just great.

It explained why Mrs. Goldstein had left a bottle of

scotch and a collection of chick-flick DVDs on her doorstep yesterday.

"Well, good for them." She shoved the money at Russell while reaching for the bag. She needed wine, grease, and a good cry. Immediately. And she wasn't willing to show weakness in front of witnesses. Not again.

But Russell held on, tugging back. "Um, it's actually twenty-seven, thirty-five."

"It's usually twenty-five with tip." She should know. She'd ordered Chinese takeout every night for the past eleven days. The first night, Russell had forgotten her fortune cookie and she had cried all over his red BIG WANG'S: 24-HOURS SERVICE T-shirt. The next night he'd brought a half dozen cookies and extra napkins.

So when she, once again, let out an ugly sniffle, Russell took a small step back.

"This is all I have," she whispered, hating how she'd once again managed to come up short.

"That's all right," Russell said. "How about you go freshen up while I set up dinner. Then after we can start the healing process." He waggled his brows and—

"Ohmigod. Are you offering a ten percent discount to Big Wang's in exchange for sex?"

"A little rebound nookie to go with the extra fortune cookies." There went the brows again.

"No and no." She slammed the door, but not before grabbing the bag of takeout.

"What about my tip?" Russell shouted through the door.

"Here's one," she shouted back. "Offering sex in exchange for two bucks might be considered offensive."

"It was a good offer." The heavily accented voice came from behind her.

Josephina turned around and saw her mother's housekeeper standing at the bedroom door clutching a stainless-steel coffeemaker to her bosom.

Rosalie shrugged one meaty shoulder. "He's right, you need a man. It will help with the pain."

"I *don't* need a man."

What she needed was a new life. She looked around what had been her house for the past few years and wondered when it had become so sterile. Clean lines, steel beams, and polished marble floors. Not a thing was out of place—except for her. Not that she knew who *her* was any-more, but Josephina decided that she'd like the chance to get to know the person she had been before—before the en-gagement, before the career-making-moment, before she let everyone's expectations and lives snuff out her own.

"Well, that's good because more of that," Rosalie looked pointedly at the takeout and added a few clicks of the tongue, "and your thighs will jiggle. Men don't like women who jiggle," Rosalie said, as though she weren't shaped like a squat pear with tiny legs that forced her to waddle every-where she went.

"Now, what do you want me to do with this?" She held up the coffeepot. It was a roaster, foamer, Frappuccino maker, and carbonator all in one—and it was Wilson's fa-vorite appliance.

"You don't have to help me pack, Rosalie," she said, although she was secretly happy Rosalie had come. She'd boxed up more stuff in the past hour than Josephina had managed all day.

For three weeks, she'd stared at the door, thinking this had to be some kind of mistake and that at any minute Wil-son would walk in and everything would go back to the way it was supposed to be. Then, last night, while watching *Under the Tuscan Sun* and inhaling a red velvet cake, she realized that she didn't want to go back to the way things were.

Even scarier, no matter how hard she tried, she couldn't pinpoint the exact moment she'd lost balance in her life and in turn lost herself. Which was why she was moving out. It was clear that Wilson wasn't coming back—he hadn't even called to see if she was okay or tell her that he was engaged to someone else. And every moment she stayed there, in the place she thought she'd grow old and raise babies, the regret ratcheted tighter around her chest, until breathing hurt.

No, she needed to leave—and pronto. Problem was, the only place she had to go was her parents' house, where the couture décor and upstate judgment would be equally suffocating, just in a different way. Even thinking about it gave her hives.

"Your mother pays me." Rosalie narrowed her eyes. "She says to come here and help you. You say you need to move. So I fill boxes. Now—"

She held up the coffeemaker again in question.

"Salvation Army box," Josephina conceded, although every cell in her body was screaming to dismiss Rosalie and fix this mess on her own. But who was she to risk her mother's wrath over a few stupid boxes?

"What about this?" Rosalie held up an old shoebox covered in stickers and glitter and enough memories to make her heart jerk painfully. Then jerk again until it somehow landed in her throat, creating a whole new set of problems. Because there, in Rosalie's pudgy hand, was a part of Josephina's past that she hadn't thought about in years.

"Where did you find that?" Josephina gently took the box and walked over to the couch.

She'd cried so much over the past few weeks, she assumed more tears would be impossible. Yet as she slipped open the lid and saw the photo resting atop a pile of letters and keepsakes, her eyes went blurry. This pain was different, as though it originated from someplace old and forgotten, and it packed the kind of power that made breathing almost impossible.

Josephina didn't know how her life had spiraled so far from center, but she did know that she hadn't felt as free as the girl smiling back at her in years. She picked up the photo and traced a finger over the rolled edge. It had been taken the summer she'd turned ten and her parents had gone on one of their trips to Europe, leaving her, once again, with her aunt.

It was one of the best summers of her life, spent making mud pies and learning from Letty how to make real ones. Which was why she was standing on a wooden chair in pigtails, pearls, and a too-big apron, with flour down her front, a whisk in her hand, and a smile of sheer pleasure on her face.

If she closed her eyes she could almost smell the bite of lemons and hear Aunt Letty's voice: *"Careful, child. If you have to beat it that hard then you're missing an ingredient. Might look perfect today but come morning that meringue will be a big pile of trouble, stinking up the fridge for days to come."*

Josephina placed the photo on the coffee table and carefully thumbed through the box. She dug past drawings and sketches—mostly in crayon and big swirly letters with hearts over the *i*'s—through magazine clippings and all of the ideas and dreams she and her aunt had cooked up for the old boardinghouse that Letty had called home, stopping when she found what she was looking for. At the bottom, postmarked six weeks before Letty had passed, sat a yellow envelope.

With a shaky breath Josephina opened the flap and pulled out the letter. The paper smelled like lilac and mothballs, and Josephina wanted to press it to her face and breathe in. A faded photo of Letty, standing on the front steps of Fairchild House in mud boots and a rain slicker, holding a jug of her finest moonshine, fell to the couch.

She remembered that last summer, sitting curled up in Letty's arms while looking out the windows of the salon as a summer storm blew past and listening to Letty recount the story about how her great-great-aunt, Pearl Fairchild, came to call the magical boardinghouse home.

According to legend, Letty had said, *the two-story Plantation-style house was built in the mid-1800s by the first mayor of Sugar, Jeremiah Sugar. It was a masterpiece designed to win the heart of the beautiful socialite Pearl Fairchild, who, moved by his romantic overture and promises of a life filled with adventure, left her family and New York behind to become Mrs. Jeremiah Sugar.*

Even the name sounded perfect. But after two months of travel, first in a train and later in a horse-drawn wagon, finally walking the remaining eight miles to the house, Pearl realized there was nothing sugary about her husband-to-be.

The man whom she had defied her parents for, had given her heart to, stood in the foyer. His slacks hung around his ankles, his face blotched red, while his pale backside engaged in rapid undulation under the housekeeper's smock, so engaged that he failed to notice her enter the residence or even pick up his beloved mayoral gavel.

Pearl never took his last name, the mayor's body was never found, and the housekeeper—prone to gossip—never had to work another day in her life, instead spending the rest of her days as Pearl's handsomely paid companion. Thus, the Fairchild House, boarding for the adventurous, was born.

Josephina turned the photo over and on the back, Letty

had simply written: *Come home, Fairy Bug. Your adventure is waiting for you.*

Fairy, she remembered, clutching the photo to her heart to keep it from breaking, was because Letty swore Josephina was born to fly. The bug part was to remind her that sometimes she had to get dirty to really live.

And more than anything Josephina wanted to live again—really live. She tucked the photo into her pocket and looked at Rosalie. "I need a car."

Chapter 2

It was official. Brett was exhausted. A little under two weeks back in Sugar and he'd already dredged the lake, helped out the local Booster Club with their yearly jog-a-thon, gotten the first set of campers settled, and agreed to play a friendly round of golf with the mayor—and local press.

He was in desperate need of some time on the course—alone, which was where he'd been coming from when he ran across—

"What the hell?" Brett swerved, narrowly missing a golfer decked out in cultured couture, stomping down the middle of the road. He pulled over to the shoulder of Brett McGraw Highway—which, in Sugar, was nothing more than two narrow lanes, one going in each direction, through the middle of a cattle pasture edged with oak trees and barbed wire—and rolled down his window

"Must have been some drive," he said, leaning out the window and watching her approach. "The nearest hole is about eight miles back that way."

He'd walked this same road more times than he cared to count as a kid, dragging a worn-out set of clubs, looking for an escape.

The leggy blonde, tugging what looked to be—a bunny on a leash?—stormed past his truck without sparing him a glance as the set of golf clubs, slung across her back like a samurai sword, nearly took out his side mirror. She wore some kind of skirt, silky and uptight and still somehow managing to hug every curve. Exposing a damn near perfect set of never-ending legs that balanced on the most ridiculous pair of heels he'd ever seen, which for some reason turned him on.

Wait, did that trailing dust mop just bark? Yup. Under the pink bows was a dog that seemed about as friendly as its owner.

"Afternoon."

Even though Golfer Barbie was clearly working to ignore Brett, he was a good ole boy and a gentleman, and would never pass a woman in distress. He pulled alongside her. She was weighted down by a bag of clubs, a couple of wheelie suitcases, and a dog with rat-sized legs. Those shoes weren't helping but they sure made her world-class ass sway in a manner that made his day suddenly seem less shitty.

"Ma'am?"

She stopped, her blue eyes narrowed into what had to be the best screw-you look he'd ever seen. The soft planes of her face folded into a scowl, pursing her lips out in offense. The dog growled.

"Ma'am?" she repeated.

Aw, she was a Yankee—her polished subtle accent giving her away—and obviously offended by his southern manners. The starched top, accessory on a leash, and stick-up-her-ass attitude told him probably Upper East Side. Not that he'd spent a lot of time in New York, although he had been with enough bored socialites looking for their wild round with the PGA bad boy to spot one of her kind.

One arm on the wheel, the other hanging out the window, Brett asked, "You need a hand?"

She crossed her arms, pulling the leash taut and cutting the yip off mid-yap, and opened her mouth to speak. Her eyes darted to the bed of his truck and then did an exaggerated roll before narrowing to two pissed-off slits.

"Nope," was all she said, and continued to head due north. The word was thrown over her shoulder and sounded an awful lot like the four-letter kind.

Brett looked back to see what had taken her from pissed off to hostile. All he saw was his bag of golf clubs.

"Sugar," he hollered. Since *ma'am* had set her off, he was hoping *sugar* wouldn't make her snap. "You can walk for five miles in any direction and you're going to end up nowhere. And there's nothing that way but Sugar Lake and an old boardinghouse."

"Good. Since that's where I'm headed," she enunciated slowly, and if Brett hadn't been so busy checking out her swing, he would have noticed she was mocking him.

Easing off the pedal again, he followed the sound of her heels smacking the asphalt, which was loud enough to be heard over his diesel. It had been a while since he'd had to chase a woman. And for the first time since he'd come back to Sugar, Brett found himself smiling. He was actually enjoying himself. And if that wasn't a testament to just how crappy his life had gotten, he didn't know what was.

"Well, how about that? Me, too. So, why don't you hop in and I can give you a lift?"

"My aunt told me never to trust a balding man."

"Balding?"

She spared him a very brief and very annoyed glance, jerking her chin toward his Stetson. "Men wear it to hide their lack of hair."

"My hat?" He hit the brakes. The dog bared its teeth. "It's a southern thing."

"Uh-huh." She kept walking.

Brett grinned. He suspected she would rather walk back to New York in those shoes than admit she needed help. "Well, I'm never one to push a lady but I am a southern gentleman and I'd hate for anything to happen to you out here on the open road. So I'll just drive along here beside you with my air-conditioning on high, maybe sipping from this ice-cold bottle of soda, just to make sure you get to where it is you're going. Okay?"

Her shoulders sank a little and she stopped. Raising a hand to shield her eyes, she took in the long stretch of pavement that cut through endless miles of sun-dried hills, which housed enough snakes and armadillos to make even the toughest cowgirl balk, only to disappear into the horizon. Her shoulders slumped a little more and...*shit*...she was gonna cry, he could sense it.

He was about to say he'd call Lavender Spenser, who owned the only tow truck in town, to check out the car he had seen a few miles back, then disappear before the waterworks started, when she spun around. And that was not the look of a woman on the verge.

Instead she glared at his truck and, dragging what appeared to be her life, stepped closer to take a peek inside. She placed her hands on the door and gave his rig an aggressive shove, smiling when it didn't budge.

Then it was his turn for inspection. She gave him a thorough once-over that was so clinical and suspicious Brett was sure it was meant to make him squirm. It did, but not in the way she intended. Because the harder she looked, the higher up that pert little nose went, the more pronounced her delicate cheekbones became, and the farther she stuck out that full, glossy lower lip of hers—and the harder he got.

"You a rapist?"

"Nope."

He hadn't considered how he must look to her in lived-in jeans, worn-out shitkickers, and a John Deere–embroidered polo that had seen better days. He had skipped shaving this morning—actually he'd skipped it yesterday, too—and his hair, in desperate need of a trim, was curling out from beneath his hat. The look screamed uneducated hick, but he'd been trying to get in a few holes without being recognized.

Not that it had worked. The beer cart girl, Lindsey—or was it Lena—gave him a cold long neck and tried for a hot kiss, scribbling her number on his scorecard when she failed.

He'd just finished his hole, a birdie no less, when people started gathering around, wanting to talk about the season, get tips on their swing, play a round with him. So he'd packed up, resigning himself to heading back toward the ranch, and maybe having a slice of Grandma Hattie's peach pie.

Opening the truck door, he stepped out of the cab, around Mrs. Madison Avenue, and her little dog, too, stretching his cramped muscles and flexing a bit in case she decided to look his way. She didn't. She was back to inspecting the truck.

He reached out his hand. "Name's Brett McGraw." When she just looked at his outstretched offering as though it was a snake about to bite, he stuffed it in his pocket and leaned back against his rig, which was conveniently parked next to a highway sign boasting his name. Crossing his ankles, he gifted her with his cover-of-*Sports-Illustrated* grin—and waited.

It didn't take long. Her eyes went wide with recognition. Two cute pink spots appeared on her cheeks and she gasped. In just about three seconds, she was going to be batting those lashes in his direction, telling him how sorry she was for treating him like he was some kind of perv, and asking—no, begging—him for a ride. And not just in his truck. At least that's what his lower half was hoping. His upper half was telling him to get back in the cab and get the hell out of there.

"Ohmigod." Her hand, the one holding the leash, came up to flutter in front of her stunned, dangling jaw. In the process, she yanked the little rat, which had its leg poised to piss all over his truck, out of firing distance. "Oh. My. God."

And here it comes... "You're that tractor salesman?"

"Excuse me?" Brett blinked. Then choked a little, remembering the ad he had done a few years back for John Deere.

Holy shit. She had no idea who he was. Meaning she had zero expectations. The notion made the hollow pit in Brett's chest, the one that he'd been carrying around for over a decade, fade a little.

"I'm right, right?" She looked back at his truck, two tons of steel testosterone with enough power to haul whatever the hell he wanted to haul. "You're the cowboy from that television commercial who sings that song while the cow pulls him around."

"Something like that," Brett said, picking up one of her suitcases and dropping it in the bed of his truck. She was the first person all day who hadn't wanted anything from him, which was probably why he was set on helping her. Finished with her suitcases, he reached for her bag of clubs, the back of his hand grazing the curve of her neck where the strap rested.

God, she was soft. She smelled like a lingerie store and some kind of flower. All he could think of when he looked at her was sex. She seemed to know exactly what he was thinking, because she shifted those two pissed-off slits back in his direction.

"What are you doing?" She clutched the bag to her chest.

"Being neighborly."

He waited for her to let go. All he got was silence. Uneasy, mistrust-filled silence.

"Good lord, Yankee, you are the most suspicious person I've ever met."

"Says the man in the creepy truck offering women rides. And who said I wasn't local?"

"Your accent. New York by the sound of it." He looked at her outfit and raised a brow. "A Madison Avenue address?" She scowled. Bingo. "And it's not creepy, it's called being a gentleman."

Although, when she crossed her arms, accentuating the generous swell of her breasts, the last thing he felt was gentlemanly.

"Now, how about you let me get on with my southern manners and load up your things?"

He gave a tug, surprised when she tugged back. Even more surprised at his reaction to getting her all riled up. And she was plenty riled. Why he enjoyed irritating her, he couldn't say. But when those eyes flashed his way, shooting off attitude and irritation, all of the bullshit in his life seemed kind of stupid.

Letting her win this battle, he let go of the bag and watched her stagger a little under the added weight before walking around the truck to open the passenger door. "You coming? Or do I need to call the sheriff and tell him some crazy lady and her ferret are loitering on my property?"

She hitched the golf bag higher in her arms, a nine-iron shifting up and out a little as if the bag was flipping him the middle finger. She looked around the miles of rolling hills and highway. "I'm on a public highway."

"No, ma'am," he drawled, playing the part of the hillbilly. "This here is all McGraw land. Sign right there says so. And that means you and Toto are trespassing."

Rooted in the middle of the highway, reluctance and exhaustion playing across her face, she looked lost. Lost and sad and maybe a bit scared. He hadn't noticed before, but under all that sass and primping was someone trying to hold it together.

Brett stepped back around the truck, stopping in front of her and softening his voice. "Look, it's hot out and will be dark soon. If that Bentley sitting in the middle of the field back there was yours, you've already walked a good couple of miles." He looked at her shoes. "Which I'm betting seemed like a lot more. At least let me give you a ride back to your car. I can drop you off somewhere or go into town and get some gas and help you get her running again."

"She's not out of gas," she pointed out, as if he'd just offended her entire sex. "My cheating bastard of an ex decided to report his car stolen. It has one of those antitheft thingies. It just stopped working."

Which would explain the shrieking horn and flashing lights. "How did it get in the field?"

"The alarm gave me a warning and I was driving kind of fast. Figured if he was going to screw with me he could search for it."

"It's probably got a GPS. They'll find it pretty easy."

"I was hoping for a pond. A deep one. Full of scum."

She shrugged, her top shifting in the process and exposing a very lacy, very pink bra strap, making him more than aware of how tight his jeans suddenly seemed. Because, well, he was a guy, and he'd been without a woman a lot longer than most people knew. "I didn't find one."

"Lucky him." Brett smiled, thinking about that strap and wondering if it matched her panties.

"Lucky him, I didn't drive it through the lobby of his career-making moment." Her hands made aggressive air quotes around the last three words, adding, "And it's bullet-proof," with more air quotes, as if that would explain away everything.

That was his cue to walk. He didn't do complicated. Because complicated usually came with expectations. And this woman had more expectations than her wheelie suitcase could possibly hold. Plus she was kind of crazy. Sexy as hell. But crazy nonetheless.

Brett could almost hear Cal's voice, not to mention the one inside his own head, reminding him how pink lace hadn't panned out so well for him in the past. And it was obvious that *this* woman and *her* pink lace were nothing but trouble. But Brett didn't get to where he was in life by playing it safe, not when trouble was so much more fun. Which was why he was determined to get her into his truck.

"If you want you can call the sheriff. His name is Jackson Duncan and he can give me the Sugar stamp of approval."

"All right," she conceded, desperation—and possibly her shoes—winning out.

She balanced the golf bag between her feet and reached into her purse. Hands fluttering through all eighty-seven pockets, they finally pulled out a cell. Pink. She punched in some keys and waited, her face going blank after about fifteen seconds. She stared at it, punching harder and tried again.

"Rat bastard!"

She pulled the phone back, wound up, and let her fly. They watched the pink metal glisten in the sun before shrinking into the horizon to finally disappear.

"Nice arm."

Ignoring his comment, her eyes went to his truck again. "How tough is your truck?"

"Chevy tough."

"Uh-huh." She gave his tire a swift kick. Not impressed. "Tough enough to withstand a head-on with a Bentley?"

"It's American." He meant it as a testament to how badass his truck was. But she mumbled something that sounded vaguely like "figures."

"You promise to take me to my car so I can get the rest of my things—"

"There's more?"

"And get me to where I'm going, untouched?"

"Yes, ma'am."

She still didn't look convinced, which made her a lot smarter than he was. This trip home was about lying low, playing it safe. Not picking up designer women with purse-sized pets. Sighing, he ushered her toward the passenger door, her fuzzy companion letting loose sounds that were about as intimidating as a Christmas carol. He reached around to help her inside, but paused, content to watch her struggle with her dog, purse, and bag of clubs. Finally realizing that they wouldn't all fit, she thrust her clubs in his face and went back to tending to the dog.

"Listen, Barbie, Toto here isn't going to pee in my truck, is she?"

"My name is Josephina. This is Boo. And *she* is male,

which means he's predisposed to making public statements whenever he feels his masculinity threatened." She eyed his truck again and smiled.

Brett looked down at the tiny dog covered in white fluff that was teased, sculpted, and pinned back with a pink bow. Two wet black eyes looked up at him and Brett actually pitied the fuzzball. Until it leaped over the center console, made himself at home in Brett's seat, and started gnawing on the steering wheel.

His mistress, on the other hand, climbed into the passenger seat, while Brett took a minute to admire the view before hoisting her clubs to toss them into the back.

"Wait," she said, grabbing at the strap.

"It won't fit. Besides, already got my own set, Jo. Nicer than," he looked at the label and mumbled, "those Stone clubs."

"Josephina," she corrected. "And how do I know those aren't from your last victim?"

"Same way I don't know if you used those clubs to emasculate Rat Bastard."

She nibbled her lower lip for a long minute and then let go of the bag. But not before she snagged one first—a nine-iron.

"Good girl. Now promise me you don't have him locked in that trunk of yours."

This time she smiled—and man, what a smile. Who knew that a smiling blonde wielding golf clubs could mess with his mind like that?

Clearing his throat, he tossed her bag, sans the nine-iron, in the back and climbed behind the wheel, looking to see if he managed to crush her dog in the process. No such luck. *Boo* sat happily on her lap, tail wagging as she stroked his head. Lucky dog.

"What's that for?" Brett nodded to the nine-iron, clenched in her hand like a billy club. "We already established you know of my commercials and I have the sheriff's support."

"I never got to call, remember? Plus, you're male, which means 50 percent of what comes out of your mouth is a lie. I'm not taking any chances."

Chapter 3

*D*on't cry don't cry don't cry.

"Hey, you okay?"

Josephina's eyes flew open and landed on the infuriating golf pro—oh, she knew exactly who Brett McGraw was. She'd thought he'd drop her off, she'd say thank you, and he'd leave. Unfortunately, he felt the need to see her safely inside.

Only they weren't inside. He was squatting in front of her, looking concerned, while she sat in the middle of Fairchild House's crumbling walkway with her head jammed between her knees, breathing like a woman in labor.

Okay, maybe she was breathing hard because she found herself eye level with his I-hit-a-thousand-golf-balls-a-day pecs and I-don't-use-a-caddy abs. Even the scruff on his face added to the whole sexy cowboy image.

"I don't know," she whispered, her eyes going back to what was supposed to be her do-over, just as it had been for her great-aunt when her fiancé died in a blaze of D-Day glory.

One look at the dilapidated old boardinghouse and she saw not one sign of paradise.

Instead, there sat waist-high mustard weed, an impressive collection of washing machines—no dryers—a rusted-out tractor and...was that an outhouse?

Good God, what had she been thinking?

She hadn't, she admitted. She'd been caught up in the lemon meringue memories of a little girl that had never wilted—but the house certainly had. Transforming the peeling paint, ramshackle porch, and what appeared to be a small posse of opossums burrowing in the heating duct into a boutique inn specializing in five-star luxury, highly personalized elegance, and southern hospitality for the city dweller was far beyond her bank account's capacity.

"Jo?" He placed his hand on her back and—great, vibes. The kind that started in the belly and if nurtured would quickly move lower.

She was homeless, carless, phoneless, fiancéless, and unwillingly attracted to a man who was too smooth, too pretty, and smelled like sex.

Josephina Harrington didn't do sex. Not anymore. Post-lingerie-landing debacle, she had decided to give up on the penis-carrying members of society indefinitely. Unless they wore a tool belt and knew something about indoor plumbing.

"I'll take that scowl as a, 'Why yes, Brett. I'm just fine. Thanks for asking.'" Brett rose to his feet, extending a hand and a slow, sexy smile that had the ability to melt panties off women everywhere.

"You know what?" Ignoring his hand, and that smile, she pushed to her feet, making her way up the porch to peer in the window. "I'm fine."

Fairchild House might be one strong breeze away from

falling apart, but at least it wasn't hiding anything. Josephina bounced on her toes, trying to get a better look inside. All she could see was sheet-covered furniture and cobwebs. Lots of cobwebs.

"Really? 'Cuz you look a little pale."

"I'm fine," she said reassuringly, wanting to punch him but settling on searching the front porch for the table with the key, which was where Letty hid it. If she found the key, Brett could leave and she could settle in for a good cry.

"I have a headache." She briefly eyed him. "Probably from the music. All that twang made my ears bleed." She went around one side of the wraparound porch. No table. "Or maybe the cologne. It's a bit strong." The other side. Nope again. "Maybe a combo." She stopped by the front door, Boo slamming into her ankle with a yip. "Where the hell is that key?"

Josephina realized she was about to cry and spun to look out at the scenery. She needed a distraction, and an oak tree surrounded by rusty appliances seemed about as good as it was going to get. Her aunt Letty's hollow promises somehow hurt worse than Wilson's betrayal. Any hope of reconnecting with that *something* she'd lost faded about as quickly as the girl who'd snorted when she laughed, baked cookies in sneakers and pearls, and woke up every morning loving her life.

She had been looking to renovate Fairchild House as a way of getting back to that magical place—rediscovering her inner awesomeness. Too bad she was so busy looking she didn't see what was really in front of her: a condemned life with a rodent problem.

Swallowing back panic, she looked at the money-pit in front of her and considered doing something irrational. Like setting Wilson's car on fire. Then demanding that her parents explain how they forgot to tell her that her fiancé accidentally slipped and fell into bed with another woman, so they could call her overdramatic and somehow blame her for the failed nuptials.

A small little whimper sounded, followed by a wet tongue laved at her ankle. Apparently Boo was panicked, too. She didn't blame him. She had ripped him out of his plush Manhattan high-rise and forced him to drive cross-country, only to find out that home was a two-story litter box.

But it was *her* two-story litter box. More important, it was eight hundred miles from Manhattan. Eight hundred miles from friends calling to say that Wilson was a jerk; that they never liked Babette; which meant they knew about Babette. Even Mr. Wang's delivery guy had known, which made her idiot *numero uno*.

Made—past tense.

She straightened her shoulders. "You guys get takeout way out here?"

"No, ma'am."

"Good," she said, ignoring the "ma'am" and making her way down the front steps.

Rounding the passenger-side door, she extracted the nine-iron from inside and went back up to face the window to the right of the front door, club swinging dangerously.

"Hold up, sugar," Brett said, snagging the club a second before impact.

"Give it back."

"You're thinking too much like a city girl." Brett raised the nine-iron above his head, palming hers like a basketball and holding her immobile when she began jumping up to steal her makeshift house key back.

With one last, failed attempt, she settled on slanting him a really hard look. "It would've gotten me in."

"Along with every mosquito and critter in the county." *Damn.* She hadn't thought of that. "Seems to me, you need someone to show you how things are done here in the South."

"Oh, and let me guess. You're just the man to show me."

"All right, I'll show you, since I hate to hear a lady beg. But my expertise doesn't come cheap."

"I am not sleeping with you."

"Sugar, sleeping is the last thing we'd be doing." He slid her a wink. "But seeing as I barely know you, and I'm not *that* kind of guy, I'll grant you one kiss."

Josephina looked at the door and knew she was going to cave. Because if a kiss was the only thing standing between her and getting inside that house, then she'd pucker up and take it like a woman. She wasn't sure what was on the other side of that door, didn't even know what to expect, except that if she failed to get inside, this moment would mirror the last fifteen years of her life. And she was tired of failing.

"Fine. Get me that key and I will give you a kiss guaranteed to rock your hillbilly world."

Big words for a woman who had rocked the world of exactly zero men in her life. Whereas Mr. McGraw was not only reported to leave members of her sex panting his name in ecstasy, he had a video with fifteen million downloads to prove it.

Grinning, Brett reached around her, grabbed the knob of the door, twisted, and there, sitting on the entry table, dangling from a life-sized bust of Kenny Rogers, was the house key.

"Kenny Rogers?"

"Letty loved her some gambler," she mumbled, staring at the key, and purposely averting her eyes from the white envelope with her name on it. "And who puts a key inside an unlocked house?"

"Better than putting a key inside a locked house," Brett said, walking closer, each click of his boots on the wood porch making her quiver. He deliberately invaded her space, forcing her to step backward, until she came flush with the door frame.

"You keep forgetting, you aren't in New York anymore, Jo," he drawled, purposely dragging out the O. "Round here people respect their neighbors."

"Josephina," she clarified, swallowing hard when he slid an arm around her lower back, his fingers grazing the skin at the waistband of her skirt.

Finally he whispered, "Now about that kiss."

Yes, that kiss, she thought, her eyes sliding shut. If this was the southern way of respecting one's neighbor, then she might legally change her name to Joie-Beth-Marie and get herself some big hair and a gun rack, because his lips looked amazing.

Scratch that. Was she seriously considering kissing a stranger just three weeks after ending a four-year relationship? Nope. Definitely not. Even if the only recent tears she'd shed had been over a bruised ego, Josephina Harrington did not go around locking lips with random guys.

"Yes, about that kiss," she whispered, resting her palms on his incredible pecs and pressing him back against the other side of the door frame. "You have to close your eyes if you want to see the fireworks."

Brett's eyes went heavy, the side of his mouth hitching up into a crooked grin, but he followed orders. Making sure his eyes were shut tight, she bent down and picked up Boo, who delivered a hot, wet, doggie kiss guaranteed to rock his world.

"What the..." Brett spat.

Boo growled.

Josephina made her way back down to the truck, giggling to herself the whole way. Ignoring the two males glaring at each other on the porch, she pulled a suitcase out of the truck. Then another.

After making a big show out of wiping off his mouth with the back of his hand, Brett stormed after her. "What in the hell was that?"

Boo, equally offended, snapped at his heels the entire way, barking him out.

"Come on, you didn't really expect me to kiss a complete stranger?" He looked dumbfounded, as though he'd expected just that. "I don't know what kind of women you've been dating." His right eye twitched at her comment. "But where I'm from, a kiss usually follows dinner and a night of dancing under the stars."

"Under the stars, huh?"

He was making fun of her for sounding like some naive schoolgirl. A reaction she was used to. But for some reason, this time, it made her smile.

"Yup, the stars and the moon and the city lights."

"Okay." Leaning forward, he rested his forearms on the bed of the truck. "How about dinner then? You, me, and a million fireflies?"

"You want to go on a date? With me?"

"A date? Why, Jo, I'd love to."

"Sorry, I don't date bald guys."

"Oh, for God's sake."

Tearing off his hat, he smacked it across his thigh. Boo barked hostilely. Josephina rolled her eyes at the pathetic display of bruised egos and—

Sweet mother of God. Her mouth went dry. Which was the exact opposite of what was going on in her panties.

Brett McGraw had thick, dark waves that her fingers

itched to dive into and explore, especially the unruly curls that were slightly damp and licked at the base of his neck. And those eyes, no longer hidden beneath the brim of his cowboy hat, caught in the sun and were the most intense shade of blue. It was unnerving.

Slipping his hat back on, he smiled, a small dimple dotting his right cheek, and Josephina felt her happy parts stand up and cheer.

This is how it starts, she warned herself. They charm you, use your family connections, and then *bang*. Yup, they *bang* their head of business development, who ends up wearing the bracelet *you* picked out last spring in Italy. Then they come home tired and ready for bed, making you feel about as appetizing as a can of Spam.

"Little curly for my taste." She set her last bag on the ground. "But, hey, thanks for the ride."

He blinked. Several times, and it took everything she had not to laugh or give herself a much-deserved high-five. Apparently, Brett McGraw didn't get turned down—ever.

His brows furrowed. Then he grabbed one of her bags, holding it hostage while examining the house. "Okay, you've seen the house. It's a heap. Where am I taking you? The closest motel is two towns over, so I'm guessing—"

"What makes you think I'm not staying here?"

He gave an amused snort and tossed the bag in the back of the truck, grabbing for another.

"What are you doing? Let go of my bag." She yanked the suitcase free and slammed it on the ground, narrowly missing his foot. Boo barked his support.

Brett took off his hat and looked at the sky as if asking for divine intervention. Her dad did that a lot around her, too.

"Look, you don't have a phone or a car, and I doubt this place even has electricity." Facts she was well aware of. "If you give me a minute to stop by my grandmother's, I can take you to Atlanta."

Josephina's stomach fisted into a painful ball. She didn't want to go to Atlanta, or anywhere else for that matter. She wanted to stay here, in Sugar, and forget everything that had happened.

"Just think, in two hours I can get you checked into a fancy room with a view of the city. A nice bubble bath, a little room service. Then tomorrow you can book yourself a flight—"

"I don't need room service. And I'm not going back!"

"Who knows what's crawling around inside?"

"I can deal with a few rats."

That seemed to amuse Brett. "You know, everything's bigger in the South."

"Are you referring to your penis?"

"No, I was referring to the size of our rats, which could carry your kissy-boo dog to their lair. But since you brought it up—"

She held up a hand. "No. And I believe it's Texas."

"Texas?"

"Yes. The saying, it's everything's bigger in *Texas*. Georgia is the peach state."

Brett's grin widened and a wicked twinkle flashed in his eyes. "Now who's talking dirty?" When she didn't laugh, Brett seemed to soften. "I'm just saying that you need to be realistic."

"What I need is for you to get the hell off my property."

"Christ, I've never met such a stubborn woman." Brett rubbed at the back of his neck. "Wait? Your property?"

"Yes, my aunt Letty left Fairchild House and all of its giant-rat glory to me."

"Holy shit. Joie?" No one had called her that since, well, him.

"Josephina—"

"I know who you are. The little blonde pixie who claimed to be able to fly, but I had to rescue from that big old oak tree."

"I never said I was a pixie." She'd said fairy. "I said that I was merely working on my levitation skills." And she had been. In her head.

"You still afraid of heights?"

"No." *Kind of.* "And since we have established who I am, that would mean you're the one trespassing, *Bart.* Maybe I should call the sheriff."

"Brett," he corrected. "And you'd need a phone to do that."

She shrugged, grabbed one of her bags, and dragged it up the stairs, smacking each step in the process, hoping he'd take the clue and leave.

"Fine," he hollered after her. "At least let me bring in your bags, check the electricity, and make sure there aren't any bears or squatters hiding inside."

"Bears? Do I look stupid?"

"No comment," he grumbled, picking up four bags at once and, with ease, setting them in the foyer before stomping through the house, mumbling derogatory things about the opposite sex.

Josephina walked into the entryway and forgot to breathe. The outside might need a nip here and tuck there...or possibly a complete facial transplant, but the inside was just as she remembered it—magical.

The entryway, circular and whimsical, spanned the full two stories. Its hand-painted ceiling highlighted the enormous crystal chandelier that hung between two staircases, which hugged either wall, meeting in the middle and creating a freestanding walkway.

When she was little, Josephina used to lie on the entry-way floor and stare at the ceiling, trying to imagine how many fairies it must have taken to create such a beautiful home. Because behind the gilded crevices of the ceiling was where fairies lived, Aunt Letty would say. And if you looked hard enough you could see their wings flutter, spreading their magical dust.

"What are you doing?"

Josephina opened her eyes to find Brett's gaze locked on her, a strange expression on his face. She realized what she must look like with her arms outstretched, palms up, eyes closed. She'd been twirling.

There were a million intelligent and worldly explanations she could have given, and a few minutes ago she would have. But instead she smiled and said, "Trying to catch fairy dust."

To her surprise, Brett smiled back. Not that his smiling was all that surprising, given that it was the international calling card of womanizers everywhere. But this smile was not contrived or given for maximum impact. It was a natural curling of lips that happened when someone was experiencing joy.

The lights flickered overhead and Josephina realized that the power was on. "Guess I've got electricity."

Brett walked down the stairs, stopping in front of her. "Running water, too. Though I'm not sure I'd drink it until it was tested."

"No bears?"

"No bears."

"Great. Then I guess I'd better get started setting up camp."

"Is that your way of telling me that you're tired of my company?"

"Pretty much."

* * *

Fairchild House sat on the banks of Sugar Lake, nestled among eleven acres of overgrown pecan plantation. As when she was young, her heart caught as the fading afternoon sun filtered through the wind-blown willows, casting a canopy of mottled shadows over the surface of the lake.

The estate, equally majestic, was made up of the main house, a detached garage, five servants' quarters, and a small wooden dock that was one storm away from sinking. Josephina's goal was to turn the house into an inn, the servants' quarters into private guest suites, and the dock into a place where people could check out small boats and fishing gear.

After Brett left, she quickly unpacked and changed into work clothes. Her goal was merely to dig a path between the porch and the garage before sundown, hoping to find her aunt's old clunker. Ten minutes in and she'd become distracted by a single yellow rose peeking out from beneath the ragweed. When Josephina had visited, she and Aunt Letty spent hours tending to her roses. Somehow being knee-deep in the dirt made her feel connected to her past and her aunt.

Desperate to uncover the beautiful rose garden that she knew hid beneath, she'd started pulling weeds. That had been about three hours ago. The muscles in her arms and thighs burned, and she was certain she could cook bacon off her shoulder blades. Fading or not, SPF five thousand was no match for a hot Georgia sun.

Josephina was on the losing end of a stubborn fistful of ragweed when she heard a phone ring. Standing up, she dusted her hands off and listened. It was coming from inside the house. She trudged up the steps and pushed through the screen door, the hinges squeaking on their axis, protesting a century of openings and closings.

The ringing came from an old rotary phone, which sat on a table next to the front door. Pushing the hair out of her eyes, she picked it up and gave a tentative, "Hello?"

The only response she got was the rustling of pearls in the background.

Josephina closed her eyes and sighed. "Hey, Mom."

If this conversation went anything like the one she'd had a few days ago while driving to Georgia, she'd need a seat—and a strong shot. Which was why she picked up the phone, dragging the extra-long cord outside, and plopped down on the porch swing.

"How was Paris?" Josephina tried again, this time forcing a smile into her voice.

"You would know if you had bothered to come. Rosalie said you didn't even want to stop by the house before you took off."

"I needed time to think." *To figure out who I am without Wilson—and without you.*

"Which is what I was giving you. But instead of figuring things out, deciding the best way to handle the situation, you made an even bigger mess."

"I didn't do anything wrong."

"You stole a car, *Josephina*."

"It was *our* car, Mom." She twirled her finger through the coiled phone cord.

"It was a juvenile attempt to get back at Wilson and you know it." She did, and having her mother point it out made her feel even more pathetic. Thank God she didn't know about the golf clubs. "You were hurt, I understand—"

"Am hurting, present tense—"

"—but to leave without a word to anyone, to me or your father, your friends, only added to the speculation."

"I called you. Told you I was going to Sugar. You said reopening the inn was impulsive, another attempt to avoid growing up and dealing with the real world." Josephina closed her eyes and willed back the tears. "You knew, Mom. You knew he was having sex with Babette and you never said a thing."

"Oh, honey. I was with my ladies club when I saw them together. What was I supposed to do, make a scene?"

"Your ladies club? God, Mom, I had lunch with Margret and Elena the day before Wilson dumped me!" Elena was supposed to be one of her closest friends.

"Your father and I told Wilson he needed to come clean. We all thought that Paris would be the best place to do it."

"So you could ruin the most romantic place on earth for me?"

Josephina could almost hear her mom rolling her eyes, mouthing to her father that she was being overly emotional.

"I wanted to be there for you, to hold you after, to cry with you." Josephina started to soften, her anger melting at her mom's words. "And to stay nearby in case you decided to do something rash."

Rash? Like put his dry-clean-only, custom-tailored Armani suits in the washer with a red sharpie and a box of glue sticks? Or rash as in cash out her savings, what was left of them, and Letty's trust, to renovate a dilapidated old boardinghouse in the middle of cow country?

"We think that you should come live with us for a while. Maybe put one of those degrees to good use. Go back to working with your father."

At present, she held a dual degree in hospitality management and interior design. When she'd realized her father had no intention of letting her work her way up the ladder like everyone else, since Harringtons were meant to lead, not serve, she left the hotel industry and went to culinary school.

She'd been hired on as the morning pastry chef at a hotel in Manhattan, one of the few her parents didn't have an inside connection with, when she met Wilson. He was charming and successful and sophisticated—and her boss. That he asked her out was surprising. That he found her unrestrained take on life sexy had floored her.

Her odd schedule, which directly conflicted with his, was wearing on their relationship and, he pointed out, holding them back. Determined to make it work, Josephina left the restaurant to become an assistant to one of the most respected event planners in New York. And Josephina was damn good at her job. So good, in fact, that Wilson began having her plan his parties on the side.

Eventually Wilson's events dominated her schedule, leaving no room for her career, forcing her to resign and make his goals hers. Which was how she'd wound up spending the past two years hosting galas and fundraisers with the sole purpose of advancing Wilson in the social scene of Manhattan.

She had been exactly what Wilson needed. Until he hadn't needed her anymore.

"Let us help you through this," her mom said, and everything inside her wanted to give in. Wanted to let her mom fix this, because she was scared and alone and she was really hungry.

Josephina wiped at her cheeks and stubbornly shook her head. "No, thanks, Mom. Your kind of help hurts too much."

Her mom's breath hitched and she let loose a few shuddery sniffles. Josephina felt bad, she did, but they had hurt her, too, and she didn't want them to fix her life anymore. She needed to fix things for herself.

"Josephina." Her father pronounced each of the four syllables precisely.

She closed her eyes and swallowed past the thickness in her throat. Dealing with her mom was one thing, but her dad had the ability to make her feel guilty without even saying a word.

"Hey, Daddy."

"You okay?"

Josephina shook her head from side to side and blinked several times against the choking burn, not caused by the sun but by homesickness. And her mom was crying. And she hadn't hugged anyone since Wilson took off, leaving her standing in pink lace and utter humiliation.

"Dad, it was mortifying," Josephina whispered, wiping her nose off on the hem of her shirt.

All she wanted was for her dad to come through the phone. To hold her and tell her everything would be okay. That her life wasn't a complete train wreck.

"It was indeed, but not as humiliating as finding out from Mason Stevenson that you stole Wilson's car and took off, tail between your legs. We're Harringtons, Josephina. And Harringtons don't run. Ever. Do you understand what I'm saying?"

"I didn't have my tail between my legs. And I had a key." Josephina let go a shuddered breath of her own. "I really needed to get to Letty's house."

"It's a dump. And you're hiding under those ridiculous plans."

"No I'm not," she defended, feeling three instead of thirty. "And Fairchild House will be a boutique inn specializing in—"

"Fifty percent of all new businesses fail within the first year."

Josephina sat on her free hand to keep from ending the call as her father recited all of the same terrifying statistics he'd used as ammo when she had wanted to open her own restaurant. Expecting him to react like a father instead of a numbers cruncher had been her mistake. One she wouldn't let happen again.

"I know what I'm doing, Dad. I have a solid business plan, a budget." Well, as solid as a plan could be when pieced together on a road trip. As for her budget, the exterior of the house alone was enough to tell her that she might have grossly underestimated costs.

"Uh-huh," her dad grunted.

"I'm meeting with the general contractor next week. He came highly recommended," she lied, purposely leaving out that his name was Rooster and he had been the only contractor in the phonebook—aside from McGraw Construction. "I went to a similar getaway in Italy and had the most amazing time."

"Tell her that Sugar isn't Italy," Josephina heard her mother say in the background, as though she feared her daughter was geographically challenged.

"I know what I'm doing."

"Okay, then tell me how many other inns like the one you've proposed have managed to succeed without the draw of an exotic destination and solid financial backing."

Josephina swallowed and tried not to show her fear. She didn't know. She hadn't had time to look into other inns, to see if what she imagined would work here in small-town U.S.A.

"I am offering people a unique opportunity to experience southern hospitality in an exclusive way. Charming old plantation home, horseback riding, tranquil lake, real cowboys. It will be a novelty for the elite."

"It's another disaster is what it is. Which is why I'm sending the jet. There's a private airstrip twenty minutes south of Sugar. I can have it there in four hours."

If she told her parents to come get her, she'd what? Crawl back to Manhattan and admit she had once again acted on a whim? Admit the house was a disaster? Admit she had failed?

She looked up at the roofline and prayed that the family of opossums would stay up in the attic. She'd heard them rustling around in the ventilation ducts when she'd been unpacking, and the bed in her childhood room would barely fit her and Boo. Because she wasn't going anywhere.

Letty'd found her magic at Fairchild House. Not that Josephina expected magic anymore, but she wanted to wake up and look in the mirror and like what she saw. That wouldn't happen if she went back to New York. It might not even happen if she stayed. But here, in Sugar, she stood a chance.

"You know what, don't bother sending the jet." Josephina closed her eyes and pictured what Fairchild House would look like when she was done. "I love you and Mom. And I am so thankful for everything you've done for me. But I've got to find my own wings now. I'm staying."

Ignoring the familiar feeling of guilt over disappointing her family, she hung up. When the phone immediately rang again, she took the receiver off the hook and dropped her head back with a thud, sending a loose screen crashing to the porch. Boo yelped and scrambled up into her lap. Resting his front paws on her chest, he licked her face.

Overhead, the head of the mama opossum peeked out of the vent and glared down at her, emitting an irritating hiss.

Oh, dear God. Did she really just tell her father that she was staying?

Chapter 4

Two hours later and no closer to finding that rose garden, Josephina showered and threw on some boxers, Aunt Letty's SHAKE YOUR SHAMROCKS T-shirt, and a pair of fairy wings she found in the back of the hall closet. She walked into the foyer, twisting her wet hair into two mouse ears on top of her head, while staring at the envelope sitting next to Kenny Rogers.

Digging into the bag of cheese-flavored pretzels, the only food that looked the least bit appetizing—besides a stash of chocolate bars that she'd already made an impressive dent in— she studied the strong yet feminine letters on the envelope.

Fairy Bug

That was as far as she'd gotten before deciding to shower, find food, clean out the fireplace, measure every cabinet and closet, alter some of the preliminary sketches she had drawn at rest-stops along her trip south, and organize her idea box. Anything to put off opening that letter. Unable to procrastinate any longer, Josephina lifted the envelope.

Seeing her childhood nickname made her throat go tight, so she took another long swig of beer she found in the fridge. Either Aunt Letty was a lush or her home was a front for a strip club. All that was in the kitchen was bar food, a healthy stash of cigars, and enough alcohol to get an entire pledge year of Kappa Delta Sigma plastered.

She dragged the back of her hand across her mouth. Coated in beer foam, powdered cheese goo, and a bit of leftover chocolate, she cringed and then wiped it on the right shoulder of her shirt. The left was already dirty. She opened the envelope and unfolded the letter.

Dear Fairy Bug,

Josephina closed her eyes and sank down to the floor, pulling her legs to her chest and nearly flattening Boo, who scrambled out from under the table. He looked up with his big black eyes and flopped at her feet, showing his support.

I hoped that you'd find your way here. This house was once your favorite place in the world, which is why I left it to you and not your parents. They wouldn't understand its magic, and I can only hope that after all these years you still might remember.

She did remember. Not that she believed in magic anymore. But when she was little, this place, and her aunt, had been heaven for an awkward girl who always felt like a hexagram in her parents' square world.

You were such a special child, too busy soaring and dreaming to get lost in the confines of life. You'll always be a special girl, Josephina, a girl whose true beauty lies in her ability to dream, and you deserve far more than a life spent conceding to expectations. This house healed my heart and gave me the courage to let go of who I was trying so hard to become and embrace who I was.

Child, with your parents, I would be surprised if you still remember how to color outside the lines. Maybe your time here will serve as a reminder. You can't make others happy until you've learned what makes you happy. When you do, grab on and never let go.

All my love,
Aunt Letty

PS. It's hard to reach with your feet on the ground, so don't be afraid to leap, child. The wings will appear. I promise.

Four reads, two beers, and an entire bag of cheesy pretzels later, Josephina lay on her makeshift bed of couch pillows and a quilt in the foyer, staring up at the ceiling, and cried.

What everyone else saw as flighty, her aunt saw as special. A pang of guilt settled in her chest. Last spring, before Aunt Letty passed, she had written to Josephina, asking her to come for a stay, to help her restore Fairchild House to its original glory.

Funny, how over the years, she'd never found the time to visit. But now, when her life was at its lowest, the only person who understood what it was like to live in her head was gone.

"This is why I don't drink," she said loudly, to any of the fairies still awake in the ceiling willing to listen. Even drunk she could tell she was slurring.

She stuck her hands in the bag of pretzels. Damn, empty. Tugging the top rim, she tipped it up, dumping the crumbs into her mouth. Correction, her hair.

She didn't know how it happened, but Josephina had worked so hard over the past few years to become the kind of woman Wilson could be proud of that she'd allowed Wilson's dreams to take over, until there was no room left for her own. No room left for Josephina. And all she'd wound up with was bruised self-esteem, a wallet full of canceled credit cards, frozen phone service, and a set of golf clubs.

Exhausted and tired of crying, she let her eyes slide shut. Somehow she knew that coming here had been the right choice. She still wasn't sure what she was going to do, but just being in this house made everything less overwhelming. If she concentrated hard enough, she could actually feel herself flying.

Feel her wings—move?

She opened her eyes to find someone staring at her. Someone who was rapidly ruining her buzz.

"Ever hear of knocking?"

"Did. All I got in response was snoring."

"I don't snore."

"Guess it was the dog then." Brett flashed his million-dollar grin. One that further ruined her mood.

"Can you point that," she whirled her hand in the air to encompass his trademarked smile, "somewhere else?"

She wanted to pretend she was immune, but feared she wasn't. His grin only widened, so she slammed her eyes shut.

Ah, blessed silence. Then, his fingers brushed her shoulder.

She growled.

Boo barked.

"Gotta say, Joie. Or should I call you Tinker Bell? Kind of hurt that you threw a party and I didn't get an invite."

"You still here?"

"Yes, ma'am."

She opened her eyes right as he reached down and brushed a hand over her belly and a few crumbs scattered to the floor. His hand moved dangerously close to the underneath sides of her breasts, sending them into party mode.

"Stop trying to brush off all of my fairy dust."

"I was actually trying to get the glob of cheese goo off your shirt before you become a sitting entrée for the rats." He winked.

She glared at Brett, who didn't have chocolate on his cheek or dinner on his shirt. No, he looked damn fine. He was freshly showered, clean-shaven, and smelled like sin.

Brett picked up a white plastic bag off the floor and dangled it in front of her nose. Something warm and mouth-watering wafted past. It was sweet and spicy and smelled like...grease.

"Is that what I think it is?"

"Double bacon BBQ burger with fries. Local specialty. Figured you might be hungry. And you might sleep better," he pulled a brand-new, adorably pink cell phone out of his pocket, "knowing you could contact the outside world if the mood struck."

"Food first." Moving slowly to make sure the room really wasn't spinning, Josephina drew in a grounding breath and sat up. Yup, the room was tilted. And swirling. And she just might need to lie back down, which she did.

Brett settled a hand on her shoulder and helped her back to a sit. He eyed the two empty bottles and grinned. "Please

tell me there are more empty bottles lying around somewhere."

"Nope." Squinting, she narrowed her eyes on the bag,
then on him. "Are you expecting a little rebound nookie to
go with my fortune cookie?"

"Is that an offer?"

"No." Josephina felt her cheeks heat, and it was definitely not from the alcohol. Feigning disinterest, she said,
"The bald thing kind of blew it, remember?"

"You might want to tell that to your hands."

She looked down. Whoops, somehow her hands had tangled themselves in the bottom of his shirt. She snatched
them back.

Rising to his impressive height, and placing his most
impressive part in her direct line of sight, Brett set the takeout next to Kenny and offered her a hand. He pulled her
up—and so far into his personal space their thighs brushed.

"Thanks for dinner," she said all breathy.

"There's an extra patty in there for Fido." *Fido* bared his
teeth, and not in a nice way. "And this," he held up the cell,
"I wasn't sure if the phone was working. I tried calling but
only got a busy signal."

A normal occurance when the phone was left off the
hook.

"It's already programmed with my number. Just hold
down this button and you can get hold of me."

She glanced at his movements. He'd programmed himself as number one—of course.

"Thanks. I can pay you back in—" She had no idea
when.

"Think of it as a housewarming gift." He slowly slid
the phone into the waistband of her boy-shorts, her stomach
quivering as his calloused fingers brushed her bare flesh.

Her eyes dropped to his mouth, lingering there long enough for him to notice and grin. But when she looked up he was staring at her the same way and they were standing awfully close. Close enough to kiss.

"You did that on purpose."

"Are you mad because I touched you or because you responded?"

Because you are making this whole "done with men thing" really hard.

"Thanks for, well, everything. It's nice to know that if I get eaten by a family of opossums I can contact the authorities so they can tell my parents. But beyond that I'm just…" Too tired to fake it anymore, she dropped the manufactured attitude. "I came here because… well, I don't know why anymore."

The charm-your-pants-off smile that was Brett McGraw, PGA Playboy and everybody's best friend, faded into something softer, something genuine.

"Because of that?" He tilted his chin toward the stack of sketches littering the floor.

Before she could stop him, he picked them up, slowly sifting through her drawings. To anyone else they might seem like pencil lines on paper, but those were her dreams, the way she envisioned Fairchild House.

Despite the panic bubbling inside, Josephina straightened, bracing herself for his reaction. She'd heard it all before. Her parents had pointed out every flaw in her plan, every reason why she would fail, completely discounting all of the work she had put into Wilson's career-making hotel.

Brett got to the last page and looked up. "Seems like a pretty big undertaking."

"My parents think it's an impossible undertaking," she replied, doing her best to sound confident. Because suddenly everything they had said was coming true and she wasn't sure if she could do this.

Brett looked around and she knew he was checking out the watermarks above the fireplace, the crack running down the far wall, the way the upper walkway seemed to sag a bit in the center. But then he looked back at her and shrugged.

"I didn't think anything was impossible when you were wearing these." He lightly tugged on her fairy wings and she felt a simultaneous tug on her heart. "This town needs an inn, a warm place for folks to stay when they come visit. Your aunt understood that. She was one of the strongest women I knew. Stood down my grandma a couple of times when I was a kid. My brothers and I used to think she was magic, a fairy guardian, she'd call herself. And I can see a lot of Ms. Letty in you, Tinker Bell."

"Thank you." Those two simple words didn't even begin to explain what he'd just done for her, but it was all she could squeeze out past the tightness in her throat.

Leaning closer, he ran a finger down her wings and waggled his brows. "Did you know I have a thing for fairies?" She laughed. And it felt good. "Hand to God. It has something to do with those skimpy little petal dresses."

She went up on her toes and kissed the cleft of his chin. "Why couldn't you have been a hog farmer?"

The room fell silent. Brett searched her gaze for a long intense moment, his own reflective and uncertain.

To diffuse the sudden shift in mood and bring it somewhere closer to manageable, Josephina gave him a playful shove. Which did nothing, considering he was built like the side of a mountain. He was also slow to move away so she backed up and held open the door. He followed, Boo prancing excitedly at his departure.

"If you need anything—" He stopped at the top of the

steps, the easygoing Brett securely back in place, and ran his eyes down the length of her body. "And I mean, *anything*. Call me."

Irritated that she was all flustered, she opened her mouth to give a breezy, not-affected-in-the-slightest laugh. Instead, a giggly and semihusky, "Not gonna happen," came out, followed by a mortifying snort.

"We'll see."

* * *

Brett rolled over, his skin squeaking against the sticky leather. He'd achieved exactly fifty-seven minutes of sleep, a kinked neck, and a bad case of bed head. Best night of sleep he'd had in three weeks.

Damn, this house was going to kill him. It was too big, too clean, hell, it even smelled like a new car. Hattie and Payton had spearheaded the decorating, making it a shrine to everything that's wrong with the world. Every inch, including the guest room, was an infusion of Minnie Pearl and Paris Hilton—redneck chic. Which was why he'd decided to take up residence in Cal's office—the only room Cal had a say in—even though cramming his over-six-foot body onto a toy-sized sofa was never a good idea.

Or maybe it was the fact that he'd accomplished jack shit since coming home to "lie low." No matter what Cal called it, it still felt like hiding.

He looked around the office and took in just how far the McGraw brothers had come. Cream-colored walls, a comfortable sitting area composed of overstuffed leather furniture. It was a far cry from the three-room farmhouse he and his brothers had grown up in.

A gallery of photos hung above the mantel. In the center

of the collection was a shot of their parents that Cal must have salvaged from the fire. His parents had been in love, all the way up until the moment they died, there was no doubt about that.

Brett found himself wondering what that felt like, to love someone so much that the rest of the bullshit didn't matter. Not that he'd ever want that for himself.

Oh, he understood the desire for that kind of love. Saw it in his parents' eyes growing up, watched how his dad's entire world revolved around a little bit of a woman. His dad's love went soul deep. That's how it was for McGraw men, they went all in. So much so that Brett knew his daddy died because living without his wife would have been too hard.

Then watching Cal's entire world crumble when his wife, Tawny, walked out was a harsh reminder for Brett to keep it simple and surface with people—especially women. If Cal hadn't had Payton to focus on, Brett didn't know how his brother would have bounced back.

Deciding a hot cup of coffee and a morning spent on the course was the only way he was going to clear his head, Brett pulled a pair of sweats out of a box and dragged them on. They were black, brand-new, and fit perfectly. Just like the other fifty identical pairs, which he got from one of his sponsors—a sponsor that he might lose.

Cal and Payton were already awake, most likely getting ready to head out for their annual father-daughter Disney World vacation. Payton was frying up some bacon and eggs. Cal sat at the table, staring at his daughter and looking surly.

"Uncle Brett," Payton said a second before she launched herself into his arms.

"Morning, kiddo." Brett pressed a kiss to his niece's forehead, then leaned a hip against the counter.

"Thank God, you're up. Please tell Daddy that wearing a

two-piece is not the end of the world." Payton's voice rang with dramatic warning—if he sided with Cal it would be the end of her world.

"I don't think he has the body to pull off dental floss and triangles." Problem was, Brett suddenly noticed that his niece did. When the hell had that happened?

"Conversation's over, Payton, so drop it," Cal said wearily.

"But it's already packed."

"Easy. Unpack it."

"I think something is burning." Brett jerked his head toward the smoke coming off the skillet.

"Grandma's teaching me how to make Daddy's favorite breakfast," Payton explained as she walked back to the stove and, pushing Brett aside as if he weighed as much as Joie's rat dog, flipped the bacon. "I made the first batch of biscuits."

Brett had tried some of her biscuits the other morning, which was why he was skipping them today. The girl was a disaster in the kitchen, but Hattie was determined to make a southern lady out of her, which included mastering all of the secrets in the McGraw recipe box.

"Now, Daddy," she said, dragging the word out until Brett considered skipping breakfast altogether. "About—"

"No means no." Cal's eyes went wide, then hard. "Remember that!"

Payton rolled hers. "All my friends wear two-pieces."

A few months ago, her standard had been cleats, scabbed knees, and a ponytail. Today she wore a flowery sundress, cowboy boots, and a sweet smile that said she was a proper cowgirl. A proper cowgirl who was going to have every young buck this side of the Mississippi knocking down her door.

"They also wear makeup and scraps of denim they think pass for appropriate attire."

"Why are you being like this? I'm thirteen."

"Twelve."

"Almost thirteen. And old enough to choose my own clothes."

"So you've said."

"I had to muck the stalls for over a month to earn enough money to buy it, which means I should get to wear it."

Brett filled up a mug of coffee and bit back a grin. Damn, that girl had Cal's number. He was already squirming in his chair, ready to cave.

Payton gave Brett a quick wink and set down a plate—eggs over easy and heavy on the bacon. "Right, Uncle Brett?"

Now it was Brett's turn to squirm. He hated being in the middle. When it came to Payton he was normally a yes man, but looking at his brother, bloodshot eyes, gripping his mug as if it were the neck of some kid who had the balls to ask his daughter out, Brett felt sorry for the guy.

He took a bite of bacon. Chewed once and forced himself to swallow. The bacon and the grimace. "Thanks."

Payton's phone chirped. She glanced at the screen and let out a dramatic sigh. "Ever since your video went viral, *all* my friends are begging to come over and meet you." It chimed again. "Kendra wants to know if she can bring her mom?"

Brett felt the tips of his ears heat. "Listen, about that, honey." He stopped. How the hell was he going to explain to his niece that the reason he'd ended up baring his butt to the world was the same reason she couldn't wear a bikini. Boobs made men do stupid things.

"Daddy already explained it."

"Did he, now?" Brett was interested in just what his brother had told her.

"Which is why I should be able to express myself." She folded her little-girl arms across her no-longer-little-girl chest. She was as single-minded as her mother had been when it came to getting what she wanted. "My two-piece is a form of self-expression, just like your tattoo."

"She's got a point," Brett said, wondering how much of his video she had seen and thinking that a teenager's two-piece had to cover more than the woman he'd interacted with. Didn't it?

"Payton, did you tell your uncle that our resort is hosting Florida State's high school football summer training program?" Cal snapped off a piece of bacon, his teeth grinding it to sawdust.

Now Brett knew why Cal looked ready to kick someone in the nuts. He knew what Brett knew. That what she'd be expressing and what teen boys would be interpreting would be two different things. He knew because he'd been one himself. Had talked many a girl out of a teenage two-piece.

He wondered how many daddies had wanted to kick him in the nuts when he was a teenager? How many still did?

Shit.

Suddenly every line, every smile, every pickup phrase he'd ever used came back to him with nauseating speed. There was no way in hell Payton was going to wear a bikini. Ever. He didn't even think she should be allowed near a large body of water. Starting today, guy was a four-letter word.

"I'm not wearing it to impress some boy." Payton laughed, breezy and fake, while bending over to wrap her arms around Cal's shoulders, hugging him from behind. "I'm wearing it for me."

Cal managed a provoked expression and turned his head, waiting until Payton rested her cheek on his shoulder.

Finally, he whispered, "Great, then you can wear it in the hotel room and putter around in the bathtub."

"That's so unfair." Payton stepped back, her lips puckering out in a perfected pout. "You never let me do anything other kids my age get to do. You're ruining my life!"

Two seconds later she burst into tears and raced out of the kitchen.

Cal pushed his plate back and dropped his head to the table with a thud. "How about you take her to Florida and I stay here with Hattie?"

"Are you crazy?" Brett said, staring at the empty doorway. Payton was usually so easygoing, like him. It's why they got along so well. "Who the hell was that? And when did she start getting—" He gestured helplessly toward his chest region.

"Don't say it."

Fine by him. He couldn't. Boobs and his niece weren't something that belonged in the same thought.

"It supports my theory that the bigger the," Cal made the same helpless gesture, "the crazier they become." Cal looked ready to punch someone again. "I swear to God, if someone had told me my kid would come out looking like my ex-wife I would have married a cross-eyed, bucktoothed, two-by-four."

"Instead of a complicated socialite with the body of a porn star?"

"God, don't remind me."

"Speaking of complicated socialite." Brett opened the bottle of hot sauce and doused his eggs. "Ran into the new neighbor yesterday. Found her stranded on the highway, so I gave her a lift."

"A lift, huh? And what kind of lift are we talking about?" Cal mumbled, lifting his own perfectly seasoned bite to his mouth.

Brett ignored him.

"Letty's girl is here?" Before Cal could savor his forkful, Hattie waddled through the kitchen and grabbed her favorite wooden spoon. White spiky hair gelled up in quills, she wore a blue tracksuit with a yellow shirt, yellow tennis shoes, and a whole lot of attitude. He wasn't sure if she was dressed for church or to run a marathon, but she was still ticked about his video. "Just like a Yankee. No respect for etiquette or tradition."

Hattie pulled out her recipe box, the one passed down from great-grandma Clover, which only made an appearance when impressing was imperative, and started flipping through the pages.

"I need to make a covered dish of some kind for her so she doesn't have to cook. Offer her a proper Sugar welcome." Hattie had already diced up the onions and was moving on to the celery. "I bet that Etta Jayne was home last night baking her up something gossipworthy. She's always trying to look charitable so she can make the rest of us look like sinners."

"She had a burger from town last night." Just the thought of her in those wings turned him on. "But I bet by tonight, she'll appreciate a nice home-cooked casserole."

"See, Cal. Poor girl had to eat greasy-spoon food," Hattie said. "Now, be a dear and grab me some of those mushrooms."

Cal shot Brett a glare. Brett smiled back. Cal set his fork down and stood. Making sure, in the process, to elbow Brett with a sharp *What the hell?* in the ribs.

To which Brett shrugged an equally expressive, *Welcome to my life, buddy. How does it feel?*

He'd spent the past two weeks measuring, mixing, and scrubbing. Not to mention taking in an earful over his wandering ways.

"Maybe some of your coconut cake. Nobody makes coconut cake like you," Brett added.

"Coconut cake," Hattie mumbled pulling out a round pan before disappearing into the pantry, dragging Cal with her.

Brett smiled. Seeing his brother take orders instead of giving them was a nice change.

Cal peeked out from the pantry. "Wait? How does a guy who is off women know what she had for dinner?"

"Just being friendly."

"Uh-huh," Cal grunted, exiting the pantry balancing sacks of sugar and flour, along with a large can of lard. A bag of dried coconut hung from his teeth.

"After we whip up this cake," she said to Cal as if this was now a team effort, "you're going to take me over there so you can watch me give her this welcome basket. Then you're going to tell everyone you see what a gracious person I am, welcoming Letty's kin with my coconut cake. Make sure you remind folks that I had a recent brush with death and still managed to whip out a blue-ribbon welcome. See if Etta Jayne can top that!"

Hattie and Etta Jayne had been best friends since FDR was in office. Also fierce competitors since the Sugar-Pull Championship of '54, when Etta Jayne was crowned Miss Peach with what Hattie claimed was a stolen "Star Spangled Banner" rendition, complete with cowbells and a flame-throwing fiddle.

"It was heartburn, Grandma," Cal reminded her.

"All folks will remember was that I was taken off in an ambulance with the siren blaring."

"You told them that if they didn't run the siren, you'd shoot them."

Hattie ignored him, ignored the fact that she carried a .45 in her handbag at all times, ignored that she'd been arrested three times for discharging her weapon in public, and went back to making her prize-winning cake.

"I'll do it," Brett offered.

"Oh, no." Cal shook his head. "Don't even think about going over there. I know that look, it's the same one you got when Katie-Sue Sherman's dad said she couldn't go to prom with you."

Ah, Katie-Sue Sherman, with her big green eyes and minuscule green dress. "That was a great prom."

"You were a freshman. And she was the superintendent's daughter. And just like Katie-Sue should have been, that new girl—"

"Joie—"

"Whatever." Cal placed his hands palms down on the table and leaned in. "*She* is off-limits."

Brett stood, leaned forward, and mimicked Cal's stance. "I never said I was interested in testing those limits."

"You didn't need to. It's all over your face." Cal exhaled, his expression going serious. "Ever since Mom and Dad died you've been running off to fill any kind of hole you could find. I'd hoped you'd take this time to relax, figure out what's next."

"I'm sitting out until the FedEx Cup," Brett said, shifting a little on his feet. "What more do you want?"

"Come on, Brett, I'm not talking about golf and you know it."

He did know it. Brett had been playing life eighteen holes at a time for so long it was easy to forget why he was running. But being here, back in Sugar, where everything reminded him of his parents—of what he'd lost—was slowly driving him insane. That empty feeling he usually didn't have the time to dwell on was slowly taking over his entire chest, and the only time it had seemed to recede was when he was sparring with Joie.

"No need to go all father-knows-best. I was just wasting time with a pretty girl," Brett said. A surge of emotion pushed through his chest, calling him a liar.

"I get it. But there is nothing safe or low-profile about a girl like that. She is exactly how you can ruin your career." Cal sat down and let out a breath. "And I just went and made her that much more of a challenge, didn't I?"

Brett liked challenges, but he didn't do complicated. It increased the odds of feelings coming into play. And more than complicated, he didn't do feelings.

Women like Joie were all about feelings—complicated feelings. Big eyes, big breasts, and an even bigger attitude couldn't disguise all the pain and vulnerability that she hid beneath all of the sass. More than enough reasons to walk away.

"You two hush up." Hattie walked around the table, her hands dug into her hips. "Knowing Etta Jayne could be over there this minute selling that girl on her corn muffins and chili is nauseating enough without you two yelling over that poor child, who, bless her heart, must have come here to finally put Letty's memory to rest."

"Which means easy pickings for a guy like you," Cal added.

"Trust me, there's nothing easy about that woman. She is prickly and stubborn and moody as hell."

"Ah, shit." Cal scrubbed his face with his hands.

"What? I gave her a ride home, brought her some dinner. *Which* she ate by herself."

"All I'm saying is that getting involved with a guy who thinks long-term is closing the bedroom door is probably not the best thing for her."

"Look," Brett said, too tired to fight with his brother. "I have no intention of anything other than being neighborly. Plus she seems serious about renovating that inn. I doubt she—"

"She's renovating Letty's place?" Hattie stood, mid-whisk, her eyes narrowed.

"Yup. She's got some pretty big plans for it." He couldn't help but smile, thinking how her eyes lit up when she talked about it.

Apron off, batter forgotten, Hattie zipped up her hooded jacket—it matched her pants. "I need a ride into town."

"What about the cake," Brett asked.

"Forget the cake," she snapped. "I gotta get to the post office. Then pick up some things for Bible study." Which Brett had a sinking suspicion came in a bottle and was weighted in proof. "You can drop me off at Dottie's after."

"Where's your car?" Brett asked.

"Jackson's holding it hostage. Says I need to get my eyes checked. Told him he needed to get his head checked."

"Sounds logical, seeing as you took out Etta Jayne's mailbox last week," Cal said.

No wonder he didn't ever date. Not only had his ex-wife shattered his world when she walked out, Cal had enough women in his life.

"Took it out with a bat, and I was doing over sixty, which proves my eyesight's fine."

She waddled toward the back door without waiting to see who would take her, just knowing that someone would. She had a pile of Brett's underwear in one arm and a stack of envelopes under her other. Which was funny, because Brett had been hard pressed to find even a single pair of skivvies last week and had to drive into town to buy some new ones. And last time he checked, those were missing, too.

"What are you doing with my briefs?"

"Selling 'em. They fetch a good one-fifty on that World-wide Interweb. Can you imagine?"

Yes, he thought taking a deep breath, he could. "What about the autographed golf balls and T-shirts I left?"

Last visit, he'd spent an entire afternoon autographing swag to help out with the pediatric ward fund for the Sugar Medical Center.

"Interest dropped 80 percent since that video aired," Hattie explained.

Brett shot a look at Cal. "The longer I'm not out on the green the less I'll be worth."

"Which is why I'm changing tactics. I've got folks from all over Facebooking me for a pair." She pointed her chin at the stack in her hand. "Worn they get double, so I took the new ones out to the barn and rolled 'em in the hay a bit. Since most folks figure that's how you spend your time these days."

Chapter 5

The sun was almost as high as Josephina's stress level and she seriously considered, not for the first time that day, doing something impulsive—like stripping down and jumping into the lake.

Even though it was large enough to support small boats and jet skis, the houses on the other side were clearly visible, and that was the only reason she was still clothed. Because if Josephina could see Brett's truck parked beside his grandmother's house—not that she'd been looking—then he could, in theory, watch her swimming in nothing but skin, which was suddenly all tingles and warm fuzzies.

With a resigned sigh, Josephina sat on the porch landing, stared out over the graveyard of washing machines, and stabbed a peach from the can. It was less depressing than the rough estimate Rooster had drawn up and dropped off earlier that morning, which sat next to an even more depressing bank balance.

That was what happened when a woman gave up her career for a man.

She speared the last peach, a tastier meal than her breakfast of pickled okra and cheesy pretzels, but not nearly enough for the day she had planned.

"Looks like we need to get some wheels." Preferably four. Attached to a working engine. She'd found the keys to Letty's car, but no car. With her luck, it was buried somewhere in the barn.

Snuggled into her side, Boo barked in approval. Apparently dog cannot live on opossum jerky alone.

She lay back, hanging her head off the top step, and stared—upside down—out at the endless miles of green, rolling hills, blanketed in bluebells and oak trees. For the first time since her last summer in Sugar, Josephina had a plan that didn't include outside expectations, and it felt damn good.

Her stomach grumbled. "We could always call our favorite cowboy for a ride."

With a growl, Boo jumped to attention, his ears back. Glaring out over the driveway, he paced the top step, his hair mimicking a porcupine ready to spit quills.

"Good point." Closing her eyes, she remembered his offer for *anything* and immediately discarded the idea. "He'd think that the kind of ride I was looking for included sweaty rebound sex."

Not that sweaty, rebound sex with a man whose smile was dialed to launch a thousand orgasms sounded bad.

"Orgasm-deprived or not," she said, trying to remember the last time she had that particular reaction with someone else in the room, "I refuse to sleep with a man just to stock my pantry."

A bead of sweat trickled between her breasts. "Unless he's got a trunk full of popsicles. Then all bets are off."

"I hear ice works, but popsicles never even crossed my mind," a weathered voice contemplated from overhead.

"According to my lady doctor, that's a myth," another, equally aged voice said.

Josephina's eyes snapped open, straining to make sense of the upside-down display in front of her. Four ladies, dressed for church or maybe a funeral, stood on her front stoop. Each had a grandmotherly shape and a quilting bee face, and each was clutching an aluminum-foil-covered dish in greeting.

All of them except the one dressed in a blue jogging suit. With a cake nearly her equal in height, the woman assessed Josephina in a way that had her sitting up and smoothing down her hair.

"Hello," Josephina offered.

The women all stared at her for a long beat, then jumped in, scrambling over each other to be the first to greet the new neighbor.

"Why look at you." The birdlike one holding a crockpot reached out and tugged Josephina's ponytail fondly. She had a long face, even longer limbs, and smelled like Joan Collins. Around her neck she wore a pair of binoculars. "You look just like Letty. Doesn't she look like Letty?"

"Spitting image," Candy-Apple agreed, shaking her head and sending her white hair, spiky enough to poke an eye out, ruffling with the movement. "It's the eyes."

"Nope. It's that fanny. Letty always carried her extra biscuits in the back," one of them said. She was short, round, and with a gray halo could have passed for Mrs. Claus, except for the permanent glare and always-packing attitude. She also had enough casserole dishes to feed a small principality and was shoving a plate of cornbread in Josephina's face. "It's cornbread, dear, to go with Dottie's beans."

Josephina couldn't help but stand, hoping that her backside looked smaller when she was fully vertical. The expression on the face of the birdlike one, who Josephina assumed was Dottie, said she should give up biscuits immediately, so Josephina shoved her hands in her back pockets.

"Don't worry, dear. Dottie always de-gasses her beans." A frail woman in a wheelchair rolled forward, offering a shy smile and a plate that seemed to jiggle. From the wheels rolling over cracked pavement or her shaking hands, Josephina couldn't be sure. Her hair was gray tufts on top of her head and she reminded Josephina of her childhood Sunday school teacher. "It's ambrosia. My great-grandmother's recipe, but with my hands...well, my granddaughter whipped it up."

"I'm Etta Jayne, now aren't you going to invite us in?" the woman with the plethora of dishes asked in a sugary voice. Etta Jayne's smile was as sweet as peach tea, but the way her plump hands stabbed into her hips, she wasn't asking, she was demanding.

Josephina attempted to invite them in and gain some control over the situation—it was her house after all—but realized it would be a waste of breath. Before she could say a word, Etta Jayne was already shuffling toward the front door.

One by one, the other ladies walked past Josephina with a "how nice to invite us in" or "such a good hostess, Letty would beam," through the entryway, past the sitting room, and into the kitchen. Even Jelly-Lou in her wheel chair managed to roll her way up the ramp and into the house before Josephina could blink.

Not only were they familiar with the layout of the house, they made themselves at home, grabbing some plates and taking up residence around the farm-style table. Right on top of her blueprints.

Josephina yanked her papers out, just before platters started hitting wood. After her talk with her mom, she wasn't sure she was ready to discuss her dreams with anyone else.

"I don't know if you remember me, I'm Hattie McGraw." She set down an impressive coconut cake and whispered, "Blue ribbon in three counties," before continuing. "Your aunt Letty and I used to take you fishing."

Josephina did remember, and her chest relaxed. These women were a welcoming sight. They were her aunt's closest friends and knew about Letty's dreams for the inn. "You taught me how to braid my hair."

She was also Brett's grandmother, and suddenly Josephina felt the ridiculous need to impress the woman.

"Always wanted me a girl and you had the prettiest hair. God gave me a son and then three grandsons. It's why I went white by fifty." Hattie patted a motherly hand on the chair below the window. "Have a seat, child, I'm starting to get a crook in my neck from staring up at you."

"Yes, please." Dottie gestured, setting her binoculars on the table.

Josephina did as asked, her heart in her throat that they thought to save Letty's seat for her, as if this were some ceremony at which Josephina was being handed the legacy of Fairchild House and taking her rightful place. Her tension evaporated, replaced by excitement and a feeling of belonging. If anyone could understand her need to do this, it would be these ladies.

"I like what you've done with the place." Hattie cut off a slice of cake and offered it to Josephina.

The kitchen was spacious, with floor-to-ceiling cabinets and hanging copper pots, which screamed country living.

The floor was checkered black and white, the exposed beams covered with cobwebs and what Josephina feared was mold. Just about everything else was yellow—the curtains, the walls, even the refrigerator. The appliances were outdated and the furniture yard-sale antique.

Besides the missing layer of dust, it looked the same. "I haven't done anything yet."

"I know." Hattie smiled, taking a bite of her cake.

Josephina did the same, but found it difficult to hold on to that smile, especially when Etta Jayne asked, "How long are you planning to stay?"

Josephina swallowed, the piece of cake getting stuck in her throat. "Actually, I'm, ah, going to reopen the inn."

All four ladies stopped chewing, expressions set between disbelief and bless-her-stupid-little-heart.

"More of a culinary getaway, really," she rambled on, desperate for them to see what she saw, buy into the potential of Fairchild House—into the potential of her. "Complete with a full-service spa and first-rate amenities, I want to create a space where guests can relax in quaint luxury."

It didn't get much quainter than Sugar. With growing up in the hotel industry and her culinary expertise, plus her eye for detail, this was the perfect opportunity for her.

The women blinked. In unison. Three times. Making Josephina's throat close even further.

"It's pretty far from town," Etta Jayne pointed out.

"Only eight miles," Josephina corrected, her voice strong and unwavering—though suddenly her confidence was anything but. "During the day, guests can explore the town, only to come home and learn how to cook gourmet, southern-inspired cuisine right here in Letty's kitchen."

"Did she say cuisine and southern in the same sentence?" Hattie asked, her eyes filled with concern.

"I don't know," Dottie whispered to no one in particular, her hand over her heart as she took in the kitchen. "I was too busy wondering how she was going to fit a bunch of Yankees in here. Unless—" Her eyes locked on the prep-island and then flew to Josephina, who shifted uneasily in her seat. "Letty taught you the key to a flaky crust at that counter. We'd jar our jellies and jams right there, every summer."

"Remember the summer Etta Jayne bought those dime store lids instead of the Kerr lids?" Hattie asked, her face pinched with sadness.

"They shot right off while we was waiting for that double batch of Letty's bumbleberry jam to set." Dottie picked up her binoculars. "You can still make out the purple rings where the jars were."

The ladies shared a look, one that was filled with memories and connection, but when they trained those eyes back on Josephina all she saw was worry and—her throat tightened even further—their fear that she was going to ruin everything.

"What are you going to do to the salon?" Jelly-Lou asked, her eyes wide and encouraging as though willing Josephina to say the right thing. And she wanted to say the right thing. She really did. But she also wanted these ladies, with their sweet-tea voices and covered-dish welcome, to understand that she was finishing what Letty had started all those years ago with magazine clippings and crayon drawings.

"Eventually, it will be a spa," Josephina answered, an uneasy feeling settling over her as the wistfulness in Jelly-Lou's eyes vanished. "I'm hoping to convert it to house a massage room, a place to do facials, and right there, where you're at, Jelly-Lou, will be the mud bath."

"Did she say mud bath?" Dottie whispered, loud enough for the entire room to hear.

"Who'd bring mud *in* the house? On purpose?" Hattie added, staring at Josephina as though she were dimwitted, and Josephina gave up. She didn't want to be rude to Letty's oldest friends or make enemies out of a group of ladies who had been sweet to her when she was younger, but she was done with people punching holes in her plan.

"It's going to take more than elbow grease and an exterminator to get this place up and running," Etta Jayne said, all the honey gone from her voice.

"Now, Etta Jayne, be nice." Jelly-Lou gave the other woman a long look that would have sent Josephina scurrying for safety. "I'm sure the girl isn't set in her ways just yet. Why, when she really thinks this through and sees how much work is needed to make that happen, she'll realize that a summer home she can come visit now and then would be a fine compromise."

"I'm not afraid of hard work." And she wasn't afraid of these old ladies. Nor did she need their validation. Letty had entrusted the future of Fairchild House to her—not her parents, or her cousins, or the little biddies glaring at her. She'd left it to Josephina, which meant Letty believed in her ability to not screw this up, had faith that Josephina could make the inn a success.

And why not? Her three-tier red velvet cake was so moist it brought people to tears in one bite. She made hosting elaborate parties look effortless. And she beat out Abigail Van Wellington for the title of Miss Dogwood three years running with her poise and kick-ass fencing demonstration.

She might not know a whole lot about running the back end of a business, but she understood exclusivity, ambiance, and entertaining like nobody's business. Reopening the inn was smart, and Josephina was the perfect person for the job. That it wasn't *their* dream didn't mean it couldn't be hers.

"Thank you, for the warm welcome and bringing me dinner"—she looked at the sheer amount of food on her counter—"for the rest of the week."

Josephina stood and headed for the living room, liking this new side of her.

"Are you kicking us out?" Hattie gasped, her hand on her chest as if Josephina had just committed a mortal sin.

"As you so wisely pointed out, I have a lot of work before this place is a bona fide, functioning inn. So, I'm sure you all understand that I need to get busy. I'm halfway to the garage with pulling weeds and I refuse to stop until I unearth Letty's car, which I know is hiding under there somewhere."

"So you're set on tearing this house apart then?" Hattie's silver crop shook with anger. "Dishonoring your aunt's wishes?"

"I'm not tearing it apart, I'm making it better," Josephina defended, making sure that her voice didn't expose how much Hattie's words hurt. "And maybe you all didn't know Letty as well as you thought. She would have loved what I'm doing here. It's why she trusted this house, and her dreams, to me. Now, if you'll excuse me, I have work to do."

At that, the women all exchanged a look, which Josephina couldn't quite decipher, but a tightening in the back of her gut said it wasn't a good sign. Not for her anyway.

Hattie opened her mouth but quickly closed it when Jelly-Lou gave her a reprimanding shake of the head.

"Yankees!" Etta Jayne marched across the kitchen, slowing to a stop as she passed her gifts. Josephina could tell she wanted to snatch them back, but southern etiquette, being what it was, dictated that she forsake the dishes and take her leave gracefully.

The other ladies followed her out of the kitchen and back through the living room, piling up at the threshold. Their eyes all settled on the formal salon, which was situated on the west side of the house overlooking the lake.

"Mud? Inside?" Dottie said with a perplexed shake of the head.

"She didn't even offer us a cold beverage," Hattie said as if that explained away everything.

After seeing the ladies out, Josephina walked back through the house and into the kitchen. She curled up with the cake—the whole cake— and pulled out her designs. In them, she had moved all the seating into the dining room and installed three islands, each with a sink, prep area, and professional-grade range. This would be a perfect place for a teaching kitchen. Arranged right, it would encourage inter-action among the guests and create a laid-back atmosphere for mastering southern fare.

Her eyes settled on the bumbleberry-colored stain, and Boo let out a small whimper. She placed him in her lap and scratched him behind the ears.

"We could always make some kind of cool wall art out of that chunk of the countertop," she said, and Boo yipped. She didn't want to destroy their memories of Letty, but she also didn't want their ideas to completely derail hers.

No longer afraid, Josephina picked up the phone and dialed.

"Y-ello, this is Rooster of Rooster's Roof and Remodels. Shoot."

"Hey, Rooster. This is Josephina Harrington. Come back," she said getting into the southern spirit. When he didn't respond, she added. "Um, Letty's niece."

"Yes, ma'am. I came out to your place this morning and checked the roof. Gotta say, it's not looking too good."

Roof. Plumbing. Electrical. She could go on.

"Didn't want to wake you so I stuck the bid to the front door. Didn't you get it?"

"Yes, I did. Thank you." *All twenty thousand of it.* Josephina swallowed, willing herself to stay strong. She'd avoided calling him because it seemed so final. And she'd been scared.

But the new Josephina no longer did scared!

Not really.

"I was hoping you could come back out and take a look at the rest of the property. I'd like to get a new estimate."

Rooster was silent for a moment. "Excuse me for saying, but that there house is a money trap. It's why your aunt left it the way she did. Fixing it up is going to cost a pretty penny."

"I have to see how many pennies it will cost before I can get a plan together. I'll pay you for any time you spend assessing the property."

"Oh, it ain't that. I just don't want you to get all broken up like Ms. Letty did when you see the figures." Letty had tried to renovate? Why hadn't she said anything? Between Josephina and her parents they could've found the money.

Then again, taking Harrington money meant taking Harrington advice, and her aunt didn't take anything from anyone: money, shit, or otherwise. Letty was a smart woman, Josephina decided. And she was going to strive to be more like her. Starting now.

"It takes a lot to break me, Rooster," she said feeling pretty unbreakable. "And I'd love it if you could give me a ballpark of what it would cost to renovate the entire house with the servants' quarters and dock included in the price."

Rooster promised he'd come over first thing in the morning and, telling herself that it wasn't too late to make her and Letty's dreams a reality, she grabbed the phone book off the counter and looked up the number for Sugar Savings and Loan.

Chapter 6

‏I might have acted without thinking," Josephina mumbled to herself as she looked at her phone. "Again."

After eleven voicemails from Wilson, ranging from annoyed to irate, and nine emails, demanding the immediate return of his golf clubs, Josephina knew that was a gross understatement.

"Please tell me there weren't witnesses," Lavender Spenser, the local mechanic and owner of Kiss My Glass, Tow and Tires, called out over the air compressor.

Two days ago, Josephina had uncovered her aunt's Cadillac parked under a field of crabgrass and next to a nest of feral cats in the side yard. Ulysses S. Grant, as Letty had named him, was green, built like a tank, got nine miles to the gallon, and played Dixieland every time she made a hard left. He also had leaky back shocks and the opossums had chewed through the fan belt, which was why she'd left it at Kiss My Glass while she ran across the street to the bank.

Spenser lay on a dolly in her grease-stained jumper, steel-toed boots, and less-than-sunny disposition. Josephina squirmed on the bench of the rusted-out pickup Spenser had been working on the entire time Josephina relayed the events that led up to her informing Wilson precisely where he could shove his Upper East Side loft and all of its contents.

"No witnesses, but it was in writing."

"Did you email it? You can claim hacker. It tends to stand up better than scorned woman."

Josephina leaned out the window of the Ford, draping one wrist on the peeling steering wheel, and yelled over the drilling of power tools. "I wrote it on this cute stationery I picked up in Spain and taped it to the bedroom door. Handmade by monks. The stationery, not the door."

"Do you have any idea how much you walked away from?" Spenser slid back under the car and mumbled something unintelligible under her breath, which was probably a good thing. Josephina already felt like an idiot; she didn't need a verbal reminder to cement the feeling.

"I don't need his money." Josephina hoped she sounded more confident than she felt.

Spenser's hand appeared and blindly grabbed some socket doohickey out of her toolbox before disappearing back under the car. "Can you start her up?"

Josephina turned the key and the truck sputtered to life. A thousand little bursts of black smoke filled the garage and made the already smothering Georgia heat suffocating.

"Shit! Off, turn it off!"

She did. The truck coughed and gasped. So did Spenser, who came out with her face the color of tar.

"So you're back, you don't need his money, and the dump is yours. Lucky you."

"I understand how, to the unimaginative eye, Fairchild

House might look like a *dump*, but to someone with a trained eye, she's a few coats away from perfection."

Spenser glared, just her eyes and forehead visible from beneath the car. "Don't let the accent and braids fool you, Manhattan. I have more points to my IQ than you do shoes. Everybody in town knows that Letty only had a little over twenty grand in her estate when she passed. That won't even make a dent in what needs to be done, which is how it got to be in its current condition."

Josephina took a bite of her stale doughnut, compliments of Kiss My Glass, and wondered if Spenser was purposely trying to ruin her good day or if she was still angry about the accidental wad of grape gum Josephina stuck in her hair during church when they'd been seven.

With an exasperated sigh, Spenser rolled out and wiped her hands off on a red rag, then dragged it down her face, making more of a mess. "Look, Joie, I'm not telling you anything you don't already know. The truth is, that place is a shithole."

"My magical shithole," Josephina said, leaning on the window frame, pride bubbling up inside. "Which is why I went to see Mr. Ryan earlier. I asked for a loan."

"I hope for his sake his grandma doesn't find out."

"Why?" Josephina asked, wondering how someone's grandmother could influence a business decision. She had gone into the bank assuming Mr. Ryan would look at her assets and laugh. He hadn't, instead saying what a good woman her aunt was, that she was sorely missed by all of Sugar, and he'd need a few days to get back to her. It wasn't a yes but it sure as hell wasn't a no.

"How much?" Spenser cut through the bull.

"Half a million."

Spenser gave a long whistle.

"What?"

"That's a whole lot of debt to take on for a house you haven't bothered to visit since you were a kid." Spenser walked to the pink box on the counter at the front of the shop.

Josephina tried not to notice Spenser's grease-stained fingers sampling all the pastries before settling on the first one she touched—a jelly-filled.

She immediately set down her own doughnut. If the sticky smudges on Spenser's jumper were any indication, this was not her first bite of the day. "It's not a house. It's a culinary getaway."

"Here? In Sugar?"

Ignoring the big glob of raspberry jelly oozing from Spenser's doughnut and her smart-ass grin, Josephina swallowed her growing nerves and looked out over the drums of motor oil and through the open bay door. Giant oak trees lined the cobblestoned walkways, covered in Spanish moss, their gnarled branches intertwined, creating a green canopy covering Maple Street. She took in the six-foot red and blue wooden bull across the street, the Confederate flag flapping above the local bar, and a man moseying across the street—the sidearm holstered at his hip as visible as his package in those painted-on Wranglers.

Ignoring the little voice in her head, the one that sounded oddly like five little old biddies and her parents, she said, "Brett mentioned that the town is in need of an inn."

Spenser looked at her. "Brett McGraw?"

Josephina shrugged, hating the heat she felt rush to her cheeks, and everywhere else for that matter.

Spenser opened the driver's door, wedged herself into Josephina's space, and rested her elbows on the frame. "You already visited with Brett McGraw?"

"Not really. I had some car problems. He found me on the side of the road and gave me a ride."

She left out the part about dinner and the cell phone.

"You two do the cowboy cha-cha yet?"

"Um, no to all implied."

"Considering it?"

"Nope."

Spenser stared long and hard as if Josephina was guilty as sin. No matter how badly she wanted to break eye contact she didn't. It was ridiculous; she was acting like some high school girl with a crush, afraid that the mean girl would find out and ruin her life.

"You got left by your fiancé at some airstrip in your altogether, while he flew off to Europe with his secretary, which means you're single. So you must be lying."

"She was the vice president of business development, actually. And how do *you* know all that?" Josephina hadn't spoken to Spenser since she was a kid, so she had only admitted to the breakup, not any of the humiliating details.

"Your mom called."

"My mom?"

Ignoring Josephina, Spenser continued. "If you're female, you're interested. Brett's sexy, charming, and loves women. And they love him right back. Women in this town have been counting the days until his return. Surprised there hasn't been another parade yet."

"Another?" As in they already had one in his honor?

"Yup. Every time he comes home for a quick visit they throw one. And the women line up, hoping they'll be the one to snag his heart for at least a night. I'm probably one of three single, age-appropriate women in a six-county radius who hasn't slept with or fallen for a McGraw. And it was a conscious decision." Spencer shivered. "McGraw men don't do it for me, which is a shame since they are so damn good to look at. And, I hear, amazing in bed."

"Brett doesn't live here in the off-season?" she asked, not wanting to think about Brett in bed.

"Brett doesn't believe in an off-season. That would mean staying in one place long enough to settle down. And this generation of McGraws don't settle and they sure as hell don't stick. They are missing the commitment gene. Well, unless we're talking about Cal—but he's only taken with one lady and she's his daughter." Spenser's smile disappeared. "Their parents were killed in a house fire when Cal was in college. Brett must have only been fourteen. All of them took it hard."

"That's terrible."

"Cal became Mr. Responsibility. Jace started picking fights. Brett, he found golf and girls, in that order. Small towns being what they are, it's hard to move on when everyone keeps reminding you of where you've been. After that video aired, the only way Cal could get him to come home for the summer was to feed him some BS story about the local golf camp being understaffed."

"He's spending the entire summer working with kids? Here?" How was she supposed to avoid him for the rest of the summer?

Spenser must have mistaken her panic for judgment. "Don't let his laid-back, life's-a-game attitude fool you. Brett, like all the McGraw brothers, protects his own. It's probably costing him millions to sit out this part of the season. He might be a commitment-phobe who has a weakness for pretty women, but he loves his family and this town."

Great, he was loyal and self-sacrificing. The guy with the charmed life that she'd created in her head was slowly crumbling, which was bad. If she started thinking of Brett as something other than an entitled athlete, she just might start liking him.

"That said, he has the attention span of a gnat when it comes to women. Translation, as soon as camp ends, he's heading out to New Jersey for the FedEx Cup."

Josephina wasn't sure why, but the thought of Brett leaving didn't sit right. She should be happy that he would be gone, not bordering on disappointment. He'd been so charming the other night—bringing her dinner, a phone, saying sweet things about her wings until her heart was fluttering. Then again, every time Josephina led with her heart she got burned.

"Well, I've done sexy and charming. I'm not looking to relive that part of my life. I'm here for a fresh start. To reopen Fairchild House."

Josephina stood and paced to the bay door, needing some fresh air and a minute to let her statement settle. It felt good, almost as good as it was to find Letty's lime convertible still sitting on the other side of the main square in town. It had disappeared sometime yesterday morning only to mysteriously resurface last night, after she'd reported it missing, smelling like cigar smoke and mothballs.

She remembered her aunt putting the top back while speeding down the highway and saying this is what it must feel like to fly. For a girl who'd spent most of her life in the confines of Manhattan, those summers at the Fairchild House had always felt like coming home.

Spenser walked around the tailgate, joining Josephina at the bay door. "Have you considered what will happen if it doesn't work out? You will have a house no one in these parts can afford to buy and a huge debt."

If anything, Spenser's question made Josephina even more determined. "Then I reassess and go at it another way."

"And what if the bank says no?"

"They can't. That would mean I would have failed. And I am done with failing." At least she hoped. "I will do whatever it takes to make this happen."

"Wow. Letty said you lived balls-to-the-wall."

"Balls-to-the-wall? Really? Me?"

"Yeah, I didn't believe her either. Not with all your lace and stupid pink bows."

"I was a kid. My mom dressed me."

"What's your current excuse now?"

Josephina looked down, taking in her runway-meets-respectable-businesswoman ensemble, and frowned. It said classy, together, sophisticated. It also said uptight Yankee.

"Letty talked about you all the time. She told anyone who would listen that someday you'd turn Fairchild House into your own adventure." That made her smile. "She was a ballsy woman, taught me to fight for what I wanted. Like going to mechanic school and taking over my grandpa's shop. When my parents refused to lend me the money to buy out Grandpa's half, Letty made up some lame Southern Business Women's Loan. She never said a word about the loan being from her, but I knew. So, I say go for it. But if you do something illegal, don't tell me."

"Because you'd have to turn me in?"

"Nope. I'd want to join you because it would piss off the sheriff." Spenser smiled and nodded at the open bay door. "And then I'd make his day because he'd get to arrest me. I hate making his day."

"Is he ticketing me?" Josephina asked, because there, across the street, next to Frank Brother's Taxidermy, Ammo, and Fine Jewelry, and in front of the Sheriff's Station, surrounded by a bunch of lookie-loos, stood one of Sugar's finest—notepad in hand and studying her car.

"That's what happens when you forget to pay the meter."

"I did pay the meter." A whopping twenty-five cents. "But I didn't park it there. When you finished working on Ulysses I drove around the block and left him under the maple tree next to your shop," she defended, not wanting to meet the town's people with a public misdemeanor.

"You saying it walked away?" Spenser joked, already headed for the open bay.

"No, I'm just saying I didn't park it there."

Josephina grabbed her purse and, making sure to smile at every single ma'am sent her direction, made her way down the cobblestoned sidewalk after Spenser, who seemed to be almost preening.

A fire hydrant of a woman dressed in an apron, flour, and a good layer of condemnation stood under a neon sign, which read: THE SADDLE RACK. It was Etta Jayne, and she was pointing a reprimanding spatula at Josephina and clucking away.

"I put a quarter in the meter," Josephina defended, hastily adding, "ma'am."

She half expected the woman to swat her tush with that spatula. She was pretty sure she could outrun the disgruntled granny, but she didn't want to test that theory.

A tip of a Stetson and three glares later, Josephina came to a halt, nearly toppling into Spenser, who had pushed her way through the gathering crowd and now stood on her tiptoes, glaring at the sheriff.

"Afternoon, ma'am." The sheriff lifted his hat, then shifted his gaze. "Spenser."

"Jackson." Spenser sent him an eat-shit-and-die glare.

This might be Mayberry, but Barney Fife he was not. The man was seriously hot. Tall, ripped, and looked amazing in uniform. She half expected him to pull out a boom box, rip off his pants, and show her his cuffs. Which should have excited her but didn't, she thought proudly. Her anti-man campaign was going swimmingly.

"This your car?" Jackson asked, writing on that little notepad of his.

"Yes, sir." She reached in her purse and handed him a quarter since she couldn't see a meter. "Here."

The sheriff eyed the coin and grinned. "I don't know whether to arrest you for trying to bribe an officer of the law, or be offended that you think I can be bought off for a quarter."

"What?" Josephina gasped, shoving the coin in her purse. "It's for the," she almost said meter, then remembered there wasn't one. "I'm paying for my parking spot."

"Parking illegally is the least of your worries, since driving a stolen car is a felony."

She was so busy staring at the big red and white SHERIFF PARKING ONLY, VIOLATORS WILL BE SHOT DEAD sign, she almost hadn't heard his last accusation. "Did you say felony?"

"Yes, ma'am. There is an 'attempt to locate' on this car as of this morning. Imagine my surprise when it turned up parked in my designated spot," Jackson drawled, his hand resting on his sidearm.

Josephina held her breath. If she wasn't so terrified of guns, she would probably have jumped in Ulysses and sped off. Because every single person who happened to be in town was now filling the streets and, it seemed, placing bets on whether the city slicker would go to the pokey or grand theft auto was cause for a public lynching.

"I'm going to have to ask you to step into my office so we can discuss the matter of this stolen car." Even when threatening felony the sheriff's voice was sexy. Low and thick and having absolutely no effect on Josephina whatsoever.

"First off, I didn't steal the car. It's mine. And secondly, I'm the one who called it in when it went missing. Yesterday," she added, making sure to point out just how misinformed his department really was.

"And who do you believe stole your—" he looked disbelievingly from the beat-up old jalopy to her corporate couture, "—car?"

"I assume the same someone who parked it illegally today."

That made him pause, giving her a chance to fully inspect his standard-issue sidearm, which, like its owner, was in impeccable condition, and looked uncompromising and ready to blow.

"Seems to me, J.D., that there's been a misunderstanding," another, equally husky voice said from behind. "This looks like Ms. Letty's car, and since Joie here is her niece, the one who inherited all of Letty's property, don't see how it can be stolen."

A warm sensation spread through her body and her heart seemed to still in her chest.

Josephina didn't need to turn to see who it was. Her nipples told her exactly whose breath tickled her ear when he whispered, "No wings today? I'm disappointed."

Breath nonexistent, she prepared herself for the impact, and turned. There stood Brett, wearing khaki shorts and a polo that had a tractor logo on it, looking cocky and mouth-wateringly irritating. His head, missing a hat today and showing off his wavy hair, tilted in her direction as if he were about to kiss her, and something entirely inappropriate began to pulse below her belly button. As if she didn't already have enough to deal with.

Why couldn't it have been some boy next door with a desk job and three cats who made her heart flutter? In true Josephina fashion, it had to be this kind of guy. A famous athlete with more notches on his bedpost than the Bible in Braille and a deadly smile that said, "I'm yours—for tonight, anyway."

"Afternoon, Joie," Brett drawled, tipping his head.

"I noticed you left out the good."

"That's not very nice."

"I'm not feeling very nice." Josephina shifted, unsure what to do with her hands. She'd never been so aware of a man's body before. Brett, on the other hand, was as cool as always.

"What the hell?" The sheriff watched as Spenser, who had disengaged the parking brake, rolled Ulysses backward, stopping under a large sign that designated him as being in a twenty-five-cent all-day parking spot.

Spenser's smile widened as she slid a quarter into the meter. "See, no crime here." She snatched the unfinished report out of Jackson's fingers, crumpling it up and sticking it into his shirt pocket with a little pat.

"Christ, Spenser," Jackson bellowed, but his eyes, Josephina noticed, kept dropping to Spenser's lips. "I should cite you for tampering with a government document."

"Oh, calm down, J.D. It's a silly misdemeanor and you know it."

"Since Joie owns the car and had no knowledge of how it came to be parked there, I suggest that she gets off with a warning," Brett said smoothly.

"I agree." Jackson picked up his radio and canceled the ATL on Ulysses, glaring at Spenser when he got to the part where he had to say he'd made a mistake about the parking designation. She gave a few complex hand gestures in response.

"You're welcome." Brett said, leaning against the fender.

"Go away," Josephina said by way of thanks, ignoring how a warm zing slid down her body.

"That's no way to greet a neighbor."

She looked up into his eyes. "Afternoon. Now go away."

At that he flat-out grinned. "You smell good. Like…" He took one stride forward, landing him right at her red-tipped toes, and leaned in, crowding her. To most people it would look as if he was just whispering in her ear or getting a better whiff, but the way his lips brushed her throat—purposely grazing her sweet spot—he was trying to get to her.

And it was working.

He buried his head even further into her neck, and she could feel him smile when he concluded, "Apple pie and," another gentle inhalation, "something spicy."

She meant to shove him back and ignore his stupid line. But then he said apple pie, and apple wasn't a line. It was observant and sweet. "The spicy part is ginger."

"God, that smells incredible."

She felt herself flush. "I was trying things out for my breakfast menu. Cracked oat pancakes with a ginger-apple glaze. I found some whiskey in Letty's cabinets."

Brett chuckled. "Sugar, if it was in Letty's cabinets it was most likely moonshine."

"Moonshine?" That explained why her skillet had burst into flames.

"During Prohibition, Fairchild House supplied most of these parts with moonshine. Letty found an old bath in the basement, which was converted into a still, and to the best of my knowledge made a batch or two every year. Passed them out at Christmas."

Josephina couldn't help but smile at the idea of Letty making moonshine.

"Sounds to me like you need a test subject for those menu items of yours," he drawled, his body still pressed against hers, his hand now on her hip. Was his accent getting thicker? "Maybe tomorrow, you can cook me up some for breakfast. In bed."

The thought of him wearing just his tattoo and her sheets made her take a step back, two to be safe, because if she didn't get some space between them she might take him up on his offer. The sound of his voice made her want to do irresponsible and deliciously dirty things. Things that would shock poor Mr. Ryan right into denying her that loan, because viable business owners did not act on impulse. Nor did they do rash things, such as licking the entire length of a man's tattoo in the middle of town.

* * *

"You look tense, sugar." She looked more than tense. She was flushed and her eyes had turned turquoise. If he didn't know any better he'd say she was as busy picturing him naked as he was her. "And by the looks of it, I have the perfect remedy."

She flushed again, then glared. She'd been caught checking him out and it ticked her off. Something he was quickly becoming a fan of.

Brett grinned at her outfit. Her hair was slicked up into some kind of complicated style. She wore a cream blouse with buttons and a collar, a gray skirt that hit the knee, and a pair of heels that, aside from her cute toes peeking out, looked stern and uptight.

She was composed, distant, and so pressed he knew he

should just walk away. Instead he found himself forming a serious weakness for those shoes, and their owner.

Even more interesting was that Tinker Bell was friends with Lavender Spenser.

Spenser was the kind of woman every guy in town wanted, but fear of being maimed kept most at a distance. The ones brave enough to try claimed she was magic with her hands, loved to get dirty, and had great aim, which made her a revered mechanic and a painful person to screw with.

"I'm not interested in your backwoods"—her gaze dropped to his fly and back up—"remedies." She sounded convincing, but her blush told him otherwise.

Unable to keep his hands off her, he tugged a stray lock of hair between his fingers, surprised it was curly and that it had managed to break free.

Her hand flew to her head in a panicked fashion, tucking it behind her ear. "It's the humidity," she explained by way of apology. "No matter how hard I try, it always ends up a mess of curls."

"I like messy." She stopped fidgeting at his admission, three other tufts curling out, and he wondered what else was untamed under all of that coiffing and uptown restraint. "And you like me. I can tell. We should go out."

"No, I do not." But instead of moving farther away, she shifted her body closer to his. "And no, we should not."

"That's a whole lot of nos and nots for someone so sure of herself."

Pretending he hadn't even spoken, Josephina clicked those heels right past him and around the back of the car.

"Nice to meet you, Sheriff." She stuck out her hand and the bastard took it, his left hand clasping hers and, Brett noticed, giving it a gentle squeeze while his eyes gave her a slow once-over. "I'm sorry about the misunderstanding."

"Jackson, ma'am. And under the ah—" he flashed a look at Spenser, who was glaring back, "—circumstances, it should be the city that's apologizing. First for the delayed response on your call and then for the parking situation."

"Mistakes happen."

"Not on my watch."

Jesus, Brett thought, watching J.D. puff out his fucking chest. Tinker Bell's magic even worked on Sugar's most self-proclaimed bachelor. He'd been through with women for so long he was practically a virgin.

"How about I make it up to you. Monday night everyone meets at the Saddle Rack. The Falcons are playing and there's dancing. First round's on me?"

Jackson was turning on the southern charm and—flirting? Brett wanted to flatten him. Joie, on the other hand, looked uncomfortable with the attention. Actually, downright shocked. *Interesting.*

"I'm afraid I have plans this Monday. Maybe some other time."

"Some other time then," Jackson said, and Brett almost felt sorry for the guy.

Almost.

Three years ago, Jackson's wife had run off with some rodeo rider, leaving behind three ugly cats and a big-ass mortgage for a house he never wanted. Brett was happy that his friend was finally ready to get out there and meet women.

As long as it wasn't Joie.

Joie looked at her watch. "Shoot, I'm supposed to meet Mr. um, Rooster in just a few minutes. He's giving me an estimate on how long it should take to fix my plumbing."

"Sugar, twenty minutes with me and I guarantee your plumbing will work just fine," Brett drawled, pulling her attention back to where it ought to be—him.

"Does that ever actually work for you?" Her brows lowered as though she thought he was an idiot. "Your sexy little smile, a flick of the hat, and a lame line in that ridiculous hick impersonation? And what? Women just drop naked at your feet?"

Hick?

People loved his accent. Especially women. He could make them weak with a single flattening of the vowel. They begged for him to whisper sweetheart and darlin' in their ear. Although he called her sugar. He'd never used that name before, but with her it fit. He knew under all that tamed order and careful control was a girl who believed in magic and wore fairy wings and was sweet as hell.

"You think my smile is sexy?"

"Didn't you hear a word I said? Never mind." Before he could respond, she yanked open the car door. With a quick wave to Jackson and a "see you later" to Spenser she hopped in and tore off, exhaust in her wake and her horn playing some kind of mariachi song the whole way.

"I like her," Spenser said, sliding up beside him.

"Why's that?" Brett asked wondering what the hell had gone wrong and why he was smiling like a lovesick loser.

"She doesn't take any of your shit."

Yeah, that was another thing he was forming a serious weakness for.

Chapter 7

⌒

Josephina lay motionless with her sheets pulled to her chin. Staring at the wild boar's head that hung above her childhood bed, she listened to the mama opossum and her clan of six shuffle back and forth through the heating duct.

Jimmy Dean, the boar Aunt Letty had helped Josephina track, shoot, and mount on the wall, made her feel safe. It was from Josephina's hog-ranching phase—a phase that had irritated her mother no end. The opossums, on the other hand, stressed her out, since she was certain her new roommates were stashing food for the winter just above the vent in her bedroom.

Not that she'd still be here come winter, she thought glumly, mentally adding to her budget the cost of the air quality specialist needed to handle the mildew Rooster had discovered behind the sheetrock in one of the bathrooms, which had gone nuclear. But she was afraid that in the summer heat the feast wouldn't make it to winter either.

Neither nostalgia nor a rude upstairs neighbor had been

why she'd woken up. She grabbed her phone off the night-stand, checked the time, and groaned.

She'd spent the past five days cleaning house, tearing down wallpaper, and pulling weeds, with still no sign of those roses. Her arms were sore, her nose was peeling, and she didn't have a single nail that wasn't chipped. She'd fall into bed exhausted and wake up feeling as if she might just be able to take on the world. Or at least ignore her parents' relentless calls.

It had been some of the best sleep she'd had in over a decade. Until something rustled downstairs and interrupted a pretty hot dream starring a bubble bath and Mr. PGA himself, and that *something* needed to die. Slow death by golf club sounded good.

A pounding vibrated the floor, followed by a growl. Josephina froze, praying it was her overactive imagination. Her mother was always accusing her of making something out of nothing. Maybe it was just Boo having some kind of bad dream and she'd heard it wrong—

Another growl sounded from downstairs. Definitely not Boo. And it definitely riled her. She gripped the nine-iron that had become her bed companion.

Oh, my God! Brett had warned her about wild animals. Josephina thought he was just messing with the city girl... but what if—?

This time the growl was followed by a high-pitched squeal.

Fumbling for the phone, she pounded the one button, smothering a hysterical laugh when it began ringing.

Brett answered, his voice low and sleep-roughened. "I was wondering when you'd call."

"Bear!" she panted into the phone.

"It's not Bart or Bear or Benny, it's Brett, and you know

it." He lowered his voice, turning the charm to full. "But if you wanted me to come over, all you had to do was ask, Tinker Bell."

"A bear—" she cupped her hand over the phone so she could whisper, "—is in my house and I think it is going to kill me."

"Ah, sugar, I was just playing with you. There aren't *many* bears in this area."

"Many or not. One is in my house. Right now. Probably plotting how he is going to track and shoot me." She glanced at the boar's head and shivered.

"Bears can't shoot." He chuckled, still managing to sound cocky and laid-back even though it was obvious she'd awakened him. Odd, since it was a Friday and she assumed he'd be out with a woman—or women, plural. Unless he was with a woman, or women, right now and he hadn't been asleep. In bed, but not asleep.

"Never mind. Forget I called."

"Don't hang up."

She didn't, because she was scared. Bear or not, something was rummaging through the kitchen; she could hear the pantry doors slamming shut.

"Oh, God, it growled again."

"It's probably just your dog."

A huge crash echoed throughout the house, followed by another ear-piercing squeal. The covers went securely over her head, wrapping her in a big, black abyss of denial. A place she was familiar with.

"Holy shit," Brett said. She could hear clothes rustling and the distinctive jangle of keys. "Where are you at?"

"In my bed. With *Boo*."

Brett moaned, but this one was low and raspy and definitely not out of anger. And she shivered from head to polished tips, definitely not out of fear. "Stay right there, I'm on my way. I mean it, don't move. If I drag my ass over there and it turns out to be some coon, I at least want to see you in bed."

"Okay," she breathed, and hung up, horrified when, picturing Brett in her bed, she heard herself purr. Rolling over to pull Boo close, she realized he was gone.

"Boo?" she whispered. Only silence in return.

"Boo-kins, come to Mama." Nothing. Just like what she was doing. Her house was under attack and she was hiding under the covers, waiting for some oversexed prince in his white pickup to come and rescue her.

Taking a deep breath, she counted to ten, flung back the covers, and clutched her trusty golf club—who knew they could be so versatile?

She tiptoed her way to the top of the stairs. Shoulders squared, she was embracing her new, independent self, ready to maim her a bear, when she saw the shadowy outline of not one, but four figures. They didn't look like bears, which was good, but they did look dangerous, huddled in a circle, most likely deciding who got to gobble up Boo.

Child, when facing down an insistent boar, toss back those shoulders, stick out that chest, and run straight at the bastard, screaming like you're going to rip his testicles off. Aunt Letty's voice flittered through her head. Letty had plenty of experience running off bastards, and her advice seemed to fit the situation.

Taking a deep breath and holding it, Josephina gripped the club, extending it forward in the traditional fencing counterattack position, let out a ball-ripping battle cry, and took off down the stairs. She'd just hit the landing when one of them spun around to stare her down and growled.

The lights flicked on and Josephina came to a halt, blinking to get her eyes to adjust. Problem was they were adjusted. And those weren't bears. Or even raccoons. It was a mob of women who looked as if they predated the Civil War. Wearing apple-stained cheeks, reading glasses, and silvery spun hair, each one was clutching a gun so big Josephina felt as if she was in some John Wayne film. And this time they weren't here to offer up a covered dish.

Dottie, the only one not packing heat, came out of the kitchen, binoculars swinging. She held a bag of pretzels under her arm, and began digging through her clutch purse, most likely to find her weapon of choice.

"Drop it, Missy," Hattie said, wagging her gun.

Josephina had seen guns before, but never looked down the barrel of one.

Holy crap! She was being robbed. By a bunch of armed grannies. And Boo, traitor that he was, yawned and pranced over to nuzzle Jelly-Lou, who was dressed in her Sunday best with a pile of poker chips and a loaded pistol.

Etta Jayne cocked a rifle and pushed her way to the front. But Hattie, dressed in saffron polyester and a terrycloth visor, jabbed her with an elbow, not giving an inch.

"Move it, Hattie."

"Not on your life, Etta Jayne. I drew first."

"I'm a better shot and you know it." Etta Jayne snapped, swinging her rifle and starting a tussle.

Then, three things happened at once. The front door blew in, a shot exploded, and Josephina saw a shower of glimmering dust as shards of chandelier fell to the floor.

*　*　*

"Move an inch and I'll shoot it off," Grandma Hattie snapped, pointing her Winchester with perfect accuracy and making Brett squirm.

"Put that thing down before you actually shoot someone. Or something." He dropped his hands, not willing to chance that she'd shoot even after he'd made his identity known.

Rounding the bust of Kenny Rogers and stepping over an empty bottle of whiskey, his gaze landed on the salon—deck of cards, poker chips, cigar butts—and then on the dog, whose front canines were sunk into his ankle.

It was a quarter to one. In the morning. And although the house, now clean of dust bunnies and smelling vaguely of Lysol and cigars, was silent, it also happened to be littered with shattered glass, cheesy pretzels, and a mob of armed church ladies.

"Bible study my ass," he mumbled.

"Watch your mouth, young man. I know where Letty kept her soap."

"Do you happen to know where she kept the broom?" Brett asked, glass crunching under his boots.

"Why you asking me? I didn't do it." Hattie slid a glance at Etta Jayne.

"Don't you dare go blaming me! My safety's on," Etta Jayne, the only person to rival Grandma Hattie as the most feared woman in town, stated, smacking her hip with the butt of her rifle. She was rumored to have teathered a cheating patron to the town flag pole, hogtied and naked.

Hattie looked at her gun and shrugged. "Whoops. Must have forgot. My apologies."

Brett sighed, feeling a knot form behind his right eye. A bear, he knew, had been a long shot, but an armed grandma and her Bible buddies hadn't even made the list of possibilities.

If his heart hadn't been racing from the frantic drive over, he'd have taken a little pleasure in the situation. The two most stubborn women he knew were at a standoff. But then he turned his gaze to Joie and any pleasure he might have found vanished.

She stood at the base of the steps, the hand above her head shielding herself from the falling glass, while the other clutched a golf club so tightly that her knuckles were purple and her arm shook. Eyes closed tight, hair a loose riot of curls, she was mumbling something that sounded oddly like the theme song to *Zorro*. She wore a pink lacy thing, which covered next to nothing, and matching tiny bottoms that covered even less. Which his lower half registered immediately.

He felt as if he was looking at the real Joie, the one she kept hidden from the world.

But what had something catching deep inside of him and sent his body into action was the moisture clinging to her lower lashes. She was shaking and kind of green and scared shitless. And she had a right to be. Grandma Hattie was terrifying enough without the benefit of a loaded pistol.

"Put that away," he scolded, shooting a look at Hattie, who ignored him completely. He cautiously approached Joie. Lowering his voice and her hand, he said, "You can put that down now."

She shook her head, eyes still firmly shut. "Not until they drop theirs."

"Sugar," Brett said lightly. "First off, you're outgunned. And even if you stood a chance, which you don't since these ladies taught me how to handle a firearm, you've got your eyes closed."

"I'm not dropping anything," Jelly-Lou, the woman who had knitted him his first baby blanket, said, petting that rat dog with one hand and raising the barrel of a Colt .45 with the other.

"Sneaking up on us like that. Where are your manners, young lady?" Etta Jayne chided.

"Me? You're in *my* house!" Joie said, eyes still shut tight, but her East Coast accent was thick and tough. And he found it incredibly hot.

"Hogwash," Dottie snapped, setting the bowl of pretzels on the table, sending a stack of poker chips crashing to the floor. "Been coming here since I was a girl. So as far as I'm concerned, this place is as much ours as yours, seeing how we took care of your aunt when you and your kin couldn't be bothered."

Tinker Bell's eyes snapped open, blue and iced over, her body taking on an irate glow.

"Out!" she shouted, convincing Brett that she might just be magical after all. No human would take on the Sunday School Mafia. "I want you all out or I'm calling the cops."

"Little Jackson Duncan? He isn't nothing but a pansy. Carries a .22," Grandma Hattie scoffed, but her voice wasn't as hard as it had been a moment ago. Joie's pinched face most likely had something to do with it.

"Look, dear," Jelly-Lou said, her tone bringing Brett back to story time at the library. "We didn't mean to scare you. We were just playing our weekly game of poker. Been going on since your aunt moved here."

"She never told me." Joie's face was a jumble of emotions.

"Reckon she had good reason not to." Jelly-Lou finally lowered her gun and wheeled her chair a little closer. "A bunch of ladies sneaking around drinking whiskey, smoking cigars, and playing cards. Talk about scandal. The Sugar Peaches would vote us out for sure."

The Sugar Peaches were the most exclusive ladies' society in Sugar County, its membership dating back to the town's establishment. No one wanted to be ousted from the Sugar Peaches, not even Hattie.

Joie was lowering her nine-iron. The handguns were re-turned to their respective handbags. And everyone looked as if they were willing to play nice. Brett actually allowed him-self to exhale. Then Grandma Hattie spoke.

"And we ain't going to let some city girl who was too busy to care when caring was needed come in and take what's ours."

"Out! Get out of my house! And don't ever come back." Joie was mad, but worse, she was hurt. He could see it in her eyes, which had slid shut again.

"Those are fighting words you're using. Better be care-ful or you might just find yourself in a feud," Etta Jayne said, putting a comforting arm around Hattie, whose eyes looked a little misty as well. Of course those two would bond when words like kin and feud were being tossed around.

"Bring it on!" Joie bellowed, club extended like a sword.

No one spoke. Silently, Etta Jayne waddled over to Joie and waited until she slowly opened her eyes. Then she spat.

Right on the floor at Joie's feet. A southern signature confirming that a feud had been called, the sides were cho-sen, and poor Joie was on the losing end. Sugar protected its own, even if it meant taking down a woman who was in way over her head. So when Hattie started sniffling up her John Hancock, Brett grabbed hold of her elbow and steered her toward the door. She dug her feet in, ripping her arm away.

Brett took in a long breath, channeling his charm, know-ing that with women it worked better than brute force. Which he was willing to use if they didn't get out of there, and fast. Tinker Bell was a sniffle away from tears and he was pretty sure that all of them, except Jelly-Lou, were tanked.

"Grandma, how about you and the ladies head on over to our place. There's some beer in the fridge, cards in the game chest. Just make sure the cigars are smoked outside or Cal will have my—" Grandma Hattie cleared her throat. "We can all get a good night's rest and work this all out in the morning." When none of the ladies moved, he added, "It's the neighborly thing to do."

It took some cajoling, a little flirting, and a whole lot of bribing—including an economy-sized pack of signed briefs—to get them gone. But five minutes later he was watching them roll Jelly-Lou down the ramp, arguing over who won the last hand.

He closed the door and turned to Joie, more excited to be alone with her than he should be.

"Nice top. That color really brings out your—" he purposely paused, loving the way her face went pink, matching her lace, "—eyes."

"Don't flatter yourself. Humiliation and lace seem to be my thing lately."

She crossed her arms in an attempt to look tough. Imagine his delight when that only highlighted those beautiful breasts of hers. Which from the looks of them were cold—or she wasn't as immune to him as she pretended.

"Sounds like a story I'd love to hear." He leaned a shoulder against the door. "Maybe over dinner. Or we could go straight for the pillow talk."

"Briefs, huh?" Joie said after a good old-fashioned eye-rolling.

"Apparently they fetch a good price online." They were back to surface sparring, so why didn't he feel relieved?

Glass crunched and a few chips snapped under his boots as he crossed the room. He glanced down at her bare feet with red tips and understood why she hadn't moved. Sliding a hand down her arm, he wrapped his fingers around the club, untangling it from hers and setting it against the wall.

Josephina stood silent, staring at the floor. Then she looked up at him and, wow. No sense in denying it. She was gorgeous.

He'd spent the better part of the week avoiding her, rationalizing that if he didn't see her this insane attraction would fade.

It hadn't. And now he didn't think ignoring her was going to work.

She had a great body, long and toned with X-rated curves, which was currently so close he could smell her shampoo. Her hair was loose, bed-rumpled, and seemed to glow under what was left of the chandelier. She was biting down on that full lower lip, which had starred in some pretty impressive dreams lately. Her nose was pert, peeling, and little too pink.

Tinker Bell had been out in the sun.

He pulled a little piece of curled-up skin off her nose. "You should wear lotion when you sunbathe. Georgia sun is strong,"

"I was pulling weeds." *Interesting.* "And I did." She scrunched her nose, making it pinker. "Guess not enough though."

He looked at her hands. They were small and elegant, even though every nail was chipped. So Tinker Bell liked to get dirty. She got more fascinating by the moment, and that was not a good thing. Especially when those blue eyes, soft and so big he was afraid that if he wasn't careful he might just fall into them, met his.

"You okay?" He stepped closer, resting a hand on either hip. His fingers brushed the exposed skin between her tiny bottoms and even tinier top.

She nodded, then thought better of it and shook her head. "The chandelier," she whispered so low he barely made out the words. "It's broken, isn't it?"

Brett looked up. "It's not that bad," he lied.

"It was Letty's favorite."

He could also tell that it was hers. Hell, she had slept under it that first night. Tonight, though, she had called him from a bed, which added a new location for his fantasies.

"I can fix it," he heard himself offer.

She shrugged, deflated. "It'll never be the same. And pretending it is, is even worse than admitting it's broke."

When she spoke like that, her voice filled with sadness and something deeper, it tore at his gut. He wanted to do whatever it took to bring back that sassy and stubborn woman he'd picked up on the side of the highway. He knew how to handle her. This woman, the vulnerable one with her heart on display, made him nervous.

"You are not what I expected, Joie. One minute you're this carefully manicured woman who is so together it's annoying. The next you're in fairy wings looking like a tornado hit and worrying yourself over an old lamp. What I want to know is which one is the real Josephina Harrington?"

"I don't know," she whispered, tugging at the hem of her nightshirt, looking as if she'd somehow disappointed him.

"What am I going to do with you?" He closed the gap, surprised when she dropped her head to his chest.

Right then, he knew exactly what he wanted to do with her. The image of her in that getup, in whatever bed she'd been calling from, was making a lasting impression. He just hoped she didn't notice.

"That's all right. No one ever knows what to do with me. Most of the time I barely know what to do with myself."

"Sounds exciting." It did. Every second of his life, it

seemed, belonged to someone else. His manager, his sponsors, his fans, his career, his family. Even now, stuck in his hometown, bored out of his ever-loving mind, it was still at someone else's request. He couldn't remember the last time he'd felt that his life was his own.

"Sometimes. But usually it just lands me in a mess."

"Like I said before, messy can be sexy." It was what drew him to her. She pretended to be carefully put together, but under all of that big-city swagger was this free spirit who felt her way through life. Unlike him, for whom every action had a monetary value and decisions were weighted by repercussions, public image, and upside.

"Or it can just be messy."

"Not on you." He traced a finger up her arm to her chin, tilting her head to meet his gaze.

A heat passed through her eyes that told him she liked his touching her, liked being with him. Determined to find out just how much she liked his hands on her, he tightened his grip on her hip, shifting closer until they brushed up against each other. He dipped his head, just enough to let her know his intent.

Her breath caught and suddenly their mouths were only a fraction apart. Their gazes held, neither talking, just sharing breath.

"Brett," she whispered again, her voice a little thick. "We shouldn't. I just got out of a relationship and you, well, it's weird that I don't even know you but I've seen your tattoo and…"

Brett smiled. So she had seen the video. Paid close enough attention to notice his tattoo, which meant she was staring in the vicinity of his ass. He didn't know if that was a good thing or not. But her dilated eyes and shallow breathing were.

It was the damnedest thing, they were barely touching and yet he was reacting as if they were naked and pressed against each other. Maybe this was what he needed, one night to get her out of his system, then he could forget about this crazy attraction and go back to lying low.

Just one night.

He lowered his head and she went up on her toes. Her eyes fluttered shut. He wasn't sure who started it, but suddenly they were kissing, her arms on his chest, his in her hair. Their lips brushed once, and then some more. Tender little kisses that made his chest tight and his jeans even tighter.

She gave a small purr of approval that was pretty much his undoing. She didn't grab or demand, instead cuddling into him all soft and vulnerable. So damn vulnerable. With another sexy sigh she pulled back, just enough so that they weren't kissing but were sharing breath, staring into each other's eyes. Hers were huge and unguarded, showing him every damn thing she was feeling.

Brett tensed, waiting—hoping like hell—for her to push him away. End this and give him an easy out.

Too bad nothing about her was easy. She wrapped her arms around his middle, pulling him close enough to bury her head in his chest, and her whole body melted into his. That one move changed the game.

He stood there, stock-still, his hands at his side. His brain raced, trying to figure out what she needed from him. Apparently it was a hug, because when he wrapped his arms around her, she let go a warm sigh that went all the way to his heart. She held on to him as if she were afraid there was somewhere else he'd rather be. Which should have terrified him, because there wasn't. He could stand there all night and just hold her, listen to those soft little sounds of hers, which turned him on almost as much as her mouth.

A sure sign that he was in trouble.

A lot of trouble. There was no room for this in his life. Nowhere for this moment to go. He was leaving and she wasn't a casual-fling kind of girl. Still, he pulled her closer, wanting to be what she needed.

Understanding his offer, she smiled into his chest and shuffled closer.

"Ouch!" She shifted her feet again, "Ow, ow, ow!"

Without asking what was wrong or giving her any more time to play tap dance roulette on a bed of glass, Brett scooped her up and carried her to the couch, trying to ignore how soft and curvy she felt against him.

Setting her on one end, he eased himself down across from her and lifted her foot. *Shit.*

"How are you with blood?"

Chapter 8

Oh, God, blood. She closed her eyes and swallowed back her dinner.

"Yeah, me either." He chuckled, but it didn't hold any humor.

She opened one eye, peeked through her lashes, and immediately felt woozy. A huge chunk of glass stuck out from the sole. All she could think of was an iceberg, and she wondered, with a tip that size, how much was in her foot?

"Get it out!"

Boo plopped down against her thigh, covered his head with his paws, and whined.

"If I pull it out there's going to be a whole lot of blood." Mr. Tough Cowboy looked kind of pale.

"And I'll bleed out?"

"Ah, sugar, you've been in New York too long. I meant that you'll most likely need stitches. Which means I need to get you to a doctor before I see the blood."

Twenty minutes and a terrifying car ride later, Josephina

sat on an exam table at the Sugar Medical Center. Brett had wrapped her up in a bathrobe—thank God—and drove like it was the final lap in a NASCAR championship race, probably afraid she'd get blood on his precious truck.

Willing herself not to look at her foot—again—she turned her head and caught a reflection of herself in the mirror above the sink. On second thought, maybe he didn't want to be seen with her.

She was wearing an epic case of bed-head and Letty's bathrobe, which was muumuu-shaped and electric-mango-colored with bulls wearing bow ties on it. And yet it was less humiliating than the teddy she had on underneath.

A flash of white doctor's robe passed by the small square window, and Josephina's belly went queasy. Doctors meant needles. And the only thing she hated more than blood was needles. Which explained why she pushed off the table, desperate to make an escape.

A strong, calloused hand came to rest on her thigh, pinning her to the table.

"In high school, I was one of the best bulldoggers in the county," Brett whispered in her ear. "And I bet I could take you down in under a second. Might even be fun."

The door opened and in walked the doctor. Tall, exquisite, and sophisticated, she flashed a megawatt smile and moved gracefully across the room with a confident ease that made men swallow their tongues whole.

"I understand you had quite the social event earlier this evening," she said, her perfect white teeth gleaming even brighter in Josephina's direction. "Well, even though the circumstances are unfortunate, it's good to see you again. Now, let's take a look, shall we?"

"Hey, Brett," she said, picking up Josephina's foot, her eyes glued to the hunk of glass catching in the light.

"Hey, Charlotte. Thanks for seeing us so quickly." Brett's hand gently massaged Josephina's thigh. "I heard you almost reached your goal for the new children's wing."

"Can you believe it?" *Charlotte* finally looked up, her cheeks tinted with pride. "I've been dreaming about this for years and it's almost here."

Josephina had read about the proposed pediatric center in the local paper, which she had found shoved up the tailpipe of Ulysses earlier that afternoon. A Texas-based company had agreed to fund the much-needed pediatric ward in Sugar. The center would support all the children of Sugar and a good portion of the surrounding area. Since the center and its building were privately owned, the actual addition would have to be paid for by the center's founders, the Holden family, who had already agreed to shoulder a large part of the debt. From what Josephina had read, the town had stepped in, planning a host of fundraisers to make up the difference.

"And a huge part of that is due to you, Brett. So thanks."

Brett just shrugged, but Josephina noticed that his ears went a little pink at the praise.

"Just a few stitches and you'll be good as new." The doctor slipped a monitor on Josephina's finger. "Now, Mr. McGraw, if you could just give us some privacy, I can have her all cleaned up and ready to go."

"You want me to stay?" Brett gave Josephina an encouraging smile. It was warm and open and real and it made her heart do dangerous things. Like set off that damn thing stuck on her finger.

The doctor flicked a glance at the monitor, currently beeping as if it was part of Defcon One.

"The minute I take this shard of glass out, she's going to bleed like a stuck pig, and since I have no inclination to clean you up off my office floor, I'm guessing this is where you say goodbye." Her gaze landed on Brett and something passed between them, something easy and comfortable. Something akin to history.

Charlotte moved to the sink to wash up, tossing Josephina a sly smile as Brett hightailed it out the door mumbling something about being right outside.

"Is there going to be a lot of blood?" Josephina asked, scooting to the back of the exam table as the doctor took the cap off the syringe.

"No; I figured you'd be more comfortable if he wasn't in here, and to be honest, your heart racing like that doesn't make this any easier."

Great. One of Brett's women—who obviously thought Josephina and Brett were doing the cowboy cha-cha—was armed with a needle and about to perform surgery on her foot.

"Before you stick that thing in my arm, I want to know if you and Brett are dating. And to tell you he's here...with me...because he was just being *neighborly*."

"Honey, this isn't going in your arm." Josephina went clammy. "And as for Brett, my granddaddy said he'd castrate all three brothers if even just one looked at me with interest." She shrugged, fiddling with the needle again. "When a Georgia state judge who is on record in support of public lynching as a form of capital punishment says something like that, it works. Not that I was interested, much to my mama's dismay. Being a McGraw makes him one of the most sought-after men in this county. And, well, my mama, being the current regent of the Sugar Peaches, would have looked the other way had I accidentally fallen into a compromising situation that would've led to a ring. Unless it happened to be the youngest of the brothers."

"Why?"

"According to my mother, Jace," her voice thickened, "bless his heart, has a past that no amount of money or fame could excuse with regards to marriage."

"I meant, why would she want you to marry a McGraw?"

Charlotte wiggled a very manicured brow. "In these parts, McGraws are gods. Their great-great-grandfather, Cletus McGraw, helped found this town, and the McGraw men are legendary for being honorable, loyal, and, as of this last generation, rich as sin. Not to mention handsome. His parents had one of the most talked-about love affairs in these parts, second only to their grandparents."

"Spenser said they died in a fire."

"It was a horrible loss for everyone, especially those boys. During a lightning storm, a bolt hit the roof and their whole house went up. Mr. McGraw got the boys outside and went back in for his wife, who was looking for Jace, not knowing he was already safe. She had asthma and passed out from the smoke. They made it to the hospital but both died an hour later, within minutes of each other, while holding hands and whispering how much they loved each other."

"Oh, my God." For a girl who never cried the room was looking awful blurry.

"My daddy was on duty that night and said that even though Mr. McGraw died first, his heart monitor continued to beat because—" Charlotte clutched her chest, syringe still sticking out of her hand, "—his wife's heart was beating through his. Can you imagine? She was literally giving him her heart, so they could go together. When she died the doctors had to pry their hands apart."

Josephina swallowed hard, her heart cracking a little more for the boy she had once known and the man she was starting to understand. "No wonder the brothers are all single. I mean, how can anyone even live up to that?" She sure as hell couldn't.

"I know. Even after all these years, people still talk about it. The whole town is waiting for one of those boys to fall. Folks thought that Cal had taken the fall with his wife, Tawny, but that was a dose of blinding lust not love, because everyone knows that when McGraw men fall, they go all in. Been that way for a century and a half. Why, to hear my mama tell it, just the way their daddy would look at Mrs. McGraw was enough to make a bystander swoon."

"How come you never dated one then?"

"Because my mama wanted me to." She smiled and Josephina found herself smiling back. "Now, close your eyes and lie back. You're looking too pale for it being so close to my quitting time."

Josephina did as she was told, feeling like a wimp.

"And, honey, being *neighborly* is Brett talk for let's get naked, feet to Jesus style."

"Yeah, well. I'm not interested in being seen naked or showing anyone my feet."

"I think it might be a little late," the doctor said to Josephina's toes, then looked at her robe and grinned. "On both accounts."

Poke. The old Josephina would have thrown up. The new Josephina, the one who was ready to take on the world, stifled a whimper.

"You really don't remember me." Poke. Poke.

When Josephina just shook her head, the doctor stuck a latexed hand out. "Charlotte Holden. Your aunt Letty used to sit me during the summer when my mama had a Peaches' meeting." Josephina blinked, still at a loss. "I convinced you to climb up that big old oak tree."

"You stole the ladder and left me up there," Josephina

said, remembering the little brunette in ruffles and pearls who had conned her into climbing the tree, then called her a liar and ran off.

"You said you could fly. I wanted proof."

"I was in that tree for most of the day." Well, until the neighbor boy rescued her, and overcome with gratitude, and one too many *From Here to Eternity* viewings with Letty, she'd kissed him.

Josephina froze at the memory, her heart going kind of squishy. Young Brett had dusted the dirt off her dress, retied the bow on her pigtails, and believed her when she confessed she was a fairy waiting for her wings.

Even though her first kiss had been with the man who had slept his way through the better part of the South and some of the outlying coastal states, she couldn't help but smile. Whether it was the memory of Brett walking her home or whatever the good doctor had in the now-empty syringe, she didn't know.

Charlotte grabbed a roll of gauze. "So you and Brett, huh? I must say I'm impressed, you move fast."

"What? No. I already told you, we're just friends. Not even that really."

"If you say so."

"He came to break up a 'social event' when a gun went off and I stepped in glass." She paused, feeling the tips of her ears heat. "Even if there was something there, which there isn't—"

Charlotte let out a disbelieving snort that somehow sounded cultured.

"I'm here in Sugar in a party-of-one capacity and penis-carting members need not apply." She considered and then added, "Unless they have a spare tire around the waist, bad breath, and their own power tools. Then all bets are off."

"That bad, huh?" Charlotte said, taking a seat on the exam table, understanding flickering in her eyes.

Before Josephina knew what had happened, she'd relayed every humiliating detail, starting with letting Wilson talk her out of seeing Letty before she died, right through the mile-high fiasco, and ending at the showdown with a golf club and pink teddy. And she didn't even cry once.

Charlotte moved to a locked cabinet, only to return with another needle. This one bigger.

"I stole them." Josephina studied the ceiling. "The golf clubs. The ones Wilson used to polish weekly."

"That a girl. You might feel a little—"

"Ow!"

"—pinch. So, a tool belt?" Charlotte went on as if she hadn't just stuck a horse-sized needle through Josephina's foot. "Does this mean you're becoming a real Georgia Peach?"

"Yup. I'm reopening the inn," she said, adding the cost of one chandelier to the already overwhelming estimate. She was hoping that Mr. Ryan would come back with an approved small business loan, but either way she wasn't leaving. She was going to turn that crumbling money-pit into the best thing that ever happened to this town—and to her.

Charlotte slapped a bandage on her foot. "Your aunt Letty was as stubborn as they come, determined to keep that house open even when the county tried to shut her down for not being up to code. Those friends of hers rallied and took on the county, making sure Fairchild House was a functioning inn all the way up until the day she passed. She'd be proud that you're reopening it, so don't let those biddies get to you. They're just seeing what you're made of."

Charlotte's words made her smile. Made the stress of securing money and patching the roof fade away, because making Letty proud was as important to her as making her dream a reality. Especially since she seemed to let down every other member of her family by opening her mouth.

The doctor studied her for a long moment. Or maybe a short moment. It was hard to tell when everything felt so good. Even her hair felt shiny.

"You know what you need?"

"A gun?"

"Well, you are in Confederate country." Josephina waited for her to laugh. She didn't. "No, I think what you need is some good old-fashioned rebound sex."

Josephina felt woozy again. The last thing she needed was a man. Especially when the man that popped into her head was a known player and heartbreaker. "Sex would complicate everything."

"If it's complicated you're doing it wrong. Look, I'm not saying fall in love. You don't even have to like the guy. What I'm talking about is a wild, no-strings romp in the hay. Good Lord, did I just say that? My mama would be horrified." Charlotte looked excited at the idea, and Josephina was quickly coming to like her. "What better way to get your life back than to remind yourself that sex is fun? That being a woman is fun?"

"I was thinking more of girl talk and alcohol." Lots of alcohol.

Charlotte clapped her hands together, a smile crossing her face. "Honey, I happen to know where you can find all three. Although I can't do tomorrow night or Thursday night. Actually my whole weekend is booked working on my platform for the Peaches. Elections are coming up and there is no way Darleen Vander, bless her vengeful little heart, is going to win the VP seat this year. I do, however, have next Monday off. You and me, we're going hunting."

"Hunting?"

"For a man."

"I'm not sure." Josephina was all for embracing this new and improved her, but she kind of wanted to do it in private. That way if she screwed up no one would know. Plus, sex with a stranger seemed so irresponsible. "I couldn't even get there. I don't have a car, well, a reliable car," she corrected thinking of Ulysses S Grant and his ongoing disappearing act.

"I could pick you up." The good doctor handed Josephina a scribbled note and helped her off the table.

"Am I done? I didn't even feel the stitches."

"I'm that good. Plus the drugs helped. Keep it elevated for a couple days and call me if the swelling doesn't go down. See you Monday." She hung her jacket on a hanger. "Don't think about it, Josephina, just come. It will be fun, for both of us."

Josephina hobbled out into the waiting room wondering if Charlotte was right. Maybe she did need a girls' night out.

Brett stood, slowly making his way across the room. He looked so strong and safe, like the sweet boy who wiped away her tears and stole her heart, that Josephina almost walked right into his arms. Then she noticed the exquisite brunette just to his right.

"Should you be walking?"

She nodded, looking past Brett to the Budweiser model whose oversized red jersey and baseball cap did nothing to diminish her hourglass curves or hide those big green eyes that were looking up at Brett as if he hung the moon. She stood next to him, her hand in his, as Brett leaned down to look at her fingers.

"It was good to see you, Brett," the groupie said, extracting her hand. She shifted that smile to Josephina and waited, finally elbowing Brett in the ribs when he kept staring at Josephina instead of giving the proper introductions.

"Hey," Josephina said, tightening the belt of her robe.

"Hey, yourself. You must be Letty's niece. I'm Glory." Again with the elbow. "It's nice to finally meet you."

"Sorry," Brett said, and Josephina could swear that he was tongue-tied and blushing. "This here is Glory Mann, best beer slinger in Sugar County. Glory, this is Joie—"

"Josephina," she corrected, offering Glory her hand.

"Letty would be so happy that you're back. She talked about you all the time."

Even though she'd heard this over and over, it was still hard to believe.

Glory looked back and forth between her and Brett and smiled. What that smile meant Josephina didn't care to know. It was followed by a long, uncomfortable silence during which Glory was grinning at Brett, Brett was staring at Josephina, and Josephina was trying to figure out what was so funny.

"I was just getting my knuckles checked out." Glory fluttered her hand in the air, the same one Brett had been holding. It was wrapped in a bandage and gauze. "Falcons lost to the Saints tonight."

Josephina waited for further explanation, but Brett was back to holding Glory's hand again, tenderly flipping it over and inspecting it thoroughly. "You should've called JD."

"Would rather deal with a couple of drunken patrons. Besides, it's only bruised—and I didn't come here to talk about a bunch of lightweight rednecks." She took her hand back and faced Josephina. "Well, I better get going. It was nice meeting you."

"You, too," Josephina said, smiling.

"See you later, Brett."

Just what *later* meant Josephina didn't want to know. But it irritated her that she was thinking about its meaning. It irritated her even more that Glory was genuinely nice. The moment Brett's gaze returned to Josephina's she stopped caring, she stopped thinking at all, because his intense stare was once more making her melt. Then he opened his mouth.

"Now that I've seen you in that silky number, how about dinner?"

"Not going to happen."

"Why?" He didn't even seem fazed.

Because I just might start liking you. "I'm focusing on me, not men."

"Who said anything about men? I just want you to focus on one man." He grinned, motioning those rough hands over his chest. That sculpted, lickable chest, which she told herself did not inspire dirty fantasies. But it so did.

"No. No man. Men. Males of any kind."

"Okay, what about sex then?"

"Nope." Her toes curled, crinkling the bandage. Maybe the doctor was right. Maybe she needed a night of balls-to-the-wall sex. And maybe she needed to remind herself of the last time she tried to spice up her sex life. "None of that either."

"Too bad. I imagine you and I would, well, it would be pretty damn sweet." He shrugged, scooping her up in his arms, ignoring her protests that she could walk just fine on her own. "I'll just keep asking."

Josephina accepted defeat and wrapped her arms around his neck, breathing him in without making it obvious.

"I'll just keep saying no."

"Until you say yes."

Chapter 9

Josephina knew the mature thing would be to excuse herself and answer the phone. Instead she sent the call to voicemail, again, and promised herself that she would call her mother back. Tomorrow.

It had been nearly two weeks since she had talked to either of her parents. And Josephina's head—and her pride—still hurt. Forcing a smile, she looked up the ladder to a pair of worn work boots sticking out of her vent duct.

"Any luck?"

"No, ma'am," Rooster, her contractor turned exterminator, said, his voice echoing off the metal walls of the duct. "Those are some sneaky opossums."

They weren't just squatting and storing enough food for the next fifty years, now they'd taken to gnawing through the wires. The little jerks had strategically hit the back power supply, knocking out the air-conditioning and the entire kitchen.

"I reckon the best way to catch 'em is peanut butter,"

Rooster said after making his way down every vertigo-inspired rung of the ladder.

"Peanut butter?"

"Yes, ma'am. On Wonder Bread with honey and a good dose of sodium fluoroacetate." Rooster rocked back on his heels, exposing his impressive spare tire. "That should fix 'em right up. Then I can get rid of their bodies for you."

"Bodies?"

"Sure enough. There should be eight or nine of them by the looks of it."

Josephina swallowed, thinking about those little black, beady eyes that had glared at her last night through her bedroom vent, and wondered how old the babies were. She had only seen the one adult, and wanted to know if she was a single mom and if so, where the father was.

"Can't we just catch them and move them to a nice place down by the river? Maybe in a tree?" Boo looked up at her with those big, black eyes and she added, "With a view?"

"Well, we could, but they'd most likely find their way back to your vents. The mama opossums like attics, because they're safe. Humans scare off any predators that would try to eat her babies."

Eat her babies? Good God! "So this is a safe house?"

"Ma'am?"

Josephina didn't get a chance to repeat her concern or ask about the percentage of single mothers in the opossum world, because her phone rang. This time it was her father's number on the screen.

Not until the phone chimed in the final stage of powering down did she feel herself relax.

Is that what the mama opossum felt when she got her babies in that vent? Relaxed? Safe from the cruel world?

Josephina looked up. The mama, eyes peeled wide,

ears back, sharp little teeth bared, looked down at her. She tried to look away, catching the last few words on the commemorative Fairchild plaque—*a boarding house for the adventurous.*

"The opossum and her babies stay."

"But they're eating up all the wires I laid—"

"Forget the wires. We can put them in some kind of metal casing, right?"

Rooster took off his ROOSTER'S ROOFING AND REMODELS: REDNECK WITH A TOUCH OF (CL)ASS hat, curling the bill of it in his palm. It was the same thing he'd done when she said she wanted three professional ranges in the kitchen. And the same thing he'd done when she said she wanted to turn the salon into a day spa. Only that time his eye started twitching and his arm broke out into a rash.

"Well, yes, ma'am. But seeing as opossums don't use an outhouse...." He eyed her. "If you know what I mean."

"But kicking them out when they have nowhere else to go isn't very neighborly, now is it?" Josephina said, knowing that being neighborly in the South was as important as going to church.

"They're not neighbors. They're hunting bait."

"Yes, well, here at the Fairchild House, they are a family looking for a safe place to start over. So thanks, but I'll figure something out." She wasn't going to let them stay permanently, but she refused to kill them. "Since I don't want to start on the kitchen until I hear back from the bank, why don't you get the power working and tomorrow we can start on the—"

Rooster's phone twanged some godawful country song.

"Sorry." He hit the Talk button. "Y-ello, this is Rooster of Rooster's Roofing and Remodels." He studied his boots while the other person spoke, then his gaze rose to land squarely on Josephina's and he grimaced. "Yes'em. Good afternoon to you, too."

Josephina felt her cheeks heat and the tips of her ears burn, which was crazy. She and Rooster had no common connections, but he was obviously talking about her with whoever was on the line—and judging from the pity in his eyes, the words were not kind.

Her heart stopped. Rooster knew Brett. Before she could stop herself she found her hand smoothing her hair down and her breath picking up. It had been that way since the night he took her home from getting stitches.

All week, it seemed wherever she went, Brett turned up. Wednesday she went to the hardware store and found him buying some kind of security system for Bitsy over at the Bless Her Hair, Beauty and Gifts, and proceeded to ask Josephina—in front of the whole store—if she needed any help picking out wood.

On Thursday, while walking Boo in the park, he was signing autographs for the Boys and Girls Club fundraiser. Just yesterday, she was at Mable's Corner Market, buying some molasses for Letty's ginger-molasses cookies and some lady items, when she walked directly into a hard, yummy wall: Brett. He was helping Jelly-Lou find dented tomato cans, which, the older lady confided, were a nickel cheaper.

Instead of calling him a stalker—or kissing him silly when she caught him denting cans behind Jelly-Lou's back—she had apologized and then proceeded to ignore him as any respectable business woman would do.

Too bad her body couldn't ignore him. Every encounter left her feeling restless and achy—and wondering just who Brett McGraw really was. She was afraid if he showed up here, now, she might just ignore him right into her bed.

"Sure enough. Here she is," Rooster said in his best church voice, thrusting the phone at Josephina. She stared at the cell, and every nerve in her body screamed *run*!

"It's your mama."

"You know my mom?"

"No, ma'am."

"Tell her I'm not here."

Rooster was already shaking his head in silent protest.

"Then tell her I'll call her back."

"Sorry, can't do that," Rooster said, not sorry at all. "She sounds worried. Says you haven't answered her calls." He lowered his voice. "And after that earful, can't say I blame you, but getting between two feuding women is about as stupid as me taking on this job when my daddy's hoping to set up house with Etta Jayne soon."

Great, he was practically related to the Granny Mafia. The last thing Josephina needed was for her contractor to walk. Straightening, she took the phone and said, "What do you want, Mom?"

Rooster's disapproving wag of the head matched her mother's tone.

"That's no way to greet your mother." Josephina bit her tongue as her mother went on. "First you ignore my calls, then turn off your phone completely, and now you speak to me with such disrespect. For all you know there was a family emergency and I needed help planning your father's funeral."

"Dad's not dead, Mom. He just called."

"That's not the point."

Yes, it was. But Josephina turned her phone back on anyway.

Rooster silently motioned that she take her time and headed into the house with Boo. A light hammering and the rustling of cabinets sounded from inside, and she was suddenly thankful for the privacy. This was embarrassing enough without adding witnesses to the mix.

"How did you find me?"

"You aren't the only one who spent summers at Fairchild House. Your grandmother sent me to Aunt Letty's every summer until I was sixteen."

That still didn't answer the question of how many people she'd talked to before finding out Rooster was Josephina's contractor *and* currently at her house.

"What do you want? I'm kind of busy." She picked up a hammer and hit the porch rail a few times.

"Yes, I wanted to talk to you about that. I was speaking with your father, and even though we don't approve of your behavior or see the potential in your project, we want to support you." That was so like her mom, to give support in the same breath as criticism. "Darling, if you agree to come home, your father will send over a crew to renovate and run the house. That way the inn is in business and it frees you from fulfilling that silly promise to your aunt."

"It wasn't a silly promise, Mom. And you're missing the point. I want to do this. I am good at this." *Damn good.*

"Of course you are, dear. No one is saying that you're not." Although her tone said exactly that. "It's just you tend to bore easily and it would be smarter to have a professional crew in from the beginning rather than trying to pick up the pieces in a few months."

There went the pearls. "I worry about you, Josephina. You've had a rough few months. Come home and let me help you get refocused and things will settle, I promise."

Refocus—meaning she'd have to change to make her parents proud.

A ball of disappointment settled in her chest. She'd

worked hard over the past few years to curb the impulsive side of her that drove her parents crazy, and their lingering lack of belief in her made it difficult to breathe. It hurt that they couldn't see that all of her past training had prepared her for this exact project. She might take a different path than the traditional one, but she was good at what she did.

A loud zap of electricity sounded from the back of the house and the lights in the front room flickered out, followed by a howl. Whether it was from Boo or Rooster she couldn't tell and didn't care. It was as good an excuse as she was going to get.

"Gotta go, Mom. I'll call you later." Feeling deflated, she hung up. The phone immediately vibrated again.

"If everything's all right, I'm going to call it a day," Rooster said. The hair on his forearms was slightly singed, but the lights were back on. "Powers up and running. Let's just hope it stays that way till morning. I can bring over some traps if you'd like."

"I don't know where I'd move them to." Josephina tried to force a smile to her face.

"Leaving them up in your vent duct isn't healthy. Plus that mama's ornery as a rattler with its tail in a knot. If you're not careful she might just rip your face off."

"Really?"

"It's been known to happen."

Just like the bears, she thought bitterly. "Well, I can't throw them out. I mean, she's only trying to protect her babies."

"It's what mamas do." Rooster placed a hand on her shoulder and gently squeezed. "Even if they go about it the wrong way."

Not knowing how to respond, Josephina quickly thanked him for the power and the use of his phone, returning it to him, and waved until his truck disappeared in a cloud of dust, thankful that she hadn't embarrassed herself by bursting into tears.

Walking into her bedroom, she flopped down on her bed. She should be grateful that she had parents who cared and loved her. And she was, most of the time. It was just that she hated everyone thinking she was nothing but a screw-up. She could make this inn a success and she didn't need their money or connections to do it. She just wanted their love and support.

There was no one to blame but herself. Her parents were only doing what they'd done for her entire life—fix her messes. It wasn't that they didn't love her, they were just trying to protect her. Which was why when her phone rang, she found herself actually smiling when she answered.

"Hey, Mom. I'm sorry about earlier."

"Actually, it's Wilson." Josephina shot up. Her smile faded and any warm fuzzies she had sent out into the universe for her mom instantly evaporated. "Don't hang up."

Josephina closed her eyes and, with a big sigh, lay back. They had spent four years together, she should at least give Wilson a chance to apologize. "Fine, you have one minute."

"Look, I want to be friends."

"Friends don't lie to each other."

"Don't be like that." His sweet tone was really starting to piss her off. Wilson didn't do sweet—unless he wanted something. "We had some good times and I don't want to see years of friendship and memories just go away. I care for you, love."

Josephina looked up at Jimmy Dean and waited for the butterflies in her stomach to start, for her heart to turn over at the familiar endearment. She closed her eyes, focused harder. Nothing.

The only stomach action she got was red-hot anger at the reminder that Wilson had been cheating on her for over a year. With a woman named Babette.

"What memories are we talking about? The ones where you were fucking your employee? Or the one where you left me stranded on a tarmac in my teddy?"

"Like you gave me an option," he bit out, not so sweet anymore.

"This is your grand gesture? Your big apology?"

She could almost see him setting his glasses on the desk and rubbing his face. "You know what, it's not. The only thing I am sorry for is trying to make it work for so long. My life, my career demands order and you're—so damn unpredictable."

"It wasn't that bad," Josephina said, her chest hollowing out a little at the truth behind his words.

"Are you kidding? Living with you was like living with an F-5." Apparently, Wilson had been watching the Discovery Channel again. He liked to watch "learning shows" so he could slide random facts into social settings and sound smart.

"And I'm sure living with me was suffocating," he said, his voice softening, reminding her of the man who had charmed his way into her heart. "Think of how that would have been in a few years, how constrained you'd have felt as a society wife. I didn't want that—for either of us. Not to mention my career couldn't have weathered it."

She looked up at Jimmy Dean again, needing his support. He seemed to stare back, smiling, as if laughing at her. She'd been a society girl her entire life and sometimes that pressure felt like a shot straight to the chest, knocking the happiness right out of her life.

"You're right," she said, trying to ignore the sting of the last part of his statement and trying to instead focus on the fact that she had gotten her closure. "Thanks for the call."

"Josephina."

She hesitated and so did he, which made her palms sweat. Wilson never hesitated.

"Mr. Nakai has invited me to a golf tournament next month in Japan. After the tournament he wants to discuss the possibility of expanding my chain to include the Pacific Rim. The clubs that were in the trunk of the Bentley were a gift from him. I can't show up without them. It would be a slap in the face."

Josephina knew exactly what that would feel like. Wilson's call had nothing to do with apologizing, or being friends, or even checking in on her. It was the last way she could be of use. He'd cheated on her, slept with another woman openly and carelessly, without any regard for her feelings, and now he wanted a favor—from her.

"Sorry. No can do."

"Don't be difficult, Josephina." All traces of the guy she loved vanished. "Your parents and I talked. I am willing to buy you out of the loft if you return the golf clubs."

That money would be more than enough to pay for the renovations. In fact, she'd have a nice nest egg left over. Too bad the cost was so high.

"Can't send you what I already burned," she lied, tapping the nine-iron that had become her faithful protector against bumps in the night and the occasional granny. Plus, who knew if there were really bears out there.

"You burned them? Jesus, Josephina. Those cost a fortune. I guess they'll cost you your inn, too, since you won't get a dime out of me now."

"Well, I hope they don't cost you a Pacific Rim expansion," she screamed, hanging up and feeling impulsive and immature.

Her hands shook as she stepped out onto the porch that sat right off her bedroom. The humidity made a mess of her hair, but for once she didn't care. The smell of dried grass, the old oak tree dancing in the breeze, and her aunt Letty's fairy statue that she'd uncovered in the rose garden chased away some of her insecurities.

In their place rose a feeling Josephina was familiar with. A feeling that, if she ignored it for too long, usually landed her in a heap of trouble. Which was why she normally kept it buried. Not today. Today it made her heart race and her body shake and her mind whisper to her to do something bold, something exciting. Live life balls-to-the-wall.

Messy can be sexy.

Feeling reckless and suddenly sexy, she raced back into her room and jumped on the bed. Standing on her mattress, she rolled up onto her toes and took down Jimmy Dean's hat, sliding it onto her head.

Her mother had been horrified when she'd come to pick her up that last summer. Covered in mud and smelling of slop, Josephina had raced into Letty's house shouting for the world to hear that she'd caught Ham Hock all by herself. She had chased, tackled, and hogtied all two hundred pounds of pork. Her mother had ripped her out of Letty's proud arms and quickly extinguished any dreams she had of marrying the boy over at the neighboring ranch and raising hogs. After that, summers were filled with ballet, violin, and classes "appropriate" for a Harrington.

And look where that got her.

Puckering up, she planted one on Jimmy Dean. If Josephina was going to make things here work, she was going to have to switch it up, go Letty on life. Embrace the mess.

There was only one way to come out of this a better person, and it wasn't by holding back.

Grabbing her purse off the nightstand, she fished Charlotte's card out and dialed before she lost the courage. Whatever Wilson thought, her parents' growing disappointment over her choices, whoever she was, she needed to break free—before she just broke.

One night, her mind whispered. One wild night and then she could go back to being the kind of person who ran a successful business. The kind of person a bank entrusted with its money.

Taking a deep breath, she rested her hand over her heart and listened to the phone ring. Her pulse pounded through her chest. This was crazy. But crazy suddenly felt right, like if she stopped trying to be Josephina Harrington and just went back to being Joie everything wouldn't be so hard.

"Dr. Holden," her voice came over the phone.

"Charlotte, it's Joie."

"It's Joie now, is it?"

"It is for tonight. That is if you're still up for a night out?"

"Now, what would a sweet girl like you have in mind?" Charlotte's smile radiated though the phone.

"Nothing cultured or proper, and something guaranteed to horrify my mom."

Chapter 10

The Saddle Rack was just like Brett remembered—packed, poorly lit, and offering up some of the best hushpuppies in the country. Lone Star was on tap, whiskey behind the counter, and a red and black Atlanta Falcons emblem hung above the mirror behind the bar, making sure anyone who entered knew whose territory this was.

Brett stepped into the bar, causing a chorus of howdys to erupt and making him wonder why he'd stayed away so long. The town might be small and the people nosy as hell, but there was something about this place that was in his blood. It was home.

A few pats on the back and several offers for a two-step later, he sidestepped the dance floor, which was in full swing, and finally made his way to the bar. "Give me a cold one."

Etta Jayne, owner of the Saddle Rack, stood at the bar next to the shotgun mounted on the wall. It was loaded and served as a reminder that she decided who got served, who got played, and sometimes, who got laid. Apparently she was still pissed at him for taking Joie's side the other night, seeing as she served him up a hostile glare instead of a much-needed beer.

After his week, he thought he'd be used to that—being ignored by stubborn women.

He'd only come here tonight because it was better than sitting at home, thinking about doing something stupid. Like going over to Joie's place and asking her out only to be shot down again.

Glory walked up, tray of empty bottles in hand, and shot him a rare smile. Not that she didn't smile a lot. The woman was always flashing those pearly whites and offering up a sweet hey. There was nothing at all sweet about this one. It was a shit-eating grin, one she reserved just for him, and one that he knew all too well.

He and Glory Gloria Mann had met sitting up on the rocks behind the eighteenth hole at the Sugar Country Club. Brett had been waiting for his daddy and Glory had been avoiding hers. They swapped secrets and spit and had been best friends ever since.

"You're looking mighty fine tonight."

Brett looked down. He was wearing boots, jeans, and a button-down. "I look like this every day."

"No, usually you're wearing some kind of logo shirt and a ball cap. With a logo. These clothes you actually paid for." She raised a brow. "Brett McGraw, you're dressed to impress."

"Can't a man come in for a drink and a little music?"

"Not dressed like that." Glory slid behind the bar and poured him a tall one. She had traded in her football attire for a denim mini and worn-in cowgirl boots, transforming herself from Falcons fan to the best beer slinger slash cocktail waitress slash bouncer in all of Georgia.

"Maybe I got all dressed up for you. Ever think of that?" he lied.

Back in high school they had kissed. It was a disaster. It was like locking lips with his sister; then she told him she was in love with someone else.

"Then why do you keep looking at the door?" She slid his beer across the bar. "Grandma told me all about your part in the gun-slinging run-in with her Bible group. Funny. You didn't mention that the other night."

"Must have slipped my mind." He purposely turned his back to the door.

"Seems to me you were all tongue-tied because little Joie Harrington is back in town," she said thorough a grin. "Or maybe your mind was occupied by what she had on under that robe."

Brett picked up the glass and took a long swig. He had no intention of discussing Joie or her robe with anyone, especially Glory.

"If I remember correctly, Joie was the girl you were going to marry and raise, what was it, goats?"

"Hogs." Apparently Brett had shared one too many boyhood secrets with his good friend.

"That's right. You were going to be the best golf player in the world and come back and buy her a pig farm."

Brett smiled against the rim of his mug as the memory from long ago resurfaced. He'd forgotten about that. He and Glory were going to get out of Sugar, get rich, and then marry their secret loves. At least Brett had gotten out. Glory hadn't been so lucky.

Glory grabbed six beers and expertly flipped open each cap. "She looks exactly like you said, barefoot, scabbed, and with the biggest blue eyes."

Except his wild-child Joie was now Josephina Harrington and she was uptown, uptight, and he would be up to his ears in trouble if Cal found out he was considering reminding her just how much fun getting dirty could be.

"Yeah, well, things change."

"They sure do, seeing as just about every single woman in Sugar and even a few of the taken ones have been throwing themselves at you since you got back. You've dated, let me think...not a one."

"So?"

"So, she still gets to you." Glory leaned across the bar and poked him in the chest with her scrawny finger.

"Nope." He shifted in his chair.

"Let me get this straight, because you know I love it when I get to say, 'I told you so.' If she was to walk into this bar, right now," she motioned vaguely over his shoulder toward the entrance, and he didn't have to ask who *she* was, "you wouldn't care?"

"Nope."

"Thank goodness, because I'd hate to see you make a fool of yourself. Again." She grabbed a bottle of Jack Daniel's and lined up four shot glasses. "Especially the way she's dressed."

Shit.

Brett choked on his beer. Setting the glass on the bar, nearly sending Glory's row of shots dominoing over, he turned to look over his shoulder. *Trouble* didn't even begin to describe his situation.

Joie, dressed more for some uptown wine bar than a honky-tonk, walked in wearing another pair of those ridiculous shoes. This time it was fancy boots with a tall heel and high sleek leather that curved around her knees, leaving only a few inches of sweet skin before the denim of her skirt started, and—holy shit—a flimsy gold top that slipped off one shoulder and cupped her very cuppable breasts.

He watched her glance around, nibbling her lip and giving away her nerves. Her eyes locked on his. He raised his hand and, like an idiot, waved. She gave a cordial smile, then ignored him, wiggling her fingers at someone else who was sitting on the other side of the bar.

He worked hard to casually crane his neck, needing to see who the hell she was greeting with those baby-blues, happy it was just Charlotte and Spenser. Not happy when he straightened and found Joie watching him.

With a quick smile that nearly knocked him off his stool, she went back to ignoring him and strode through the crowded dance floor, those hips of hers swaying with determination.

"Admit it," Glory said, resting her forearms on the counter. "You knew she'd be here tonight."

"Nope." But he'd hoped.

Brett took a sip of his beer, this time managing to swallow without making a spectacle while he watched Joie slide onto a bar stool. There was no point in trying to hide his intentions from Glory. She always saw right through him.

Glory set down the dishrag, her expression going solemn. "Some of us never get a second chance, Brett. What if this is yours?"

"You always were a romantic."

"So are you and you know it. You didn't come back home to lie low or because Cal guilted you into it. Besides your family, you could care less what people think of you or those stupid sponsors. You came home to figure out what's missing, what you lost. Sure you went off and won that god-awful green coat."

"Jacket," he corrected.

Glory shrugged, sliding a beer to the guy two seats over. "Whatever, the point is that golf was the means, not the dream."

Maybe that was his problem.

A few days before that video hit the networks, Brett had played a damn near perfect round, winning a decent-sized purse. After the handshakes and autographs and interviews he'd gone back to his hotel room—alone—feeling restless as hell. It was as if something was missing, had been missing for a while. Then he saw Joie with her travel-sized rat and golf clubs, clicking her way down his highway—and suddenly, all the BS didn't matter.

"You saying I should open a hog farm?"

"No, I'm saying you should take things slow with Joie." She held up a hand, silencing him before he could make some comment about just how slow he'd take Joie. "Everything's always come easy for you, and when it wasn't, people made it easy—golf, college, friends, women. Especially women, because you go for the ones who are easily impressed. With Joie you're different, off-balance, like you have to work to make her like you."

"Sweetheart, I wouldn't have to do much more than wink and flash her a smile and she'd fall into my bed."

"And then what? A hot night. Maybe two? Then she gets catalogued like all the rest." She set down some pink concoction in a glass and spread her hand to encompass the women in the bar.

"I thought out of everyone, you knew me better." But when he looked around, a bunch of eyes batted back in his direction. Several of which were just a few feet away, giving him *the look* and waiting for Glory to leave so they could pounce.

"Hey, Brett," one of them said, taking an aggressive step

forward and proving Glory right. Her eyes said they'd met before. Her body language said she was ready to get reacquainted.

"Hey, there...uh..."

"Summer," Glory said, saving him from an embarrassing situation—making it easy on him. *Damn it.* "I was just headed over with your drinks."

"Actually, Summer was just headed home. Weren't you?" Darleen Vander interrupted, her hand coming to rest on Brett's arm.

Darleen Vander was a distinguished Sugar Peach and three years his senior. She'd invited him to homecoming her senior year and took him to her daddy's hunting lodge instead.

Stacked, dyed red, and flashing her newly naked finger, Brett had to admit that Darleen was still an attractive woman. She was also making it clear to everyone in the bar she intended to leave with him tonight.

"I wanted to come over and personally express just how grateful the Sugar Peaches and I are that you so graciously agreed to pose for our calendar." She stepped closer, getting as personal as one could get and still be clothed. "As you know, it's our biggest fundraiser."

"So you said."

"In fact, this year we are donating all the proceeds to help build the new pediatric ward for the Medical Center."

You and everybody else, Brett thought. Half of the organizations that had come to him for help with their fundraisers were donating all the proceeds to pay for the new wing at the Medical Center. It was all Hattie and her ladies choir talked about—well, when they weren't figuring out how to take down the new neighbor.

"Can you imagine," Darleen went on. "The Sugar

Peaches Pediatric Center? Our founding members would be so proud. And with you showing up to personally sign people's calendars, we're sure to win."

"And here I thought this was all about the kids," Glory said, her eyes big and innocent.

Peaches like Darleen made a career out of doing charity work, and spent their life reminding women like Glory exactly who the charity was for. So Brett wasn't surprised by the hostility between the two.

"You are absolutely right, Glory Gloria Mann." Darleen separated the 'A' and attached it to the 'Mann" making it sound like, "Glory, Glory, Amen." A locker room name coined by a bunch of jocks in high school who had, at one time, brought tears to his best friend's eyes. Now it just brought resignation. "This is about securing a much-needed children's ward for our town. I'm sorry, I wasn't sure I heard what you and your mama were doing to help? Oh," Darleen gasped, clutching her pearls. "I am so sorry, forgive me. I forgot."

Forgot, my ass. Everyone knew that Glory's mom had run off with someone else's husband, leaving behind a confused six-year-old with her wheelchair-bound grandma.

Brett plucked the pink drink off the bar top and handed it to Darleen. "You have a good night with the girls, Darleen. And make sure to tell that boy of yours hey for me."

"Sure will, but maybe we can have a drink later?" she asked, taking the glass, unable to hide her surprise when Brett turned back to Glory, placing his hand on hers, asking without words if she was all right. He had hoped that things had gotten easier on her the past few years. Seems they hadn't.

After Darleen strutted off, he said, "If you want me to, I'll tell the Peaches I can't do the shoot. Blame it on Darleen."

"No." She slid her hand out from under his and busied herself wiping down the bar. "Charlotte has put everything into finding the money for the Medical Center, which this county desperately needs. I won't let one mean woman screw that up."

Glory measured the distance from Darleen to the bar and adjusted her voice accordingly, "Look, Brett, I know you didn't have sex with every bunny who's claimed to have driven your driver. But you've had your share of women."

He had. Darleen being one of them. And not just in high school. He'd run into her a few years back in Atlanta. She had been newly divorced from husband number two and he'd been coming off a great season. Ever since, they had made a habit of falling into bed—attached to a box spring or four mud tires, she wasn't picky.

If he came home and she was between husbands, they hooked up. No drama, no strings, just sex with no expectations. Although the last few times, the sex hadn't been all that great. And Darleen had been pushing for some kind of commitment.

Which was why, when he'd first come back into town and she'd invited him over for dinner, making it clear that her son Tribble was at the ex's house for the entire week, Brett gave her some excuse about having to help Cletus prep for the summer camp. And now that he'd met Joie, Brett had no intention of picking up where he and Darleen left off last winter.

Watching her saunter from one table to the next, whispering, while her friends stared Glory down, Brett wondered how he could have ever slept with a woman like that in the first place.

God, maybe Glory was right. He was a pig. Exactly the kind of guy that Joie avoided.

"She does like me, by the way. Joie, that is," he defended. "Said I was sexy."

"Oh, I'm sure she did." Glory topped off each glass of Jack. "Girls like her aren't won with charm and smooth words. Take this slow, put some elbow grease into it, and actually get to know her. See where it goes." Her gaze flicked to Darleen, who stood in the wings, still available and waiting. "Or do a total McGraw thing, go for the easy win, and blow it. Problem is, you might just spend your whole life wondering."

Glory picked up her tray of drinks and slid out from behind the bar. "Believe me, Brett, wondering, even for a heartbeat, sucks. When it's your whole life, it's more like a sentence."

Chapter 11

Josephina was debating changing her order from an apple-tini to a margarita. From the outside, the bar looked like a typical southern dive. A single-story brick structure complete with red awnings over the paned windows and a neon sign asking *Ain't it time you fell off the wagon?* Once inside Josephina couldn't decide if she was in a rodeo, bar, or strip club.

Black-and-white checkered tiles spanned the room and outlined a circular wooden dance floor that was packed with people two-stepping. At one end was a long mahogany bar, at the other a padded pit with an electric bull. But in the center sat a small stage with a disco ball, a church pew, and two metal poles, which she was certain weren't used for pole aerobics.

An unwelcome tingle raced down her spine. Without even looking up she knew who she'd find.

Brett leaned against the opposite side of the bar, looking relaxed and way too tempting in a pair of well-worn button-fly jeans and a dark blue shirt. Same place he'd been when she'd walked through that door ready to ask him for a dance and a roll in the hay.

This time when their eyes locked and he smiled, it was slow and sure instead of shocked, as he'd looked when she walked in—not the look a woman set on seduction wanted to get from her potential one-nighter.

He raised his beer in salute. She tried smiling back, instead shifting uncomfortably in the chair, her legs sticking to the cheap vinyl, which matched the cherry-red tablecloths.

Josephina looked back to her friends and blinked. Charlotte, wearing black slacks, a lavender cardigan set—angora, no less—and pearls, looked as if she should be sitting on that church pew, not a bar stool. And Spenser was in ripped jeans, motor oil, and a black tank top that said LUBE THIS. Her hair was thrown up in a messy ponytail.

Suddenly Josephina's off-the-shoulder, silky shirt and hooker-high boots seemed wrong, on so many counts.

"Remind me again why I'm the only one dressed for this hunt? A hunt that was supposed to be a team effort?"

"The only kind of hunting I do is with a gun," Spenser said around bits of chewed hushpuppy.

"This is my hunting outfit." Charlotte placed an affectionate hand on Josephina's and gave it a few friendly pats. "Of course, it's also my Sunday tea outfit, since this is a small southern town, and when a woman does something like this, although *I* admire it greatly, people talk. And I can't have my mama hearing the prattle come morning."

Josephina froze, a heat burning up her neck, and forced herself not to look around to see who was staring at her. "People know?"

"Honey, this is Sugar," she said. "Everyone knows everyone's business, and yours is particularly interesting, seeing as you're Letty's prodigal niece. Her single niece."

Josephina looked around the bar and found everyone staring back. Everyone.

"After a while, you'll get used to everyone being in your business," Spenser said with a sigh that wasn't all that convincing.

"Oh, God," she mumbled, resting her head on the bar top. "What was I thinking?"

"That he has a great ass."

"*That* you are a beautiful, single woman in desperate need of some s-e-x." Charlotte needlessly lowered her voice for the last part. Over the steel guitar and Friday night commotion, not to mention the humiliation pounding through her ears, Joie could barely hear her.

"I need to find a new candidate." Which was not going to happen. Casual sex was one thing. Casual sex with a stranger. No way. "I mean, what if he knows?"

"Oh, honey, he knows. The chemistry between you two could power the cotton mill on the outskirts of town."

"It's not chemistry. It's called irritation."

"It's enough to split atoms," Spenser said, smiling.

"Will you stop frowning. It causes wrinkles." Charlotte pressed her two index fingers to either side of Josephina's forehead and tugged. "Wrinkles over a man you are destined to have a fling with, I might add."

"I think he's busy." She was frowning again, damn it.

Charlotte peered around Joie, and through the crowded bar. Brett was surrounded by several scantily clad, adoring fans. All female. All attractive. All ready to go.

"Don't get tied up on their account. They can't help themselves. And Brett, well, that's just what happens to McGraw men. They sit down, women line up. It's like some bizarre magnetic force that they were born with. Even after their daddy, God rest his soul, married a northerner, women still adjusted their pearls and took notice when he came into town."

"He married a Yankee?" Josephina asked, rather shocked.

"No, their mama was from Atlanta, which was sinful enough since there were willing women right here in Sugar."

"Well, I'm not the line up kind of gal. Did that once, didn't even know there was a line, and somehow I ended up at the end."

"That's why you need to do this. The man wants you. See how he's listening to Darleen, nodding and smiling and doing all the things a southern man does because his mama raised him right?"

Darleen. Even her name sounded like southern royalty. "You do realize that is the same southern charm that had some bimbo riding him like a bull and showing her goods on national television."

Spenser stopped chewing. Charlotte's eyes narrowed, her mouth pursed delicately in anger.

"What?"

"Those McGraw men do love women, but Brett would never purposely record something like that on film. We may live in a small town and talk a little different from big-city folks, but we are good southern people," Charlotte said, her eyes glassy with hurt.

"I didn't mean it like that," Josephina said.

"All right then, my mistake," Charlotte said, her voice as sunny as if Josephina hadn't just offended the entire South and a good part of the Midwest. "Now, look how he keeps frowning at Jackson standing behind you."

She didn't have to ask who Jackson was, since the sexy sheriff stopped chalking his pool cue to flash her a smile that was heartthrob worthy. Not that her heart—or any other part of her for that matter—throbbed.

She watched Brett take a sip of beer and over the rim of his glass send Jackson a hard look. The sheriff, however, cracked the balls, sending two solid-colored ones into the corner pocket while simultaneously sending Josephina a wicked grin and a wink.

She spun back around on her bar stool. "He just winked at me."

"Well, of course he did. The fact that it surprises you means you're worse off than we originally thought."

"The fact that you're entertaining hooking up with Jackson means you need your head checked," Spenser grunted.

"Ignore her." Charlotte shot Spenser a reprimanding look. "Now turn back around and smile."

Josephina did, and to her amazement he smiled back.

"Well, aren't you popular," Spenser mumbled.

"Oh, God." Josephina's hand flew to her mouth. "Are you and Jackson—?"

"What?" Spenser nearly swallowed her tongue whole, she was sputtering so much. "Me and JD? No way. I like my men good-looking and with a sense of humor."

Charlotte laughed. "Those two have had it out for each other since childhood. Spenser spent most of her money in high school buying eggs and toilet paper specifically for Jackson's car." Charlotte lowered her voice and without turning around, leaned closer to be heard over the game playing on the flatscreens around the bar. "So don't listen to her, because Jackson is a major catch who up until tonight has shown zero interest in getting caught. He is currently single, lives in that gorgeous blue and white Victorian off Maple, carries a gun, and is rumored to use his cuffs in *and* out of uniform."

"If he doesn't date how do you know he likes it kinky?"

"Before he married, he spent a lot of time with the two older McGraws, which meant he was quite the ladies' man. Oh, and like Brett, he's had his eye on you since you stepped into the bar."

"He has?" Jackson was hot. With sun-kissed hair, a lip-smacking body, and wearing dark jeans and a Stetson, he looked as if he'd fallen off the page of some Hottest Cowboys Calendar. Maybe Mr. July. But she was more interested that Brett had been staring.

Jackson tipped said Stetson and his smile widened. At the southern gesture, she blushed—well, tried to—as Jackson rearranged his hat and took a step in her direction. She waited for that heat to build in her belly, for a zing of awareness to make her melt.

Josephina sighed. Not even a tingle.

Jackson was only a few feet away when he hesitated and stopped. His smile faded to a frown and Josephina realized it was because she was frowning.

All she could picture was him and those cuffs, and she started hyperventilating—not in a good way. Armed, handsome, and kinky didn't do it for her. His brows raised in question, not that she blamed him, as she was sending off all kinds of mixed signals.

Josephina spun back around. "Oh, my God. What am I doing? I saw something glimmer on his belt and thought handcuffs and freaked out. I suck at this."

"No, you're just out of practice. You've spent the last few years using moves from college on a guy who wasn't interested."

Ouch.

"I don't think I've ever had moves. College or otherwise." She looked up and down the bar. What was taking so long with the drinks?

"Oh, you've got moves. That whole wild child wrapped in suffocating sophistication."

Spenser snorted. "Says the woman wearing pearls and a sweater set."

"It was a compliment." Charlotte glared at Spenser, then pointed Josephina in the direction of the mirror behind the bar. "You are a woman with womanly needs. There is nothing wrong with two consenting adults partaking in some good old-fashion adult fun."

"He is sexy as hell." Spenser held up a finger and began ticking off all the reasons to say yes. "Smells like a good time and, most important, wants you. Which works in your favor, because you are in desperate need of a lay. It's simple. No commitment. No getting to know each other. No broken hearts."

It sounded so easy when put like that. Problem was, for Josephina nothing that involved emotions worked out easy, and Brett seemed to stir up more in her than just lust. "I don't think I can go through with this."

"Take back the control, honey," Charlotte said, squeezing her hand. "Be bold."

"Men do it all the time," Spenser added. "You came to Sugar to start over, find adventure. Well, your adventure starts here. Tonight."

"Look at him," Charlotte whispered. Josephina did, and her *adventure* looked mouthwatering. "Do you think Brett is sitting over there feeling guilty as sin because he's looking at you as though he wants you to take off everything but the boots?"

"Making whoopie is not sinful," Etta Jayne cut in, setting down two beers, a shot of bourbon, and enough pointed stares to advertise that she'd overheard—no appletini, though. "What's sinful is that top of yours."

"What's wrong with my top?" Josephina looked down. It was slinky and sexy and she'd thought it was perfect for the occasion. Plus looking at her top caused her hair to curtain her face, hiding the embarrassing red tint in her cheeks and giving her something to think about other than Etta Jayne telling Hattie she was planning on seducing her grandson.

"It's gold."

Josephina looked at Charlotte, who managed an elegant eye-roll. Together they had picked out this outfit because Josephina had wanted to make the perfect statement. Although her darling new boots didn't quite say sexy cowgirl as she'd intended, the whole ensemble worked well with her figure and purpose.

Spenser, however, had taken one look at her top and burst out laughing.

"Now, Mrs. Allan, that shade is fitting for Josephina. Look how it makes her skin just glow."

Etta Jayne, in obvious disagreement, gave Josephina a disgusted look and turned to leave. The bar was suspiciously short on appletinis.

"Excuse me," Josephina said, not wanting to start another feud but really needing a shot of liquid courage. "I think you forgot my drink."

"That there's a drink, isn't it?"

"Yes," Josephina said, straightening and trying to emulate Charlotte's elegant take-no-shit posture. "I'd prefer something a little more fruity."

Etta Jayne narrowed her eyes and leaned in really close. "You want fruity? Then go to the Gravy Train. They've got pie."

She snagged a hot basket of hushpuppies from a passing waitress and slammed it on the bar. Josephina did her best not to squeak.

"Maybe order a backbone while you're at it." Etta Jayne leaned in as if imparting national secrets. "You're wasting your good years letting that pansy fiancé of yours still run things."

"Ex-fiancé," Josephina corrected. "And he is not running things."

"Child, my Ralph died while making love. To another woman, a stripper, in church."

"In church?"

"Sugar Baptist Church," Etta Jayne said with a single, firm nod. "It wasn't a Sunday, mind you, but he was a deacon, with key privileges, which he thought gave him other privileges. So I dragged that pew of sin in here and placed it right next to those poles as a reminder. I could have let his cheating ways ruin my life, but I didn't. Cuz then he'd win."

"Etta Jayne," Charlotte chided. "You know that Ralph isn't dead. He's living over in Mobile."

"With that stripper. Same as dead." Etta Jayne dug her hands into her meaty hips. "So what I was getting at before I was interrupted was when the itch takes over, I say scratch it. No shame in that. Why even your aunt Letty, God rest her soul,"—Etta Jayne nodded to the WILD TURKEY WEDNESDAY HALL OF FAME—"she used to say that falling in love's like a roller-coaster, at first it's exciting, thrilling. But in the end, all you wind up with is bugs in your teeth, ratty hair, and a queasy stomach."

Josephina squinted at the collage hanging behind the bottles of liquor and smiled when she got to the faded Polaroid, third one from the top. Sitting on the bar and giving two drunken thumbs up was a sun-weathered woman surrounded by eleven empty shot glasses, two young bucks, and a crowd of Stetson-wearing silver foxes. "Is that Letty?"

"Yes, ma'am. Still holds the county record." Etta Jayne

gave a semiwelcoming smile. Well, she wasn't baring her teeth as she had been a minute ago. "She'd say skip the queasy part and go for the good stuff."

"You are absolutely right, Mrs. Allan," Josephina said, feeling freer than she had in months. She could be carefree. No-nonsense. She didn't even have to think like a man in order to have a one-nighter. She just needed to think like her great-aunt's niece and be Joie, the woman who runs her own life and takes crap from nobody.

Someone on the screen must have made a touchdown, because the bar erupted into a chaos of cheers.

"I'm going to have sex with Brett and then tomorrow go back to being Josephina Harrington, successful proprietor and capable businesswoman."

And there went the teeth. "You're setting a love trap for Brett?"

"Nope." Love implied gas. "A sex trap," Josephina corrected, raising her voice enough to be heard over the sound of the sports fans behind her.

"Is that kind of like a Yankee snipe hunt?"

Josephina shifted on her stool, knowing it was Brett behind her by the way her thighs quivered. This was not how she'd envisioned her night going.

"It's stupidity is what it is," Etta Jayne snapped, and waddled off. And here she thought she was making friends and influencing people.

Old ladies, two. Josephina, zero.

"Well, if you will excuse me, I think I just saw someone I know walk in." Charlotte, the worst wingman in history, sent Josephina a not-so-sly look.

Brett laughed. "Charlotte, you've lived here your whole life. I don't think there's anyone in town you don't know."

"Isn't that fabulous," Charlotte sang, sliding off the

stool, grabbing Spenser, and effectively leaving Josephina to face Brett alone.

Almost able to hear him smile, she remained facing the bar, kicking herself for thinking she could pull this off and wishing he would take a hint and leave. To her vast disappointment he didn't.

She kept her eyes glued to her beer, watching the foam slip slowly down the side and pool on the counter. She wanted to forget the whole thing, drive home, crawl under the covers with Boo, and die silently of embarrassment.

Hiding from her mistakes was what she was good at.

How else could a woman of thirty hold multiple degrees and yet have no career to speak of? It was why she found it easier to grab on to other people's dreams, because then she couldn't mess up her own.

She felt him slide onto the stool next to her and reach out, taking her fingers with his. Tugging her around, he adjusted their bodies so that they were facing each other and their knees were brushing.

"Hey there."

"Hey," she whispered back, peering up at him and knowing that despite the dark lighting he could see her blush. He wasn't so much smiling as looking concerned.

"I was going to offer to buy you a drink, but seeing as you already have one, how about a dance?" His accent, she noticed, got thicker every time she saw him.

She knew she should let go of his hand, it was making what should be nothing feel like something, but she liked how his fingers fit around hers. "I figured your dance card would already be full. Wouldn't want you to let down your adoring public."

He shrugged. "The only girl I'm interested in dancing with tonight is you."

She cringed at the reference that put an expiration date on what she was feeling. Although that was silly. Brett was a master at casual and she was trying to master the concept, so the honest remark should've made her relax. It didn't.

"Brett—"

"Well, you finally admit to knowing my name." He was smiling, but for some reason he seemed nervous.

With his free hand, he reached out and followed the neckline of her shirt, from one shoulder, across her collarbone, to the other arm, pulling the fabric farther down as he went. Her brain went fuzzy.

"Don't let anyone give you a hard time about your shirt. Gold looks good on you. Even if you are in Falcon territory."

Josephina looked around and took in the red paraphernalia, the sea of Falcons' jerseys, and closed her eyes. Why couldn't she, just once, make the right kind of impression?

"And I'm guessing gold would be—"

"Saints color. New Orleans Saints. The Atlanta Falcons' biggest rival. Actually, it is one of the longest-standing rivalries in southern football history." Before she could come up with some sophisticated comeback, he asked, "Why are you always wearing those ridiculously high shoes?"

"They aren't ridiculous! I will have you know that I…that…they're darling," she said stiffly, shoving at his chest.

He didn't budge, except to capture her hand again and hold it there. The bar was alive with excitement, people cheering and clinking mugs so hard that beer sloshed over the rims and onto the floor. But all Josephina could focus on was the frantic strum of his heart as it vibrated against her palm. Everything else disappeared until it was just them, and she felt her embarrassment fade, her body relax, and something inside her go all warm and mushy.

Brett, on the other hand, was actually sweating a little, which gave her the courage to tell the truth. "I wear high heels because I'm only five-foot-three and they make me feel taller. It's hard to be taken seriously when people are literally looking down at me."

For a moment, Brett sat silent, just watching her, the earlier humor replaced with understanding. He stood, moving so close she could smell his soap, and it smelled sexy and woodsy and made her nipples stand up and take notice.

She had to force herself to stay still, to not lean forward and kiss her way up his chest. He tugged her to a stand, their bodies brushing, and even in her heels she had to crane her neck to meet his gaze. He was solid muscle and man, but instead of feeling insignificant, she felt feminine.

"My mama was a tiny thing, would barely reach my chest if she were still alive. She was the strongest person I knew. You remind me of her," he admitted in a rough voice while tucking a strand of hair behind her ear.

A shiver when through her body and the smug grin that broke out on his face told her he noticed.

"Are you going to dance with me or do I have to beg, Joie?"

The way he said her name made her legs wobble. How could she survive dancing with him when all of his good parts would be touching her good parts and making her think about getting him naked? Acting impulsive in private was one thing; letting the whole town see her wild side would be disastrous.

"I don't know," she said, finding this whole casual business confusing. "I don't really know how to dance country."

"It's called two-step and I'm a great teacher." Taking her hand, he turned her in a little spin. When she stopped she was flush against his chest. He leaned in, his lips brushing her ear and his voice warm with emotion when he whispered, "Think of it as twirling with a partner. I already know you're an expert when it comes to twirling."

From a distance they looked like two people about ready to hit the dance floor. But something far more powerful was happening. No lame pickup lines. No arrogant playboy. Brett McGraw was becoming a man with depth and a soft heart. A heart, she decided, that made casual impossible.

He leaned in, his lips brushing her ear. "No pressure, Joie. When you make up your mind, just let me know."

And then that long, easy stride of his carried him across the room, past his waiting fans, and down a hallway at the back of the bar, leaving Josephina wondering what had just happened. How had he attached emotions to what was supposed to be cut and dried?

Just before he turned the corner, he was stopped by Glory, who whispered something in his ear that made him smile. A genuine smile that was warm—real. The waitress went up on her toes, kissed him on the cheek, and Josephina looked away, calling herself a dozen different kinds of fool.

Focusing on the flatscreen over the bar and hating herself for caring, Josephina wondered how, once again, she'd let a man's agenda completely overshadow hers. She'd come here with a plan, a good one, and with one twirl and the flash of a dimple—an extremely potent dimple—she had completely dismissed her manhunt.

She glanced at the photo of Letty and—*oh, my God*—squinted to read what was scrawled on the bottom of the Polaroid.

Letty Fairchild, living balls-to-the-wall.

Josephina looked over her shoulder and found Brett still standing in the same spot, his gaze locked on hers. He raised a brow and shot her an altogether different kind of smile. One that said he knew how to make a woman melt with pleasure, and he wouldn't even have to get naked to do it. At that, something zinged through her body. Something that was bold and sensual and gave her the freedom to let her wild side take over.

Chapter 12

W hat the hell is wrong with you?" Brett asked himself in the bathroom mirror. He hadn't meant to ask Joie to dance. Was pretty sure it would end with them in bed. No, he *knew* it would end with them in bed.

And why in the hell would that be a problem?

He banged his head against the mirror a couple more times. How was he supposed to do this whole take-it-slow-and-get-to-know-her thing when every time he looked at her he pictured her naked? And every time some other guy looked at her—and they were all looking—he felt like killing them?

"You don't do jealous." Brett reminded himself.

He had been fine all night. Watching her from a distance, plotting how he was going to ask her on a date. Then Jackson sent Josephina a smile, one that gave him a 99 percent chance of getting laid, and Brett came two clicks away from busting the sheriff's teeth.

He knew that smile. Had perfected the same one. Intended using it tonight.

Damn it! What was it about Josephina Harrington that had him acting like a jealous boyfriend? She was complicated and irritating and a complete disaster.

And open and adorable and intensely real.

Hell, she got to him, and Brett hated that. The smart thing to do would be walk away. Too bad he wasn't feeling smart at the moment.

The door swung open with such force that it must have shattered a wall tile or two. Brett looked up. The woman he'd been obsessing over was leaning against the door jamb, breathing hard, and her eyes were wild—almost as wild as her golden mass of hair, which hung down to the middle of her back.

Crazy, sexy hair.

"You lost?" he drawled, going for casual and failing miserably.

"What makes you say that?"

"You don't strike me as the kind of lady to follow men into the john."

"Maybe I…" She stopped talking and looked around. Taking in the urinal and condom dispenser, she gasped as if just realizing where she was, then hitched her chin higher, if that was even possible. "Maybe I do this all the time."

"Sure you do. Tell me"—he crossed his arms over his chest—"after you threw open the door, what was your next move going to be?"

She glanced to the floor, but her face remained firm. As if determination drove her. "I was thinking I'd *move* toward you."

Air caught in Brett's lungs. His eyes roamed from her plump lips all the way down to her spiked boots, wondering if that skimpy Saints-colored shirt, which was so thin he could see her nipples budding, would slide the rest of the way down her arm with one simple tug.

"What if someone comes in?" he asked, trying to call her bluff. One of them had to act responsible, and at this point he was afraid it wouldn't be him. He was no better than those teen boys Cal wanted to castrate.

For a moment she looked panicked, as if she were going to bolt back to safety, only she didn't. She pushed away from the wall and took a single step closer to him. "So what if they do?"

Not good.

"Look, sugar, how's about we go have us that dance?" He grimaced at how his accent kept sneaking out. Whenever he got rattled he started smoothing out his vowels and dropping his Rs.

Like now. Standing here, with her, in close quarters, when he was trying to do the gentlemanly thing. Hard task, when there was obviously something more than just scorching chemistry between them—although it had tractor loads of that.

Nope, this something made him want to run like hell and take her up on what her eyes were offering, all at the same time.

"That's why I came in here." She continued toward him, her hips swaying and tugging the hem of her skirt higher with every step. "To tell you, I made up my mind." Not stopping until she was standing between his feet, she placed a hand on his chest. "And I don't want to dance."

"Okay." He took a step back. "You hungry? Maybe we could go grab a bite?"

The universe was conspiring against him, because for every step back he took, she took one forward.

"Not hungry. For food anyway." She paused and tilted her head to the side as if trying to get a read on him. Whatever she saw on his face made her grin. "Brett McGraw, are you running from me?"

Yes. "No, ma'am." His back hit the wall.

She ran both hands up his chest and back down, stopping just short of his waistband.

"Sure seems like you're coming after me, though."

And that wasn't a Joie move at all. She'd been ignoring him for weeks. But now? The woman was stalking him like a mountain lion would its prey. Which shouldn't matter, but for some reason, with her, it did.

Her hands instantly stopped the exploration of his chest. Her smile faded. And those eyes, those blue doe-eyes that kept him up at night, no longer broadcast heat and wild promise but uncertainty and—*aw, Christ*—shame.

"Oh." She dropped her hands and took a shaky step back. Her fingers flew to her hair, smoothing it down. Something, he realized, she did when she was nervous. "I did it again, didn't I? You were just flirting with me while you were waiting for Glory to get off. I made something out of nothing."

If this was nothing, he didn't think he'd survive something.

"I'm such an idiot." She took another step back, and right before she turned to bolt, he reached out and clasped her hand.

"It's something, Joie," he said, pulling her toward him, so close that her body, soft as hell, pressed up against his. Without hesitation, Brett pressed his lips to hers, landing with enough pressure to let her know just how much of a something there was between them.

He didn't want her thinking Glory was the woman he

wanted. And he sure as shit didn't ever want to see her look as vulnerable as she had a second ago.

He pulled back slightly. "I was waiting for you. I was waiting to see if you'd change your mind and wanted to dance with me."

"You don't have to pretend to make me feel better."

"I'm not pretending," he whispered, his voice all but disappearing under the muffled hum of the music. "Trust me, there is nothing I want to do more than make you feel better."

His hands slid down to the small of her back, pulling her body into his and pressing her against his hard proof.

Bad move.

Her blue eyes zeroed in on his mouth and he felt her body melt into his. A heat started well below his belt buckle, and somehow slid upward, settling into his chest.

"Joie," he heard himself sigh when her hand wrapped around the back of his neck and she tugged him down, lightly pressing her mouth to his.

He stood perfectly still as she gently—nervously—nipped and coaxed his mouth. He tried to recall all the reasons why they should wait. But then her soft palms slid under his shirt up his chest, making her intentions very clear as she gingerly traced every inch of his torso with her fingertips, sending his body into overdrive.

"I want you, Joie," he groaned against her lips. "I have since I saw you walking down that highway."

At his comment her mouth turned more aggressive, and so did her hands. She yanked them out from under his shirt, only to push him up against the wall. Her body was tense and her movements desperate.

Something's not right, he dazedly thought. This wasn't Joie. Her hands were all over him, pulling him closer, but he'd never felt so separated from her.

"Want you, too," she murmured, tunneling her fingers through his hair. As if desperate for his taste, her mouth was back on his, kissing the hell out of him.

He felt himself unraveling, splitting at the seams. And it wasn't from her mouth working his, although if he were being honest it was one of the hottest kisses of his life. No, what got to him was the underlying vulnerability behind every sweet stroke of her lip.

"Slow down, sugar. You're not making this easy." He tangled his hand in her hair, his fingers gently stroking the base of her neck. Her pulse exploded under his touch.

"Really?" She exhaled against his mouth, sending a warm puff of air skating across his damp lips. "Let me help with that, then."

She slid her hands up her thighs until they disappeared beneath her skirt. When they came back out they brought a pair of—*hello*—sheer black panties with them.

Sheer. Black. Panties.

He was so screwed. He told himself to look away. But then she started shimmying and wiggling—which did amazing things in moving her shirt lower—and the scrap of lace slid to the floor. And yeah, he looked. Hell, not looking wasn't even an option.

He ran a hand down his face and acknowledged just how fucked up this whole situation was. For the first time in his adult life, Brett had wanted to take it slow. But the girl next door stood looking at him, panties around her ankles, her eyes promising one hell of a ride.

The game had changed somewhere along the way and he was pretty sure he wasn't playing with a complete set of rules.

Her heels tapped on the floor. *Click.*
Ah, shit. Neither was she.

Click. Click. Click

Stepping out of those panties, she made her way back to him, those damn heels creating the sexiest click against the tile, just as they had that day on the hot pavement.

"Does that clear things up, Brett?"

Fuck yeah it did.

Her fingers tugged at the buttons on his shirt, quickly unfastening each and every one. He was mentally reciting all the reasons this was a bad idea when those lush lips of hers trailed over his chest and his dick was too busy praying that she'd head south for a visit to read the memo that this was not happening.

Not here and not now.

"What are you doing to me, Joie?" He ran a hand down her back and lower—telling himself that he was just doing a little recon, checking to see if he could feel a difference sans the panties.

He could.

"Like I said. I want you." She kissed his neck, his chin, his jaw. His brain went fuzzy when she licked his lower lip, giving a little nibble before letting go.

And wasn't that a miracle, because he wanted her, too. Bad. Untamed, fairy-wing-wearing Joie could *kiss*. She also knew how to render a man stupid with those hands of hers, hands that were doing a little recon on their own, right down his back to his ass, and—*sweet baby Jesus*—around the front.

"Sugar, want doesn't even begin to explain what I'm feeling," he said against her lips. "Which is why you should be telling me to stop."

"You're right." She positioned herself closer, doing a little shimmy with her hips that blew his mind. "We should stop."

"We should," he agreed absently as he skimmed his lips down the delicate ridge of her throat. "Getting caught making out in a bathroom with a New York socialite would send my sponsors running."

"Thank God I don't want to just make out." She kissed her way to his ear, her breath hot against his skin when she added, "And I'm not a socialite. I'm a business owner."

"I've always had a thing for business owners," he said, and felt her smile against his neck.

"Let me guess, it's the skirts."

He pulled back. Her eyes were heavy. Heated.

"Maybe it's just you I have a thing for," he admitted, trailing a single finger up, gently skimming over the swell of her cleavage, loving the way she whispered his name.

So he did it again, and her hand dropped to trace the hard ridge of him through his denim.

Yeah, it was her all right. One brush of her hand and breathing seemed to piss off his chest, so he gave up, instead focusing on how incredible she felt. How amazingly soft her hand was as it glided up the front of his pants and then—*bingo*, button popped—back down underneath the waistband of his jeans.

That was his cue to stop, to tell her that he wanted to take his time, wanted to make this perfect, wanted to make her see how special she was. No, that last part was a "needed to," only Joie wrapped her sweet fingers around him—holy shit—they were magical, working him with the exact amount of pressure to make his eyes roll to the back of his head and his hips buck into her hand.

Clearly, his dick was in complete control, overruling every rational reason why they should slow down, because instead of putting on the brakes, he found himself gauging just how big the stall looked. Joie's gaze followed his and she started leading him closer and his hands went to her hips, backing her up, and *Jesus* they were an inch away from doing it against the stall door—and his life being complete.

Except then he'd be that guy, the one who had bathroom sex with an incredible woman, okay, amazing bathroom sex because yeah, it would be off the charts, but it would still be sex in a public place where anyone could walk in and see. And she would never forgive herself. And he didn't want that for her.

"Not here," he rasped, gripping her hips and backing her against the wall when she had him one stroke away from saying fuck it and giving in. He captured her hands and anchored them above her head. With a gentle squeeze on her wrists he said, "Not like this, okay?"

She nodded breathlessly, staring at him for a long, intense second. Brett traced his fingers down her smooth forearms, over her collarbone, promising himself that he would stop there. Too bad Joie had other ideas, which included dragging his hand a little lower to rest on her incredible breasts.

They were even better than he imagined. Almost better than the sexy little sounds that fell from her lips when she fisted her fingers tightly in his hair and took his mouth in a searing kiss.

Almost.

God, he could kiss her for hours—days. Loving the way she tasted, the way her lips teased and nibbled, the way she all but climbed up his body trying to get closer.

She must have misunderstood the "not like this" part of the conversation, because she switched things up again, changing the rules. Clutching the condom dispenser for balance, she lifted her leg and locked it behind his back. The tip of her boot snagged the waist of his pants, digging into his skin. The sting of that sharp heel across his ass was freaking life-altering.

"Counter," she whispered, her voice sounding as surprised as he felt when she started rocking against his thigh. Two seconds of that little slice of heaven and he could feel her body tighten, feel his resistance slipping. "Get me to the counter."

Un-fucking-believable. They were both still clothed—well, mostly—and he was pretty sure that she was two rocks away from—

Brett tore his mouth away, his ears struggling to hear over the pounding of his heart.

"I'm almost there," she moaned. And Brett wanted to be the guy to take her there. He really did.

But there it was again. The worst sound he could possibly hear. The distinct snap of boots on tile. Definitely not Joie's and definitely coming closer.

"What was that," she breathed.

Brett looked into those wide, worried eyes and swore he'd kill whoever walked through that door, and then himself, because he was about to become something that he never wanted to be—Joie's regret.

"We're about to have company."

* * *

"What?" she stared in utter disbelief.

Brett gave her flushed face and well-kissed lips one last look and then shoved her backward, directly into the stall. She found herself plastered against the cold tile wall.

"My underwear!" she shrieked right as Brett shut the door in her face.

Through the crack in the stall, she eyed the scrap of lace

on the floor. Too far to just grab and in a place that whoever was about to come through that door would have to
step over. All she could think of was how she needed them
back. It wasn't as if she had sewn her initials into them, but
that didn't stop her from freaking out. From thinking that, if
seen, a big scarlet S—followed by an L-U-T—would appear
on her forehead.

She made a move for the door, but it was too late. The
footsteps stopped, right outside the bathroom. Brett stepped
into the stall as well, taking up all the space, and closed the
door behind him, locking it. Shutting the lid, he grabbed a
seat cover, draped it over the tank of the toilet, and uncere-
moniously plopped her on top of it.

"What are you doing?" she whispered.

"Making sure those heels of yours, sexy as they are," he
set her feet on the toilet seat and worked on buttoning his
shirt, "stay hidden from view. Doesn't take much for people in this town to talk, and two sets of shoes in the men's
stall will be front-page news by breakfast. Especially a pair
of city boots like those."

He thought her shoes were sexy?

If the door hadn't opened at that precise moment,
Josephina might have started kissing him again. What was
wrong with her? She'd almost had sex. With a man she
barely knew. In the dirty bathroom of a honky-tonk.

Using the condom dispenser for leverage.

At the sound of a zipper lowering, Josephina slapped
her hands over her eyes. Closing them wasn't enough. Because the man Josephina saw through the crack in the stall,
wearing tasseled loafers and starched slacks, sporting a very
distinctive bald spot on the top of his head, was none other
than Mr. Ryan, Sugar's number-one loan officer—and the
man who held the fate of Fairchild House in his hands.

"This can't be happening," she whispered into her hands.

The sound of flushing told Josephina it was okay to look. The water and rustle of paper towels gave her hope that she might even get away without being seen. The sudden halt in his step had her eyes flying open.

She looked up at Brett. He glared through the crack in the door, his face going even harder when a tasseled toe nudged the pile of lace. She had been so busy trying to have her one wild night, she never stopped to think what her impulsive behavior could cost him. Brett had even tried to tell her earlier and she'd brushed it off.

No wonder she drove her family nuts.

She brushed the backs of her fingers against his knuckles. When he looked over she cupped his face and mouthed, "I'm so sorry."

If anything his jaw tightened. Before she could stop him he opened the door and closed it behind him. She couldn't see beyond Brett's back.

"Hey, Bill."

"Brett." Bill chuckled, as if he should have known all along. "Been a while."

"Yeah." Brett bent down and grabbed her panties, sliding them into his pocket.

"Looks like you've had a good homecoming." It was meant as a compliment. Josephina listened for the high-five.

It never came. Just a half-chuckle and a "Well, you know me."

To anyone else he'd come off as cocky. Josephina, though, could hear the strain in his voice, the way his chuckle came out more tired than bragging. If she wasn't so ready to chalk him up as some dumb jock, she'd say he was sick of playing the PGA Playboy. But he was willing to play it if it meant saving her from embarrassment.

"Hey, thanks for helping Lucas with his grip the other day. His coach swears it added twenty yards to his drive. He might even move him up to varsity if his game keeps improving like it has."

"He's a great kid. Got a hell of a swing." She could almost hear Brett shrugging off the compliment.

"Well, I owe you. Maybe this weekend we could play a few holes?" Bill's voice was dripping with so much hero worship, Josephina wanted to tell him to just pucker up and kiss Brett's ass directly. "My treat."

"Why don't you bring Lucas along?"

And that was why, she realized, everyone loved Brett. Everyone in town, it seemed, had some story to tell her about what a great guy he was, how he'd done something selfless, helped some citizen in need. He was superman to them. Through hard work he had managed to turn everyone into his friend, earning their respect while still keeping it casual.

What she was slowly starting to understand was that, while Brett was loyal and giving, he kept the vulnerable part of himself hidden. He wanted everyone to think he was this easygoing, no-problem kind of guy. Which he was. But he also had a really big heart that went way deeper than people gave him credit for. Always so busy making everyone else's life easier, he didn't take time for what he needed.

Josephina didn't understand why he was like that, but she knew that she didn't want to be just another in a long list of people in his life who stood by and let him take responsibility for their stuff. Not that she was *in* his life; no one was really *in* with Brett McGraw, but she was not going to hide in a stall and let him take the fall and ruin what he'd created with these people. She'd started this mess and she would fess up. Even if it meant losing her shot at a loan.

Josephina stood, her heels making a sound on the tile floor. The bathroom grew uneasily silent. She tried to open the door. Brett stood firmly against it. She pushed again. Not even an inch. She wanted to kill him. First, for being the kind of guy who'd want to protect her. And second, for blocking her view.

"Well then, I guess I'll leave you to your, ah," there was a punctuated pause and she felt the banker's eyes trying to peer through the door, "night, then."

Brett didn't say good-bye. He didn't move either, until the door shut and they were once again alone. She told her hands to open the door, only they didn't listen very well, opting to engage the lock instead.

"Joie?" Brett was standing right on the other side. She caught a glint of his stretched-out shirt and mussed hair—with her fingerprints all over it—through the crack in the stall door. "You going to open up?"

Her legs gave way and she plopped down on the lid. She closed her eyes and shook her head, as if he could see. Moments ago it had been confidence and desire directing her life. Now it was humiliation.

After a silent moment, he knocked, the sound making her hand fly to her mouth. "Come on, sugar, open up."

"Go away."

"Not going to happen. Now open up so we can talk about this." He sounded calm and safe, as if with one hug he could make everything okay.

Josephina stared down at her feet and contemplated sticking her head in the toilet. Knowing it would only make her a wet idiot, she closed her eyes and debated. Put on her big-girl panties and open the door to face the situation head-on. Or barricade herself in the stall and wait him out. Either way she needed panties.

She let out a frustrated groan and stomped her feet a few times. She'd come here to find herself. Okay, she'd come to *Sugar* to find herself. She'd come to the Saddle Rack to get laid. She'd failed at both, accomplishing nothing except to make an even bigger mess of things.

Run, her mind screamed. *Open the door and run like hell.* She could pack up Boo and be on her way home in twenty minutes. But she'd already done that, and Fairchild House had begun to feel like her home.

"I can stand out here all night until you decide to open that door. Or you get hungry." Her stomach growled on cue. "Thing about golfers is we get paid a lot of money to stand still and be patient."

The metal of the stalls groaned under his weight as Brett leaned against the door, making himself comfortable and letting her know he wasn't going to leave.

"Yeah. Well in school they called me Job because I was gushing with patience."

Brett didn't answer. He didn't have to. They both knew she was lying. Josephina had the patience of a pigeon. Five minutes in that stall and she'd start weaving church hats out of toilet paper and used gum.

She eyed the roll of paper and wondered how many hats it would make. Her hand reached out to touch it, test its durability.

"I can hear you fidgeting."

She let out a sigh, really hating that he already knew her so well. "Fine, but you have to promise not to look at me."

"What?" He was smiling. She could hear it.

"Turn around or I won't come out."

When he pushed away from the door and turned to face the wall she slowly stood. Peeking through the crack, she made sure he wasn't looking in the mirror and took a minute to appreciate his incredible butt. Good Lord, how could one man own all that hotness? There must have been a shortage on sexy genes for at least a year after he was born.

"Stop staring at my ass and open the door before someone else comes in here."

"Close your eyes."

"Joie." His calm sounded a little thin.

"Fine." Straightening her shoulders, she opened the door and faced her problems as any grown woman in her situation would do.

She walked up behind him and, praying his pants were still unbuttoned, yanked them as hard as she could, all the way to his ankles, and ran like hell.

"What the—?"

"Sorry," she hollered over the slamming of the door as she made her way toward the bar and right into the arms of Mr. Ryan, loan officer and sole witness to her failed sexcapade.

His eyes widened with surprise, then even more with understanding. And Josephina Harrington did what she'd spent her life perfecting.

She ran.

* * *

Josephina drove fast, and always to the right, to avoid another rendition of Dixieland, but no matter how hard she tried she couldn't shake Brett. Or the look on Mr. Ryan's face when he put together just who was taking Sugar's Redneck Romeo for a one-night rodeo in the men's room.

This was what she got for letting her impulsive side roam. Which was why she'd texted Charlotte that she was leaving and run to her car.

She tore down the driveway, slammed the car in Park, and stormed up to Brett's truck.

Ripping open his door, she demanded, "Stop following me!"

"Who said I was following you. Maybe I liked listening to your car's horn. Dixieland, catchy."

She crossed her arms across her chest. Not amused.

Sighing, Brett hopped out of his truck. "I wanted to make sure you got home intact."

She stuck out her hand. "Then give me my panties back."

"Go out with me."

"No."

"Then, no."

She tried not to notice the way his face went a little slack at her rejection, and instead threw her hands in the air, released the mother of all grunts, and turned to make a punctuated exit.

"Hang on, sugar." Brett's arm, warm and strong, snaked around her waist, pulling her back against him. Every nerve ending hummed to life and she had to squeeze her thighs together to ease the building pressure. She was still a jumble of hormones, and feeling his heat seep into her only made things worse. Not to mention it made her heart warm and slowly turn over.

Never a good sign when she was already reminding herself that what he was offering was the exact opposite of what she needed.

Her earlier behavior might have already sealed her shot at making this inn a success. Allowing herself to fall for Brett would destroy her chance at happiness. She had come to Sugar to discover who she was, not to disappear into another relationship. And if she'd managed to get lost in a mundane guy like Wilson, her chance at maintaining her identity with Brett was a big fat zero.

"Just one date, Joie," he said against her neck, his calloused hand sliding across the patch of bare skin between her skirt and shirt.

Goosebumps erupted everywhere he touched, and even the places he hadn't. His goody bag pressed tight against the small of her back and was packed full of party favors. Apparently, all for her.

"It's late, I'm tired, and I just want to go to bed," she lied, not bothering to move when his little finger dipped beneath the edging of her skirt. Okay, she moved, but only to give him easier access.

"I already told you I wasn't that kind of guy," he whispered against her ear, his hands doing some whispering of their own. "And I know you're not that kind of girl, Joie."

And that was her cue to move. She stepped away, hating that her chest felt like it was pressing in—and not in a good way.

Hell, she didn't know if she was capable of pulling off a one-night stand and walking away unharmed. But that's what this time here in Sugar was for, to figure out who she was. So how the hell could he be so confident in his assessment of her?

That was the point, she admitted sadly, he couldn't. And instead of letting her figure it out, he made the decision for her. "Good-bye, Brett."

Of course, he didn't budge.

Suddenly tired, she gave up and headed for the front door. He kept pace with her up the steps and across the porch. Under the moonlight, he relaxed against the railing, watching patiently as she dug through her purse for her house keys. "Go home, Brett."

"Not until you agree to dinner. Or a movie. Maybe a ride."

She looked up at him, since he was now leaning against the door frame, a towering mass of testosterone and sexual power, and rolled her eyes.

He reached into the back pocket of her skirt, pulled out the missing keys, and dangled them in front of her. "I don't know where *your* mind's at. I was talking about a date, which included horseback riding."

"A date?" She snatched the keys. "No way am I spending several hours with you. Five minutes in a bathroom and everything came unglued."

"Not everything."

Didn't she know it.

With a long sigh she turned to look into those devastating eyes. They were crinkled around the corners from that easygoing smile he always wore and sparkled with humor, but tonight they also held a hint of uncertainty.

She understood that feeling. She had thought tonight would be exciting. Fun. A night to remember what it felt like to be free. Feminine. Sexy. Maybe even have herself an orgasm. Or two.

It hadn't turned out that way and she was out of second chances.

"My life is crazy. Between my disaster of an engagement, trying to get this inn ready to open, and earn the respect of the people in this town, I'm not looking to date anyone right now."

"All right," he brushed a finger across her temple, "what are you looking for then?"

"No strings, balls-to-the-wall sex." No hesitation. No shame.

When Brett just stared at her, apparently too shocked

to respond, she shrugged and busied herself with unlocking the front door. Too bad her hands were shaking so hard she couldn't even get the key into the slot. Another recurring problem.

"That's what you were looking for? Balls-to-the-wall sex?"

Her hand slipped at his tone and she dropped the keys to the floor. She bent to get them and his hand covered hers, strong and sure. They both stood, but he held on until she met his gaze. All signs of humor gone.

"Were you using me, then?"

She blinked. "Is that a problem?"

He looked at her a long time and an unsettling feeling settled over her. "Yeah. It is."

"What did you think this was?" she asked, trying the key again, because looking at him with that laid-back, life's-a-game façade missing did funny things to her chest.

"A date."

This time she laughed. "In the bathroom? Be still, my beating heart."

"I was getting ready to ask you out." He sounded defensive and a little unsure. "And you're the one who cornered me."

Yes. Yes, she was. And that he reminded her only added to the humiliation. And the fact that he wasn't listening to her.

"I'm sorry if I read this all wrong and offended you in some way. But even if I was thinking about dating again, which I'm not, you're not really a long-term kind of guy."

Brett started. "Who says I'm not long-term?"

"Brett, you're the PGA Playboy, king of one-night stands."

As soon as the words left her lips she wanted to take them back. She opened her mouth to apologize, but from the way Brett stood, silently staring at her as though he must have misunderstood, the lines around his mouth becoming more pronounced with every second of understanding that passed, she knew she'd gone too far. In the process of trying to make herself feel better, she'd hurt him.

He gave a tight nod and silently took the keys. In one try he slid them home and twisted, swinging open the door.

"Funny thing about that, Joie. I thought I'd introduced myself as Brett McGraw." He handed her the keys and turned on his heel, but not before Josephina saw the raw disappointment in his eyes.

Heart heavy, Josephina watched him make his way down the steps, into his truck, and down the driveway—a cloud of dust in his wake and her panties in his pocket.

Chapter 13

Twenty minutes later, Brett found Cal, slouched over a bowl of cereal at the kitchen table. His eyes were bloodshot, and if Brett looked hard enough he'd bet he'd find a gray hair or two, no doubt thanks to Payton, who was already upstairs sleeping.

Hattie was in the office, counting her latest eBay earnings and estimating how much money they had left to raise for the new pediatric ward. Which left Brett with the choice of dealing with his nosy grandma or his know-it-all older brother.

"Payton said you caught her talking to some kid and flipped," Brett said, repeating what his niece had told him when he'd called to wish her a happy birthday.

"She was flirting. In that two-piece. And he was fucking eighteen," Cal growled. "Nearly killed him. Then Payton. Burned the bikini."

Satisfied that Cal was in an equally shitty mood, Brett grabbed a bowl and a spoon and joined him at the table. Except for Cal slurping up his milk, they finished their bowls in silence. Both poured another.

"Heard Grandma and Etta Jayne issued a feud on the neighbor girl," Cal said around a mouthful of Cheerios.

"Yup." Joie was the last person he wanted to talk about. He could still taste her sweet lips and the bitter rejection.

"Also heard you were keeping that low profile you promised."

Since Cal already seemed to know every goddamned thing that happened while he was gone and Brett was tired of his brother's shit, he didn't bother to answer, instead doing some slurping of his own.

"Look at you, acting all pissy like a woman. Would it have anything to do with 'lying low' tonight with our lace-wearing neighbor at the Saddle Rack?"

"She wasn't wearing lace tonight." *At least not when she left.* "And how the hell do you know if she was there?"

"This is Sugar. And there was a post about it on Hattie's blog."

Brett swallowed. "Grandma has a blog?"

"Facebook and Twitter accounts, too. She says it's to increase traffic so she can sell more of her quilts. She's got over a million followers. Want to know how she gets them?"

No. He did not.

"She writes about her favorite superstar grandson, posts baby pictures, even gives up-to-the-minute information about your life. Kind of like a reality show in journal form." Cal dropped his spoon and the smug grin. "Jesus, Brett. You took a girl out in a robe and teddy?"

"I took her to the emergency room for stitches. And fuck you."

Cal was silent, assessing Brett in a way that told him he'd given away too much.

"Holy crap. You didn't get any."

"What makes you think I went looking?" Brett took another spoonful.

"You're always looking." Cal raised a brow. "Plus, you're wearing a shirt with buttons." His expression went slack a second before he started laughing. "I was right, *you* didn't get any!"

At his brother's remark, Brett surged to his feet, slamming his bowl into the sink and rinsing it out. When Cal fell silent, Brett turned to face him, giving his best screw-you glare.

Cal studied him for a few moments, going serious. "Odd thing is, usually you'd just give up, move on to someone who was interested. You didn't do that tonight. Why?"

Good question. One with a pathetic answer, which Brett didn't care to share with anyone, let alone his pain-in-the-ass older brother.

The truth was Brett liked one-night stands—almost as much as he liked a challenge. And although Joie was a challenge, what she wasn't was a one-night stand. He'd had enough of them to recognize that no matter what Joie was telling him, or herself, girls who believed in fairies and remodeling money-pits were looking for more of a happily ever after. And part of him, a part that he had ignored for most of his life, wanted to be that guy—for her.

For a minute there tonight, a short minute, he thought he could. Then she reminded him of who he was: Brett McGraw, easygoing playboy who spent ten months out of the year on the road, where every new city brought a new bed and a new girl—or so the papers said.

The press got part of it correct. He did tend to take the easy path in life and love, which usually led to just a few nights. Not a future. The part that they missed, though, that

Joie missed, was that deep down Brett wanted to commit himself completely to someone else; he just didn't know if he had the balls to try. He'd lost his ability to stick the night his parents died.

Growing up surrounded by the kind of love his parents had shared, only to have it ripped away in a single night, had taught him how powerful love could be—and how easily it can all be taken away. He craved the connection that he'd witnessed from them, that he had shared with them, but the idea of putting himself out there only to lose—he didn't know if he could handle that kind of pain again. So he'd always kept things casual—until tonight.

"Just following your orders to lie low," he lied. "Keep myself out of trouble. Plus, she's really wrapped up in that inn."

"Son of a bitch," Cal mused, leaning forward in his seat as if straining for a closer look. "It finally happened, didn't it? You found the one girl in all of Sugar that doesn't want to sleep with you and you're sweet for her."

Brett gave a harsh laugh with absolutely no humor in it. Because she wanted him all right, just not the way he wanted her. Man, karma was a bitch.

"I'm not sweet for her."

"Really? Because the last time I saw you this wound up was when..." Cal shook his head and unfolded himself from the table. "I don't think I've ever seen you like this."

Brett gave him the finger.

Cal laughed, a stupid-ass grin following him across the kitchen. "You know what? I take back everything I said. Watching you make a fool of yourself over some woman is worth the risk. So, chase away, little brother. Chase the girl next door."

At the reminder that Joie was next door, for the foreseeable future, Brett felt his stomach hollow out. The idea of seeing her around town, across the lake, sitting on her front porch swing, made him want to pack up and hit some balls. Say, in Hawaii.

"Yeah, well, she doesn't want to be chased."

"Even better." Cal elbowed his way to the sink, slapping Brett on the shoulder. "Perfect way to stay out of trouble and the media, if you ask me."

Brett wasn't asking, because he feared he was already head deep in a sand trap. And this time he had no idea how the hell to swing his way out.

* * *

Josephina stood on the forth rung of the ladder with a sheet of wallpaper over her head, a cutter in her left hand, and a scraper in her right. No matter how long she stood there or how many times she chanted balls-to-the-wall, she couldn't gather the courage needed to crawl up one more rung.

Hands clammy, she sliced the wallpaper horizontally and watched it slip the whole five feet to the floor. She crawled down, then flopped into an overstuffed armchair, hating how her heart felt as if it was going to explode right out of her chest.

Her phone rang. Pulling it from her back pocket, she answered. "Hello?"

There was a tense silence, some heavy breaths, and teeth clicking as though someone was biting through fingernails, then, "Um, hey there, Miss Harrington?"

Josephina sat up. "Rooster? Are you all right? When you didn't show up yesterday I got worried, then when you didn't return my calls—"

"Yeah, about that." The knot that had settled in the pit of

her stomach yesterday tightened. "Seems I've got me some back problems and I don't think I'll be able to get out to your place for some time."

Josephina rolled her eyes at how he emphasized the last two words, implying that Hattie would be crowned Miss Peach before he'd ever come back to her house.

"So by back problems, do you mean the weight of five overbearing and nagging grannies obliterated your spine completely?"

Rooster stuttered and gasped for so long, Josephina almost felt sorry for the guy.

"Look, don't worry, Rooster. I get it. I'll send you a check for the work you already completed."

He mumbled some apology and they hung up. With a weary sigh she leaned back and took in what she'd spent three and a half hours accomplishing. The wall looked like the rest of the room, bare plaster up to her head and dusty roses spanning the remaining fifteen feet of the wall.

Josephina sighed. This was what happened when one's contractor went MIA, then up and quit, forcing one to make do with limited demolition skills.

She closed her eyes and laid her head back. After four years of interior design school and three more spent in the field, Josephina Harrington couldn't manage to take down wallpaper.

Accepting defeat—for now—she walked over to Kenny, pulled back his head, and took a handful of candy corn. Last week, she'd wisely replaced the poker chips with corn syrup, carnauba wax, and yellow dye number 5. She shoved them into her mouth and savored the sanity the sweetness brought.

Licking her fingers, she scrolled through her contacts. She had already expanded her knowledge of construction, but unless she found a book on how to install window flashing with a chapter on overcoming vertigo, Josephina needed to find another handyman. She had told the bank she'd be up and running by summer's end—meaning she had a lot of work to do.

* * *

Brett stood under a MEMAW & PA-PAW'S GROOM, FEED, AND RESCUE banner with a goat humping his leg, a pug clutched in his arms, and Mrs. Wilkes's hand cupping his ass.

"Smile." She squeezed. "And don't you worry about nothing. This is going up above the register. Right next to the one from last year. You're still our hometown hero."

Brett silently swore. He was exhausted, smelled like livestock, and hadn't eaten since breakfast. Today was his day off, but he was feeling guilty, and helping Mrs. Wilkes with her grand opening groom and vaccine drive had become a tradition. So he smiled, took the photo, and went back to hosing off a donkey.

The tradition had started six years ago when Brett's season was sponsored by one of those chain pet stores that, according to Memaw Wilkes, spent its big bucks putting hardworking folks like herself out of business. To help balance the scales, and his guilt, Brett had agreed to be her spokesman and help out every time he was in town.

Today was no different. Only this time the money went toward the new wing at the Medical Center, and his guilt came from how he'd spent the past forty-eight hours. Instead of listening to the part of him that wanted to make Cal proud and protect Jace, Brett had ignored his brother's advice and gone to Illinois for the tournament. His fans were expecting him, his sponsors counting on him, and his name was on the ad.

Oh, and it was a thousand miles from a certain blonde socialite he couldn't get out of his mind.

Unfortunately, he'd missed his flight—and a scheduled interview with ESPN—lost by a stroke, and ended up in an elevator with Dirk Stone and his daughter Bethany. The press went apeshit. Cal threatened to beat his ass. Jace had to go underground for a while, moving to Daytona to work for an old army buddy. The only bonus was that Hattie had doubled her money on eBay.

The last thing Brett wanted to do was come out here, with everyone smiling at him as if he hung the moon, and groom Ms. Mann's armadillo, who sat patiently in the wheelchair with his owner.

Not only was Jelly-Lou Glory's grandma, she was also Brett's childhood Sunday school teacher. Wondering if the woman who taught him the Ten Commandments on a felt board had watched him making the beast with two backs on national television had his chest constricting and his hands sweating.

"Afternoon, Ms. Mann," Brett said, forcing his legs to move and his arms to scoop up the armadillo. Before she could tell him how sorry she was for his predicament, or make some crass comment about Bethany and her family, he rushed out, "Is Road Kill here for his oatmeal-cucumber bath?"

"Yes, he is. It works miracles on his dry skin. And I just love when they put those cute little bow ties on him." She patted Brett's hand. "But don't you worry yourself, I can have one of the others wash him."

"That's all right. If I can handle Ms. Longwood's geese, Road Kill will be easy."

"I'll do it, Uncle Brett," Payton said, resting her hands on the wheelchair handles.

Brett looked around for Cal. Didn't see him, but noticed that a group of senior boys had their eyes fixed on his niece. Brett glared until the kids ducked their heads.

"Does your dad know you're here?"

Payton held out her arms in response. Dressed in a pair of head-to-toe blue coveralls and a ball cap, the kid looked miserable. Especially when it was pushing a hundred and her teammates were flittering about in shorts and tank tops, making plans for a BBQ at Sugar Lake.

A BBQ Payton wouldn't be going to. Wanting to make some summer cash, his niece had taken up tutoring at the library. Too bad for Payton that her first customer had been eighteen, on the varsity football team, and more interested in anatomy than algebra. Too bad for the kid, Cal showed up early and nearly tore his head off. Payton's tutoring career came to a premature end, and she was sentenced to three weeks' community service—with the elderly.

"Grandma asked me to bring you this." She held up a paper bag. Brett's mouth watered at the grease-stained bag. "It's fried chicken. She wanted to make sure you ate."

"It's also a ruse." Jelly-Lou looked around and dropped her voice to a conspiratorial whisper. "To give you time away from all the shameful gossip about you and that girl. Vultures."

Brett looked at his niece and shifted on his feet. "The press can be—"

"Not the press, dear. The nosy people in this town. Sinners, every last one of them. They've got a pool going to see if she's carrying a McGraw in the oven."

Brett choked. "That video was taken two years ago."

"Not Miss Stone," Payton clarified. "Miss Joie."

"Joie? But I haven't...We aren't even seeing each other."

"Neither were we." His niece looked over her shoulder at one of the guys and gave a sad smile. Brett almost felt sorry for her...until he looked at the boy in question.

Payton wasn't showing a speck of skin but the kid smiled back all the same. His eyes, however, said he was still thinking about anatomy. He was leaning against the wall, arms crossed in a way that flexed his biceps, showing off a stupid-as-shit boy-band tattoo. All Brett wanted to do was walk over and kick that grin off his face.

"God, you're as bad as Dad," Payton cried. "We didn't do anything wrong and now, because Dad freaked out, everyone's treating us like we did. I thought *you'd* understand. Guess I was wrong."

She tossed him his lunch and scooped up Road Kill. Tears in her eyes, she stormed off before Brett had a chance to set things right.

Shit.

"It's the hormones, dear." Jelly-Lou patted his hand. "Now, go on and eat up. Maybe even take a little nap. You look worse for wear. Don't want to add sleepless nights to the speculation."

Brett looked around. Every single person in that parking lot was staring at him. The minute he locked eyes, each and every one of them sent a big nod and smile. Too big.

Having a hard time breathing, he thanked Ms. Mann, made a note to apologize to his niece, and headed for his truck.

As he rounded the back of the building, kicking himself for disappointing everyone, he plowed into someone with enough force to send that person tumbling. He heard a startled gasp followed by an angry yap.

Quick on his feet, Brett grabbed hold to keep them from falling into the Dumpster. When his arms met soft curves, silky hair, and needled teeth, his brain registered that this was not just someone. This was the last person he wanted to face right now. And her dog was practicing lockjaw on his arm.

Joie looked up through startled eyes, the sexy scent of whimsy washing over him. They stood there, with her wrapped around him, his hands low on her back, the smell of tossed-out dog food turning in the hot summer heat, and Brett felt all of the tension seep from his body. Which was as ridiculous as the goofy grin he wore.

To his amazement, Joie grinned back. Her hair was swept up in a ponytail but she was back to wearing her trademark uptown wear. Boo, who had on a baseball hat and stupid-ass doggie tennis shoes, growled, which meant he'd finally let loose the death grip on Brett's arm.

Boo barked and sank his teeth back in.

"Boo," Joie scolded, taking a step back. Brett would have put up with Needle-Teeth if it meant keeping her in his arms. "I'm sorry. Did he hurt you?"

He looked at his arm briefly. Seven little puncture wounds, when turned sideways, seemed to make a smiley face. He glared at the dog. "Naw, a little thing like that couldn't even hurt a kitten."

Boo lunged, trap snapping.

"Bad, Boo," Joie scolded, setting Fido on the hot cement and turning her attention back to Brett.

Boo pouted.

Brett preened.

Joie took his arm, her cool hands sending a sexual kick right to the gut. "I don't know what's gotten into him, he usually loves people. Are you sure it doesn't hurt? Maybe we should see if they have anything inside to clean it out."

"I'm fine." He placed a hand over hers, stilling it.

Her focus shifted between their hands and his eyes several times. Her lips parted on a breath and then, sadly, she stepped back. "I guess you have enough soap on you to ward off germs anyway."

He dropped his gaze to get his mind off those lips, which did him little good. Because now he was focused on her shirt, which was white. And sudsy. "I got you all wet."

She looked down at her designer blouse and shrugged. "Who knew a flock of geese could be so dangerous?"

And just like that, any hope of him getting brownie points for helping animals in need was blown. How bad-ass could a guy look when he'd been taken down by an angry mob of geese?

That she knew, though, meant she'd been watching him.

As if reading his mind, she flushed and said, "I was on my way to meet Mr. Ryan about my loan. I have a two o'clock."

Knowing it couldn't be that late, Brett looked down at his watch. Tinker Bell was early.

"I know." She smiled shyly. "I was so afraid I'd be late, I ended up being an hour early. I was going to see if Spenser wanted to grab a bite at the Gravy Train when I saw the sign for Memaw and Pa-Paw's grand opening," she paused, confusion lining her brows, "which seems odd since the sign next to it marked their sixtieth anniversary of being in business."

Brett felt himself flush, and it wasn't because of the triple-digit temperature. "Whenever I come home, if it falls on the eighteenth, Ms. Wilkes has a grand opening. She says it doubles her profits and helps get the locals to vaccinate their animals."

"The eighteenth?"

Brett blew out a breath, hating that what he was about to say made him sound like a tool. "She calls it her 'eighteen hole-in-one'. For eighteen dollars you can have your pet vaccinated, clipped, and groomed."

Brett watched to see the reaction that would cross Joie's face. To his surprise, she didn't look at him as if he were either some hero or a tool. Instead her eyes went soft and she placed her hand on his shoulder, gently tracing a finger down his arm, leaving behind more than just the need to have her naked and moaning his name.

"By none other than Mr. Hometown Hero." She shook her head, her ponytail brushing from side to side, reminding him of the girl he'd rescued from Letty's old oak tree. "That must be exhausting."

"Grooming animals all day?" He lifted a shoulder, trying to play off how tired he was.

"No. Always trying to manage everyone's expectations."

Brett didn't know how to respond, because managing expectations had become so second nature, he didn't even recognize when he was doing it anymore. But instead of explaining that letting down the town that had rallied behind his family after his parents' death felt like a betrayal of their memory, he stood there like an idiot, staring into her eyes and nodding, hoping he met her expectations.

"Look, about the other night."

Joie placed a finger against his lips and stepped closer. Wrapping her arms around his waist, she tucked herself firmly against him and just held on.

Brett closed his eyes and melted into her, loving how grounded he felt. These days, most of his time was spent in flux, balancing his needs against the needs of those he was responsible for. Yet this little pixie of a woman stood there, offering him something nobody in his world usually took the time to give—support.

A minute or fifteen might have passed before she gave him a final squeeze and stepped back. Her face was open and unguarded, and he wondered what she saw that made her lips turn up into a sweet smile. Before he could get any answers or even wish her luck on her appointment, she slid her hands up to cup his face and placed a gentle kiss on his cheek, then silently headed down Main Street toward Spenser's garage—her dog strutting behind her.

Brett watched until she disappeared into the open bay of the shop.

Heart beating too fast, appetite nonexistent, Brett tossed the chicken in the Dumpster and headed back to help Ms. Wilkes close out the day. Washing pets was a perfect distraction from what had just happened and gave him time to put the past few weeks into perspective.

Time he'd no doubt spend obsessing over what the hell he was going to do with the neighbor girl who drove him to distraction. He hadn't even tried to get her into bed. And that scared him more than the sight of Mrs. Winslow and her pet alligator.

* * *

Brett was exactly where he wanted to be—sitting on Joie's front porch swing with Joie sitting on him in nothing but her blonde curls and tanned skin. Her legs tangled around him, pulling him closer as she arched back, sending that wild mass of hers sliding across his thighs.

Oh, my! she moaned, rising up only to slowly slide back down. She felt incredible, the way she wrapped her body tightly around his as if she never wanted to let him go. Couldn't let him go.

Her mouth worked his before heading south, down his

chest, until she untwined their bodies and dropped to her knees on the weathered wooden porch. She took him in her hands, her eyes huge with appreciation, and licked her lips. Her gaze flew to his, heated and full of wonder.

Would y'all look at that?

That didn't sound right. Brett opened his eyes and…

"Jesus Christ!"

"Watch that mouth, there are ladies present," Grandma Hattie snapped, her voice crackling with outrage.

Brett opened his mouth to say—what? He had no idea, because standing next to Hattie were her poker buddies. With cameras. Their arthritis-riddled fingers and walkers having no effect on how fast they could snap off shots.

"Dottie, you hold him down while Jelly-Lou gets that Stetson on him," Etta Jayne said, reaching into her fanny pack and pulling out a professional-grade lens.

"I bet it'll get triple the money," Hattie said, her sausage fingers rubbing together in the universal sign for "pay up or shut up."

A flash went off. When the green and yellow spots finally stopped dancing, Brett saw a smiling Etta Jayne, wiggling her pudgy little fingers at him.

He looked down. Nothing but underwear. *Great.* He adjusted the afghan over his waist and stood up.

"Little late to pretend modesty now, don't you think?" Etta Jayne looked her fill, and Brett could feel the heat creeping up his neck and inflaming his ears under the intense scrutiny. "You used to run naked through my sprinklers. You ain't got nothing I haven't seen before."

"I was a kid."

Etta Jayne shrugged.

Brett ran a hand though his hair, which he was sure looked more like sex-ruffled than bed-rumpled. He'd have to sweet-talk his way out of this, because if those photos wound up on the Internet, Cal would kill him. The good news was that, since they were all women, he was pretty confident he'd walk away with all three cameras and his pride.

"Now, ladies." Brett unleashed his award-winning smile.

"Don't you flash those dimples at me," Hattie scolded, stepping forward. "Here's the deal. We aren't making the kind of money we used to with your autographed golf balls, and the town is still short for the new wing."

"And these pictures will be like having our own printing press," Dottie said.

"Pictures that you will hand over immediately," he threatened. "Because new wing or not, that"—he eyed the camera—"is not leaving this room or I'll be too busy cleaning up my career to MC the Sugar Ladies Baptist Choir Summer Concert."

"We're counting on that money, and you already agreed," Jelly-Lou said, panicked, rolling her wheelchair closer.

"He doesn't look very agreeable right now," Dottie whispered to Jelly-Lou.

"He's a McGraw. Man of his word," Etta Jayne countered, staring Brett down.

"A fact that I hope you all remember and take to heart," Brett said, glaring at his grandmother. Hattie took a seat on the couch and glared back.

With a sigh, Brett grabbed his jeans off the floor and tugged them on. If he was about to be blackmailed into helping out with whatever harebrained scheme they had going on, he wasn't going to endure it in his skivvies.

"Here's the thing, son." Hattie tossed him a shirt off the floor. He smelled the pits and pulled it over his head.

"We've played cards at Letty's place every Monday night since that tornado tore through Sugar in the spring of '58. The same year I lost my Ray. And no Yankee is going to come into our town and ruin over fifty years of tradition."

"And drinking," Dottie added.

"And since Letty's niece got her knickers in a twist, we're short a location," Hattie said.

"What does this have to do with raising money for the medical center?" he asked.

"Well, you want these photos and we need someone on the inside." Dottie steepled her fingers in front of her mouth, excitement pouring from her. "Feeding us information about Joie's schedule."

"So basically, I'm being blackmailed by the Sunday School Mafia?" Not a single lady had the decency to look even a little embarrassed.

"We need someone to keep her busy so we can continue having our Monday nights there until we find a place." Jelly-Lou said, her eyes big and innocent-looking.

"Or she gives up and goes home," Etta Jayne mumbled, cutting to the heart of the matter.

"And you were hoping that that *someone* would be me?" he asked, the throbbing behind his right eye escalating.

All four women nodded vigorously, suddenly looking like quilters instead of extortionists. Not that Brett wouldn't mind spending every Monday night holding hands and showing Joie just how beautiful Georgia was. Hell, just the thought had him smiling like a damn teenager. But he wasn't willing to betray her trust like that.

"Look, I know how important Mondays are to you." He did. Hattie had never missed a one. They'd even invented Re-Run Monday's at the Saddle Rack during the off-season, knowing that football would attract a crowd and distract folks from noticing that the Bible study ladies never carried Bibles. "But it doesn't justify spying on Joie."

"No one will know the truth," Jelly-Lou said. "The whole town knows she was looking to have relations with you."

Relations? Yes.

A relationship? Not so much.

"It's not going to happen, ladies."

"Well, now, see, I was telling everyone down at the Gravy Train about what a good job you did on building me my ramp," Jelly-Lou said with a smile that let Brett know he'd just been buttered. "Then Hattie reminded me how you paid your way through college, helping Cal build houses."

"Rumor around town is that she's in need of a contractor," Hattie said.

"She's already got a contractor."

The women studied their shoes. *Ah, hell.* With his thumb and forefinger he pinched the bridge of his nose. The smart thing to do would be to walk away. His gut was telling him that every second he stood there listening to their crazy-ass idea, it became more likely he'd get sucked in.

Then again, as Brett was fast learning, he didn't always do the smart thing.

"What did you say to Rooster?"

"Seeing as his daddy is interested in being my gentleman friend." Etta Jayne crossed her arms over her chest, jamming her fists in tight. "And this being a family feud, it would be outright disloyal for Rooster to keep taking a paycheck from that woman."

"*That woman* is your late friend's niece and rightful owner of that house."

"Wasn't how it was supposed to happen and you know it," Jelly-Lou said gently, rolling forward until she was right at Brett's toes.

He looked down into her soft eyes and knew that something else was going on. These ladies were stubborn and a pain in his ass, but they weren't outright mean.

"Only one of us belongs there," Dottie said, and the others "Amen-ed" and "God's truth-ed" but Brett was too tired to point out that there were four of them, not one.

"And it ain't her," Etta Jayne spat, and okay, *she* had a mean streak as wide as the Gulf, but it was usually backed by pure intentions.

"Not like she has the money to pay him anyhow, seeing as she was turned down for the loan," Dottie added.

"The loan she wanted to make Letty's dreams come true? And the loan that *your bank* turned down? What were you all thinking?"

This time they all had the decency to look ashamed.

His heart hurt for Joie. He knew how much she was counting on that loan.

Why hadn't she told him? Because she was stubborn and proud and one hell of a strong woman who would see admission as a sign of failure.

It had been four days since her second meeting with Bill Ryan. Brett wondered when Rooster had stopped showing up at the site. How long it took her to realize she was in this all alone. Then cringed at the idea of Joie forty feet up, swapping out roof shingles and cleaning gutters.

Brett dropped to the couch and took Hattie's hands, noticing how fragile they felt. "What's really going on, Grandma?"

With a sigh, Hattie dropped her gaze to focus on her lap. When she looked up, all of the stubborn bluster was gone and in its place was a deep sadness that Brett felt clear to his bones.

"We're not ready to let go, son. That house—" Hattie

stopped and took in a shaky breath. "It's all we've got left of her. It's not that her girl isn't a proper southern lady, or even that she's a Yankee. She's just got all these ideas and plans and we need a little while longer with our Letty, just as she is."

Letty had only passed last summer, and he knew his grandma was struggling with moving on. All of the ladies were close, but Letty and Hattie had bonded over losing their husbands the same year. And even though it didn't excuse the way they'd treated Joie, Brett understood what it felt like to let go of someone you love when you weren't ready.

"How long do you need?" Brett asked, rubbing a hand down his face.

The ladies shared a look.

"You can't have it forever," Brett added, reading their minds. "But maybe I can make it so that everyone walks away with what they need."

"Letty's birthday is the end of next month, and we wanted to do right by her memory—you know have a party in the salon, like we do every year."

"Why don't you just tell Joie? I bet if she knew what you were planning she'd let you use the house," Brett said, knowing it was true.

"That girl would hear party and want to help, but we need to do this the southern way." Which Brett assumed consisted of cigars, poker, and copious amounts of moonshine. "Meaning no Yankee to ruin our traditional mock apple pie contest and moonshine shoot-off."

He wasn't sure if the shoot-off portion of their tradition referred to how they got the moonshine into their mouths, or mixing target practice with drinking. But he did know one thing. "Mock apple pie was invented by the Pilgrims." All four ladies looked at him blankly. "*Meaning* it would be a Yankee tradition."

"Hogwash," Etta Jayne snapped, all a-bluster. "Doesn't matter anyway, this here tradition started with just the five of us in that salon and it needs to end with just the five of us."

Brett felt his heart give a little. He wanted his grandma to have her good-bye, wanted Joie to realize her dream of opening the inn, and—*Lord help him*—he did not mind the idea of watching Joie traipse around in coveralls with paint in her hair and dirt under her nails.

Man, his body was already humming. And since all he did around here was watch his competition gain on him or have his every move documented by Hattie, Brett formed a plan. One that would make everyone happy—and his life a whole hell of a lot easier.

"All right, here's my offer. I'll help her with the house, make sure that she leaves the salon alone until Letty's birthday. But then you've got to find a new place to hold your poker game, and no more causing trouble for Joie. She's had it rough enough without the Hatfield-McCoy welcome you all rolled out. No more talk about her dog having rabies. That Ms. Longwood's missing geese are now in her down comforter. Or that she blew Letty's estate on enhancing her...peaches."

Although he knew enough to assume the other rumors were false, he had firsthand knowledge to discount the last one. Firsthand knowledge that had him grabbing his keys and trying to remember where he put that tool belt.

"Now hand over the cameras and we have a deal," he said.

They all crossed their arms at once, their stubborn chins raised in defiance.

"This is the only offer you ladies are going to get. Understand?"

The women remained tight-lipped. So did Brett. He could outwait them all—and he did.

"Fine," Hattie caved, her tone letting him know that she wasn't happy about it.

Brett was scared they'd all want to spit and shake on it, but Etta Jayne finally held out the camera and Brett allowed himself to breathe. Until he opened it.

"Where's the memory card?" he asked, checking and rechecking the card slot.

"What kind of grandma would let someone take indecent photos of her grandson?" Hattie tutted, giving Brett a little pat on the cheek before standing and making her way to the door, her cronies waddling in her wake.

"Oh," he said, feeling a little grouchy that he'd been played—by a bunch of old ladies, no less. "And stop stealing her damn car."

Hattie turned and feigned shocked horror at his accusation.

"I've seen that ugly tank parked behind the shed, so don't look at me like you are all Sister Maria. Walking into town in those shoes can't be good for her back."

Although it did wonders for his fantasies.

Chapter 14

Josephina had spent the past few days trying not to cry. The day after Rooster quit, she'd gotten word from the bank that she wasn't a "solid investment," but if her father were to cosign they might be able to reach a deal. To which she said, thanks, but no thanks.

Knowing she wasn't a contractor or even a decent do-it-yourselfer—something she intended to take up with the author of *Remodeling for Dummies* as soon as she figured out how to change the blown fuse so she could get the electricity back on and email them—she was determined to plunge ahead.

Yes, it was unfortunate Rooster had quit and that she'd been denied that loan. Those things would make it harder, but not impossible. Neither Josephina nor Boo was willing to give up. For the first time in her life, Josephina was going to finish. Even if it meant remodeling every inch of the inn herself.

She pulled on a pair of boots, lace-up, with steel toes, in

an adorable shade of fawn—her latest online find—grabbed her tools, and started knocking out a door-sized hole in the partition between the kitchen and the dining room. When finished, the open archway would bridge the gap between food preparation and food appreciation, making the meal a complete experience. It was also a great way to blow off some seriously pissed-off steam.

By ten Josephina had worked herself into a sweaty mess with a major bone to pick. That those ladies had been coming to her aunt's house all those years didn't give them the right to dictate what happened to the inn or destroy people's dreams. She had assumed the position of doormat for most of her life. No more.

She jumped up and swung, her makeshift sledgehammer failing to make contact with the wall. Her arms were burning and her back screamed, but she had to finish this before she'd take a break.

Josephina took another swing, finally admitting that she wasn't tall enough. So she jumped.

"Damn it all to hell." Swinging in midair wasn't giving her enough leverage to break through the sheetrock. Plus there was a framed photo hanging on the kitchen wall of Letty and her poker buddies, grinning down on her as if amused.

Stomping into the kitchen, past the ladder and a tempting pitcher of sweet tea, Josephina grabbed a napkin, then a chair. Placing the napkin over the photo and the chair directly under the still-square arch, she climbed up and went to work. She would beat that wall until it was the perfect arch, then soak in a nice bath while sipping her sweet tea and locating the chapter on framing. Followed closely by the chapter on drywalling and finishing.

"Afternoon, neighbor."

The sexy greeting came from nowhere. Josephina spun around, sending the chair teetering on its legs. Her arms flailed as she tried to regain her footing. But she was too far from any sound wall. The chair's legs went left, hers went right, and then she was sailing through the air in the camel pose, a position she had been working to achieve in yoga for three years and suddenly mastered midair while plowing into Brett.

His chest slammed into her cheek, her knee clocking him between the legs. He gasped as they tangled, stumbling back a few feet before crashing to the floor.

Josephina lay on hardwood, her body sprawled across his, her right eye twitching erratically, when a pair of capable hands ran down her body to settle on her ass. And squeeze.

She smacked Brett on the chest but didn't move. After two weeks of looking at Rooster's belly, followed by six days of only Boo and the opossum family for company, Brett was a welcomed sight. Boo, on the other hand, felt the need to bare his teeth and growl.

"What?" Brett asked Boo, who merely snarled in his teal track suit and collar. "Just checking to make sure the lady's all right." His blue eyes met Josephina's, and she might have involuntarily moaned.

"I'm fine. And you've only checked my butt."

"I know." Another squeeze. "You took a pretty hard fall."

She shoved off his chest and stood.

Brett got to his feet in one fluid motion and turned around, showing her his butt. It looked spectacular in worn denim that was faded in all the right spots. "Mind checking mine, then?"

Josephina stuck her hands behind her back to keep from taking him up on his offer. "What are you doing here?"

Now that his mistress was off the enemy, Boo pranced over to the front door and sat, as if telling their guest it was time to hit the road. Brett ignored Boo and inspected the piles of broken sheetrock, the sketches and magazine tearouts she had taped to the china hutch—and the big unfinished hole in the wall.

"I guess I could ask you the same thing."

Embarrassment hit hard. She was aware of how ridiculous she must look. Standing in the middle of a ground zero wearing cutoffs and an old college tank with a pink bandana tied around her head.

"Making a walk-through from the dining room to the kitchen. Letty wanted it to have rounded edges with scalloped molding." Josephina nodded toward the hanging sketch that Letty had sent her years ago. "But it's looking more square than arch-shaped."

"Ah, sugar, say it ain't so." He spoke as if actually in pain while he looked at the hole in the wall, then back at the golf club. The one Josephina was using as a sledgehammer. "With a driver?"

She picked up the golf club and swung it at the wall, taking out a good-sized chunk of plaster and sheetrock. "Who knew how handy these things were?"

She pulled back and, midswing, stopped. Her eyes slid closed as the bitter and earthy aroma teased her nose.

"Ohmigod. Is that…" Sniff. Sniff. "French roast?"

"Yes, Ma'am. Glad I set it down in the entryway before coming in here."

She walked right past him, dragging the club as she went. "I haven't had fresh-brewed coffee since my car started disappearing."

He turned and looked out the window. She followed his gaze and rushed out the front door. "You found my car!"

Brett joined her on the porch, iced coffees in hand, and sat on the top step. Extending her coffee, he patted the boards next to him. "It was having a sleepover with mine."

Josephina rolled her eyes, but took the caffeinated gift and sat. Inhaling deeply, she took her first sip. "Mmmm… this tastes so good."

She licked her lips and found Brett staring at her mouth. He was even sexier than she remembered. The wide, strong shoulders, those big blue eyes, and that just-rolled-out-of-bed hair. He was luscious.

He tugged on one of her braids. "If it makes you feel better, my grandma and her thugs called off the feud."

"Then why did I wake up to a bathtub full of bullfrogs this morning?"

Brett grimaced. "Yeah, sorry about that. The truce flag was raised just a couple hours ago."

Josephina hugged her legs to her chest and rested her cheek on her bent knees. "Why are you really here?"

"Thought you could use a handyman. One with more than a bag of clubs for tools."

With a heavy sigh she leaned into Brett, resting her head against his shoulder. Tenderness washed through her when he dropped his head on top of hers. They sat like that, in comfortable silence, staring out over the lake and sharing space. The air was warm, and aside from the water gently lapping at the dock, the lake was surprisingly calm. No wind. No clouds. Just stillness. And a strong shoulder to lean on.

Usually she had the need to entertain when people were around, but with Brett she felt she could just be.

* * *

How long they sat there, Brett didn't know. It was as if the rest of the world went away. No scandal, no impending interview, not a single celebrity favor. Joie seemed to make everything fade into the background. Here, at Fairchild House, with her soft body leaning into his, only the two of them existed.

Until a cold and moist nose wedged itself between them, digging its way into Brett's side. Small little needle teeth sank into his hip. Brett elbowed the dog with all the force of a gentle breeze and the thing let out a sorry-ass yelp as if Brett had backed over him with his pickup.

"Oh, Boo," Joie cried, easing away from him to pick up the dog, who sent Brett a shit-eating grin and then snuggled into Joie's glorious breasts. "Are you okay?"

Brett had built houses with his bare hands, could last eight seconds in the pen, and had made enough money in professional sports to buy a small country. There was no way a five-pound ball of fur was going to one-up him.

"I bet he got his paw stuck in one of these loose boards. Didn't you, boy?" Brett scooped up the rat and dropped him inside the house, making sure to secure the screen door.

Boo lunged at him. His nose slammed against the screen and he bared his teeth. Brett bared his back.

"He should be safe now," he said, glancing inside to assess the damage.

The piles of sheetrock and debris weren't going to be a problem, but getting the rest of that wallpaper down was going to be a pain in the ass. The entryway ceiling was at least thirty feet up.

From what he could tell, she'd had the roof and plumbing fixed. The wood on the porch and dock still needed to be replaced. Large water spots covered the ceiling, continuing down parts of the west wall and giving him reason for worry.

A few of the light fixtures needed to be refurbished and, based on the lack of light, the electrical was still shoddy.

She needed that loan. No amount of do-it-yourself was going to make up for the lack of funding. But maybe a heavy-hitter endorsement could make up for her lack of credit with the bank.

Joie was leaning into the railing, staring out at the lake. He took a second to appreciate the way the denim rode up, exposing more of those amazing legs and pulling the fabric taut across her perfect ass.

"I heard about the loan." No point in dancing around it. Even if his grandma hadn't told him, all it took was five minutes on the Internet. Between Hattie's blog and the *Sugar Sentinel*, there wasn't a person in Georgia who didn't know that Fairchild House was in dire straits with no chance of funding.

"Going back home isn't an option."

"Because of Rat Bastard?" he asked, joining her at the rail.

"Because my father would take it as a white flag that I was giving up."

"You could always ask him for a loan."

Her body stiffened for a moment before she took another sip. "I have to do this myself. Letty said magic comes from the journey, and *this* is my journey. Taking money from people who expect me to fail would be worse than failing."

"We can't win everything."

"Says the four-time Masters champion."

"I thought you didn't have time to read up on me." She blushed. God, he loved that blush.

"I read about how, because of you, the Memaw's groom-a-thon made three times their projected goal, putting the Medical Center that much closer to getting their children's ward."

Now it was his turn to blush.

"It gave me an idea," Joie said, her fingers brushing his knuckles, so absently that Brett didn't think she was aware that she was touching him. His body manned up all the same. "I could host some kind of event here, like Mrs. Wilkes did. Only with food instead of livestock. An evening of wine and friends."

"I'd come."

"As long as you were only a guest," she clarified, and he felt something in his chest turn over. "I could invite all my friends from New York, the town, a big everyone-get-to-know-each-other and see the new-and-improved Fairchild House. I'm not Brett McGraw, Golf God, but I have a pretty impressive black book."

He smiled. "I bet you do."

"I don't want to be the person who loses Letty's house. When I was little we would spend hours talking about reno-vating the place and making it new again. She told me this place was magical, healed the spirit."

"Do you believe her?"

"Yes." She smiled and everything seemed to brighten. "This was the only place I felt free as a kid. I want to share what I found here, and I have to make it happen on my own. Prove to myself that I can stand on my feet."

"You don't need to prove anything, Joie."

"I don't?" she whispered.

"No."

For her this wasn't about a broken heart or bruised pride. Rebuilding the inn was about finishing her aunt's dream and finding one of her own. Some might claim she was being un-realistic about the odds of success, but not him. He admired her for turning down her parents' money.

"But you do need a contractor. And I know just the guy."

"I don't have any money, Brett."

"That's not a problem, sugar. You couldn't afford me anyway." He waggled a brow. "But I'm willing to work it out in trade."

Instead of walking away, as he expected, she placed her hands on his chest in invitation. "Oh, yeah?"

The heat from her touch shot through his body. It would be so easy to take what she was offering. Brett almost did, until she slid her hands down to intertwine with his. He watched the way she unconsciously knotted their fingers, her thumb brushing over his knuckles before tightening her grip. His eyes flew to hers, locking, and everything inside him softened.

Shit. Shit shit shit.

Glory was right. He didn't just want sex with Josephina. Okay, he wanted sex and he wanted her, but he also wanted more. He wanted to feel like that guy who'd helped a crying girl out of the old oak tree. He wanted her to kiss him because she thought he was decent and a good guy.

Besides his family and Glory, Brett didn't have a lot of experience with relationships. Oh, he had sponsors and fans and the people of Sugar and women—lots of women—but ever since the fire he had avoided relationships, purposely seeking out women who, like himself, weren't interested in anything other than sex without strings. Because no strings meant he didn't have to put his heart on the line. Not that his heart was on the line now, but there was definitely something more at risk than a few nights of fun.

Which was why he lifted her hand to gently kiss her fingers and found himself saying, "Not that kind of trade. Unless you're ready to go on a date; then we can talk."

She released a frustrated sigh and pulled her hand back.

"As for my fees, I'm willing to work every day after I

get done with my campers and full days on the weekends. In return I get a dinner that isn't fried and a room to keep my things."

"As in move in?"

He'd been talking about a place to leave his tools, but now that she brought it up it sounded like a great idea. She might not be willing to agree to a date—yet—but when the evenings came and there wasn't much to do but watch the sun go down, he'd finally get that dinner. And maybe she'd start to see him for who he really was.

"You are in the hospitality business, are you not?"

She nodded, looking confused and adorably annoyed. Right where he wanted her.

"Now isn't that auspicious. You need a handyman who's willing to work cheap. I'm looking for a place I can actually sleep and dinner conversation that doesn't have anything to do with fundraisers. It's a win-win."

She eyed him warily.

Brett put his hands up. "You can always say no, of course, and I can head back home. I'm sure you can handle it all yourself. I mean, you have that club."

With a heavy sigh, she said, "You do real work and bill me at the end of the project for your hours and I will add the total, minus the cost of room and board, to my mounting debt, which I will pay back...as soon as I can. And I really need to focus, so if this is going to work then I need you to promise: no parties, no women, no dates and no, underwear is not optional when sleeping."

"Does that mean it's optional when we're awake," he teased, and she smacked him. He caught her hand and trapped it against his heart. "No going commando, got it. As for the not dating, I'm glad you're ready to be exclusive."

"That's not what I meant and you know it."

"No?" He feigned confusion. "Well then, you have my word, I promise to ask you out every day until you say yes." He bent down, getting eye level, and when she was good and flushed, he kissed the tip of her very burned nose and said, "Now, where should I start?"

She rolled her eyes. "You got a tool belt?"

"In the truck."

"Then you're hired. First job, figure out what's wrong with my breaker box." She stacked the boards in a pile and hauled them up. "Oh, and Brett, make sure you wear the belt."

* * *

Three days later, Josephina shoved the last scrap of wallpaper into the trash bag and knew it was quitting time. Her arms were sore from scraping off glue, which was littering the wood floor, she had a big bruise on her forehead from running into Brett's elbow—and sharing breakfast, lunch, and dinner with a man who made her motor hum only added to her aches.

True to his word, he had asked her out every day. And every day it became harder to say no.

Today had been the worst, she thought as she watched the play of Brett's muscles while he supported a plank of rotted wood over his head. He was all rippled and gorgeous and flashing that orgasm-inducing smile. The one that curled up slightly at the corners, saying he'd caught her drooling. Again.

"A simple yes is all it would take," he said in that southern-boy way that made her heart warm. Along with some other, more pertinent, parts.

"I have no idea what you're talking about." She stepped sideways, right into a bowl of nails, knocking them over.

Then, blaming Brett for taking up too much damn space, she picked up the handsaw off the floor and reached into her back pocket for a pair of gloves—coming up empty.

"I've got an extra pair in my tool belt," he said with humor in his voice as he jerked his chin toward his goodie bag, um, tool belt. "Right there in the center pocket. You see them?"

Oh, she saw them all right. She also saw how incredibly amused he was.

"Don't move." Eyeing him, she cautiously reached into the pocket, careful not to touch any of *his* tools. She grabbed the leather gloves and jerked her hand back.

Doing her best to ignore his laughing, she crawled up to the fifth rung of the ladder and sawed away the remaining few inches of beam. Between the sexy smiles and "accidental" brushing of bodies, Brett kept her in a constant state of unbalance.

"So to clarify, you're saying you don't want to go out with me," he mused.

"We're roommates, Brett," she sighed, sawing through the end of the beam and wondering why she kept repeating herself. "And we can be roommates with benefits. But dating roommates wouldn't be a good idea."

"Why is that?" he asked, lowering the beam to the floor. This time she was certain he was flexing his arms on purpose.

"Because we'd go out, have a good time, come home, and have sex. Only instead of just amazing no-strings sex it would be complicated by all this other stuff, which would make things weird. Eventually I'd be short one contractor, miss my opening date, and wonder what happened."

Not wanting to look at him, she set the saw on the top of the ladder, ready to move to the next spot.

"First off, I'm in this for the long haul, I gave you my word on that."

Josephina turned around to ask him if he was talking about the inn, but then she forgot how to speak. Brett blocked her descent, climbing up behind her to the second rung, which brought him eye level. He gripped her hips and backed her up against the ladder. "And, sugar, sex between us wouldn't be amazing, it would be earth-shattering."

That's what I'm afraid of.

He sculpted his hands down her sides to her thighs, paying extra attention to her bottom on the trip back. She rested her hands on those biceps she'd been watching all week so she wouldn't fall over as the air whooshed out of her lungs.

Hell, she'd suffered from severe oxygen deprivation since the minute she found him this morning, standing on the front porch, latte in one hand, a cheese Danish in the other, and the sun cresting behind him.

The man redefined "sexy contractor." The faded college T-shirt clung to his impressive chest. And the hotter it got, the clingier the material became. Which was why four o'clock was Josephina's new favorite time of day. It was when Brett shucked his shirt. And the tool belt he wore weighed down his jeans, giving her a prime view of chiseled abs and lean hips, and highlighting his yummy parts.

And that wasn't even the most tempting part. Nope. The more she saw Brett as a normal hot guy, the more the never-going-to-date-him rule seemed to blur, and the harder he became to resist.

"I suck at relationships," she rushed out, more for her than him. "I get so lost in the other person that Josephina goes MIA. I can't do that again. Not now when people are counting on me. When *I'm* counting on me."

"It's just a date, Joie. I'm not down on one knee." He sounded so sincere her heart pounded as if he were.

"Date implies the start of something, and you're leaving." *And if I let you, you might take my heart with you when you go.* "And I'm staying here, in Sugar."

With a single nod, Brett let her slide past him on the ladder. He wasn't giving up, not by a long shot, she could see that in his eyes. But he was letting it go—for now.

The last of the sun's rays disappeared behind the hills and Josephina stood back to assess the damage. The air quality specialist was coming back out tomorrow. He had already come through earlier that morning, marking places that tested positive for mildew or mold.

To cut down on costs, they'd agreed to let Josephina remove all of the wood and sheetrock where mildew and mold was detected. The result was that sheetrock, beams, and ripped wallpaper covered the first floor, her hands were scratched and irritated, and there was a fine layer of dust covering everything, including her and Boo. Oh, and the beautiful wainscoting, which was original to the house, was torn open in sections spanning the entire west side of the house.

There was three times the amount of mold found than the original estimate, which meant three times the cost and three times the destruction. Fairchild House looked as sorry as Josephina felt. And she wasn't sure, even with Brett donating his time, how far her budget would stretch.

After paying Rooster for the hours spent on the roof, plus the cost of supplies, and now with spore-removal estimate 2.0, Josephina was quickly running out of cash. She needed a few more sets of hands, a phone call from the bank telling her they'd made a mistake, and a bath—since she was certain her hair was housing a small family of sparrows and she smelled like day-old Spam.

Brett, however, looked completely intact and smelled like man. A big, bad-ass man who slung hammers for fun and could rip out an entire bathroom, including a claw-footed tub, without breaking a sweat or marring that beautiful rock-hard body with so much as a speck of dirt, making her feel a little inferior in the do-it-yourself department.

Resting his hands at the nape of her neck, Brett ran his fingers up into her hairline, working out the kinks and bringing body ache to a whole other level. She tried to fight back a moan, losing when he stepped into her. His warm body pressed up against her back as his thumbs followed the line of her muscles, sliding under the straps of her tank top and making her entire body liquefy.

"It'll be all right, Tinker Bell. A few coats of paint and she'll look good as new."

At that, Josephina couldn't help but laugh. It would take a complete team from HGTV to put this house back together.

"Okay, maybe a little more than paint, but trust me when I say this place will look beautiful when it's finished. In fact, you're going to be booked solid as soon as people see what you've done." He sounded proud.

Of her.

Unable to resist, she let her head fall back against his chest. Borrowing some of his confidence, she studied the room and pictured it painted, accessorized, and full of customers. Paying customers. A smile touched her lips and she felt herself sigh.

He slid one big hand around her waist and down her stomach, pulling her against him, her back flush with his front, all of his good parts easily recognizable and causing recognizable reactions in her own. Reactions that weren't appropriate to have for a roommate slash employee, especially since they weren't naked roommates.

"I can't be booked solid, not for another two years. By the time I finish with the dock and the main floor of the house I'll be out of money. And by main floor I am excluding the kitchen."

That was the part that really got to her. She wouldn't have enough money to do the kitchen until *after* her grand reopening. She had been counting on the money from that loan to get the three professional-grade ranges and stainless-steel counters that she had picked out. The only problem with her plan was in order to host the event the way she wanted to, she needed a place to cook in high volume, which she couldn't do until she got the money from hosting the event.

Not that it mattered. She still hadn't come up with a marketable idea that would attract people. An impromptu poll revealed that half of her friends were conveniently booked for the three weekends she had been considering. The other half needed to check their schedules. Her mother begged her to join them in Spain. And even with the feud called off, the town hadn't been as excited about the reopening of Fairchild House as she'd hoped.

"It'll get there," Brett offered.

"If I don't lose the house first."

She turned to face him, but when he didn't loosen his grip she found herself nose to chest with him. Taking full advantage of their position, he nuzzled her neck. She felt every single muscle in her body stand at attention only to melt into a puddle.

"Brett." It was meant to be a warning, but it came out more of a plea.

With a soft groan that sounded like, "I know," he pressed

one last open-mouth kiss on the underside of her jaw, then lifted his head and stared directly into her eyes. "You won't lose this house, Joie. That I am sure of."

She waited for him to put conditions to his bold statement. He didn't. He was dead serious. The intensity in his face, the way his eyes stayed locked on hers. It was an expression she had seen before, but never as the recipient. Until now.

That's when Josephina knew she was in trouble. She'd promised herself she would keep it casual. But the way he held her, spoke to her, believed in her—the way her body responded—felt like a whole lot more. Something akin to strings.

The last man she'd tied herself to made her feel protected and safe, only to sever their string so fast it left her world spinning out of control. She didn't want to tempt fate again so soon, especially when Brett was turning out to be the kind of man who could steal a lot more than her identity.

Chapter 15

Brett looked around the dining room and smiled as he lowered the gift bag to the table. They'd been at it a week and already the room looked fantastic.

Clear of a full Dumpster of demolition debris, the once mauve walls were now painted a sophisticated chocolate with light blue accents, giving the space an elegant and inviting warmth. Josephina must have been up with the sun, because she had also managed to sand down Letty's old dining table and it looked ready to be finished.

"How did your campers do today?" Josephina asked from the kitchen.

Pulling out the chair, Brett took his seat, knowing that in about two seconds Joie was going to come walking through that arch, carrying loaded plates, sweet tea, and a million ideas of what project she wanted to tackle next. They had gotten into an easy habit. He was out of bed and at the driving range by dawn to ensure he got in his thousand hits before working with his campers. When lessons broke for the day, he hightailed it out of there so that he could spend lunch with Joie, catching each other up on their day before they started tearing down walls and installing toilets.

Sometimes they would eat in the kitchen. Yesterday they had some kind of Thai chicken wrap while sitting down by the dock. Last night they'd eaten on the front porch, but today he wanted to eat in her newly remodeled room so she could enjoy the signs of her hard work starting to pay off.

"I reheated last night's chicken and made it into a sandwich. There's more in there if you're still hungry——" She stopped, tray in hand, eyebrows raised in question at the bright pink bag sitting at her seat.

Her hair was tied in a messy knot on top of her head and her breasts pressed tight against the little top she wore. By the time he got to her faded, well-worn, hip-hugging cutoffs he was half-hard. It was almost enough to make him forget why he needed to hold out, make him wonder if sex without strings was such a bad thing.

"What's that?" she said, breaking the spell.

"Something for you." He patted the chair.

"Really?"

Eyes lit, face flushed, she set down the tray and took the seat right next to his. She scootched closer, their knees brushing under the table, and all he could think of was how she had wrapped that leg around his waist while those perfect tens were in his hands. Or how if he shoved the plates aside, he could lay her on the table, slide off her top, and lick every inch of her.

"Open it." He handed her the bag.

Josephina placed it in front of her and daintily pulled out every scrap of tissue paper that Glory had put in there, folding them into little squares. Three sheets in, she gave up the pretense and crumpled the rest into a ball, tossing it to the floor and scaring the dog. Brett smiled. Partly at the dog, but mostly at how Joie tried so hard to hide her messy side.

Peeking into the bag, her eyes went wide, before landing on his. "A tool belt?" She pulled out an extremely pink and frilly belt, filled with nails, gloves, and girl-sized tools.

Despite the air-conditioning, which he had gotten working yesterday, Brett found himself sweating. Glory might have had a hand in wrapping it, but Brett had come up with the idea and picked it out himself. And now, what had seemed like a sweet gesture made him feel like a tool.

"I love it." She hugged it to her as she rose from the chair. She inched close enough that Brett could smell her shampoo and feel the heat of her skin through their clothes. It took every ounce of control he had not to pull her down on his lap and finish what they'd been skating around for weeks.

She held the belt to her hips and swayed back and forth as if it were some kind of new dress.

"Help me put it on." She spun around, giving him the chance to appreciate how nicely her ass filled out those denim cutoffs.

He buckled the back, letting his fingers linger for a moment before forcing himself to lean back in his chair. "You were always looking at mine. So I figured you would want one of you own."

Her eyes ran down his body and then she looked away. Taking in where the bottom of her belt hit, Brett smiled with the sudden realization that maybe it wasn't the tool belt she was checking out after all. Her pink cheeks told him he was right.

"Thank you."

She laid a hand on either shoulder and, leaning down, gave him a gentle kiss on the lips. A chaste brush, something

friends would share, but it lit him up. Especially when she
eased back, her head still ducked to look up at him.

Damn, this was not helping.

The angle was just right, and he could see straight
down her top. Yellow lace and all. She'd straighten if she
knew she was giving him a peepshow. And he'd take her
to bed if she kissed him again, which from the look of
things she was considering. So he kept his distance and enjoyed the view.

"You're welcome." He took a deep breath. The present
was a segue into talking about money. She was desperately
underfunded and Brett had a surplus. The trick would be to
get Josephina to agree to a personal loan without making her
feel like he didn't believe she could do it alone. "I found a
place that sells those stoves you wanted for half the price in
Atlanta. They even deliver."

"Half off is still too much," she said, her fingers playing
with the hair at the back of his neck.

"Not with a loan. We could—"

With her hands busy, driving him slowly insane, she
leaned forward, just an inch, and pressed her lips to his.
Not kissing him, just silencing. "I don't want to talk about
money or loans right now." Every word was underscored
with a teasing brush of her lips. "I'm in a good mood. And
I'm hungry."

Him, too. And not for what was on the table.

She tried to move away, but he stopped her, his hands
tightening around her hips. "Then we talk about it after
lunch, Joie."

"Yes, sir." She began to straighten at the same time he
leaned forward to...what? He wasn't sure. She had him so
wound his whole body was humming. Especially when his
movement brought that yellow lace a whole lot closer.

He heard her breath catch, his own chest doing some sputtering. One glimpse at those glazed eyes and little smile that was all trouble—and he was screwed.

"Joie, this is a bad idea," he mumbled, even as he steered her sweet ass toward him until she was straddling his lap.

"Sure doesn't feel bad," she whispered, shifting closer and driving a screwdriver into his hip, the hammer catching him between the legs.

He grunted.

"What?" her eyes crinkled in confusion.

"Your tools pack a punch."

They both looked down at her tool belt and he groaned, but for a whole other reason this time. The hem of her shorts had all but crawled up her thighs, leaving little to the imagination, and making his pants even tighter.

"So does yours."

"Seems to be a problem I've been having lately." He unbuckled her tool belt slowly and placed it on the table. Gripping her ass, he pulled tighter, showing her just how dire that problem was becoming. "What are we going to do about that?"

"I have some ideas on how to alleviate that particular problem," she said softly, her tone doing crazy things to his heart.

"So do I." He ran a hand up her back to the nape of her neck, his fingers tangling in her hair, the other hand settling right below the dimples on her lower back. She dropped her head back and he leaned in—because why the hell not—and trailed kisses down her neck.

God, she smelled good, like hot chick, sweet tea and—*Holy, Christ*—she shimmied farther down his thighs, bringing all of the parts that mattered into complete, mind-blowing contact. As if that wasn't tempting enough, she nipped at his mouth, delivering a sexy little love bite while she rolled her hips right into him and—lucky guy that he was—she did it again.

With a low growl, he took over, delivering one hell of a smoking-hot kiss. She must have agreed on the "smoking-hot" part because her hands fisted in his hair and she purred into his mouth. *Ah, man*, her mouth was a little slice of heaven.

"I thought you wouldn't sleep with me unless I agreed to go out with you?" Her legs came around his waist, locking behind the chair, encasing him between her thighs. It would be so easy to slip those shorts of hers off. He had a condom in his back pocket. A box of them in his bedroom. And a bulge in his pants that wasn't going away any time soon.

"I said no sex. And I meant it." He really did, which was why he had to voice it, as a reminder.

"But?"

"But—" He cupped her knees and slowly slid his hands up her thighs. "I never said anything about making out."

"Are we talking a few putts around the tee?" She leaned back, resting her hands behind her on his knees. The position caused her thighs to widen and her hair to slide across his legs.

Brett's eyes dropped to take her in. She was dusted with sheetrock, flushed from the heat, and her breasts—a place he'd spent hours fantasizing about getting up close and personal with—pushed provocatively against her shirt. She was sexy and sweet and so damn primed he could feel her body hum with anticipation.

Oh, there was no way he was going to put it in the hole, not without some kind of date first, but he sure as hell wasn't stopping at the fairway either.

"That depends on if we're having dinner tonight."

"I already picked up some salmon at the store today. With wild rice." Again with the hip roll.

Two could play at that game.

"I was thinking more of a nice steak in town." His fingers worked their way beneath the scrap of cotton she called shorts so he could palm her ass. He felt her breath catch and—lucky guy indeed—his hands met silk. Sexy, skimpy, and just loose enough to slip his fingers under.

"That sounds a lot like a date." Her hands fell between them. One worked the button of his fly, while the other worked him, tracing the hard ridge of him through his denim and then making things interesting by cupping him and delivering a gentle squeezing—followed by a not-so-gentle one that had his body begging for release.

"That feels a lot like we just made it to the green, sugar. So unless you want to putt this thing back and forth with no hope of making the shot, why don't we agree to a casual dinner at the Gravy Train?" At this point he was desperate, and horny enough to settle for a single dance at the Saddle Rack.

"I don't even think I can wait until after lunch, let alone dinner." She sat up, wiggling her hips until he could feel the heat of her cradling his hard-on.

With a groan he pulled her to him, their bodies molding tight against each other, their mouths meshing over and over until her hands started fiddling with his belt buckle, and he wasn't certain why they should wait. He knew more about her than any other woman he'd ever known.

She was sweet, and funny, and liked cream in her hot tea. She had a thing for cheese Danish, despised condiments on design alone, and even though she curled up with him on the sofa at night to watch ESPN, she thought golf was boring. And she got him. Honest to God, got who he was at his core and never expected anything from him but honesty.

And honestly, right now, he didn't think he would be able to say no any longer. Not when their kissing turned gentle and neither of them was ripping at the other like that night in the bar. This time there was more: more feeling, more heat—more connection.

He would be content to kiss her all night. The way she melted into him, languidly stroking his tongue with hers, told him she was feeling it, too. He was getting to her. Which was a good thing, because she had gotten so far under his skin, she was there to stay.

"Brett," she whispered between kisses.

"Hmmm?" He took her mouth again, only to slant his head and go in for another taste.

"Your phone," she breathed. "It's ringing."

"They'll call back."

Which, after several more heated exchanges, they did. He tried to ignore the phone, tried not to focus on how he was going to destroy the son of a bitch who was on the other end, but Joie pulled back, resting her forehead on his. "It could be an emergency."

With a sigh he dug the phone out of his back pocket and looked at the screen. He dropped his head back and released a deep breath. Joie was flushed, her hair disheveled from his fingers, her lips swollen and, like his, most likely numb from kissing so long. And she was about the sexiest thing he'd ever seen, so it nearly killed him to say, "I need to get this."

"Of course," she offered, climbing off his lap and looking anywhere but at him. "I should probably—"

"Yeah," he breathed, noticing how he could still taste her lips on his.

"Okay, then, um . . ." She collected their lunch dishes and quickly disappeared into the kitchen, her sexy swing making him regret taking the damn call. But nothing would make him regret those kisses.

Brett stood, biting back a groan when gravity hit, and paced painfully to the window. "Afternoon, Bill," Brett said, his voice harsher than he expected.

"Got your message," Bill said, and Brett could hear him struggle between professional and overeager. "As it worked out, I've got a clear morning tomorrow, figured I'd call the club and get us a 7:00 a.m. tee time if that works for you. We can tee off and then talk."

Brett took in the missing sheetrock, shoddy electrical, and then took a deep breath. Letting it out he said, "Seven is perfect."

* * *

"Loosen your little finger, just a bit." Brett hooked his pointer finger around Tribble Vander's little one and shook it, earning a grin from the boy. A hard task, since the kid was scared that his mama had forgotten him.

"Like this?" Tribble asked, his hands now loose but his shoulder still too tense.

Tribble was one of the local campers. Smart kid, small for his age, and couldn't drive worth a damn. But he had heart and was having a hard time adjusting to his parents' divorce. Which was why, when Brett came out of the locker room and found all the campers gone for the day, except Tribble, Brett called Joie and told her to start lunch without him.

They'd been hitting balls for over an hour, waiting for him to be picked up.

"Now drop your shoulders, relax into it…there you go. Now swing."

He stood back and watched the boy whack the ball. Brett

let out an appreciative whistle when it went a whopping ten yards farther than the last one, and most of that was on the roll.

"Did you see that?" Tribble said, his eyes wide with surprise.

"I sure did," a sultry voice came from behind. "Maybe you'll grow up to be a golf pro just like Mr. McGraw."

"Really?" Tribble grinned to his ears.

Brett ruffled his hair. "Sure, practice hard enough and you can be anything you want. Now, go grab your stuff. You need to rest up for tomorrow. We're working on distance."

"I am so sorry I was late." Darleen looked primped and relaxed, as if she didn't have a care in the world. And that pissed Brett off. "But I can't say I am disappointed that I get to see you."

He waited until Tribble was out of ear range. "If you're going to be late, you might want to give the front desk a call. That way Tribble won't get scared. He thought maybe you got confused on whose day it was to pick him up."

"Please forgive me if I put you out. I had a last-minute rush on an account at work and lost track of time. I did try your cell phone, several times, as a matter of fact, but it went to voicemail. However…" Darleen said as Tribble came back, placing her hand on her son's shoulders, "to apologize for any inconvenience I may have caused, why don't you come to our place for dinner. My friends say I make the best pot roast in three counties. But you already know that."

"That would be awesome," Tribble said.

Brett was at a loss. He always made sure Tribble was at his dad's when he stayed with Darleen. Messing with kids, unless you were planning on committing, was not cool. And Darleen, up until today, had seemed to share his sentiments.

So why was she changing the rules? And why did she think this tactic would work?

Brett ran a hand through his hair, unsure how to get out of this with Tribble as a witness. Which was what, based on the calculated pout of her lips, Darleen was counting on.

He didn't doubt that she loved her son, but her using Tribble's relationship with Brett to get him back in her bed made Brett feel like exactly the kind of man the press accused him of being. And for the first time he was ashamed, because he had been raised better. His parents, his grandmother, and Cal made sure of that.

"Sounds great, but I already have plans tonight, partner. Maybe tomorrow you and I can share morning snack time."

"Yeah, all right." Tribble looked disappointed about dinner, but the blow was softened with the idea of spending time with his coach tomorrow.

Brett remembered the first time Cletus had shared a meal with him, and he had worn the same look of wonder that Tribble did right then.

"Maybe another time, then," Darleen said, invitation clear in her tone.

Brett tipped the bill of his cap respectfully. "Thanks for the offer, but I'll be leaving soon."

Darleen's lips thinned, but she quickly recovered with a smile. "I noticed your truck's been parked out front of the Fairchild place the past few weeks."

"Just helping the new neighbor with some remodeling." His tone was final, offering no further discussion on the topic. The last thing Joie needed was Darleen digging up gossip for the Peaches' weekly newsletter.

Twenty minutes later, Brett pulled into Joie's driveway. He wanted nothing more than to swing hammers side by side with his stubborn roommate. He also wanted to take her to bed, but sadly that would have to wait. They hadn't locked lips since the other afternoon in the dining room, but she was caving on the no-date stance. He could see it in the way she watched him when she didn't think he was looking, how she unconsciously touched him while talking, and how she hesitated before turning him down.

In fact, earlier that morning, over a full stack of her cracked-oat pancakes with ginger-apple glaze, he'd suggested that they end their week with a cool drink and a twirl around the Saddle Rack's floor. She opened her mouth and startled the crap out of both of them when nothing came out. After another failed attempt, she cleared the table and hustled out of the kitchen, claiming she needed to shower.

He put the car in Park and smiled. It wasn't a *Yes, Brett I'd love to go out with you.* But it was a lot closer than her usual *Not going to happen, Playboy.*

A little extra swagger in his step, Brett slammed the truck door and did a double-take. Barreling out the front door was a frazzled Joie, wearing a conservative hair style, a sleek power suit, and—he noticed with a smile—a delicate chain snaked around her ankle with dangling silver fairies. Even when she tried to look tough, her whimsical side came through.

Before he could ask what she was doing all dressed up, she bounded down the stairs and launched herself into his arms. He buried his face in her hair, loving how she smelled. He also loved how she molded herself up against him, radiating so much excitement she was bouncing on her toes.

* * *

"I'm so glad you made it home before I left. I had to tell you, but I didn't want to call and interrupt if you were still with one of your students."

Josephina pulled back to look at him. She was still in

shock, so it took a minute to gather her thoughts. Telling Brett was almost as exciting as her news.

"Mr. Ryan called me today. And guess what? They decided that Sugar is in need of an inn. And since Fairchild House is listed as a historical property, they reevaluated their previous decision and I got the loan."

Brett didn't look surprised, he looked pleased, as if he had known all along that her idea was sound. He opened his mouth, but she was so excited she cut him off. "But the best part is, I did it all by myself. No Dad. No Wilson. Just me. Can you believe it?"

He didn't speak, but kept smiling—really big.

"Did you hear me?"

"I never had any doubt." He pulled her into his arms and whispered against her hair, "I'm proud of you, Joie."

"I can't stop thinking that this is a big step. There's no going back. If I sign and something goes wrong—"

Brett stepped back and clasped her hands, which had been worrying the hem of his shirt. "Joie, this loan is a great thing. You would have made it regardless, but the money will make it a little easier."

"Thank you."

She waited for the panic to subside, for her heart to slow to a more normal pace, and when it did she froze.

Josephina had been waiting for his approval, for him to reassure her that she could do this. She had put off signing the papers on her dream, telling Mr. Ryan that she wanted to look them over. In reality, she wanted Brett to look them over, because his support would give her the courage to sign on the dotted line.

"Let's go inside and talk about what this all means," Brett said, tugging her toward the porch.

"I can't." She pulled him to a stop, because in that moment she realized she might just follow him anywhere. "I am supposed to meet Mr. Ryan to sign the papers in twenty minutes."

Her appointment was for tomorrow, but suddenly she didn't want to wait.

"Then dinner. You and me. Tonight. To celebrate." He looked so hopeful, and she wasn't surprised that she wanted to say yes. She'd been wanting to say yes since the day he'd shown up on her front porch, tool belt on, ready to get to work. But she couldn't.

"I have plans with Spenser and Charlotte." Plans that she'd agreed to that morning. Part of her wanted to cancel so she could spend the evening celebrating with Brett. The other part—the part that remembered how many times she'd done that for Wilson, had her saying, "I'm sorry."

And she was. But she was also never going to be the kind of person who blew off friends, commitments, or her dreams for a man ever again.

"Don't be sorry." Brett cupped her cheek. "It's your night to celebrate. Go. Have fun. Plus, Cal called earlier asking if I would come over. Apparently he's imprisoned Payton for the duration of the summer for smiling at some punk at the market and he's in desperate need of estrogen-free company."

Her heart fluttered right up into her throat. He was going to cancel on his brother for her? Wilson would have never done that.

"But, Joie," he looked her dead in the eye, "we will have our dinner."

Chapter 16

The Saddle Rack was already packed with locals, and a few fans who obviously followed Hattie's tweets. Brett was used to the stares. It happened everywhere he went. What he wasn't used to was the whole reason he'd agreed to come into town when Cal offered to buy him a drink.

Wearing a top that was barely legal, a cream skirt that had ridden up to show off those amazing legs, and that little charm around her ankle that made him hard, Joie sat three tables away. Feigning a deep interest in Spenser's and Charlotte's conversation, she was smiling prettily and doing everything to avoid looking his way.

"Are you going to do it or not? Either way I need an answer." Jackson waved a hand in front of Brett's face. "Jesus, you didn't even hear a word I said."

"He was too busy staring at Joie's fuck-me pumps." Cal slapped Brett on the back.

"Screw you." He was looking at her ankle, wondering why he was crammed in a booth between Cal and Jackson instead of over at the table celebrating with Joie. Although crashing girls' night would have looked even more pathetic than showing up here with his buddies. "And I heard what you said, JD. Count me in."

"Ah, hell. Remind me to eat before I come." Cal grimaced. "Last time you manned the grill my pancakes were about as appetizing as a short stack of skeets. And the bacon was overcooked."

"People don't care if the bacon is charred black, they come to see the famous Brett McGraw in a stupid-ass hat and apron." Brett cringed at Jackson's reminder. "Skeets or not, that year we doubled our ticket sales. And since this year's money is going toward that new wing at the Medical Center, the Sheriff's Department is hoping to quadruple the turnout."

"And Brett's ugly mug on the tickets is just the thing your team needs, right?" Cal said, amusement gone.

"I'm not going to lie, so yeah. When the guys asked if Brett would do it, I said I didn't see why not, so they put him down as the cook." Jackson looked at Brett. "Then my dad started advertising that you were the celebrity host for his golf tournament on the same day."

Brett groaned. He'd only agreed to the mayor's tournament because the money went to help the new wing at the Medical Center.

"I can't believe that the pancake breakfast is the same day as your dad's tournament."

"Same as the Sugar Ladies Summer Concert, Payton's cheerleader carwash, and some calendar signing for the Peaches," Cal offered helpfully.

"Why didn't he mention that when he brought up the tournament to begin with?"

Cal laughed. "Man, you really stepped in it, Brett.

Everyone in town wants their name on that pediatric center and they figured whoever had you would bring in the most money."

"Wait, the center will be named after a person?"

"Person. Organization. The biggest donor gets to decide."

He'd been played. By every person in this damn town.

"You're telling me this now?" Brett asked, wondering how, if at all, he was going to pull this off. He was hiding out from the press because he couldn't keep it in his pants. His niece had grown boobs and twirled her hair when guys were around. And his grandma had blackmailed him into spying on the woman he was living—but not sleeping—with.

Now he had, by his own stupidity, somehow become the great white hope for Sugar's new pediatric center, placing himself in the middle of a town feud where they'd set him up to choose, knowing he couldn't turn a single person down.

Cal shrugged. "Figured you already knew."

"How the hell would I know?"

"Well, maybe if you didn't spend all your time eye-fucking Joie, you'd have noticed that a feud was brewing, pitting neighbors against neighbors. And you, brother, are at the center of it."

"Hattie's feud with Joie?"

Cal shook his head. "The superintendent has staked a claim on you for the same weekend as the golf tournament. Last I heard the local Boy Scouts troop and Future Farmers of America had joined the fight. There's also a town pool going around on who's going to win, by how much, and if Judge Holden will finally get his lynching, courtesy of the Peaches."

"My money is on your grandma," Jackson said, and both men starting laughing.

Brett took another long pull of beer, draining it and setting the empty glass on the table. Where was the pitcher? And the vacation in his vacation? He'd had exactly zero down time. Between his campers, helping out around town, and working at Joie's, he was exhausted.

Actually, that wasn't entirely true. His time at Joie's was as close to perfect as it got. Swinging hammers felt good. Watching her prance around in those cutoffs while ripping up subfloor was even better. Sitting at the kitchen table and sharing a meal with her made him wish for things he shouldn't be wishing for.

"You need to get laid," Jackson said.

"You're the one who elected himself town poster boy for celibacy when Sadie walked out."

Jackson scowled. "I've had women."

"Ones on the Internet don't count."

"What crawled up your ass, McGraw?" Jackson snapped.

"Nothing."

"Yeah? 'Cuz how I look at it is if I wanted to be nagged about not dating I would have gone to my grandma's for dinner." Jackson blinked, then a slow as shit grin spread across his face. "Holy crap. You've been sweating it out over at Joie's place and you haven't sealed the deal."

"Sweating it out?" Cal laughed. "Hell, the moron has moved in. Is renovating her place for free. And he has to sleep in the guest bed."

Actually, it was worse than that. Not that he'd tell his brother, but he now slept on the couch, since the only finished room when he'd moved in had been downstairs, right below Joie's. At night he could hear her moving around, pulling on her pajamas, clicking out the light, sliding into those sheets. It was enough to drive him nuts.

"We're taking it slow."

Jackson choked. "Four of the pussiest words in the English language. Oh, how the mighty have fallen."

Cal rested his elbows on the table and leaned in. "Admit it. You have a thing for Joie that goes beyond one night, and it scares the shit out of you."

Brett released a hard breath. He studied Joie, who quickly averted her gaze, but not before color stained her cheeks. Brett opened his mouth just as Glory came over with a pitcher of cold beer, a strained look, and the perfect excuse to change the subject.

She set the beer on the table, followed by new frosty mugs and kept her gaze solidly on Brett, even when she was dividing up the pitcher and handing Jackson a refill on his soda. Not an uncommon reaction when she was around Jackson. Those two had a past that Brett had made clear he wanted no part of.

"So, does Joie know?" Glory whispered, balancing the tray of drinks on her shoulder.

A sick feeling sank to the bottom of his gut. "Know what?"

"That you're sweet on her?" Cal interrupted and Jackson laughed.

"You know I hate gossip, but, well," her eyes flew to Joie and then back to him, "it seems that Joie got that loan from the bank. But Darleen's claiming it didn't go through her department, which according to her means something is screwy."

"Shit." Brett pinched the bridge of his nose. He had every intention of telling Joie that he'd arranged the loan. After hearing her determination to complete the project, even after the bank denied her, he wanted to do something to help her, to show her that someone believed in her dream.

He'd set up what was supposed to be a private conversation with Mr. Ryan and used his account to secure a
third-party loan through Sugar Savings and Loan. The loan
was between the bank and Joie, but his funds were held as
collateral.

"Does she know?"

"Who? Joie?" Cal laughed. "Hell, Brett, the whole bar
knows that she got that loan. Why do you think people have
been sending her drinks all night?"

Brett glared at Jackson. "Is that who you bought a
drink for?"

Jackson shrugged. "Bought the first round for the
whole table. A group of lovely ladies, out for a night on
the town."

"I just wanted to make sure you knew that people are
talking and to say you should tell her." Glory looked at Joie
and then back to him. "The sooner the better. The longer secrets go, the harder they are to admit. Until one day it's just
a wall between you and everyone else."

* * *

"Although we are beyond words about you acquiring that
loan, what we want to know is"—Charlotte looked in both
directions and smoothed out her daffodil-colored skirt before leaning in to whisper—"are the rumors true?"

Josephina knew what, or rather whom, she was referring
to. There was no point in lying. They would find out soon
enough that, in typical Josephina fashion, she had managed
to turn the One-Night-Romeo into a roommate who tinkered
with her fuse box instead of her toy box.

She looked over her shoulder at Brett, who was sitting
with his brother and the sheriff—where he'd been for the

last two hours. He looked amazing in boots, a pair of button-fly jeans, and an ease that was anything but polished.

He looked up and their gazes collided and held, sending her entire body into hyperdrive. She tried to play it off, act unaffected, but when he sent her a wink whose exact translation was, "I'm getting to you," she realized that she was in trouble.

She turned back to the girls and admitted, "I wouldn't know."

"Excuse me," Charlotte asked, obviously dumbfounded by the news. "Come again? I don't think I heard you right."

When embarrassed, Josephina's voice tended to shift toward shrill, one of the many things she had inherited from her mother and wished she could dispose of. Which was why when she spoke the words, "I. Said. I. Wouldn't. Know," every person in a ten-foot radius, including Brett, turned to look.

Lowering her voice she went on, "He wants to take things slow."

"Honey, his truck is parked out front of your house from sunup to sundown. He isn't dating anyone in town," Charlotte said. "In the South that's like taking out an ad in the *Penny Saver*: 'Big-city girl and hometown hero living in sin.'"

And wasn't that just great. Joie knew that in a town this size, it wouldn't take long for people to notice Brett wasn't hanging up his hat at home. She'd just been hoping people wouldn't care.

"We're not *living* together. He needed a place to hide out and I needed a contractor. And he said he wants to date first."

Both women sat, mute. Blinking in unison.

"Hold up," Spenser said. "Are you saying that you

threw yourself at the PGA Playboy and he refused to sleep with you?"

"Yes. And thank you for that lovely recap. Now can we all agree that I suck at romance and move on?"

"He asked you out on a date? This is great." Charlotte tapped her fingers on the rim of her Baptist cocktail. "When is it? Where is he taking you? Oh, and what are you going to wear? I have a fabulous little red dress that I bought when I lived in Atlanta and never wore. It would look great on you."

"I told him no." Which made her either incredibly smart or the biggest idiot on the planet. Because instead of fully enjoying her night out, she'd spent most of it stealing glances and wondering how much time had to pass before she could politely excuse herself. Now that the loan was official, and she had done it on her own, she found that she wanted to be celebrating with him.

"Why on earth would you do that?" Charlotte gasped, hand over her heart. "What if you're the one?"

"I'm not *the* one. I'm a challenge and he's up for a chase. Playing with me serves as a good distraction." But the minute the words came out of her mouth she knew they weren't true.

Charlotte placed her hand on Josephina's, her expression serious. "McGraw men don't play. Not with women's hearts. If he says he wants to take it slow, then honey, Brett McGraw, self-proclaimed bachelor, wants to do a whole lot more than date you," Charlotte said, all dreamy and clutching a wadded cocktail napkin to her heart.

"He's leaving."

"He's interested," Spenser argued.

Something Josephina was well aware of. It didn't fit into her new plan, which was all about control and professionalism. And it didn't help that when she walked in tonight and saw Brett every cell in her body had screamed out for her to rush over to his table.

He'd greeted her with only a smile and a wink, so she told herself to order a drink and give the man some time to visit with his fans and friends, of which there were plenty. Then his table had looked so intense she hadn't wanted to interrupt. Now she just felt silly because he'd hugged nearly every woman in the bar, except her, and she wished he would get up off that incredible butt and come over already, so she could be put out of her misery. Instead he sat, casual as ever, sipping a beer and watching her.

She grabbed her purse and stood. "I hope Brett finds his *one*. But it's not me." A small pang radiated through her chest because the reality was, if she allowed herself to, she could easily fall in love with him, only to have him leave. "And right now, the only thing I am interested in is a hot shower and a soft mattress."

"Well, shoot, sugar." His voice was so smooth, the words seemed to pour from his lips. "I already showered, and as you know my mattress is kind of lumpy, but I'm willing to take a dance in exchange."

The thought of pressing their bodies together and swaying for even three minutes had her sweating. Although he hadn't tried to kiss her since the other day in the dining room, every time they were within a foot of each other they somehow managed to touch. His arm accidentally grazing the side of her breast as they installed the new vanity and shower fixtures in the bathroom, his hands on her hips, steadying her as she climbed up to the sixth rung on the ladder to put up the shower curtain rod.

Josephina should have said no, told him it was impolite to eavesdrop, but all she could think about was his hand resting at the base of her neck. His skin was hot against hers as his fingers, rough and calloused from working on her house, made small patterns, reaching up under her hair.

Brett looked at her. "You okay? You're a little pink."

"Too much sun and too long a day. Which reminds me." In an effort to put some distance between them, she stood right as the front door shot open with a bang.

The bar went silent because there—with her Falcons-themed velour track suit, a .45, and half the town in tow—stood Hattie McGraw, her frosted posse, and the entire Sugar Ladies Baptist Choir. Hattie's greeting was to raise the gun, smile when her gaze landed in Josephina's general direction, and pull the trigger.

Ceiling and shards of plaster scattered to the floor. To Josephina's surprise, she was the only one who took cover. Everyone else went back to business as usual. Pool games picked up, the DJ kept playing that twangy stuff Brett liked—and Brett, casual as ever, leaned down to help Josephina up off the floor.

"You okay?"

"I think so." Dusting off her knees with her free hand, she whispered, "I swear that woman is out to kill me."

"Ah, there's no reason to be scared." Brett gave her hand a patronizing little squeeze. "She's all bark."

Hattie lowered the gun, pointing it directly at Brett. "There he is!"

"Damnit, Grandma," Cal bellowed, moving forward. He stopped the second Hattie swung the gun to him. "You could have shot someone."

"Don't you use that tone, boy. And I ain't never shot someone I hadn't intended on. I came here to talk to your brother and nothing is going to stop me, you hear?"

Cal threw his hands up in sheer frustration.

"Now, Hattie," Jackson said quietly from behind, making his way toward the weapon. "We talked about this. You can't go around discharging your weapon in a public place without me arresting you."

"You can't arrest her." A regal woman with carefully coifed white hair stepped forward, her tailored dress and pearls swishing as she pushed her way through the swarms of people now filling the bar. She grabbed Hattie's gun and positioned it to the right and down, low enough to have Brett squirming. "Not until her grandson comes clean."

Josephina felt Brett's hands go clammy. "All bark, remember?"

"Grandma," Jackson sighed, rubbing the back of his neck. "You were supposed to wait for me at the church. I was going to come get you when choir practice ended in an hour. And since when do you and Hattie agree on anything?"

"When justice needs to be served," Hattie announced. "As soon as Brett tells all these good folks that he promised to MC the Sugar Ladies Summer Concert and politely decline participating in *their* fund-raising events we can all go back to our lives, and Kitty and I will go back to disliking one another."

"Ah, Christ," Cal muttered.

"Not so funny now, is it?" Brett grumbled.

"He is not canceling Sugar's First Annual Golf Tournament," Kitty glared at Hattie and Josephina recognized her from the paper as the mayor's mother, which made her Jackson's grandmother.

Kitty Duncan worked the crowd like a pro, shaking hands and showing off her pearly teeth before stopping in front of Brett. "Are you, son? A lot of people are counting on you and your friends turning out, including my son. The mayor plans to make this a tradition, a way to bring in commerce to the good people of Sugar."

"I don't see how the mayor can expect to hold him to that tournament." Memaw stepped forward from the choir, her blue robe looking more like a muumuu. "When he's already agreed to help me with my dog and cake walk."

"What about the Catfish Catch and Cook-off?" someone hollered from the back.

All at once, everyone began shouting about how Brett had promised this, or agreed to help with that, how without him their events would fail. Rumbling about raising funds, the new center at the hospital, and being a man of his word filled the bar.

She counted at least six commitments on the same day that Brett had agreed to. And right then, Josephina understood why he never stayed long in Sugar. More important, she knew exactly what it felt like to be at the root of everyone's disappointment.

"Hey!" The shout echoed over the noise, bringing all the arguing to a halt. Josephina was surprised to find that it came from her. Even more surprised that everyone was silently staring—no, glaring—in her direction. Well, except Brett, who was looking at her as if she had grown a mullet.

"Hi, everyone." She gave a lame little wave and instantly shoved her hand into her pocket to make sure she didn't repeat the gesture. "So, Brett has found himself in a place all of us have, at one time or another. He has unintentionally overextended himself."

"Overextended or not, he made us a promise and in this town that means something," Etta Jayne snapped. "We are counting on that money for the Medical Center."

"Right, the Medical Center. So you mean to tell me that all of you just happened to pick the same day for your event? That is some kind of coincidence." Josephina laughed. Everyone else remained silent.

Everyone, except the mayor's mother, whom Josephina had planned on inviting to dinner. In hospitality, having the local officials behind you, Josephina had learned from her father, was as important as the capital, because without permits and local support it didn't matter how much money you had.

"And just what are you implying?" Kitty asked, shock lacing her words.

The bar fell quiet again. This time the uncomfortable kind of quiet, as everyone stared at Brett, waiting for him to do the right thing. She wasn't sure what the right thing was, but she knew that there were so many people placing their hopes on Brett that he had no choice but to disappoint someone. And being the kind of guy he was, letting down anybody wasn't in him.

"Which is why Brett came to me earlier this week and asked me to plan a big event. Like a celebrity fundraiser," Josephina heard herself say. "One that incorporates everyone's ideas and increases the chances of finally funding the children's ward."

"And why would he ask you?" Hattie asked, sounding hurt.

"It's what I did before."

Before she had given up everything for a man who didn't want what she was offering. Something she couldn't let happen again. But Brett had helped her when Rooster had walked, and now it was her turn to return the favor. This was a completely different situation. At least that's what she told herself.

"We can call it Sugar's First Annual Pucker Up and Drive." Utter silence. "You know sugar, like pucker up," she made kissy lips, "and drive," she mimicked swinging a gold club.

All she needed was a *ba-dump-cha* of the drums. Because the only response she got was silence. Uncomfortable, isolating silence.

"Joie," Brett whispered. "You don't have to do this. I can figure it out."

"I know." she whispered back.

"How will we know who raised what?" the mayor's mother asked.

"Um," Josephina swallowed. She could do this. The fact that the bank had enough faith in her to give her that loan gave her the courage to continue.

"Since all of the proceeds were intended for the same cause, I don't think it should matter." The looks on the faces in the mob told her she thought wrong. "If we all pool our efforts we will probably increase the overall profit. More money, more kids get treated, right? It's a win-win." Repeating Brett's earlier words, she looked up at him and smiled.

"Well, you'd sure come out the winner, having all these people out at your new inn," Etta Jayne accused.

"What about the money? You expect us to trust some northerner with the money?" Someone who sounded a lot like Rooster yelled, followed by a couple of "yeahs" and an "amen."

"Hey now," Brett defended, his hand tightening around hers in a protective gesture that made her heart stutter. "As far as I can tell, Joie's the only one here trying to fix this mess, so hear her out."

"Thanks," she whispered, a warm feeling pushing through her chest. "And it's a fair question. Fairchild House would be the perfect place. There's lots of room, plenty of parking in my field, and the lake's right there for the...uh...fish-off? As for my time and the use of my property for the day, I would be happy to donate them both."

There were a few tuts and whispers, and Josephina felt as if everyone was judging her.

"Hush up now," Charlotte shouted, startling herself and then smoothing down her dress. "Y'all are so busy arguing over whose name is going to go on that sign, no one is understanding that without the money there won't be a new wing. And I've worked too hard to let that happen. Yankee or not, she's the only one making any sense. So I stand firmly behind Joie's idea."

"Thanks, Charlotte." Josephina smiled at her friend, feeling for the first time since moving here that she belonged—at least a little.

"Joie," Brett said, his voice rough. "They're talking about three weeks from now. If you agree to plan this event it will mess up your timeline for the inn."

"It just means we have to figure out a way to get it done faster. With the loan I can hire a crew, make it go faster."

"Yeah." He rubbed a hand though his hair. "We need to talk about that—"

Not wanting to hear any of his doubts about her ability to make this happen, she shook her head. "This is my town now, too. I want to help." She addressed the crowd before he could respond. "So if anyone has any questions about the Pucker Up and Drive..." Nothing. "Give me a call."

With that she turned and headed for the door. Brett reached for her hand, which she shoved in her pocket as she skirted around the crowd. After the way he'd looked at her, as though she was someone amazing, one touch and she would forget her plan to stay immune and fall right into him.

She picked up the pace, hoping to outrun him. Too bad he had long legs, which were in excellent shape.

Before she knew it, they were standing by her car, silent while Josephina searched through her handbag for the keys.

To her dismay, the parking lot was completely deserted, providing them with too much privacy for comfort's sake.

Less than a foot separating them, they stared at each other, which made Joie reach down and fiddle with the keys in her hand. Brett stilled her movement with his, taking her keys, then threading their fingers. She felt herself leaning toward him and admitted that she needed his comfort right now.

"Joie, look, about—"

"Don't worry about anything." She'd run because she was afraid he wouldn't want her to host the event, that he feared she'd screw it up. And after staring down that angry mob, she was suddenly tired of fighting. She just needed someone to believe in her. "I can handle this, Brett. I won't embarrass you, I promise. Actually I'm really good at this kind of thing. I practically orchestrated Wilson's career-making moment."

He tucked a finger under her chin and raised her gaze to his. "I never thought you'd embarrass me, Joie. You're just so busy with the inn, I didn't think you'd...No one has ever...Thank you."

"You're welcome." She felt herself blush.

"Look"—he cupped the bill of his hat and drew it down lower on his forehead—"about the money."

Oh, right. The money.

She cleared her throat. "I meant to tell you, but you seemed busy with guys' night and your fans and then the angry townspeople with their pitchforks. I just kind of blurted it out." She took a breath. "It's official. I signed my life on the dotted line. Woo."

He traced his thumb across her cheek and she forgot how to speak. "I'm never too busy for you."

"Because I let you hide out at my house?"

"Because of this," he whispered, then lowered his head and kissed her.

He brushed his mouth across hers and all thoughts of being in control evaporated under the heated little tingles starting at her lips and spreading south. She instantly switched gears, her hands sliding down his chest. She was amazed at how the rock-hard muscles bunched and tightened under her touch as her arms slipped around his waist.

She expected hot and demanding with the ability to melt her panties off. Instead, what she got was altogether different. A gentle brush of the mouth. A languid touch, so tender the air whooshed out of her lungs.

His hand curved around her waist and he tilted his head, getting his hat out of the way, as he deepened the kiss, gently loving her with his mouth. She opened for him immediately, her tongue seeking out his.

Slow down, part of her was screaming, this was too much. With each caress she was being dragged further and further into his world, until one day she would look up and be surrounded by only him. She was already planning his big charity event, and falling into his bed would be dangerous.

Another part of her, the part that flooded her body with heat and slammed her heart against her chest, was so loud it kept her from hearing anything except her resistance crumbling to dust.

Brett pulled back enough to look into her eyes. His expression was nothing like that cocky playboy she'd met on the side of the Brett McGraw Highway. It was a look of hopeful uncertainty.

"Joie," he whispered. He gave her room to breathe, time to step away and pretend that everything hadn't changed.

She tried to convince herself to walk away, get in her car

and drive home before they couldn't go back. Only she must have taken too long, because he tightened his arms around her waist and buried his face in her hair.

Her good sense clearly impaired, Joie stepped into his embrace as if it was the most natural place in the world to be—and she knew. There was already no going back.

Brett wasn't the shallow womanizer everyone made him out to be. Sure, he could smile and melt every heart in the room and, okay, he oozed southern charm. But he had offered to help her for no other reason than that he was the kind of person who genuinely cared for others. It showed in the way he treated his family, how the people in town responded to and protected him. What got Josephina the most, though, was his unwavering belief in her.

"Ask me again," she said into his chest.

His hand ran beneath her hair, hugging her tighter, so when he spoke his breath tickled her ear. "Joie, will you allow me the honor of taking you to dinner? In public," he added hastily.

She lifted her face to his and smiled. "Why, Brett McGraw, I thought you'd never ask." She latched on to his belt loop and tugged him closer. "Can we go home and make out some more?"

"Yes, ma'am."

Chapter 17

⌒

At seven sharp, Josephina turned onto Maple and pulled into the first cobblestone driveway. Ulysses had just finished his second rendition of Dixieland when she took her third tour of the parking lot, which was packed full of mud-splattered trucks and a few worse-for-wear Cadillacs. As Ulysses revved up for an encore, she eased her car over the concrete stop, through a dirt lot, and parked under a tree housing some suspicious-looking mockingbirds.

"It's just a date." She rested her head against the steering wheel and groaned.

No matter how many times she said it, it didn't stop her hands from sweating. Even though it was silly to be nervous—seeing as they had cohabited for the past few weeks—Josephina wanted tonight to go perfectly.

After a deep breath and mumbling the entire theme song to *Zorro*, Josephina stepped out of the car, the thick heat immediately causing her skirt to curl up at the hem and vacuum seal to her skin. She stared up at the flock of birds overhead. They looked harmless enough, but then so did opossums.

Smoothing down her skirt, she tiptoed around gopher holes, over what she hoped was a log and not an alligator, breathing a sigh of relief when she made it to the parking lot without breaking an ankle.

She had insisted that if this was a first date then Brett would shower and get ready at his grandmother's house and they would meet at the restaurant. Showering with only a wall separating them and leaving in the same car seemed too domestic. Plus she wanted to show up wearing an outfit guaranteed to make Brett ache. Only fair considering she hadn't had a decent night's sleep since he moved in. And with her little black dress, which was held together by a single wraparound bow, he didn't stand a chance.

Josephina didn't know if she was ready for strings, especially with him leaving in a few weeks, but she did know that she would regret not seeing where this led.

Tossing back her shoulders, she looked at the restaurant and suddenly felt overdressed. The Gravy Train was a one-story wood-sided A-frame that sat on the corner of Maple and Oak, and looked more like a ranch house than an eating establishment. Complete with a wraparound porch, a guard dog named Jessie James, and a dinner bell, the Gravy Train was not only the local feeding hole but—since Skeeter the cook was rumored to be sweet on Etta Jayne—one of the many businesses that sided with the Granny Mafia.

Going for balls-to-the-wall, she fluffed her hair, hoping the humidity hadn't turned it to frizz, and waltzed by a white pickup parked by the front door, next to a sign designating the spot as belonging to Brett McGraw. She patted Jessie James, who stuck his nose in her crotch and drooled on her toe in greeting, on her way into the restaurant, where the

SUGAR'S TWICE AS SWEET 259

scent of slow-cooked ribs and something almost exotic filled her nose.

Josephina inhaled long and slow, trying to decipher what could make southern BBQ smell so...incredible. Not that she didn't appreciate southern fare, she loved it, but this smelled like...

Josephina didn't get a chance to finish her thought, because every eye in the joint was now turned to her.

The ones belonging to Hattie and her crew were the easiest to spot, since they were aimed with lethal accuracy. Maybe this was a bad idea. A sign that she should get into Ulysses and Dixieland her behind home.

The grannies crossed their arms and glared.

Definitely a bad idea. There was no way she could sit through this meal. Not staring at the man she intended to seduce into bed while his grandma was three tables away.

Chicken or not, Josephina took a step backward and right into a warm wall of manly smelling muscles. Brett's arms came around her waist, his body encasing hers in a way that made her feel protected and safe. As if she belonged.

"Having second thoughts?" he whispered, making her thighs quiver.

"No, well, maybe," she admitted. With Brett behind her, his front pressing against her back, she mustered the courage to glare back at the old ladies. "Maybe we should just go somewhere else."

"Why would we do that, when this place has the best ribs in the state and"—he leaned in, dropping his voice—"it's only a few minutes from home?"

Brett's palms glided over her stomach as he gripped her hips to turn her. She looked up into those eyes, made even bluer by his shirt, and forgot to breathe. Even in jeans and a dark gray button-down he radiated pure sexuality.

"You didn't think you could wear that," he looked down at her dress, "and expect me to make it through dinner and an hour drive home."

"We can always skip dinner and go straight home."

"As tempting as that sounds, Miss Joie, I want to enjoy a nice meal, maybe a glass of wine, and make cow eyes at you from across a table."

"They serve wine here? Funny, I was under the impression that the only thing served in this town came in a pitcher or a shot glass."

Brett pressed his hand to the small of her back and led her toward the back of the room, past the firing squad. If he took issue with charming a girl into bed while his grandma was five feet away, he didn't show it. He merely nodded his head, in that respectful southern way, and smiled at each and every lady as he said, "Evening," before steering her into a corner booth with high seatbacks for privacy and a sign that read, YOU NOT A MCGRAW? THEN SKEDADDLE.

* * *

"I hope you're hungry," Brett said after the hostess took their drink order and disappeared.

"Starved." Her mouth twitched up at the corners and her eyes, which had been bouncing between him and his grandma's table, heated and locked on his. Oh, she'd built up an appetite all right, he thought with a smile, it just wasn't for anything on the menu.

Brett sympathized. Seeing her in that dress had his mind racing, picturing him slowly unwrapping her until she was sprawled out naked across her bed. Naked except for the heels. Her hair was down, wild and curly, just how he liked it. Her heels were red, high, and over the top. He knew damn well she had chosen that outfit with the single purpose of driving him crazy.

It was working.

He had held out for weeks in the hope that he'd get the chance to take Joie out, prove to her and to himself that he could be relationship material. And yet, right now, the only material he could focus on was the silky material hugging her breasts as she reached over and grabbed one of the menus.

"You don't need that." He plucked the menu out of her fingers. "I was planning on ordering for both of us."

"I like to order for myself, thank you." She snagged the menu back and made a big deal out of studying its contents, which was a waste of time, since he'd called ahead and prearranged their entire dinner.

"I know you are more than capable of ordering. It's just I know what's good here, what the house specialties are."

"Uh huh," she said biting her lip in a lame attempt not to laugh as she read from the menu. It didn't work. "Like the McGraw Slaw? Or, wait, should we order the Hole-in-One Hot Brats?" She cleared her throat and continued. "Guaranteed to make your top blow."

Brett felt embarrassment creep up his neck. He snagged the menu and tossed it on the table behind them.

"Here's your drinks," Skeeter said, moseying up to the table. The man was slow as molasses, wielded a mean spatula, and never left home without Lorain—a .45 Desert Eagle—strapped to his hip.

Skeeter set down a basket of croquettes and his famous hushpuppies. Followed by two drafts. Odd, since Joie had ordered an appletini—a drink that he'd made sure Skeeter had all the ingredients for when he'd called in their order.

"Now, I got the ribs smoking out back and made sure to set aside one of my peach and passion fruit cobblers—"

"I think there was a mixup with the drink order, Skeeter." Brett slid the beer to the edge of the table. "The lady ordered an appletini."

Skeeter stole a glance behind him and wiped at his brow. "But beer goes better with ribs."

"Better or not, you and I both know that if a lady orders pecan pie and all you have is peach, then you'd better go plant yourself a pecan tree and pray for rain."

Joie's eyes darted to Skeeter, who picked up the beer, foam sloshing over the rim as he tried to set it on his tray. Her face went soft and something close to understanding and apology flickered between the two.

"It's okay, Brett. Really, beer is fine." With a forced smile she took the beer back and sucked down a big gulp, leaving a thin line of foam on her lips.

Brett looked toward his grandma and her friends huddled around the table and felt his jaw clench. This was no longer about a drink or even the inn. This was about the North and the South all over again. The Civil War might have ended in 1865, but in that second, with their stern looks and chapel posture, Brett knew that the battle still raged and they were asking him to choose sides.

And every damn person in the place was watching to see where Brett McGraw's loyalty fell. Family or female.

"Refreshing," Joie said. "Thank you, Skeeter."

Even when unwillingly placed in the center of a scandal, a place Joie had avoided at all cost, she still acted compassionately, placing Skeeter's comfort above her own. The town was determined to make her feel like the outsider, yet she was the only one looking out for their people.

Skeeter swallowed and ducked his head. "You're right welcome, Miss Harrington."

"And your hushpuppies," she took in a deep breath, "smell incredible."

She picked up a hushpuppy and studied the cornmeal ball thoroughly before taking a delicate nibble, as if it were some fine wine. Then she let out a moan that had Brett thinking of something else entirely.

"My God, that is phenomenal. Is there lemongrass in these?"

"Um, yes, ma'am. I spent some time in Vietnam after the war."

"Asian-infused southern cuisine." She took another bite, her tongue sliding over her lip. "Brilliant." Her eyes went wide with excitement. "Would you be interested in doing a few classes at Fairchild House when we're up and running? People would line up to learn from you."

And Brett saw it happen, Skeeter's face flushed and he gave a half-smitten smile. Joie had spun her sugar and won the old man over with her sweetness.

"Why, I never really considered—"

A scolding throat cleared from behind and Skeeter shot a worried look over his shoulder. The man who did two tours of Vietnam, the second with only three fingers on his trigger hand, was sweating over a bunch of old ladies and their feud. And Brett knew what he had to do.

Eyes on Hattie and in a voice loud enough to carry across the bar but charming enough to be polite, he lifted Joie's beer and said, "Mighty southern of you to buy us our first round, Grandma. But I think you misunderstood, the lady ordered an appletini."

The restaurant fell silent. It was as if the collective gasp sucked all of the air out of the room.

Brett had just called out his grandma's manners in front of God and a good quarter of the town.

Hattie would take his head off the next time they were alone, but he refused to falter.

The silence stretched on, getting thicker by the minute. Brett crossed his arms, flashed a dimple, and waited. He could outwait anyone, even his grandma, if it meant making Joie feel welcomed in Sugar.

Hattie gave a final furrow of the forehead and then plastered her most welcoming smile on. "Well, you heard the man, Skeeter. Bring the lady her city drink."

Skeeter scurried off without another word and all eyes returned to their respective plates. Conversation resumed and the restaurant hummed with the usual quitting-time energy.

"Thank you," Joie whispered.

"You can't thank me yet, you haven't even tried his croquettes." Brett picked up one of the dumplings, dipped it in the sauce, and held it to her lips.

He thought she was going to refuse, and he wouldn't blame her if she did. Sitting in that booth was like being onstage and having the whole town watch their date play out. Then, with a smile that said, *Let's give them something to talk about*, she opened her mouth and took a bite.

"Oh, my God, that's heaven," she moaned, and Brett had to agree. Feeling her lips brush his fingertips as she finished off the second half of the appetizer was on par with the sexiest thing he'd ever seen. "There's Thai chili paste in there."

"You didn't think I brought you here because the menu is named after me, did you?"

She nodded and he laughed. He'd brought her here because he knew she loved food, and the Gravy Train was one of the few places around that offered a unique take on...well, anything.

"If you think that is heaven, wait until you taste the ribs. Skeeter soaks them in Baijiu and hot mustard, then smokes them until the meat falls off the bone."

He licked off the remaining sauce and went for another one.

She watched him eat, her expression heating to the point that he started squirming in his chair. Brett didn't do nervous around women, but there was something about Joie that kept him off-balance.

Since the day he'd seen her walking down that highway, he had known they were building toward this moment. It was only their first date, but it felt like he'd known her forever. Just being with her made him happier, and hornier, than he could ever remember being.

"I think we should get some to go."

"What?" Brett choked down the croquette he'd been swallowing. "Is this because of my grandma?"

Joie shook her head, those gorgeous curls spilling over her shoulders. "It's because I want to be with you."

She rested her elbows on the table and leaned in, the neck of her dress dipping low enough to give him a generous view. "I want you naked in bed, and if you think I can sit here staring at you for the next hour and not touch you—"

"Skeeter, can you make that to go?" Brett asked, grabbing her hand as he stood.

He'd been an idiot to think they could sit here, in the middle of town, and not undress each other with their eyes all night. Sliding his fingers more deeply between hers, he threw a couple of bills on the table and tugged her toward the exit.

Fuck the takeout.

* * *

Josephina's whole body shook as she tried to open the front door of her house. She'd never felt so nervous or alive. Brett's strong hand was resting at the small of her back, but he could have been deep inside of her from the way her body was reacting.

With his free hand, he took the keys and opened the door. Once inside she tugged him toward the staircase but he pulled her to a stop.

"What?"

Before he could answer, Boo's head peeked over the back of the couch. The minute he spotted her his whole body started wiggling. Tail wagging so hard it moved his whole being, he trotted over.

Brett looked down. "I'm giving you two minutes to do your thing. After that I'm locking the door and you won't get back in until morning."

Boo let out a snort and then, snout in the air, made his way outside.

Brett shut the door and walked back toward her. Never stopping, never hesitating, he just walked right up into her space as if he belonged and took her mouth. His lips were amazing, full and skilled, all patience and finesse. He kissed her as though he couldn't get enough, which worked for her, since she was pretty sure that this was the best kiss in the history of the world.

In fact, kissing Brett was like being reborn, like she was being kissed for the first time. It was needy and desperate and—magical.

Kind of like his thigh, which was currently tucked between hers, putting on the pressure and driving her right out of her mind. Nuclear-powered tingles exploded though her body and it was all she could do not to un-buckle his belt and drop his pants. Especially when his thigh shifted higher, pressing harder, creating a delicious friction.

Friction was good. Friction was freaking great. But she wanted more. So she went to work, leading her hand to the cause. Okay, both hands, since one palmed his ass to pull him closer, while the other slid around the front to his— *oh, my.*

"Aw, sugar," Brett groaned, his head falling back. "You keep that up and it will be over in three seconds, and I want to do this right. In a bed. Taking my time. Loving you all night."

That last part had her nipples going into party mode. But the bed? Was he serious? After weeks of foreplay there was no way she was going to make it upstairs. That he hadn't attempted to move, except to push harder into her palm, told her that it would not take much to get him on board.

She gave a little squeeze. "Impatient, remember?"

Maybe it was more than a little squeeze, but he didn't seem to mind. Nope, Brett's eyes dilated and she knew it was game on, because he let out a relieved groan and all of his finesse and hard-won patience evaporated. His mouth took hers as hands slid up her thighs and under her dress, gripping her ass. Then he lifted. Her feet came off the ground, her heart fell to her toes, and Josephina felt sexy. Desirable. Wanted.

How long had it been since she had felt wanted? Too long to remember.

"Wrap your legs around me."

Worked for her. She even let out a relieved gasp when her back came flush with the wall and her happy parts got up close and personal with his. Anticipation set her body on fire and her hands to work, tugging at his belt buckle. Brett's hands were skilled, shoving her dress to her waist and running the tips of his fingers along the edge of her silk panties, then up the center, making her gasp.

"You're soaked."

"I have been all night," she admitted, smiling when his belt clanked open.

"Then I have been neglecting my dately duties."

If Josephina was having trouble getting his jeans unbuttoned before, she was helpless when he pushed her silk to the side and slid one finger in. When another joined the party, she knew without a doubt that this was the best first date ever.

Wanting him to feel the same, she gave up on his fly and slid her hand inside his jeans, sighing when she found him already hard. She stroked him, his body jerking at the contact, and his hands faltered, nearly dropping her. So of course she did it again. This time she didn't have to scream for him to take her to the table.

Brett had figured out that part for himself, launching into action and moving them across the room at record speed.

She moaned when her bottom met a cold, hard surface. But it was a deep, needy moan that escaped when Brett nudged her thighs wider and settled between her legs. He was sheathed and ready, sinking into her before she could do more than tug her panties to the side.

And good God, time stopped. She didn't want to move, didn't want to breathe, afraid that if she did it would all be over. And it couldn't be over. The feeling was just too amazing.

He was amazing.

"Brett," she breathed, not sure how to explain what was happening. It was as though all of the emotions and expectations collided into a ball of hot need low in her belly.

"I know," he groaned, placing a kiss in the curve of her

neck. His hands tightened on her hips, pulling her toward him, until she felt full, complete.

Digging her heels into his lower back, she urged him even closer, with such force that they tipped back until she was flat on the table and he was flat against her. A great combination—that hard, male weight, pressing into her soft curves felt so good she couldn't catch her breath. All of the fantasies she had built up over the past month couldn't even compare to the real thing.

Not even bothering to brace his weight, Brett drove into her and she came hard and embarrassingly fast. No that it deterred him, since he continued pumping, creating hundreds of aftershocks before he quickly followed her over.

Still splayed across her, and buried deep inside, Brett pulled back. His hair sticking in every direction, his shirt missing the top few buttons, he looked as dazed as she felt.

With a contented sigh, Josephina turned her head, surprised to find Kenny staring down at her. In fact, her mind was so muddled that when Boo yipped to be let back in, Josephina found herself wondering why the hell they had waited so long. Sex with Brett was unlike anything she had ever experienced.

"You okay?" Brett whispered.

Josephina nodded, unsure if she had enough left in her to actually form a coherent word. And when she spoke her voice came out breathy. But she was breathy. "That was—"

Boo barked. Loud enough to wake the entire Sugar Lake neighborhood.

"Just the appetizer," Brett whispered, slowly easing out of her. He helped her sit up and pressed a sweet kiss to the side of her neck.

With one last look, he discarded the condom and went to

the door to open it. Boo sprang in, ears back, tail up. He was on high alert.

"Now go on," Brett told Boo and pointed to the couch.

Boo walked over to the table and sat firmly under Josephina's feet, which still hung lifeless off the end of the table. Too much bliss could do that to a girl.

"Sorry, buddy. Tonight she's mine. We talked about this. You knew it was coming."

With a resigned sigh, Boo gave Josephina one last big blink of the eyes, kind of like Brett had a moment ago, and tapped across the floor to curl up on the couch. He even turned his back as if giving them privacy.

Josephina couldn't help but smile. "You had a talk with Boo?"

"Yes, ma'am. I've learned always to express my intent when there is another man in the house." Brett tugged her to a stand and her dress back over her body.

"And what was the consensus?"

"That he'd have to start sharing." Brett eased her against him, his hands moving deliciously up her spine.

"Boo's not big on sharing."

"Neither am I." Josephina felt a slight tug and then her dress fell to the floor, leaving her in nothing but her Falcons-red panty set and matching pumps. "God, you're beautiful."

Ready for the second course, she reached behind to undo her bra.

Brett caught her hand. "Not yet. Now we take it slow, and that means I get to finally look at you. All of you."

Josephina resisted the urge to cover herself, but his gaze was so hungry and intense she wasn't sure what to do with her hands. Not that she had time to figure it out. With an appreciative grunt, Brett scooped her up and headed for the staircase.

"What are you doing?"

"Sugar, I have waited weeks to see you like this. I'm going to take my time enjoying every inch of you. First with my hands." He started up the stairs, firmly cupping her butt.

"Then with my mouth." He ran his tongue over the lace edging of her bra, while he placed her on the mattress.

After delivering a well-placed, well-executed kiss that spanned from her breast all the way past her belly button and lower, he straightened and stood back, his eyes raking over her body. Neither of them moved or spoke. She watched him watching her, and the raw lust in his expression made her bold.

She pushed up on her elbow, moving so that one bra strap—*whoops, how did that happen?*—slid off her shoulder. "Then what?"

His eyes rose to meet hers and a slow, lethal smile curved at his lips. "Why don't you slide off those panties and I'll show you."

Josephina reached behind her with one hand and then changed her mind. If he wanted a show, she would give him one. Her eyes never leaving his, she traced the lace trim with the tips of her fingers, slowly tugging down the fabric and letting her breasts spill over.

"I changed my mind," Brett said, his voice thick and strained. "I want to be the one to undress you."

Reaching behind with one arm, he pulled his shirt off. Next came his jeans, underwear included, exposing a tribal tattoo that started on his upper rib cage and ran the length of him, down to his hipbone and disappearing behind his back, where Josephina knew it stopped at the dimple above his butt. It also exposed the most incredible erection she had ever seen. She tried not to openly stare, but the man was gorgeous.

Before dropping his jeans to the floor, Brett reached into the back pocket and pulled out a strip of condoms. Holding it by two fingers he let the packet fall open, revealing a six-pack—minus one.

"Pretty cocky there, cowboy."

"It's called confident optimism." Tossing the condoms on the bed next to her, he covered her body with his, and she sighed at how good it felt. Their naked skin touched, sticking in the summer heat, as he pressed her hands above her head and into the mattress. "And the cocky doesn't start until portion three of the evening."

She laughed and he kissed her, slowly and languidly, as he had all night, intending to enjoy every second of it—and every inch of her. He kissed the side of her mouth, nibbled on her lower lip, and dipped his tongue inside for a kiss that seemed to go on forever.

Her fingers, on a mission of their own, ran down his tattoo, tracing the slightly puckered lines all the way to his ass, then along his hip and around to the front. She couldn't help it if in the process, the backs of her fingers grazed the tip of his erection. Twice.

"Jesus, Joie," he said, rolling on his side to face her. "This time it's going to last."

With his rough hands, he traced her lips, her breasts, her every curve, leaving nothing unexplored. He was killing her, his fingers teasing up and around, mapping every inch of her from belly button to the tips of her toes. By the time he got back to her center, sliding his finger under the elastic of her panties, her body was so amped she was shaking.

At least she'd die a satisfied woman, she thought, when his fingers eased under the silk and then into her—and the wait was worth it. His calloused fingers against her achy skin felt so delicious her whole body clenched, pulling him deeper. He stroked her gently, slowly building the pressure, until the tension knotted in her stomach, in her every muscle—and she wasn't sure how much longer she'd be able to hold back.

She was pretty sure she asked for more, but he ignored her, instead taking his sweet-ass time, nipping at the underside of her breasts until she was certain she was going to die. His tongue traced mindless patterns over the lace, making sure to cover every inch of her breast, except the nipple.

With an impatient moan, she arched up, trying to show him what she needed, and Brett smiled against her skin. And just when she thought he was going to take off her bra and move to the other breast, he covered her with his mouth, pulling so hard she felt it all the way to her core. He slid in another finger, and she felt the pressure intensify until he gave a gentle nip right as his thumb pressed down on the right spot and she exploded, crying out his name.

Body limp, nerves humming, Josephina opened her eyes to find Brett watching her. He wasn't so laid-back or easy-going anymore. His face was tight and his body taut.

"Do you have any idea how gorgeous you look when you come?"

She slowly shook her head, amazed. Two orgasms. In one night. She didn't even think that was possible. Not for her. She looked down and laughed. "I still have my underwear on."

"Not for long." He slid her panties down her legs, over her heels, and off, his hands exploring the entire way. Her bra came next. "The shoes stay on."

"Only if we promise to skip over point two on your presentation and go straight to the third item on the list."

Brett grinned. It was wicked and hot, and Josephina felt her body start to heat back up. "And that would be?"

Reminding herself that she was living life at full tilt, she explained, "I want you. Inside of me. I believe you said I could have it slow and long and all night."

"Best item on the menu," he drawled.

Tearing off a foil packet, he covered her body with his, and she felt him pressing at her entrance. Her patience gone and her body demanding release, Josephina rose up and took him in one hard thrust.

"Fuck," he rasped, his fingers digging into her right hip.

When they could both breathe again, he withdrew and then sank back in, slow and easy, giving her exactly what she needed, until she forgot to be nervous. Forgot about his grandma and her parents and the stupid feud. Until all she could think about was him, and her, and this moment.

"Is this okay?" he whispered.

It was more than okay. It was amazing. And she hadn't felt amazing in years. As if she were at home in her own body. As if being *her* were enough. So to show him just what he did to her, she tightened her thighs around him and Brett let out a low moan. "The lady requested slow and long, so I'm trying for slow and long. But, Christ, Joie, you aren't making it easy."

"I changed my mind. The lady wants it hard and fast," she panted, surprised at her words, but inwardly proud. She was done living by everyone else's rules, wanted to live life with no holds barred.

Josephina arched up off the mattress and circled her hips.

"Yes, ma'am," Brett growled, and proceeded to do just that. He hooked a hand behind her knee and brought it up flush with her hips and drove in, going deep and hard and hitting places that she'd long ago passed off as myth.

He picked up the pace, pushing her pleasure well past amazing and into sudden meltdown. The familiar heat built, spreading out and curling her toes. Brett dropped his hand between their bodies, circling the right spot. With one slide of his finger, Joie exploded and everything inside her shook.

Brett gave a last thrust and she heard him moan out her name. Then he collapsed on top of her. Josephina's leg fell to the side, her arms hung limp around his back as she lay there, silently listening to the pounding of her heart and their heavy breaths as they struggled to take in oxygen. Outside of opening her eyes, it was impossible to move. Not that she wanted to be anywhere but there, under this big mass of yummy man.

After a long moment, he rolled over, taking her with him. Brushing a strand of hair off her forehead, he planted a kiss on her temple. "You are amazing."

"I was just thinking the same thing," she whispered, forcing herself to hold it together.

Those three simple words affected her far more that they should, because she couldn't remember the last time someone had said something so sweet to her. Not since Letty. And she wanted to curl into him and never let go, which was when Josephina knew she needed to lighten the mood before her heart did something stupid—like fall for a guy who was bound to leave.

"You're not so bad yourself," she said, smiling up at him.

"Not so bad?" Brett cupped her face between his hands and brought her lips to his. "I guess I'd better get to work on raising your opinion of me."

She held up the remainder of their condom strip. "You only have four swings. Think you'll come in under par?"

"Sugar, I made three aces with two swings, and I still have part two in tonight's itinerary to see to." He trailed open-mouthed kisses down her chest to her belly, nipping at her hipbone. "Plus, if we run out, I got a box in my room. Costco-sized."

Chapter 18

Josephina pulled her gold-sequined ball cap low on her head and tried to remind herself that this thing with Brett was temporary. But the more time she spent with him, the more she felt herself hope for something more.

He was charming and thoughtful and the best lover she'd ever had. But it wasn't just the sex that had her heart spiraling out of control. It was how he could challenge her while never making her feel that she could disappoint him. He seemed to like her, quirks and all. And somehow managed to make her laugh in spite of her parents and the old biddies driving her insane.

The showdown at the Gravy Train was only one of the many ways Brett had tried to ease Josephina's way into Sugar societal acceptance. And it was working. People were actually smiling at her when they went into town, asking her about Fairchild House, and offering their help on the Pucker Up and Drive. It was as if she was finally making a place in Sugar. The only thing about Brett that she didn't like was that he was leaving in just a few weeks.

Looking up at all of the spectators in the stands, Josephina squared her shoulders and forced herself to focus. Surrounded by half the town of Sugar, she stood ankle deep in mud, wearing denim, camouflage, and a huge target on her back. With more than a dozen women, and the prize being Brett, Josephina knew it was about to get down and dirty. Especially when she saw Darleen from the bank, who had been so nice when she'd applied for the loan, look from Brett to Josephina, her vision tunneling in and turning hard.

"There's still time to change your mind," Darleen offered with enough sweetness to give Josephina a cavity.

"I'm good," Josephina said, eyes on her guy.

"I would just hate for you to wind up empty-handed *and* dirty." Darleen smiled at Brett, big and inviting, her eyes never leaving his when she continued, "Because anybody can sink their claws into one, but it takes a real woman to tie 'em down."

Josephina eyed her Romeo, with his two hundred pounds of slicked muscle and sheer testosterone, and knew that taking this one down by force would be a painful lesson—for the woman stupid enough to try.

Fairy Bug, Aunt Letty used to say, *where's the sense in chasing a male into a pen who don't want to be caged? Especially when a pile of slop and a gilt in heat will do the trick.*

Josephina smiled. Rather than corner this big guy, she was going to seduce him right into her arms.

Bodies tensed and mud squished under shifting feet as the clock counted down. At zero, a heartfelt "Sooiee" boomed through the high school speakers, cutting the silence.

Grunting and squeals filled the pen as the women zeroed

in on their boars, determined to be crowned Miss Sugar Slick. That the prize was a round of golf with none other than Sugar's golden boy only increased the odds that someone was going home in an ambulance.

To Josephina's right, Darleen took off in a sprint and, knocking down a fellow Peach, gunned for the smallest greased pig, Bacon Bits. Bits was small but fast, squeaking right through Darleen's fingers and making a hard left to circle the pen.

Josephina's eyes never left Romeo, who, the heavyweight of the seventy-sixth annual Sugar Slicked Pig Roundup, stood stock-still in the middle of the pen. With the body of a tank and a don't-fuck-with-me glare, Romeo was the one pig every woman avoided and the one that if you gave him a chance would rip your face off.

With a single snort, Romeo created a three-foot radius of intimidation around him.

Ignoring the other women, Josephina slowly made her way to the center of the pen. Stepping over a downed contestant and narrowly missing a charging Bacon Bits, she reached into her pocket, pulled out a handful of sugar cubes, and dropped to one knee.

Romeo would come to her in his own time. Her job was to wait until he figured out that all she wanted to give him was a bit of sugar.

* * *

"I ain't but just hollered *sooie* and that Yankee is already done for," Hattie said, shaking her head.

"She isn't done for, Grandma. She's got more pluck than that," Brett said, leaning back on the bleacher, his eyes never leaving Joie.

"Well, I'm going closer so I can get a picture when that boar takes her out. Payton showed me how to upload photos on Twitter and I just bet my Tweeps would love them a picture of a Yankee bathing in manure."

He didn't know what Tinker Bell was thinking, kneeling in the middle of a greased-pig contest, but he knew she would rather jump in the pile of slop than lose to a Peach. Especially since there were ten-to-one odds that the city girl would wind up with a mouth full of mud. They were calling it the When Pigs Fly Odds, and Brett was going to make a killing.

"As long as you don't disappear when I come to collect, Grandma."

Hattie's white spikes disappeared into the crowd, but not before Brett saw a single arthritic finger flip high in the air.

"Looks like you were betting with the wrong head," Cal chuckled.

"Maybe."

"Maybe?" Jackson looked at Brett and shook his head. "There's no maybe about it. You're not sleeping on the couch anymore and it's clouding your judgment."

"She'll win." Brett grinned as Joie plopped down, legs crisscrossed while mud seeped through her jeans, soaking her delectable backside. Her lips and body moved as if she were wrapped in a deep discussion. She nibbled on something then extended her arm in offering to big old Romeo.

The other women were hollering and diving in the mud, and there sat Joie, in her own world, talking to a pig.

"Win?" Jackson barked. "She's squatting in the mud, holding out her hand like she expects the pig to shake it." *Not giving a rat's ass that everyone was whispering or that Hattie was taking her picture*, Brett thought. "Plus, she's wearing a Saint's hat."

"She just likes the color," Brett lied. Joie would have picked out that hat on purpose, knowing it would piss off the Sunday School Mafia.

"He's got it bad." Jackson shouldered Cal. "His eyes have that dazed look to them. Like he's been in bed for hours but hasn't slept a wink."

Brett shrugged, not caring that Jackson and Cal were exchanging glances. Brett knew what he looked like, gazing at Joie all the time, following her around town like some lost puppy. But he didn't give a shit how pathetic he came off. He only had a few weeks left before the FedEx Cup and he intended to spend every second of it with her.

"So I take it that she didn't kick you out after she found out about the loan," Cal said.

"Nope." Which wasn't a lie. Brett hadn't told her. He planned to, just not tonight. Tonight he wanted to help her shower off every speck of mud while she wore nothing but that crown she was about to win.

"Hold up," Jackson said, his voice going low with disbelief.

Brett and his brother looked back down at the arena floor.

"Well, shit," Cal mumbled, no doubt counting the bills he just lost.

Brett stood to get a better view. "Who's the idiot now?"

In the middle of a muddy war zone sat Joie—her gaze locked on Brett's with a smile that got his heart pumping—petting her pig. Reaching into her back pocket she pulled out a gold leash, dangling it from her fingers, and the damn animal actually lowered his head while she slid it on.

Brett shook his head, knowing exactly how the boar felt. The poor guy never stood a chance.

All the ladies but Darleen stopped and watched as Joie and Romeo strutted over to the judge's table. Darleen, who had wrestled her pig to the ground, knotted off her rope and stood, wiping mud off her cheek.

Joie paused to pull off her camouflage shirt, exposing a pink tank-top underneath, and tossed it to Darleen.

"You got a little something, right there." Joie waved her hand to encompass Darleen's entire body. Then she turned back to the judge's table and when the sun caught the gold glitter affixed to her top the crowd erupted.

In bold letters, spanning her generous chest, sat two little words that took her from New York socialite to Sugar's sweetheart: Got Wings?

Tinker Bell had indeed found hers. She was playing by her own rules, no longer afraid of what people would say, taking a stand for her right to live here in Sugar. And in the South that makes you "People."

Brett had already made his way down the bleachers and hopped the rail by the time the Sugar High School principal spoke.

"Well, I'll be. It looks as if we've got ourselves a winner," the principal said into the mike. He held up the Miss Sugar Slick crown and the crowd cheered some more. "It's with great surprise and pleasure that I crown the winner of the seventy-sixth annual Sugar Slicked Pig Roundup and Miss Sugar Slick, Miss Joie Harrington—"

"Hang on, Mr. Jessup," Brett interrupted, taking the crown. "As the sponsor of this event, I believe that pleasure is mine."

"What kind of pleasure are we talking," Joie whispered, looking up at him through her lashes.

The moment those baby-blues hit his, Brett was lost. She was the sexiest damn thing he'd ever seen. Covered in mud and glitter with a pig on a leash, Joie Harrington wove her way into the place in his heart that Brett had long thought dead.

Skeeter's camera flashed, capturing the moment for the *Sugar Sentinel*, as Brett crowned his fairy princess. It kept right on flashing as Brett pulled her into his arms and kissed the hell out of her in front of God and Hattie. Oh, and Romeo, who was grunting something fierce and trying to wedge his way between them.

"I call for a recount," Darleen snapped, snatching the crown off Joie's head and stopping Brett before he went too far and embarrassed them both. "She didn't follow the rules. She didn't hogtie her boar."

"Well, hang on there, Ms. Darleen," Skeeter said, sending Joie an encouraging wink. "The rules state that this is a roundup, not a hogtie."

"Mine's technically tied," Joie said. "But you can have the crown if you want. I just wanted the golf lessons." She sent Brett a sexy grin.

He'd give her lessons all right.

"I don't want the crown," Darleen shouted. "And you used a leash. I roped and tied mine and you just bribed yours with sugar."

"That's because sugar's twice as sweet."

* * *

Careful not to step on the paint-coated tarp, Josephina made her way to the kitchen and tried not to think about Brett in the shower. Just the sound of the water running gave her way too many ideas. She set the table and was putting the final touches on dinner, her body humming with desire, when Brett padded into the kitchen. Bare feet, jeans hanging low on his waist, he toweled off his hair before pulling on a black T-shirt.

He looked so right, standing in her kitchen. Actually

he seemed to belong in nearly every room of her house. She had thought living together would be awkward, especially after sex. It was anything but. Their daily routine was so smooth it was almost choreographed. They seemed to have settled into each other as if this was how it was meant to be.

Brett grabbed two beers from the fridge, popped the caps, and, instead of sitting at the table, joined Josephina at the counter.

Standing directly behind her, he placed his beer on one side of her, and hers on the other, effectively caging her in. "Smells good."

"Uh-huh." She busied herself with serving up dinner to keep from leaning back into him. Even though they had just spent the last hour testing out the new master bath, she wanted him.

"It's chicken and dumplings." Dang it, her voice was all breathy. It didn't matter that he wasn't even touching her. He was so close she could feel his heat seep into her pores. Feel his breath on her neck.

"Wasn't talking about dinner." A second later he was pressing forward, his hands slowly working their way around her waist, his nose burying itself in her hair, and she went from breathy to breathless.

"Dinner's getting cold," she whispered.

"It'll keep."

She jerked a little when his fingers, chilled from holding the beer, met the bare patch of skin above the button of her shorts. Sliding his hands under the hem of her shirt, he eased them back until his thumbs worked circles at the knots in her lower back.

"I'm just working out some of those knots you seem so fond of," he innocently explained.

"Okay." That was all the answer she could get out. His hands continued working their magic as the refrigerator hummed, Boo yipped for his dinner, and her body slowly turned to Jell-O.

"When did you learn how to make chicken and dumplings?" His lips brushed her ear.

"It's Lettys' recipe," she sighed, leaning forward, giving his strong, capable hands complete access to her sore muscles. "She used to make it for me when we would celebrate something big."

She felt him smile. "And what are we celebrating?"

"I told my parents about the loan and about the Pucker Up and Drive."

Brett's hands never slowed, but she felt a slight hesitation. "What did they say?"

Unable to stand still at her good news, she straightened, turning in his hands. "At first they were surprised that I managed to secure one, which kind of hurt. But after a lecture on how I could have gotten a better rate and that I should have just borrowed the money from them, my dad actually sounded proud."

"Of course he did." Brett dropped his hands and took Boo's plate, setting it on the floor. Boo glared for a brief second and then lapped up his dumplings.

"No, you don't get it." She carried their two plates over and set them on the table. "He even canceled a trip to Brazil to make sure he and Mom would be here for the fundraiser and grand opening. He wants to see what we've done and thank you in person for helping me with this *mess of a project*." She did her best to keep her smile intact as she threw air quotes around the last few words.

Brett joined her, placing a beer at each plate. Although he sat in his usual way, leaning easily back in the chair, legs sprawled out as if he didn't have a care in the world, there was a tightness to his expression that said he wasn't easygoing about her parents' call.

"Don't let him do that. Don't let *anyone* minimize what you've done here, Joie. This event, the remodel, everything was you. I just earned a few peaceful nights of sleep by swinging hammers."

Josephina told herself it was ridiculous to get teary-eyed over his words. Brett was just a protective kind of guy. The reminder still didn't stop the swelling in her chest or the warm flutters in her stomach because he was extending that McGraw protectiveness toward her.

She moved the food around her plate for a second, wondering if she should go on, especially since he was looking a little nervous. She had a feeling that if she told him exactly how much of an impact he'd made on the inn he would get uncomfortable, just as he did when people around town thanked him for his help. But he deserved to hear how much his belief in her meant.

Setting her fork down, Josephina walked around the table and made herself right at home on his lap. "It's about more than paint and siding, Brett. You believed in me. No one has ever done that before."

* * *

The next night, Boo sniffed his dinner twice before showing Josephina his tail as he plodded gamely over to the entryway and plopped down. Ears alert, tail completely still, he looked out the screen door.

"Boo, come eat. He's not coming," Josephina said, pushing back her own plate.

The moment she set down the paint cans and started

dragging furniture out of the salon, Brett had made some excuse about meeting Cal at the Saddle Rack and high-tailed out of the house. Without their usual dinner. It hadn't seemed like a big deal until Josephina sat down at the table and realized she had come to enjoy his company. Dinner with Brett was fun and easy. She liked having someone to share her day with. Someone to talk to about her crazy parents, to celebrate the little accomplishments on the inn.

Okay, it wasn't just someone. It was Brett. She liked having him around. More precisely, she loved having him around and that terrified her. Somewhere between ripping up subflooring and wrestling hogs she had fallen hard. And he was leaving.

Appetite gone, Josephina picked up her plate and dumped the remains of her tarragon chicken and polenta in the trash. She was just rinsing it when she saw something streak across the boat dock.

Walking to the screen door, she strained to see through the night. The moon was high and after a few seconds her eyes adjusted. She grabbed a flashlight and one of the drivers from Wilson's golf bag before quietly sneaking onto the back deck to end this.

Hattie, as of now renamed the Hillbilly Hellion, was at the front of the pack. Hard to miss in her kiwi green and condemnation, she waddled up the dock with tree trimmers in one hand, making complicated gestures with the other. Behind her, creating more noise than a street corner preacher in Manhattan, two others slunk in and out of the shadows. At the dock, sitting in the boat with her hand on the motor, was Jelly-Lou, loudly whispering orders and directions, which all ended with "God willing."

Josephina did some slinking of her own, down the back

steps so she could track their every move. Crawling through the rose garden, she crouched behind a hedge, blindly reaching for the garden hose and coming up short.

"Thisaway," Etta Jayne hissed.

"What?" Hattie hissed back, so loud that it was most likely heard in town.

"I said, thisaway."

"Don't you tell me whichaway to go. Been coming here since Christ walked the earth. I know where it's at!"

Both women took off toward the side of the house, jostling and elbowing for position, neither giving an inch until they reached the side wall.

Josephina didn't know where Dottie had disappeared to and whether to call the cops or giggle at the old ladies—until she heard the metal of the tree trimmers sliding open and saw an explosion of sparks followed by a loud boom that ricocheted off the water and around the lake.

All the lights inside the house went five hundred Kelvins brighter, illuminating the entire backyard long enough to make out the shocked expression on each of the ladies' faces, including Dottie, whose head peeked out from under Ulysses's hood. A second later, the lights of all the houses around the lake flickered out like dominoes, one by one, plunging the entire area into a sea of black.

Boo took off, his little claws skidding their way across the back porch and down the steps, his bark somewhere between small-dog-defending-his-home and elation at seeing his friends. *Traitor.*

"Lord Almighty, Hattie, I thought you said no one was home," Jelly-Lou announced.

"Well, you thought wrong." Josephina flicked on her flashlight, shining it in their eyes.

There was a brief oh-shit moment, then Dottie's binoculars hit the dirt and they all took off, making their way around the hedges, every biddy for herself.

"Oh, no, you don't," Josephina snapped, stepping over the hedge, determined not to let them get away. "You broke it and this time you'll fix it!"

Two steps and Josephina felt herself sink. Up to her shins in mud and soaked clay. She lifted her foot, and the suction was almost loud enough to drown out the now-obvious spray of the hose, which, based on the saturation levels, indicated that someone had turned it on hours ago. The same someones who were currently hobbling across the dock.

This was not happening. She was not going to be bested by a bunch of mean old ladies. She was going to catch them, call Jackson, then press charges, finally ending this feud.

Josephina sprang into action, leaping back over the hedge and making her way through the rose garden. Ignoring the pebbles cutting through her bare feet and the thorns scratching at her arms and legs, she stubbed her big toe on Letty's ceramic fairy and rammed her knee into a rusted washing machine, getting to the dock just in time to see a green fanny bend over and yank the boat's starter cord.

The engine sputtered and then caught, and all the ladies cheered as the boat slowly backed away from the dock.

With enough momentum, Josephina could leap and probably clear the boat. But the dock wasn't all that sturdy and neither was the boat. And although Jelly-Lou wasn't in her wheelchair, Josephina wasn't sure if she could swim.

Boo, on the other hand, had no reservations about scurrying his little doggie butt down the dock and taking a flying leap. Josephina froze, part of her screaming, "Get 'em, boy," proud that he was protecting what was his. While the other part wanted to cry because he was so little and the lake was so big.

But when Jelly-Lou reached out and caught him midair, and he crawled up her chest, tail wagging and licking her face, Josephina felt something inside her break a little.

"That's my dog," Josephina shouted over the engine.

"And this is our town," Etta Jayne hollered back, her voice echoing off the lake's surface.

"You have until tomorrow morning to bring him back or I call the cops," she yelled into the night. The only response was the wind brushing through the old oaks.

At first Josephina thought that the ladies were lashing out because of the salon. That they were mad about losing their place to play poker, and in a way she understood. Now, all Josephina understood was that this was personal. It wasn't the salon or her inheriting the house.

They didn't like her. They never would. And with them running the town, it wouldn't take long before everyone else started looking at her differently.

Sure she had made a few friends, but if pressed, Josephina had no illusions that they would pick her. Mean or not, these old ladies were grandmas to half the town, and surrogates to the other half.

And Josephina was not a part of that equation.

* * *

Brett found himself in a corner booth at the Saddle Rack wedged between Cal and the wall. What a sorry excuse for a Friday night. It was either listen to Hattie's newest get-rich-quick scheme, which included a conference center, a camera crew, and some kind of jock itch cream, or go back over to Joie's place, apologize for tearing out of there, and drag her to bed. Since both would give him an undesirable outcome, he chose to knock back a few with the guys.

The day had been normal, lots of stripping and nailing and brushing—and guilt. Then he'd walked into that kitchen and found her in pajama shorts and a light pink tank top, her hair in a messy knot on top of her head. She was barefoot, shower-fresh, and sitting at a table that had been set for a family. And he couldn't do it.

He couldn't sit across from her, sharing their day, looking her in the eye, and not tell her about the money. The more time they spent together, the less he thought about going back on tour. And the more he realized just how badly he had fucked up.

"Joie's parents are coming to the Pucker Up and Drive," Brett admitted. "They're excited over Joie making the inn a success and called to say they are bringing some of their friends."

Cal gave Brett a disappointed look. "You haven't told her about the money yet, have you?"

"It hasn't come up."

"And what did you say when she told you the bank changed their mind about the loan?"

"That I was proud of her." Same thing he said every time she'd brought up how surprised she was that Mr. Ryan had reconsidered and found her risky endeavor a sound investment.

"You're a sick son of a bitch. You push yourself into her life, make her fall for you, *sleep* with her, and this whole time you're letting her walk around town preening about her loan. Lying to her. If some bastard did that to Payton I'd kill him." Cal shook his head, his voice going low. "And so would you."

"You don't think I already feel like shit?"

"Yeah, well imagine what she's going to feel like when she finds out." That was Brett's fear. She would be hurt and sad, but in the end she would question her ability. And that Brett couldn't live with.

"After her parents and that bastard of an ex, she pretty much thinks everyone expects her to fail. If she knew I gave her the money, she'd lose all belief in herself." Brett leaned forward. "What the hell was I supposed to tell her?"

"The truth. Same thing I gave you when Mom and Dad died and you started screwing around." Cal shook his head. "Saying you believe in someone and actually believing in them are two separate things. What's the point in taking it slow with her, trying for something real, when you can't even be honest with her?"

"I don't want her to doubt herself."

"That's bullshit and you know it." Cal leaned forward too, right into Brett's space. "You think it's easy for me to step back and let the people I love fall and make mistakes? You? Jace? Payton? Tawny? To put it all out there for everyone to see and then let the other person decide if they're going to make it or rip your fucking heart out when they don't?

You're scared, Brett. You're scared that Joie's going to screw up and lose Fairchild House and then leave. Leave Sugar. And leave you."

Brett's chest tightened. "Okay, then what do you suggest I do?"

"Man the fuck up. Put it on the line. Tell her about the loan, about how you feel, and let her decide if she wants to forgive you. If she loves you, she'll figure it out."

"And what if she decides she doesn't."

"Then you'll have to figure out if you love her enough to let her find her own happiness."

"I never said I loved her."

"Yeah. Tell that to yourself a couple more times and

you'll start to hear what a complete ass you sound like."
Cal stared at Brett long and hard, and then shook his head.
"Christ, Brett, you don't even see it, do you?"

"What the hell are you talking about?"

"You asked me to start building you a house on the other
side of Mom and Dad's property. Why else would you think
about settling back in town?"

Before Brett could come up with a good reason, other
than the obvious, Jackson walked up.

Dressed in jeans and bed-head, the sheriff appeared to
have been called in on his night off, and judging by the way
he gripped his sidearm, he was not a happy camper. "I hate
to break up this brotherly love fest, but I just got a call from
dispatch. Seems I am supposed to go arrest your grandma
and figured one of you might want to come with me."

Cal sighed. "Don't tell me she was caught skinny-
dipping again."

"No, seems she's wanted for destruction of private property, county property, and dognapping."

"Ah, hell," Brett said, already headed for the door. "Cal,
you handle Grandma. I'm going to check on Joie."

* * *

Brett skidded off the highway onto Fairchild Lane, kicking
up gravel and sending his truck sideways. Anxious to get to
Joie, he didn't slow down even though he couldn't see more
than five feet in front of him.

The moment he'd left town, he'd understood just how
much trouble Hattie was in. Sugar Lake, usually glimmering
with twinkle-lit docks and glowing houses, was black. Kind
of like his mood right now.

Cal had called and confirmed that their grandma had, after

swearing to him otherwise, paid Joie a visit and reinstated the feud. She'd stolen Ulysses's battery, cut Joie's power—accidentally blowing a transformer and plunging the entire neighborhood into darkness—and dognapped Boo.

Brett crested the final hill, gunned it through the canopy of moss-covered oaks. His truck came to an abrupt halt as he stopped to take in the scene before him.

On the front porch, surrounded by some kind of torches, Joie sat on the swing, knees hugged to her chest, staring out at the lake. He wasn't used to seeing her so still. The woman was constantly in motion. Even when she fell asleep watching TV her right big toe made small circles. Tonight she looked small and defeated.

Brett killed the engine, stepped out of the cab, and couldn't help but grin. Closer inspection showed that it wasn't tiki torches. She'd lit two of Rat Bastard's drivers on fire and stuck them in the ground.

He made his way up the steps, careful not to singe his clothes, and eased down next to her. She didn't say a word, and when he scooped her up and sat her on his lap, she just slid her arms around his neck and cuddled close. They sat, silently rocking in the swing and staring out at the lake, which now that Brett's eyes had adjusted was lit by the moon.

"Boo's gone," she whispered.

"I know. Cal's going to bring him home in the morning." He heard a muffled little sniffle. *Shit, she was crying.* "I can go get him now."

"No, they're probably feeding him bacon gravy and frosting his hair with highlights so he could be the newest member of their posse. Right now they're most likely teaching him how to gnaw through electrical wires. He'd be mad if he had to miss out."

After a minute she quietly said, "When I was little and a storm would roll in, I would get scared and Letty would wrap me up in a quilt and we'd snuggle in the salon while she told me stories about fairies and Pearl Fairchild."

She sniffled again, this time with a little more quiver, and he dropped a kiss to the top of her head. He hated that she was crying. Hated that his grandma had made her feel this way. Mostly, he hated that her body sagged with defeat.

"And sometimes, after a long day of pulling weeds or gardening, we'd eat ice cream out there and paint each other's toenails. She called it the after-soil-spoil." She snuggled deeper into him and, man, that did crazy things to his chest. "She always said the one thing people need more of these days is a little pampering. It's how we show love." Her arms tightened around him. "I'm not taking away their salon to be mean, I'm doing it to honor what Letty and I talked about. What we dreamed of. A magical place that pampered those brave enough to find their adventure."

"And Letty would love every bit of it," Brett said against her hair.

"Then why do I feel like every time I get one step ahead, I get tossed back two? Sometimes I wonder why I'm even trying." She looked up, her eyes a piercing blue, filled with a confused hurt that kicked him in the gut.

He took her face in his hands, his thumbs brushing the tears away. "I'll talk with Hattie in the morning and this will all go away, I promise."

"You can't make them like me, Brett." She shrugged. "Which means I've spent the past seven weeks trying to make a place for myself in a town that doesn't understand me and with a group of people who don't care enough to even try. The worst part is that, once again, the family of the man I'm falling for hates me."

Brett's breathing probably stopped, but it was hard to tell, since his heart was beating out of his chest. *The man I'm falling for.* It was the closest Joie had come to giving a verbal commitment that she was in this as deep as he was.

"She doesn't hate you, sugar. Even if she did, it wouldn't matter to me." He looked in her eyes so she could see the truth there. "You and your silly dog and this rodent-infested inn matter to me. You, matter to me, Joie. If they can't see what an amazing woman you are," he cradled her lower lip between his, "it's their loss."

"What if it's not them? What if it's me? And no matter how hard I try, no matter how many times I open myself up, it's not enough?"

He shook his head. The truth was, he knew exactly how she felt. Had been there more times than he cared to admit, and with good reason. But these last few weeks had changed him—she had changed him. Around her, Brett could just be Brett, and she never asked him to be anything more. Joie was genuine and so easy to love. That she doubted that about herself broke his heart.

Brett looked up at the sky, glittering with stars, and back at Joie. "Get your shoes. I want to show you something."

Brett walked Joie to the edge of the lake, letting go of her hand when they reached the dock. He untied the weathered dinghy and pushed it into the water, letting it sit for a minute to check for leaks. When none appeared, he held a hand out to Joie. She was wearing a tank top, a pair of men's boxers, and mud up to her knees. And, he had a sinking suspicion, no bra.

She looked at his hand and then to him. "Where are we going?"

"Trust me, Joie." The minute the words left his mouth he knew he was in deep shit. Her lip trembled slightly, her eyes got shiny, but in the end she took his hands without hesitation.

As he helped her onto the boat, he knew that Joie had just gone all in and he was a lying sack of shit. He started to tell her about the loan, but when he saw the lingering self-doubt in her eyes he knew he couldn't be the cause of more.

Not tonight.

Chapter 19

L ook up." Brett leaned back against an old support beam of what was left of his childhood home. Wrapping his arms around her waist, he eased her between his legs.

Tired of fighting, she dropped her head back against his chest and looked up at the sky. Millions of stars flickered against the black backdrop.

"It's beautiful," she whispered, struggling to hold all her emotions inside.

His family's property, the old oak tree, the crumbling structure and dreams surrounding them, everything rushed at her at once, leaving the overwhelming need to cry.

"Sometimes when I was a kid, things got so bad I didn't think I could breathe anymore without the pain killing me. I'd sneak out my bedroom window at Hattie's and come here to watch the stars. There were so many of them that after a while I didn't feel like I was slowly suffocating."

"How long did it take?" Josephina wanted to know. She

felt as though she'd been drowning in everyone else's expectations her whole life. Tonight, Hattie and her friends had held her head under the water, and Josephina was afraid she'd never manage to find her way back up.

"Sometimes I'd stay all night, sneaking back in right as Hattie started banging on doors announcing breakfast. If she knew, she never said a word."

"She knew. That woman makes it her business to know everything."

"I'm sorry," he whispered against her ear.

"For what?"

"Tonight. The Feud. The event. A lot of things." His breath skated down her neck, sending tingles even lower. "I need to tell you something."

"Like how many other girls you've brought up here?"

"To this place?" He threaded their fingers together and held tight. "Not a one. After the fire—" he shook his head. "No one. Not even Glory."

Josephina looked at what was left of the structure. There was no roof, few walls, and nothing that would identify this as a place of safety and happiness. The wood that wasn't scarred black had been beaten away by the weather. The very fact that the house hadn't been rebuilt told Josephina just how deeply the boys were affected by their parents' death.

"Was that your mom's kitchen?" she asked, pointing to a crumbling rock and concrete structure.

"Yeah, and right here, where we're sitting, was my bedroom." She felt, more than saw, him waggle a brow.

"Brett McGraw, you lured me to your bedroom *and* between your legs." She rubbed against him and she could feel the thick, hard length against her back.

"Yes, ma'am." He leaned down and nipped her earlobe.

"How come they didn't build the house closer to the lake?"

"Why do you ask?" He craned his head around to look at her profile.

"Just curious." She turned and their faces met. Immediately, his eyes zeroed in on her lips—just her lips. Her breath caught and she waited for him to kiss her, but as the seconds went on, and he continued to stare, the tension grew past the physical into something deeper.

"Where would you build it?" He studied her, silently assessing.

"I would build it closer to the lake, over by the beautiful oak tree we docked under. But I'd put a small chef's garden outside the kitchen, just like your mom had." She broke the connection to look past the kitchen into what she knew used to be a small family garden. "I would probably turn this building into a barn, salvage parts of the original structure. And of course"—she turned her head to face him again, and went for a little humor to cut through this web he was weaving over her—"I would put a pig pen right here where we're sitting."

Easygoing Brett looked so unsure of himself, so intent on her every word, as though her opinions really mattered, that warmth spread through her heart.

"I remember when you rescued me out of that old oak tree," she whispered.

"You were wearing pink ruffles and these cute pigtails." He gently tugged on her hair before sliding it aside so he could press a kiss to her bare shoulder. "Eyes full of tears, crying up a storm over how you were waiting for your wings so you could fly down."

"And you believed me."

His hands slid to cup her face. "Sugar, you wrapped those arms around me and planted one so big on my lips,

I would have believed you if you said you were a Falcons linebacker."

"Did you know that you were my first kiss?" she said, surprised at how shy she felt at the admission.

Brett tilted his head and whispered against her mouth, "Did you know that you were mine?"

Brett cradled her lips for a long, languid, wonderful moment. When he finally pulled back, Josephina asked, "Is that why you offered to buy me a hog farm?"

"No." He pressed a dozen little kisses along her jaw and hairline. "I was going to build you a hog farm because when you talked about it you smiled, and I would have done anything to not see you cry again."

When he didn't laugh or even smile, Josephina's heart did a flip right up into her throat. If she hadn't loved him before, she hopelessly fell right then. Fell in love with a man who was destined to leave her.

"Why did you bring me here, Brett?"

"Because I want you to stay." No hesitation. "I want to see you happy and settled here in Sugar."

"Letty left me that house, and no matter how much those ladies throw at me, I'm not leaving." She paused to swallow. "But you are."

"I could come home." His hand slid through her hair.

"What, between tournaments?"

"We could make it work."

"That sounds like a lot of empty nights in between."

His hand fell and he leaned back. "Are you afraid I'd cheat?"

"What? No." She wasn't. He might have slept with his fair share of women, but Josephina knew when he committed himself to a relationship he wouldn't stray. It went against who he was as a man.

With a sigh, she found herself looking up again, leaning against Brett and letting the vastness of the stars work their magic.

"Wilson was gone so much over the last two years I think we spent more time apart than together. I don't want another relationship like that. It hurts too much. I deserve more. We both do." She closed her eyes and forced herself to put it all out there. "I want roots, Brett. And you're leaving the day after the fundraiser."

He exhaled hard. "So where does that leave us?"

Walking away now wouldn't make the blow any less painful. And knowing that she'd opted out of what could be one of the most important relationships of her life because of fear wasn't going to happen. Nope, Josephina would open herself up to the time they had left and make sure when he went back on tour, went back to his life of twenty-four-hour commitments, there would be no regrets about going half in.

"I figure you have a little over two weeks before you have to leave for New Jersey. That gives us sixteen days and nights to get each other out of our systems." Even as she said it she knew it was a lie. The way his arms slid around her waist, pulling her to him as if afraid she'd slip away, said that he knew it, too.

"What if I can't get you out of my system?" he asked.

"It still doesn't change the fact that you're leaving."

Tipping her head to the side, she wrapped one hand around the back of his neck and tugged his mouth toward hers. She kissed him partly because she didn't want to talk about his leaving, but mostly because she couldn't go another minute without letting him know just how much he'd come to mean to her. She couldn't say the words aloud without the threat of tears, but she could show him.

On a groan, Brett's hands tightened on her waist, brushing over the naked skin of her stomach, the friction of his hands on her making it impossible to catch her breath. He started a careful ascent, around her navel and over each rib, with agonizing slowness, until he was cupping both breasts.

She felt him smile at the discovery that she wasn't wearing a bra.

"God," he growled. "I knew it."

"You want to know what else?"

Sliding her hand under her tank, she linked her fingers with Brett's. The feel of both their hands on her breast was so erotic she realized she could sit there until morning, with Brett thoroughly exploring her with his hands and mouth.

Fingers still laced, she guided his hand down her stomach, under her pajama shorts, and right where her lace and silk should have been.

"Hot damn, girl," he moaned into her mouth as his fingers grazed her moist, heated skin. "Naked and wet."

"It's your fault. You say sugar in that sexy drawl and my whole body melts."

Now that she had his hand right where she wanted it, she tried to untangle their fingers.

"No, stay with me." His grip tightened around hers before slowly sliding their fingers back and forth across the sensitive flesh.

"Brett," she whispered when they both cupped her. Her breath caught and she pushed into their hands, needing more. She had never felt like this, this out of control with need. It was naughty and wild and so damn right.

"Sugar," he purred, sliding two fingers in, and she almost came apart. "Look up."

Resting her head against his chest, she did as told, dropping her knees to the side, just in case he needed more room to work. And Brett, she learned, took his work very seriously, slowly loving her while she stared at the stars.

All of her fears and troubles started getting smaller and smaller as that place in her heart, the one now reserved for Brett, got larger and larger until she felt as if her chest would explode trying to hold it all in.

In that moment, their bodies lit only by the moon, the debilitating need to please her parents, to prove to the town that she could make Fairchild House a success, to protect her heart from disappointment, disappeared. In its place was a desire to live—really live and experience everything life was offering.

Feeling bold, Josephina slid her own finger inside. Brett hesitated for only a moment before slowing his rhythm and giving her time to match his. They fell in sync easily, gliding together.

"That's incredible," he said. "Sexy as hell, but incredible."

Yeah, it was. She loved how they moved together, how their belief in each other dissolved everything until all that remained was their desire and the man that she loved.

"I'm going to come just watching you," he whispered into her hair, his breath ragged and hot.

Well, if that didn't steal her breath, then the way their fingers slid in and out, picking up the pace and leaving nothing unexplored, had Josephina teetering on the edge. But when his lips took hers, soft and full of emotion, she felt tears threaten.

No man had ever appreciated her the way Brett did. She could see it in the way he looked at her, feel it in the way he kissed her. And dear God, the man could kiss.

"You are so damn beautiful," he said, and warmth swelled, starting low in her belly and spreading through her entire body. But where it settled was in her heart.

A mix of emotions, which were too intense to hold back, rushed over her. She felt her muscles tighten around them and her chest expand until she felt so much of everything that she was afraid to breathe. Afraid that if she gave in there would be no going back. Not for her. Not with the way he was holding her, slowly taking up residence in her heart.

"I've got you, Joie," he promised. And she believed him. "Just let go."

She did. Against her better judgment, she pushed down the fear and she let herself fall—right into him. The stars overhead went blurry and she shattered, his name a strangled cry that cut through the still night air.

Neither moved. Neither spoke. Josephina sat there, cradled against him, their fingers still intertwined, and their gazes locked as they clung to each other. She could feel his heart pounding through her chest.

Every breath, every touch, every cell in her body was saying, *I love you.*

And Josephina could have sworn that his body was whispering the same thing.

* * *

A few hours later, Brett lit the last candle and dropped another pile of pillows on top of the sleeping bags and quilts. Satisfied with his surprise, he shucked his jeans and crawled under the makeshift bed, wearing the same stupid-ass grin that had been plastered on his face for the past week. Making love under the stars had only made it stupider. So had taking his sweet time in the shower with Joie, helping wash off every speck of mud.

"What are you doing down there?" Joie stood at the bottom of the stairs holding a candle. She was wrapped in a silky pink robe, which only came to her thighs, and, based on his advantageous position, not much else. "Waiting for fairies?"

"Waiting for you." Something he found himself doing a lot lately. Something, if it meant having this woman in his bed, he wouldn't mind spending the rest of his life doing. Even though the thought of a life past tomorrow made him sweat, and thinking of a life past Joie scared the shit out of him.

"I guess I'd better hurry up then." She glided across the room, limbs loose, hips swaying, eyes dancing with mischief. She moved like a woman who had recently been well-loved. Which she had. Twice.

He waited until she got to the end of the quilts and pulled back the blanket, loving how she licked her lips. He wasn't wearing much of anything either.

"So I'm guessing a fun game of strip poker is out of the question," she said, her voice laced with mischief.

"Not the game I had in mind."

Joie traced the V of her robe, letting her fingers dip under the belt. With a slow pull, the belt fell away and the robe pooled at her feet. No T-shirt, no lace, no silk. Just her. All grace and curves.

And damn, was she beautiful.

"Is this more like what you were thinking?" she teased.

Brett grabbed her by the waist and in record time pulled her under him. His hands glided over her body, loving how her eyes flamed and she nibbled her lower lip when he hit a good spot. "Not quite, but we're getting there."

"How about now?" she asked, taking matters into her own hands. Literally. "We getting any closer?"

Brett exhaled hard, absorbing the sensation of her cool hands curving around the hard-on, which he'd been sporting since he realized he couldn't get the power working and would have to make do with candles. Then he thought of how her naked skin would glow under the flickering light and he was done for.

Slowly she stroked him. They didn't kiss, or speak, or move, just fell into each other's gaze as she took her time exploring him and blowing every last fuse in his brain. Even if her hands weren't on him, the way she looked up through her lashes, as though he was a part of this magical world she had created, would have melted his heart.

"So close it scares me," he whispered, lowering his head and kissing her.

He took his time exploring her mouth. At first just her lips, the top one, then the bottom, eventually sliding his tongue across the seam. She opened up for him and he took it deeper, pushing them to the next level. Hell, everything between them went deeper with each breath they shared.

Tonight was about connection, about opening up and admitting that he didn't want this to end when he went back on the circuit. He was going to rebuild on his parents' property. Finally move home. And he wanted Joie to be a part of that.

Needed her to want to be a part of that.

Brett took her hands and pressed them above her head, her touch too much to handle if he expected this to last through the night. Rolling on the condom, he settled back between her legs. She pressed herself closer, which was fine by him, especially when she wrapped those silky legs around his middle, and her arms tightly around his neck, igniting a wave of desire that went straight to his heart. Brett held her tighter, kissed her a little harder, putting everything he was feeling out there for her to see.

Joie rolled her hips, rocking up against him, sliding her body against his, creating a natural friction that was damn near close to heaven. Cupping her head with one hand, he slid the other under her back, creating a barrier against the floor as he moved in and out, their bodies never more than a breath apart.

He kept kissing that mouth of hers, lost in how her body felt plastered to his, as if afraid that the magic would vanish the moment they rolled out from under the chandelier. Then Joie arched her back and squeezed even tighter as Brett exploded and felt every one of her muscles melt into a puddle beneath him.

Face buried in her hair, he listened to their hearts slowly return to a normal rate.

Without breaking her hold, she peered down at their tangled bodies, her hands in his hair, her legs locked around his middle, feet pointing to heaven, and smiled. "Letty was right. You can't get your wings with your feet stuck to the floor."

"Wings?"

"Uh-huh. I think I finally found mine," she whispered, staring up into his eyes as she pulled him back down for another kiss. "Because I feel like I'm flying."

* * *

Brett woke to a wet nose nudging one arm. Too bad for the dog, he had a naked woman lying in the other, snuggled so tightly against his body he couldn't tell what limbs belonged to whom. And he didn't care.

Last night had changed everything. He felt it in his chest. They had made love until the sun started to crest the hills, each time more magical than the last. Brett smiled at his word choice. Cheesy as hell, but when talking about Joie it seemed to fit.

A little whimper echoed in his ear.

"Five more minutes, buddy," Brett whispered, pulling Joie closer and tracing his hand over her hip and down her thigh. She moaned and pressed back into him, her ass sliding against him and putting the "good" in his morning. "Make that an hour."

"I figure you have about two seconds before that dog bites it off," a voice said from the doorway.

Making sure the covers concealed Joie, Brett turned and grumbled, "What are you doing here, Cal?"

Joie squeaked and pulled the quilt over her head.

"Was about to ask you the same." Cal's tone was easy, but his expression could cut slate.

"None of your damn business. Now, if you could get the hell out, that would be great."

"Morning, Cal," muffled out from under the covers as a warm hand found Brett's and gave a quick squeeze.

"Morning, Joie." Cal blushed. Good, the bastard was embarrassed. "Sorry about barging in. But no one was answering their phone."

"The power's still out," Brett explained, adding, "and my cell is in the truck."

Cal's brows furrowed. "Really? The power at our place came back on last night."

"Yeah, well, Grandma didn't shove hedge cutters into your fuse box." Brett took a deep breath, noticing Joie still hadn't come out from under the covers. "Since we have established the source of the blowout, you can leave."

Joie smacked Brett's back. The reprimand was loud enough to make Cal smile.

"Hattie is on the warpath; she's got everyone riled up and on their way over here." Another squeak from under the covers. "I headed them off. You've got about ten minutes tops before they come breaking down the door. Just enough time to take a cold one. Oh, and I brought her dog back."

"Boo!" Joie came out of hiding for the dog, which bounded over to her and delivered wet doggie kisses.

"Thanks, bro." Unable to move without flashing his brother, Brett nodded, his irritation ebbing.

"Yeah, well, next time I get to rescue the girl." Cal rubbed his arm. "That thing has the jaws of a bear trap. She reminds me of my ex."

"He is usually a good dog," Joie defended. "I'm so sorry, Cal."

"Don't be." Brett brushed his lips across hers, not bothering to correct her. That dog was a menace, but to her Boo was family. "Cal called Boo a girl. He deserved a little nip."

"Nip? Hell, she—"

Boo growled, showing his masculine teeth.

"—*He* nearly chewed through my steel-toed boots to get to my ankle."

Brett looked at Joie, who he could tell was nervous about another run-in with his grandma, and back to Cal. "Can you try to buy us another few minutes?"

"I can try." Cal pulled out his phone but didn't sound too confident. "We still need to talk before everyone gets here. I have something to show you."

Brett didn't like the sound of that and he didn't want to end a perfect night with a lecture from his brother.

"Want to borrow my shower?" she whispered after Cal disappeared into the salon.

She stood and pulled on her robe, which was a damn shame, so Brett stopped her right before she tied the belt. Taking her by the lapels he held it open, letting his gaze run the length of her, and then gave each breast a kiss.

"No, I want you in the shower but somehow I don't think

my grandma would see it as rude to barge in." He gave one last look and tied the belt. "Why don't you go get cleaned up and let me deal with my family?"

She looked hesitant. He didn't blame her. He was asking her to go hide while he handled things.

"Please."

To his surprise she nodded and then said the only three words that could send his entire world crashing down.

"I trust you."

Chapter 20

~

Shit." Brett grabbed for the paper in Cal's hand.

"You're so far in it, no amount of charm will get rid of that stench."

Cal was right. Brett didn't even have to open the magazine to understand that his entire life was about to go to hell. Worse still, he'd brought down Joie with him. His hand fisted as he read the headline and imagined ripping the journalist's throat out.

PGA'S PLAYBOY MCGRAW PLAYS IT FAST AND LOOSE AND PAYS THE PRICE—TO THE SUM OF HALF-A-MIL.

He hated the media. Hated himself right about then. He'd fucked up. Big-time.

"At least tell me that you came clean about the loan," Cal said. Brett's guilt must have shown on his face. "Aw, man, what were you thinking?"

"That I had time. That once she got the inn up and running she wouldn't care." Brett ran a hand down his face. "I'm going to lose her over this, aren't I?"

"I don't know," Cal admitted quietly.

Brett opened to the first page and scanned the article. There was too much personal information, too many details about the loan, about how he and Joie were childhood friends, about her disaster of an engagement to Rat Bastard for this to be a speculative story. Someone had sold him out.

He tried to breathe. His lungs told him to screw off, which was what Joie was going to do the second she saw those papers. Since he'd won his first Masters and gone from small-town nobody to overnight sensation, Brett had known that his luck would run out, that one day his play-it-loose reputation would bite him in the ass. He just never expected the fallout to affect the ones he loved.

"Shame on you, Brett Gentry McGraw," Hattie scolded from the doorway. Dressed in a silver track suit, she held a covered dish in one hand and a wooden spoon in the other. Beside her, all in church wear and enough condemnation they looked ready to spit—or shoot—was her backup. And pulling up the rear, in sweats and department-issued attitude, was one of Sugar's finest.

"Even with all you put me through as a boy, bless your heart, I never once spanked you. But after seeing how you treated that girl, in Letty's house, I reckon it's time to say, 'Bend over.'" Hattie raised her spoon and smacked Brett in the chest.

"How I treated her?" Not wanting to lose an eye, Brett grabbed the spoon. "You ladies know as well as I do that the only reason someone talked was that this feud of yours gave them permission to." Brett tried not to sound angry, but he was.

The folks of Sugar protected their own, and his grandma and her friends had gone to great lengths to make sure Joie was never seen as belonging. He was also angry at himself for being so worried about pleasing everyone else that he let down the one person who mattered.

"A feud, if you remember, you promised would cease."

"And you promised to keep her busy. Not charm your way into her sheets," Dottie countered, shaking her head. "Which is why Darleen talked to that reporter."

"Darleen?" He didn't know why he sounded so surprised. She had been trying to tie him down since that night he'd run into her after he'd scored a fifty-nine in Atlanta.

"Bill already let her go from her position at the bank, which is a shame, with her being a single mom," Dottie added.

"And if you decide to press charges for divulging personal information," Jackson finally spoke, "then it would be my place to take a report, which is why I am here at seven-fifteen on a Sunday morning. My only day off, I might add."

"But know this," Hattie said. "If you do, then I will be forced to make a separate report citing you for thinking with the man downstairs. And I'm not talking about the devil!" Hattie poked him in the chest with one pudgy finger. "Not that I'd want Darleen for a daughter-in-law, that woman is nuttier than a pecan factory. But she's desperate for a husband and has a child in the house looking for a daddy. She's been telling folks for years how she was going to land you, and you never gave her a reason to doubt it, until you started parading Letty's girl around town." She shook her head. "I raised you better than that."

"At least the world doesn't think her services equate to a half a million." The voice was so small, so full of hurt and confusion, that Brett felt his chest tighten to the point of pain.

He turned around and there, still in her bathrobe and bare

feet, holding a tray of sweet tea and breakfast muffins, was Joie.

On one side of her, holding a half-dozen magazines, was one very pissed-off mechanic. On the other, holding what used to be a very expensive golf glove in his teeth, was a very pissed-off pooch.

His chest hollowed out as he saw the pain wash over her face.

"Joie." Brett took a step forward and Boo lunged, fangs exposed.

"I was going to get in the shower when Boo had to go out. Then I realized that I should bring out some cold beverages for your family, you know, show them that I really want to make amends, make this work. But Spenser showed up at the back door with these magazines. So I came in here to show them to you and heard you all talking. I guess the joke's on me, huh?"

"No. No joke," Brett said. "I know what it sounds like, but the God's honest truth is, I wanted to spend time with you. Let you see who I really was."

"I see who you are, Brett. I'm just sorry it took me so long." She glanced around, as if suddenly realizing just how many people were in the room witnessing this moment. Her face flushed with humiliation. "I think I liked the playboy better. At least he was honest about his intentions."

"It's not like that." He took a step forward, but she backed away, setting down the tray. Her hands were shaking so hard that the tea sloshed over the rim of the pitcher.

"What's it like then? Please tell me." She pressed her free hand to her stomach. "Because it sounded like you lied to me about why you wanted the job and then lied to me about the loan."

Brett exhaled a hard breath. "I knew after Bill turned you

down for the loan the only way this feud was going to go away was to agree to be your contractor. That way you had a second set of hands and I could make sure the salon was intact for Letty's birthday."

"We wanted to say our proper good-byes to Letty, dear," Jelly-Lou admitted. "Brett told us to just ask, that you would let us. I'm sorry now that we didn't."

Josephina didn't even blink. "And the loan?"

"I played a round with Bill and tried to get him to reconsider loaning you the money. He said it was just too risky for a bank their size. We struck an agreement, one that was supposed to be confidential." He slid a look at Dottie, who immediately studied her shoes. "Before I could explain, Bill had called you and half the town knew. Then you were so damn proud of that loan, I didn't want to take that away from you."

"So you lied to me instead?" She looked at him as if he'd shattered her world. "You told me you believed in me, that you knew I could do this. I believed you, Brett. I believed you so damn much that I started believing in myself."

"I did believe in you. I do. I knew you could do this."

"Really, because letting me walk around deluding myself about how I got the loan doesn't seem like the action of someone who believes in me."

"I didn't tell you because I knew you wouldn't take the money."

"That was my right!"

"I know, but I was so scared of losing you. I wanted to make sure you had every reason to stay."

"You lied to me, Brett. Made a fool of me in front of everyone?" Her face fell as she took in the crowd, and he knew what she was thinking. That he was as big an asshole as her ex. "Is this some kind of game for you people? Make her fall for the hometown hero and then break her heart so she'll leave? Do you all hate me that much?"

"No. Don't you get it?" Brett pleaded. "I don't want you to leave."

"Well, then, it looks like Brett McGraw gets what he wants again. Because I don't have anywhere to go. This was my do-over, my chance to make something for myself, and you took that away." She pulled in a shaky breath at the last word. "At least my parents and Wilson told me to my face what they thought." And that's when her face crumbled. "I guess that's not the *neighborly* way."

"We don't hate you, child," Hattie said, her voice low and soothing. It was the same tone she'd used when he or one of his brothers tore up a knee or elbow. "We were just trying to see to Letty's wishes."

"Grandma," Brett warned. Joie was a second away from crying and he knew what Hattie was about to tell her would shatter her world.

"This is her business, too, and she has a right to know," Jelly-Lou said. "Go on and tell her, Hattie."

"Tell me what?"

Hattie walked over and took Joie's hand. "A few months before Letty passed, God rest her soul, she talked about changing her will, leaving Fairchild House to the four of us. The will was drawn up, but she passed before she got a chance to sign it."

"Which meant I got the Fairchild House by default?" Her big blue eyes went wide, her body tensed. Joie was preparing for the blow. He almost looked away, not sure if he could handle what was about to happen.

"I'm sorry, dear," Jelly-Lou soothed. "We told her to reconsider, but she was adamant, she wanted the house to remain a sanctuary for the adventurous. And you were so busy with your life, Letty was afraid you'd lost your connection to the magic of the place."

"But what about the letter Letty left me?" Joie whispered.

All the ladies exchanged a look, but it was Jelly-Lou who spoke. "Letty wrote you that letter a long time ago, but we figured that despite everything that happened, she'd want you to have it."

Joie didn't need to speak for the whole room to feel what had just happened. Her heart had cracked in two. She had just lost the only person who saw the magic that was Joie. The only person who made her feel accepted enough, loved for being just who she was.

She studied his face, and the look she gave him pretty much ripped open his heart. "Did you know? About Letty not wanting me here?"

Brett grasped for the words to make this okay. Maybe it was his hesitation, or maybe she just got him better than anyone else ever had, but she took a step back, away from him, from his family, from the town.

"I was just trying to protect you." It sounded like a bullshit answer, but it was all he had.

Her chin shot up and her big blue eyes darkened with sorrow. "I didn't need your money, Brett. I just wanted your respect, which you protected me right out of. And I let you do it. How sad is that?"

Panic flooded his chest. He was losing her. He could feel it. She never judged him, never expected him to be anything other than himself, and he had destroyed everything they had built.

Her phone, which she had set next to Kenny last night, started ringing.

Dottie, being the closest, picked it up. "The screen says

it's your mama. You want me to answer it? Explain what's going on?"

"No. If she's calling then she already knows."

Joie took the phone and stared at it, waiting for the ringing to stop. No one spoke. When the phone chimed that she had a voicemail, she put it in her robe pocket.

"Now, if you'll excuse me, I don't feel much like serving any kind of cold beverage today, so I'll ask you to gather your covered dishes and southern manners and get the hell out of my house. Because until I decide otherwise, it's still mine."

She turned on her heel and took off up the stairs.

Ears back, tail high, Boo strutted over to Brett, lifted his leg and pissed on Brett's bare feet. After a quick wiggle of his hips to ensure that every last drop hit the intended target, Boo trotted after his mistress.

* * *

Josephina held it together until she heard the front door shut, the sheets were securely over her head, and Boo was snuggled at her feet. Three boxes of tissues, two pillowcases, and a T-shirt later she had finally pulled it together. Until she heard someone banging around outside and her lights flickered back on and started up again. The sobs lasted straight through breakfast, dinner, and Jimmy Kimmel, stopping only when her tears, combined with a pity-party-sized bag of cheesy pretzels, had congealed into a paste covering her hands, face, and the right side of her hair.

Every time she thought she had her emotions under control, she'd remember standing in the foyer, covered only by silk and humiliation, facing down yet another firing squad in starch. The tears—and pretzel craving—would start back up, deep in her chest, vibrating upward until she sounded like a beached seal.

Josephina wondered how she had managed to get herself in this situation again. How she had once again trusted a man who hadn't believed in her.

A lifetime of practice.

Boo yapped in the distance. Giving up on sleep, she tossed back the covers, pulled on a pair of cheese-stained yoga pants, and went downstairs. Boo needed to take his morning march around the exterior of the house, re-marking every corner that the mama opossum had marked last night. She needed to eat something that didn't contain the word cheese.

As she passed the entryway, her cell, which she'd shoved inside Kenny's bust so she wouldn't have to hear it ring anymore, was still ringing. Knowing it was either her mother, whom she didn't want to talk to, or Brett, whom she wasn't emotionally ready to handle, she ignored it.

Boo stood at the front door, his little body doing the got-to-go wiggle.

"All right," Joie said. "I'm coming."

She unlocked the deadbolt, and Boo's wiggle picked up in intensity. So did his yapping. If she hadn't been so delirious, she wouldn't have been so surprised when she opened the door and came face to face with the last person she wanted to see.

By all that was holy, why did she have to confront Brett while wearing cheesy-goo and leftover makeup?

"Joie." Brett rose to his feet.

He looked exhausted. Miserable. As if he'd slept on her porch all night. And even though his hair was standing up in the back, his face was covered with stubble, and he was wearing the same jeans as yesterday, he looked so damn handsome it hurt.

"Boo, come." But Boo was already out the door. He fluctuated between exaggerated wagging and growling, as if unsure of how to greet the visitor. Josephina knew exactly how he felt. Which was why she had to shut the door, before she wagged herself right into his arms.

"Please, just give me a minute," Brett said, his voice pleading, his eyes red from lack of sleep.

"One minute." Josephina crossed her arms over her chest, hoping to cover up her FAIRIES DO IT BETTER shirt and the hard-to-miss proof that he still turned her on. The man had lied to her, publicly humiliated her, and yet her body still ached to be connected to his. Pathetic.

"Darleen and I used to have a thing, never serious, just sex."

Humiliation, raw and potent, scorched up her throat at the casual way the words spilled off his tongue. Would he one day talk about what they had shared so casually? Her heart told her no, that the connection between them had been special—magical. Then again, Wilson had claimed to love her.

"But I haven't been with her in months," he said, as though that made everything better. "There hasn't been anyone in a while, except for you."

"I don't care about Darleen."

The tension around Brett's mouth relaxed a little at her announcement. Not wanting to give him false hope that they could come back from this, Josephina patted her thigh and called for Boo to come inside. He positioned himself stubbornly at Brett's boots.

Feet together, chest puffed out, Boo snorted his opinion. He didn't want Brett to leave. Problem was, neither did Josephina, but she knew the longer she held out hope, the longer it would hurt.

"Okay," Brett paused, as if finally able to breathe. "About the loan—"

"You don't get it, Brett." Josephina took a breath of her own, willing herself to make it through this with her pride intact. "The string—it broke. And no amount of talking, or apologizing, or time can fix that," she explained, her heart breaking with every word. "So, please go. I can't do this again."

Josephina called for Boo one last time, and when he didn't respond, other than to lick Brett's ankle and whimper, she stepped back inside, and any pretense that she could hold it together crumbled. The clicking of the door was so resolute, so final, that it knocked all the air out of her body.

Afraid she'd collapse, Josephina leaned against the door and let her head fall back, praying for the strength to walk away.

"We're going to have our talk, Joie." Brett's voice came through the door, followed by his boots on the wood porch. They stopped right on the other side and she could practically feel his strength radiating through the wood.

When he spoke again, it was as if he was whispering in her ear. Low and heated and melting her resolve. "You know how I like to take my time when we make love?"

Take your time? The man was the most thorough lover she'd ever had. Even thinking about how diligent he was made her thighs clench. And her heart ache.

"Well, sugar, you haven't even begun to comprehend how long I'm willing to dig in. So you take your time. I'll be waiting right here when you're ready to talk."

Josephina looked around at the sophisticated dining room, the clean lines of the foyer—it all looked wrong. This place was no longer a passion they shared. They would never sit over a meal and talk with pride about how far they'd come. There was no more joy in this for her.

Everything would forever remind her of Brett—and how much he'd hurt her.

* * *

Eight hours later, the heat had finally dropped to a balmy ninety-three. Brett's stomach was in knots, the sun was finally setting, and he hadn't heard a peep out of Joie. Not a one. She hadn't even come out to check on Boo, who was sitting on the stairs next to Brett, his sad little muzzle resting on Brett's thigh.

"Sorry you're in the doghouse, buddy. Never meant to bring you with me, but the loyalty is appreciated."

Boo's eyes—just his eyes—moved up to connect with Brett's and the poor guy let out a whimper.

"I know. She has to come out sometime." The dog looked about as confident in Brett's assessment as Brett felt.

"That's the sorriest picture I've ever seen," Hattie said, hopping out of Cal's truck, Cal right behind her.

Brett didn't want to face his family. Not yet. He was still mad at his grandma and he didn't want to deal with Cal's I-told-you-so bullshit.

"If you're here with dinner, I'm not hungry." He was starved, but knew he wouldn't be able to eat unless it involved sitting at Joie's table. "And if you're here to apologize, then you might as well go home, because she's not taking callers and I'm first in line."

"I'm here to take you home before Jackson hauls you in for soliciting on a lady's stoop," Cal explained.

"And what the hell do you think I'm soliciting?"

"According to the papers, sex," Hattie said.

"Did you have to bring her?" Brett pointed to his grandmother, who was now pacing the porch and peering through the windows.

"She was with me when Spenser called. Since you haven't bothered to answer your phone all day and Spenser only gave me ten minutes to drag you home before she called Jackson to arrest your dumb ass, I decided to head straight over," Cal said. "So why don't you come home and let Joie cool off?"

"She told me that she doesn't want to talk about it. That it's too late. Not that I blame her."

"She didn't change it none," Hattie said, her face pressed to the salon's window. She sounded perplexed and out-and-out astonished.

"Not yet. But she will." Brett grabbed Hattie by the arm and dragged her off the porch. If Joie was hesitant before, there was no way she would come out with spiky gray hair and judgment plastered to her windows.

Hattie dug her feet in and Brett felt anger boiling up. If he didn't get to see Joie, then there was no way to make this right. No way he'd win her back.

"Did one of you ever stop to think that maybe this was what Letty wanted? That Joie came here to finish building the dream *she* had shared with Letty?"

"Letty would never want this." Hattie waved a hand at the inn.

"Really?" Brett said, surprising himself with how harshly the question came out. "Because I saw the sketches and plans, and half of those were Letty's, including the salon. She wanted to pamper her guests, give them a place to recharge."

"Post-soil-spoil," Hattie whispered, recognition setting

in. Taking his face between her crinkled hands, her voice wobbled as she said, "Oh, Brett, I was so scared that she was going to ruin what Letty had worked so hard to build. When she started talking fancy people's getaways and mud tubs, we got scared, all of us. I didn't even think—"

"Yeah, well, this town should have had more faith in her, Grandma," Brett said, including himself in that equation. "Because as far as I can tell she was the only one thinking about Letty."

"I did that girl wrong, and it breaks my heart that I wound up hurting her. And you."

"Mine, too, Grandma." Because the damage went so much deeper than anyone realized and Brett didn't know how to fix it, didn't know how to make Joie's world okay again.

"But she waltzed in here with her big-city ideas and we didn't know her from a Democrat. She isn't our people."

"I wanted her to be *my* people." Brett patted his chest. "Do you get that? She thinks golf is boring. She doesn't take my crap. She makes me want to stay in Sugar, put down roots, be a better man. The kind of man Dad was."

Saying you believe in someone and actually believing in them are two separate things.

"Christ." Brett's lungs stopped working.

Cal had been right. Time and again she'd given him the chance to be the kind of man she needed, but instead of giving her the same consideration, he'd tried to manipulate the situation, control it so she wouldn't fail—and in turn leave. Leave Sugar. Leave Georgia. Leave him.

Too bad that he'd turned out to be just like all the other a-holes in her life. A selfish liar.

"So you finally figured it out," Cal said, clapping him on the back, a smug-as-shit grin widening across his face.

"Yeah." Brett leaned down to give Boo one final pat.

"How bad is it?"

"Bad enough to let her find her happiness."

* * *

A week later, a pounding came from right outside Josephina's window. She shot up, taking the blankets with her and sending Boo flying to the ground. He landed with a thump, his big doggie eyes glazed over and confused. She knew how he felt. The sun was barely even peeking over the mountains, a strange person in a prison-yard-orange track suit and a trucker's cap was levitating outside her second-story window and, according to the bedside clock, she had achieved less than two hours of sleep.

Another sound shot through the air. This time it sounded like a gun going off.

"Not this time, Annie Oakley!" Josephina said, pulling on a pair of sweats.

Try as they might, she wasn't leaving town. Well, at least not until her mom arrived on Saturday with Rosalie in tow to help pack up Josephina and her dreams for the move back to Manhattan.

She hadn't wanted to leave, even promised Spenser and Charlotte that she wasn't giving up on her dreams for Fairchild House. But after hiding out for the better part of the week, she realized that whatever magic had originally drawn her to Sugar was now buried under a pile of broken string. Strings that hurt so much, there were moments when remembering to breathe seemed too daunting.

It was one of those moments in which her mom had convinced Josephina that the best option was to come home. But she'd be damned if she'd let these old ladies get the last word.

Grabbing Letty's shotgun off the wall, she charged down the stairs, out the front door, and stuck her barrels in the first face she saw.

"Christ!" Cal jerked up, stumbling backward over the leg of the ladder and down two steps, landing on the ground. "What are you doing?"

"I can ask you the same. And since I'm the one holding a gun, I guess you get to answer first."

"Finishing up your house." Cal looked at the gun but didn't move. "I thought you were more of a blunt object kind of girl."

"Sent my ex's clubs to Japan last week, just in time for his big Pan Pacific Moment." She'd even cleaned them up. Aside from the drivers that she'd used for torches they looked good as new. Durable suckers. "And what's *she* doing up there?"

Not only were there a dozen men in steel-toed boots and professional-grade tool belts, Rooster on the roof, her girlfriends waist high in weeds, but Hattie was on top of a really high ladder, cleaning out the gutters in an orange pants suit.

"Work release."

Josephina couldn't help but laugh at just how that conversation went down. A laugh that died in her chest even before it could surface as she began adding up the daily rate for all the bodies currently swinging hammers. "I doubt everyone here is on work release. Even if they are, there's no way I can afford all these people."

What really got her heart thumping, though, was the thought that one of those tool-belt-wearing studs might be her stud. She didn't want to see him like this, here, working on her house. Didn't want to think about how hard it would be to watch him do what they had spent the summer doing together, knowing it would never happen again.

"He isn't here," Cal said softly. "He went back on tour. Played a game yesterday in Canada."

"Oh." *Canada?* Josephina's heart dropped to her toes.

"As for the cost, I figure that after what my family put you through, think of it as a gift." He sent her an apologetic look, and cautiously added, "Plus, Brett wanted to make sure your place was ready for your parents' visit."

"Because he didn't think I could do it alone?"

"I couldn't do this alone, and I've been building houses since I was a teenager." He reached out his hand. "Now you going to give me the gun so I can get up? Or would you rather shoot? At this point, either decision is fine with me."

Josephina didn't give up the gun, but she did rest it across her legs after she sat down on the top step.

Cal dusted off his backside and, walking in the way only a McGraw man could pull off, dropped down next to her. They sat silent, watching two men tear off the rotted siding on the closest of the servants' quarters. When finished, Josephina had imagined glass block walls, billowing gauze, and oatmeal-colored Adirondack chairs for her Hampton Suite. Now when she looked at it, she had a hard time picturing anything. Maybe because clean lines and loft décor implied couples getting away from the big city for the weekend, and Fairchild House with its fishing and hiking and welcoming landscape was almost made for families.

Letty had always said that the house came to life when Josephina visited because only children could sense the magic hidden in the walls. Magic that she was walking away from.

"I'm leaving on Saturday," she blurted out.

She watched as Cal looked from her to the ground, before running a hand over his face. "You think that's what Letty would want you to do?"

Tears sprang to her eyes at the familiar feeling of disappointment. "I don't know anymore. She didn't even mean to leave me Fairchild House. I got it on a technicality."

"She'd tell you to suck it up and use whatever magic was being offered to get this place up and running."

"That magic being Brett's money and your charity?"

"Oh, my guys aren't charity. And Brett may not always think with the right head, but when it comes to money he's all about calculated risk and return on investment. I'm not sure about all of what's going on between the two of you, but I can tell you that my brother would never have invested in you if he didn't believe you'd make it."

Josephina looked at her toes, unwilling to let him see the emotion in her eyes. She wanted so badly to believe that Brett had faith in her ability to make Fairchild House a success. "I intend to pay him back every penny."

"Good, then add my guys to what you owe him, since I'm billing him for this mess, and prove that you are Letty's niece by making a good life for yourself here."

Josephina snorted. "In a town that hates me?"

"They don't hate you."

She shot Cal a disbelieving look, and he had the good manners to grimace.

"They just have a hard time with change, and you blowing into town, renovating Letty's place, showing up everyone with your fund-raising skills, stealing the golden boy right out from under them." Cal looked out over the oak trees and lake. "That's a lot to take in for a town that took eleven years to agree on a color for the new town hall."

"Town Hall is white."

"Exactly."

"The inn was mine to do with as I chose," she said, feeling, for the first time in days, a sense of ownership of the house. "And I only offered to plan the Pucker Up and Drive to end all the arguing and feuding."

"It is yours. And you stepped up with the Pucker Up and Drive to protect Brett." Cal nudged her shoulder with his. "And, Joie, in this town arguing and feuding is as important as church and football. It's how we show our love."

"Kind of like pampering," Josephina mumbled, thinking of Letty and the inn and just how far she'd come.

She took in a deep breath and looked around. Maybe the town wasn't the only thing fighting change. She had come here with her big-town ideas, never thinking that there were people right here, in Sugar, who needed pampering, too.

"So what do you say? Do I send my men home?"

She shook her head and smiled. "I wouldn't want to be thought of as un-neighborly."

"Good girl, now can I have that gun so my men can get back to work?"

Josephina handed Cal the gun and stood. The plaque that she hadn't bothered to read since her first day here was now polished and glimmering in the morning sun.

FAIRCHILD HOUSE
HAS BEEN DESIGNATED A HISTORICAL NATIONAL LAND-MARK.
BUILT IN 1838 BY, JEREMIAH SUGAR, THE FIRST MAYOR OF SUGAR.
UPON HIS DEATH IN 1839 HIS BRIDE-TO-BE, PEARL FAIRCHILD,
TURNED THE RESIDENCE INTO A BOARDINGHOUSE FOR THE ADVENTUROUS.

Josephina might suck at love but that didn't mean she was a failure. Staying meant she'd have to see Brett from time to time, and it would hurt, but Pearl had mended her broken heart here, and so had Aunt Letty. Josephina would just be another in a long line of strong women, sharing the magic of this house with those adventurous enough to search for it.

That's it, she thought, knowing what she needed to do. And it was exactly what Fairchild House was made for. More imporant, it was what this town needed. What she needed.

Her eyes rested on the servants' quarters. "Where was the medical center planning on keeping the families while their kids were receiving treatment at the new ward?"

"They haven't figured it out yet. Why?" Cal asked, a smile tugging up one side of his lips.

"I was thinking that there is an awful lot of fairy dust around here."

Chapter 21

That's no way for a lady to behave," Josephina scolded, snatching her hand back a second before it got ripped off.

"Come on, sugar," she cooed, once again offering up her peanut-butter-laced finger. "You know you want some."

The one remaining set of beady black eyes blinked at her from inside the vent and took a tiny step closer. The problem was the other set of much larger eyes, which were accompanied by razor teeth and a terrifying hissing sound that filled the air vent every time Josephina got close to luring the last baby out.

Using her bare toe for leverage, Josephina pushed off the top of the ladder so she could reach the extra inch she needed to grab the baby opossum by the scruff. The mama lunged forward, going for Josephina's face.

"Shame on you, Mrs. Pearl," Josephina tutted. "What kind of example are you setting, trying to rip off somebody's face? Especially when that somebody happens to be your neighbor."

Backing out of the vent, the metal cutting into her stomach, Josephina cuddled the shaking little baby to her chest. She tipped her catcher's mask up on her forehead and unzipped her backpack, which she had secured to the roofline, and smiled at the five sets of eyes and whiskers looking up at her.

She placed the final baby in the pouch, zipped it up, extracted a set of leather gloves, and grabbed a handful of cheesy pretzels. Gloves on, mask firmly in place, she slid the upper part of her body back through the narrow passageway.

The minute she came into sight, the hissing started up again. Fangs bared, Mrs. Pearl leaped forward, claws in the air, and slammed against the catcher's mask. Josephina held her ground, letting Mrs. Pearl know that she wasn't budging.

She felt for the opossum. She really did. Mrs. Pearl was only trying to create a safe space for her babies. Too bad her ideas on remodeling were in direct conflict with Josephina's—no matter how cute the little guys were, sketchy power and leaky roofs would not pass code.

Mrs. Pearl lunged again, only to stop about an inch from the leather-gloved hand.

"All bark and no bite. I know some other ornery ladies just like that. Maybe when you get settled in your new house we should invite them over for poker and moonshine."

Josephina set down a cheesy pretzel, then another, leaving a trail of crumbs that went to the end of the vent. Straddling the top step of the ladder, she snapped her eyes shut, trying to ignore the sweat building behind the mask.

"You got the ladder?" she hollered down.

"Yes, ma'am," Rooster said at the same time as Boo barked. "Although, you know that I think this makes about as much sense as those clothes you put on your hound. I could have had them out weeks ago."

"Yes, and they would have been traumatized. Sometimes all people need is a little understanding and patience."

"They aren't people," he mumbled, but she knew he held the ladder all the same.

After what seemed like an hour, a pink heart-shaped nose covered in a smattering of white whiskers poked its way out.

"Come on, Mrs. Pearl. Your family is waiting." She slid the backpack through her arms with the pouch resting against her chest and pulled open the center zipper.

Mrs. Pearl leaned forward and, with her eyes firmly on Josephina's, sniffed the inside of the bag, her body softening when she saw her babies. Slow as molasses, Mrs. Pearl made her way into the opening and immediately started licking her brood. All the babies fought to get on their mama's back. Giving them privacy in such an intimate moment, Josephina swallowed hard, zipped up the pack, and slid it on her back.

"Well, look at that. Letty's girl is catching herself a coon."

Holding on to the top rung, the Pearl family securely on her back, Josephina chanced a glance. She wasn't sure if it was altitude sickness, cheesy pretzel overdose, or the pressure of the catcher's mask on her forehead, but she had to blink several times to make sense of what she was seeing.

On her porch, in Bible-blue choir robes, stood the poker-playing posse and the entire Sugar Ladies Baptist Choir with a covered dish in one hand and a hymn book in the other, fanned out as if they were about to bring it on home. In the center, holding a mile-high cake with three silk blue ribbons hanging off the lip of the plate, was Hattie, the smell of coconut and vanilla cutting through the thick summer air.

"No coon. Just a family of opossums that I'm relocating." Josephina carefully made her way down the ladder, feeling ridiculously proud. She'd just helped out her first family and the biggest busybodies in town were there to pay witness.

"Relocatin'?" Hattie asked, and the women all started mumbling amongst themselves, their murmurs picking up speed, but so did Josephina's heart. Maybe they had come to support her after all. "You could have had your face ripped off?"

Then again, maybe not. "I'm fine, just trying to earn my wings."

"Aside from losing her good sense, Miss Joie wasn't ever in any danger, ma'am," Rooster confirmed.

When her feet hit the wood of the deck, Josephina, making sure her back was to the choir, closed her eyes and willed her breakfast not to make a second appearance. She hung on to the ladder and took slow, calming breaths. In and out.

Okay, maybe *fine* was an overstatement. But she had faced her fear of heights, and rodents, and lived to tell the tale.

When her hands stopped shaking and she was certain that her face was a color other than green, she handed the backpack to Rooster. "Why don't you go put them in their new house?"

Rooster mumbled something about women as he disappeared behind the barn.

Josephina walked across the porch, down the steps, and, without a word, tilted back her mask. When Hattie didn't move, just kept shooting Jelly-Lou sharp looks every time Jelly-Lou shoved her forward another inch, Josephina decided to offer the first branch. "Can I offer you all a cold beverage?"

A small smile spread across the older woman's face and

she gave Josephina a long once-over. Something flickering in Hattie's eye that Josephina had never seen before with regard to her—respect. "Huh, well, look at you."

Josephina stepped back and looked down. Besides the baseball mask and leather gloves, she was wearing jean cutoffs, a camouflage tank, two braids, and no shoes. She looked as if she was ready to walk the redneck runway. And it felt good.

"What's all this?" Josephina asked, addressing the army of covered dishes. Even though just about every person in town had been by this past week to help get the house ready for tonight's Pucker Up and Drive kickoff potluck, Josephina still wasn't sure if these casseroles came in peace.

"It's our part," Hattie said. "Figured with all the painting and decorating, you could use some help setting up for tonight. So the ladies and I decided we'd be that help."

"In your robes?"

"No." Hattie glanced at the choir, who all gave her an encouraging nod, "Brett called right in the middle of "Holy, Holy, Holy." Just hearing his name made her heart sink to her toes. "Reminded me that it would be right neighborly for us to offer up our culinary prowess for this weekend, seeing as you're doing all of this for the hospital."

Josephina put her hands on her hips. "Did you just say culinary and prowess in the same sentence?"

"Now, people who live in fancy houses shouldn't go slinging cow chips, child. It turns everything to shit." Hattie's smile went full-blown. "And it's triple-blue-ribbon prowess."

"And?" Jelly-Lou rolled forward, gently nudging Hattie from behind.

"And it took best in show at the Sugar County Fair in '67," Hattie said, holding up her cake, while glaring at Jelly-Lou.

"It was runner-up to my pineapple surprise cake in '67, and you know it," Etta Jayne clarified. "But I think Jelly-Lou was referring to us."

One by one, each of the four ladies who had made Josephina's life hell stepped forward. They all exchanged a sad look, but it was Hattie who spoke. "And we're sorry. Sorry about the feud, about stealing your car, and cutting your power, and dognapping Boo. And about putting those toads in your bathtub."

"And the chandelier," Jelly-Lou added, Josephina's heart aching at the reminder. Brett had been unable to find a place that had the right kind of glass to fix it. "We're real sorry about that. We know how much it meant to you."

"Don't forget to apologize for telling everyone that her peaches are enhanced," Etta Jayne said.

Thirty sets of critical eyes dropped to Josephina's chest, even Rooster's, who appeared from the side of the house. Dottie pulled out the binoculars.

Josephina cupped her breasts, showing them the natural jiggle. "One hundred percent real."

"So Brett said," Jelly-Lou informed everyone.

With a resigned look, Hattie held Josephina's hand and led her to the swing. Still clutching tightly, the older woman took a fortifying breath and her posture crumpled—right along with Josephina's heart.

"Go on, Hattie," Jelly-Lou encouraged.

"Yeah." Dottie rested a hand on Hattie's shoulder. "The girl deserves to know."

The last time Josephina had heard those words her world had literally cracked in two.

"Please," she whispered. "I can't take anymore. When I got here the place was a disaster, a guy that I was sleeping with gave me money, then lied to me, you all hate me, and there was a single mother opossum in the ceiling with her babies and I was too much of a city girl to kill them so I relocated them."

"But you stuck it out. You dug your heels in, broken heart and all, and made it happen," Hattie said quietly, taking in the changes to Fairchild House—the remodeled servants' quarters, the rose garden—and gave a watery smile. "Letty would have been so proud."

"Yeah?"

"More than proud, dear," Jelly-Lou said, rolling up the ramp. "We all are. You are Letty's girl inside and out."

Hattie took both of Josephina's hands in her own meaty ones, her voice serious. "Lord knows, after how I treated you, I have no right asking for favors, but seeing as this is Sugar and we're neighbors, I'm asking. I made such a mess of things and I need your help to fix it. I love that boy more than anything and I chased him off."

"He'll cool down," Josephina said, trying to soothe the older woman and knowing it was true. She knew firsthand that when it came to his family and this town, Brett was loyal to a fault.

Hattie shook her head. "He phoned about twenty minutes ago from the road. He packed up his truck this afternoon and is headed back out on the circuit."

"But the Pucker Up and Drive is tomorrow."

Hattie nodded, a small sniffle escaping.

"He loves this town and he's worked so hard on this fundraiser. Why would he leave?"

"For you," Jelly-Lou said.

"For me? Why?" she asked, but she already knew the answer, and it hurt her heart.

If she had understood at the time that staying here meant forcing him out, she would have left. He belonged there tomorrow. Her heart whispered that she belonged there, too. That she belonged there with him.

"He didn't want to ruin your moment." There was no blame in her voice, just a deep sadness. "I've never seen that boy as happy as when he was with you. And I'm sorry I didn't see it for what it was until it was too late."

"Too late for what?" Josephina whispered. All of the blood rushed to her head, pounding and making it hard to hear. A lump grew in her throat, expanding until talking became painful.

"Cal and his crew are building Brett a house on the back side of our property."

"By his parents' house?" She tried to swallow but couldn't. "Why would he build a house?"

That seemed like a lot of commitment for a guy who considered the world his stomping ground.

"Before he left, he was thinking of retiring after this year," Hattie admitted. "Told Cal that he wanted a place he could come home to. Raise himself some hogs and maybe start a family with a stubborn Yankee."

"Hogs and a family?" *Stubborn Yankee?* Josephina was breathing too hard, the words all spiraling around in her mind too fast; she was afraid she'd misunderstood. Because suddenly everything and nothing made sense.

Josephina hopped up. "Rooster, hold that ladder!"

"Yes, ma'am."

Josephina grabbed the binoculars from around Dottie's neck and slung them around her own. She crawled up to the top of the ladder and straddled the top. Lifting the rubber eye cups to her face, she scanned the landscape. Finding the big oak tree, she moved the lenses to the right and her breath caught.

A concrete foundation lay on the west side of the property to the left of a gigantic oak and butted up to the bank of the lake—right where she'd told Brett she'd place a floor-to-ceiling window. Next to where she'd imagined the kitchen door was a fenced-off bed. Enclosed in rod iron, the soil had been tilled and it was the perfect size for a small chef's garden. Farther off, near the old structure, was the beginnings of what appeared to be a barn and a roped-off area that she could only assume was for a pen.

That was all Josephina could make out before her vision went blurry with tears.

"But he lied to me," she yelled down.

"He loves you, dear," Jelly-Lou hollered back. "Not that that makes his lying all right, but love makes people do stupid things. Why else would a man give up his home, his family, his friends? He gave you that loan for the same reason he left everything behind, so that you could have your fresh start."

"He wanted you to be happy here," Hattie added.

Josephina felt everything inside shift. The anger, the hurt, the heartache, it all faded, leaving only one realization.

"But I'm not. Happy, I mean." Not without him.

Taking the ladder three rungs at a time, she raced down and, pulling together a mental plan, she fished her cell from her back pocket and thrust it at Hattie. "I'm trusting you with my most precious asset. My black book."

"Should we tell her it's just a phone," Dottie whispered.

"In the contact section you will find the name and number of every person you will need to pull off this event. And the calendar lists every event that takes place over the next seventy-two hours, who has volunteered, and who's bringing what. I'm expecting to raise enough to build Charlotte that pediatric ward."

Jelly-Lou took the phone. "We've got this covered."

"Yeah."

"What did you lose?"

"Everything." The minute he said the word, he knew it was true. She was everything to him. He loved golf, his town, his family, but the one thing he couldn't live without was the woman standing in front of him. The woman who, if she gave him a chance, he'd spend the rest of his life making happy.

"Aw, shit," Brett barked, tugging off his Stetson and pacing to his truck, only to slap his hat against his thigh on the return trip. "Aw, shit! I did it again." His boots kicked up dust as he walked his line, back and forth. "I came back here to tell you that I screwed up. Screwed up the best thing that has ever happened to me and I'm not even done apologizing and I already messed everything up."

Those heels, the red ones with the pointy toes, tapped on the asphalt.

"God damnit, Joie, here's the thing," he said, gripping his hat and spinning around. "I'm in love with you. And I bought you a fucking pig."

Now it was her turn to stop. Her eyes filled with tears and her hand trembled slightly as she clutched her chest. "You bought me a pig?"

"I know, a real man would have brought a ring, but when I saw Bubba's Boar House and found out he had a new litter of piglets..."

As if on cue, a shrill squeal erupted from inside the cab.

"You bought me a pig!" Before he could respond, Joie flung herself into his arms. She was halfway up his body, her legs circling his waist, by the time his hands came around her.

And right there, on the Brett McGraw Highway, with a pig in the cab and cheesy pretzels sticking to his shirt, he kissed Joie. And when she kissed him back, Brett knew he was one lucky son of a bitch.

By the time they eased apart, Joie was sitting on the hood of his truck, wearing his hat, and they were both breathing heavy. But at least he was breathing, which beat the hell out of what he'd been doing this past week.

"I love you so much, Joie. When I'm with you I want to be the kind of man my dad was."

"Funny, when I'm with you I just want to be me. And that's never happened before," she whispered. "That's why I had to find you."

Brett felt his heart stumble. "You came to find me?"

She burst out laughing. "Why else do you think I'd be in the middle of the highway in heels and shorts?"

"I don't know, because I am one lucky SOB." He looked down at her shoes, resting on the grill of his truck. "And if you bring up those shoes one more time we will have to continue this conversation in the bed of my truck."

"I was going to Atlanta to catch you before you got on your plane. To tell you that if you wanted me to, I'd come with you to the tournament," she said, flashing those baby blues at him from beneath her lashes—and God almighty he loved this woman.

"You hate golf."

"But I love you." She kissed him long and slow. In response he pulled her flush against him, and melted into her, showing her in that one kiss everything that she meant to him and in return promising her every one of his twenty-four hours.

The piglet let out another squeal and Brett groaned. "So, can we not tell anybody that I proposed with a pig?"

"As long as you help me get out of these heels."

Epilogue

⟳

Well, isn't that a man for you," Charlotte said, taking in Brett at the top of a very tall ladder.

"That he is. All man." *And all mine*, Josephina thought as Brett held the new nameplate, while Cal secured it into place. The way Brett's worn jeans pulled when he leaned forward did the most delicious things to his backside. The copper sign, which he had placed a twenty-four-hour rush on and which now hung next to Fairchild House's historical plate, did some serious melting of her heart.

FAIRCHILD HOUSE FOR THE ADVENTUROUS
 PROVIDING TEMPORARY HOUSING AND PERMANENT
SUPPORT
FOR CHILDREN DEALING WITH LIFE-THREATENING ILL-
NESS
AND THEIR FAMILIES.

When Josephina had finally stopped worrying about proving herself a success and started thinking like the women who came before her, she realized that Fairchild House was not only an ideal getaway for city slickers, it was the perfect place for families to stay when they needed a lot of hope and a little fairy dust.

Fairchild House was part hearth and part magic, and who better to appreciate that than the children who would come from all over the state to find treatment at Sugar Medical Center's new pediatric ward? Which was why she had converted all of the servants' quarters into family-friendly apartments and added kid-friendly cooking courses to her lineup.

"I still can't believe we can start construction on the new wing," Charlotte whispered, her voice thick with emotion. "I really didn't think we'd manage to raise all the money. And if it hadn't been for you I don't think we would have."

"*Your* wing," Josephina corrected. "And I just meshed everyone's ideas together."

"Well, my daddy, bless his heart, still hasn't made an official announcement of who will be heading it," Charlotte said with perfect southern decorum.

Brett dusted off his hands and slipped them around Josephina's waist. "You may have meshed everyone's ideas, but this weekend was all class and heart. It was a Josephina Harrington event, no question."

Josephina smiled as she leaned back against him and looked out over the porch at the crowded yard.

The event was, by far, the pinnacle of Josephina's event-planning career. Fairchild's grounds looked beautiful. The dock twinkled with lights, every pecan and oak tree on the property had candlelit Mason jars hanging from it, and in the middle of it all was a picnic area. She'd even had her first city dwellers check in as paying guests—her parents, Rosalie, and three couples she knew in New York, including a travel writer, a hedge fund chair with a soft spot for pediatrics, and a couple looking for the perfect destination wedding.

Cal and his crew had worked around the clock to make sure the inn was ready for guests and, as a surprise, built a dance floor with a stage for the band, which had kicked into high gear as soon as the sun went down. And, as the mayor was about to announce, they had made enough money to fund the new wing *and* to purchase two much-needed hyperbaric chambers.

As if that weren't enough, Brett had found a man in Savannah who specialized in antique glass. By using the leaded glass from the old broken-out windows in the servants' quarters, he had managed to patch the chandelier to where it looked better than new. Better because Brett had insisted that one of the stems be left broken.

The way the light caught the jagged glass made it look magical, he'd whispered last night while making love to her and showing her just how magical it could be.

Francesca Harrington stared past all the décor to the pen located at the side of the house and gasped. "Is that a pig pen?"

"It's a petting zoo." Josephina laughed, placing a hand on her mother's to stop the clacking of pearls, which had started the moment she'd arrived. Josephina bet that when the lamb, ducks, and two goats were delivered tomorrow, and the final coat of paint went on the mini–Fairchild House—new home to Mrs. Pearl and her opossum brood—her mother would bypass the gin and tonic she was sipping and go for straight gin. No tonic, no ice.

"The kids will love it," Charlotte chimed in. "A perfect distraction from days at the center."

The music slowed to a halt and the mayor made his way onstage. With The Sugar Ladies Baptist Choir taking positions behind him with their church robes swaying in time to the town anthem, he thanked the people of Sugar for pulling together and gave a heartfelt speech that brought out a hearty "Hallelujah" from the choir and made Josephina proud to call herself a resident of Sugar. Opening the envelope with the winning name, which had been selected by silent poll, the mayor chuckled, turned his gaze on Josephina, and spoke.

"Well, I'll be. By an overwhelming show of support, the name for the new wing at the Sugar Medical Center will be the Fairchild Pediatric Ward."

Josephina turned to Brett, his face blurring behind all her tears. "Did you have anything to do with this?"

"No, ma'am." He cupped her face, tracing her tears with the pads of his thumbs. "This mess has you and your aunt written all over it. It started when you waltzed into town in those shoes and that Yankee pride and ended when you refused to give up. That kind of strength and determination says Fairchild through and through. And what better name to give a children's ward than one that stands for living life balls-to-the-wall."

"You do like my shoes." Josephina wrapped her arms around Brett's neck.

"I love your shoes." He kissed her good and hard. "And I love you."

"I love you," she whispered back, sinking into him.

"I still say it was rigged," Hattie snapped.

Hattie made her way to the front porch, three gray heads bobbing in unison behind her, with the poor mayor in tow. "We raised more money than those Peaches! And you're gonna tell everybody." Hattie pointed to Charlotte, who blanched.

"Grandma," Cal sighed, pinching the bridge of his nose. "It doesn't matter who raised the most. It was raised, the town is happy, and the new wing will break ground next month."

"It matters when Darleen is claiming that the Peaches were the biggest donor."

"Well, Darleen was responsible for a large portion of the funds," Charlotte politely informed Hattie. "If you hadn't forced her to hand over the check she got from the tabloids for selling that story, I wouldn't have the money to hire the extra nursing students."

"Yeah, well now she's claiming that since she raised more, the Peaches get to head up this year's Miss Peach Pageant. She's even talking about lowering the age limit so her niece can participate."

"The more the merrier," Cal sighed.

"Glad you feel that way, seeing as Payton was talking about going out for it herself. Heard her gabbing to that yahoo football player with the pansy-ass tattoo down by the dock. He was particularly interested in the bathing-suit portion."

"Like hell!" In one fluid motion, Cal was over the deck's railing and hightailing it down toward the lake.

"Grandma, you know as well as I do that Miss Peach doesn't have a bathing-suit portion," Brett chided.

"How would you know?" Josephina smacked his chest lightly.

"Dated a few." He dropped a kiss on her nose and whispered, "But it's false advertising."

"How's that," she kissed him back.

"None of those Miss Peaches are as sweet as you."

The last thing Cal McGraw wants is for his daughter to win the Miss Sugar Peach Pageant. Swimsuit category? Over his dead body. So when he is drafted to join the committee, he hatches a plan to change the rules from the inside. But he never counted on co-chairing the committee with the wild and sensual Glory Mann . . .

Please see the next page
for a preview of *Sugar on Top*.

Chapter 1

Glory Gloria Mann had never been arrested before, just as she'd never had to spend the night in jail, so she wasn't sure of the exact protocol, but she knew bullshit when she heard it. And Deputy Gunther's excuses were starting to smell worse than her manure-crusted pants.

"I bet if you called over to the Sugar Country Club, they'd tell you Judge Holden is somewhere between the third and fourth hole," Glory said, pinning Deputy Gunther with a glare.

"The sheriff's on it, Miss Glory," Gunther said, shuffling nervously from foot to foot. He was built like a bull, only with puppy-dog eyes, a gentle smile, and a soft center. Glory had always liked him; he was one of the few football players who hadn't made her time at Sugar High miserable.

"So you said. Three hours ago." When he silently lowered his eyes to the floor, she added, "Come on, Gunther, I'm freezing and tired and you and I both know that the sheriff is just trying to mess with me."

His ploy was working. She was about two minutes from tears. The ugly kind.

She'd been arrested, booked, and locked in a concrete square. She hadn't eaten since her second break yesterday, or slept in over forty-eight hours, and her midterm, which she'd busted her butt studying for, had started over an hour ago—meaning the only way she was going to pass that class in time to apply for the Community Outreach Manager at Sugar Medical Center was if she aced her final.

Gunther looked from the empty front office back to her and the tips of his ears went pink. "I guess I could let you have another call. Just one, though. And you have to use this."

He dug through his pocket, handed her his cell, and Glory felt her heart tighten painfully.

"And call who," she mumbled softly. Not that it mattered. It was already too late.

Gunther's eyes darted to the floor again.

They both knew that the sheriff wanted to milk the situation, just as they both knew that whatever obscene bail he convinced the judge to set, neither Glory nor her grandma could afford it.

Her best friend, Brett, could afford it, and he'd pay it in a heartbeat, which was why, in her moment of desperation, she'd called him.

Too bad she remembered *after* she'd left a voice message that he was in California and that she'd promised herself never to put him in a position to choose between his best friends again. She was trying to keep her distance, give Brett and his new wife, Joie, the space they deserved as newlyweds.

Last year he'd added Sex-Stud YouTube sensation to his impressive credentials, a title that almost cost him his career as a professional golfer. The last thing he needed was more people whispering. And any time Glory so much as smiled at a man, people whispered.

"That's all right, Gunther." Glory tightened her arms around her bent legs and dropped her head to her knees. Her body ached to be back at home, in her own bed, with the covers pulled securely over her head—fast asleep.

"Can I at least get you a blanket? Maybe some hot coffee?"

"That'd be nice."

"All right, then. Sit tight."

An aching sadness tore through her chest and Glory didn't answer—couldn't—afraid of what might come out. She felt her tears coming closer to the surface and the last thing she needed to add to her night was a public pity party. But she was locked in a cell, facing a possible F on a test she was more than ready for. Her only crime being—she was too damn nice.

"I didn't steal the stupid tractor," she whispered to herself.

"I know you didn't, Miss Glory."

She slowly lifted her head, startled to see Gunther still standing there. And damn it if the tears didn't spill.

"Ah, don't cry." Gunther fumbled for his handkerchief. "The sheriff's not a bad guy. He, well, some people don't know how to let go."

Ain't that the truth?

Glory made her way to the cell door, took the offered hankie—a difficult task since Sheriff A-hole had insisted on keeping her cuffed—and wiped her eyes.

"Thanks. It's just been a really shitty night."

With a solemn nod he made his way toward the end of the corridor—toward freedom. Only he stopped in the doorway and turned back to face her.

"For the record, I never believed what everyone said about you and Coach Duncan. I was even planning on asking you to Homecoming back then. But then you transferred schools."

"I decided to homeschool," she corrected.

Actually, she'd made such a mess of her life that she'd quit. Not her education, just the school part.

Gunther shrugged. "Yeah, well, I would have still asked you."

Glory watched silently as he disappeared around the corner. What was she supposed to say? The guy who caught a seventy-yard pass in the middle of a thunderstorm but couldn't manage to pass basic algebra without cheat notes; the same guy whose only shot at getting out of Sugar was a football scholarship—which never happened because Damon Duncan resigned the week before playoffs—hadn't blamed her. Or at least thought enough of her to risk social annihilation so he could escort her to a stupid dance.

"Hey, Gunther."

He poked his head around the corner. "Yeah?"

"I would have gone." Glory cleared her throat. "To Homecoming. If you had asked, I would've gone with you." She gave him her sincerest smile. "Your wife is a lucky lady."

With a sheepish nod he was gone, the security door shutting with a resounding thud behind him. And Glory was alone. Really alone. Something she'd had thirty years to master, but never quite gotten the hang of.

She paced in front of the bars, feeling a little caged and a lot scared. She had been cuffed, fingerprinted, photographed, and processed, for God's sake. Glory Gloria Mann was a criminal with a record.

At least she and her mama had something more in common now. Not that she planned on seeing her mama anytime soon. If Julie-Marie Mann hadn't bothered to come see her daughter when she'd been suspended for "inappropriate relations" with an older man, she didn't think that a grand theft auto charge would do it either.

No matter how hard her life got, and senior year had been hell, her mama had never shown up. Not even to stand by her daughter's side when she was wrongly accused of having sex with a faculty member—when in reality all they'd ever done was kiss. She hadn't shown up when Glory had been bullied or teased or chose not to walk the stage with her classmates even though she graduated with honors. Nope, not once in the entire time that Glory's life was falling apart did her mama even call to see if she was all right.

A sniffle escaped as she walked back to the lone steel bunk at the far side of the cell and plopped down, the mattress expelling enough dust bunnies to give her acute asthma. Exhausted, she leaned against the concrete wall and closed her eyes, but her entire body shook as a cold chill seeped through her thin tank top and right into her soul. Glory was still soaked straight through from the summer storm. And wet undergarments and catnaps did not coexist. Not in Glory's world.

She had just given up hope of Gunther finding that blanket when the heavy metal door unlocked, startling Glory to semialert and bringing her to her feet. With a gracious smile, she walked to the front of the cell—and stopped short.

The door swung open and in walked Sheriff Duncan. He strode down the corridor, a ring of keys in one hand, a gun strapped to his hip, with a smile so smug it made her heart die a little.

She'd learned senior year that if she wanted to live peacefully in Sugar, avoiding people with the last name

Duncan was crucial—especially ones that had Sheriff in their title. It was scandalous when Damon Duncan, home town hero and Sugar's favorite football coach, lost his job for being involved with an underage student. That the offence happened at the Duncan Plantation during the Miss Peach Pageant, with a girl from the wrong side of the tracks, made it downright blasphemy.

Walking the school hallways after that was humiliating and terrifying. The nasty looks and even nastier comments were bad enough, and some of the students started the De-Peaching of a Miss Peach campaign, posting doctored photos of Glory around the hallways. Guys started giving Glory the wrong kind of attention. And one day while walking home she was propositioned by a truck full of pissed off jocks, who blamed her for the football team not making it to State, and Glory broke.

She wanted to graduate like everyone else, wear a cap and gown and make her grandmother proud, especially since Jelly-Lou had sacrificed so much to see that Glory got a good education and had choices in life. But the thought of walking across that stage, having her classmates shout cruel or embarrassing things in front of the one person who believed in her, was too much, so she quit. She let the Duncan's and the bullies take away something that she was proud of.

She glanced down at the cuffs cutting into her wrists and sighed. If she didn't get out of here soon, she'd miss another chance to prove that she was more than her last name. She only had a month left before she'd graduate nursing school and fulfill her dream of working as a registered nurse. And to do that she needed to get out of there and call her professor.

But that wasn't what inspired her sudden urge to make a

noose out of shoestrings and be done with it. No, what made her chest lodge itself painfully in her throat was that Jackson wasn't alone. He'd brought friends. Two of them, to be exact. Deputy Gunther and—she swallowed.

Oh, God! It couldn't be.

Being stuck in the slammer all alone was terrible. But this? This was so much worse. At least alone, there was no one to witness her humiliating moment. No one to pass judgment and suddenly wonder if she really was just like her mama. No one to shake his head and say, "What have you gotten yourself into this time, Glory?"

And when she said *no one* she specifically meant Cal McGraw.

Glory's heart pounded against her chest, so hard and fast she was afraid she might just pass out. As far as everyone else knew, her connection to Cal was nothing more than his being her best friend's older brother. Which was sadly true. But to Glory, Cal was much more. Always had been. Not that he knew that—or even if he did, that it would change things. She'd long ago given up hope that he would see in her what she saw in him.

Forever.

Panic welled up and she was mentally struggling to keep it together when his intense blue eyes locked with hers. She wasn't sure if it was a low-blood-sugar thing, since she hadn't eaten in nearly twenty hours, or if the huge lump in her stomach had slowly expanded its way to her throat, cutting off her air supply. But Glory knew that if this was karma, he packed one hell of a punch.

One look at the six-foot-plus wall of sexy contractor-for-hire encased in butt-hugging denim and high-octane testosterone making his way toward her cell and Glory knew that her day, which was already smothered in cow patties, was about to turn into a gigantic pile of 100 percent, grade-A shit.

* * *

"Looks like you made bail." Jackson sniffed the air and grimaced.

Brett owed Cal big-time. When his kid brother had called earlier that morning, asking him to post bail, Cal had no idea how it would screw with his day.

Glory was the last woman he wanted to see. She was a walking wet dream, and Cal wasn't interested in going there—ever. At least that's what his head said; his dick, on the other hand, gave up listening the second he saw her in that thin tank top that showed off every womanly curve she owned. Which was why he'd always kept his distance.

A hard thing to do when Gunther was huddling protectively at the cell door, making Cal wonder just how badly Glory had been treated. Jackson was all but smiling, and Glory looked as if she was one smart-mouthed comment shy of bursting into tears. Something he figured she'd done earlier, since she was sporting two faint tear tracks down her pale cheeks.

It was obvious from the way she was doing her best to ignore him that she wanted him there about as much as he did. Brett had his loyalties, but so did Cal. Another reason he should head out. He'd posted her bail, she was alive, and—

What else did Brett expect him to do?

But instead of excusing himself, he stood there, staring and wondering if A) she was wearing a bra, B) if so, what color it was, and C) how the hell a woman who looked like she'd been bathing in manure could look so damn good.

God, he needed help.

"What the sheriff was trying to say is that you're free to go, Miss Glory," Gunther corrected with a glower.

"Why don't you go make sure the paperwork is all filed properly, Deputy?" Jackson said.

"Seeing as how you forgot to mention that your daddy called, I figured I'd come in and tell her the good news myself," Gunther said to Jackson, before turning to face Glory and lowering his voice. "Mayor Duncan is dropping all charges. And I hope that you will accept our apology for the oversight in telling you. I know that last night was pretty awful."

Apparently not as awful as his statement, because Glory didn't move. Those big mossy green eyes of hers zeroed in on Gunther, wide and expectant, waiting—for what, Cal didn't know. From the way the deputy stood silently shifting his weight, he was as confused. Jackson just looked pissed.

"So, that means you're free," Jackson grumbled, turning the key. "For today anyway."

The cell door slid open and the clanging of metal echoed in the silent corridor, but Glory didn't move.

"How long?" she whispered, and that small catch in her voice did something to Cal's chest that had him sweating. She cleared her throat, threw her shoulders back, narrowed her gaze at Jackson, and tried again. "How long ago did he call to have me released?"

"About three hours ago," Jackson said.

"Three hours?" Glory tucked her arms under her chest and glared.

The movement pushed her breasts slightly up, answering questions A and B—no, and he was fucking toast—and proving what Cal had long suspected but diligently ignored: Glory Gloria Mann had one spectacular body. She had legs to her neck, a surplus of curves, and enough sex appeal to make Cal forget why he stayed away from women like her.

Not that he was interested—because women like Glory were tempting and tantalizing and a whole lot of trouble.

Serious trouble, Cal warned himself even as his eyes slipped over the length of her—incarcerated, coated in sludge, but damn near the most incredible woman he'd ever seen.

He forced his gaze away from her chest, and when they settled on her face he called himself a hundred kinds of bastard. Because the way her lips trembled, she was in desperate need of a champion in her corner.

Not your problem, buddy.

Cal had enough problems of his own without adding another woman to the equation, especially a woman who came with more baggage than he did, and who was a walking talking reminder of the kind of heartache that came with chasing wild. So he shoved his hands in his pockets and stomped down every protective instinct that gnawed at his gut.

Nope, his days of playing the shining knight to a beautiful lady were long over.

"The mayor said he figured that stealing his tractor was a prank gone bad. But then he found this in the parking bay. Right next to an empty bottle of moonshine." Gunther approached the open door and held out his hand. Resting in his palm was a single red poker chip with THE FAIRCHILD POKERS engraved in gold.

Cal looked at the ceiling and groaned.

"I've never known you to be a big gambler, Miss Glory."

Gunther also knew what everyone in that cell now knew. Cal's Grandma Hattie and her Bible-toting poker cronies had stolen Mrs. Kitty's tractor. Not Glory. She was just trying to put the Prowler back before things got out of hand. But why hadn't she just told the truth? They could have avoided this entire effed-up situation.

She strode out of the cell and, stopping in front of Jackson, held out her cuffed hands. "Take them off. Now."

"Your sentencing is Monday at nine," Jackson said, slipping the keys into the hole. He paused. "So don't think about taking a vacation between now and then."

"Sentencing?" Those gorgeous eyes went wide with confusion. "I thought Mayor Duncan dropped the charges."

"He did." Jackson smiled, a little too smugly for Cal's liking. "Against my advice. But there are still the resisting arrest and assaulting an officer charges to be dealt with."

"Assaulting an officer?" Cal laughed. He couldn't help it.

Glory was all of five-seven and a buck-twenty to Jackson's towering six-plus feet. With her dark hair pulled up into a ponytail and those flannel pajama bottoms, which were fuzzy and pink and kind of adorable, she looked more like a coed than a criminal. And the only thing her sleepy state and vulnerable eyes dealt Cal was a kick to the gut.

"You can't be serious," he heard himself say. "There is no way you're claiming that. And why the hell is she still cuffed?"

"Can, and am. What part of assaulting me and my men did you miss?" Jackson sounded betrayed. "And since I'm not easily swayed by a pretty face and neither is Judge Holden, I think these charges will hold."

"For Christ's sake, Jackson, just uncuff her so we can go." Jackson shot Cal a look, serious as hell and he knew just how Brett had felt all these years being stuck in the middle of this feud. "Look, I don't know about you all, but I have more important things to do than stand around arguing about a silly tractor that she may or may not have stolen."

"Right," Glory clipped off. His comment only seemed to make her more upset.

Jackson released her hands and as Cal watched Glory rub at her reddened wrists, a slow anger began to twist in his gut.

"I believe that Judge Holden will be swayed by the truth." Glory picked the chip out of Gunther's hand and settled on holding it when she realized she had no pockets. "And I happen to be an excellent poker player. So thank you for returning this."

And with that she strode toward the exit, her backside every bit as tantalizing as her front.

"Hold up, are you admitting to stealing my grandma's tractor?" Jackson said, hot on her trail.

"I'm not admitting to anything," Glory shot over her shoulder, her tone dripping with smart-ass. But Cal noticed that her hands were trembling as she pushed open the metal door—and it wasn't just from the cold. "Does it even matter? What is a grand theft auto compared to assaulting an officer, right?"

Chapter 2

May or may not have stolen, my ass," Glory mumbled as she yanked open yet another door. She stomped past the break room, past three glaring deputies, and—ignoring the steady drizzle—across the parking lot, not stopping until she reached the steel gate enclosing the Sheriff's Department's new parking area.

At eight feet high, with crossbars too small for a baby coon to squeeze through, the only way out was up. Glory stood on her tiptoes and reached to grip the top of the fence—crap! Make that twelve feet.

The light drizzle turned more end-of-summer storm, and she looked back at the closed door and swore. She had no phone, no way home, and no jacket.

Even worse, Glory thought, resting her head against the bars and letting out a stifled sniffle when she looked down and saw that her ducky galoshes were ruined, Jackson's little stunt had cost her the chance to graduate nursing school summa cum laude. He had probably even cost her her dream job.

Charlotte Holden, head of family medicine at Sugar Medical Center, had taken a chance on Glory, putting her recommendation behind Glory's proposal that, if approved by the hospital board, would make her the Community Outreach Manager for the soon-to-be built Fairchild Pediatric Ward. The position would be working directly under Charlotte, whom Glory admired and respected, and working with kids—which was what Glory wanted to spend her life doing. And although she was pretty sure that her current situation counted as an "excusable absence" for missing her exam, it wasn't as if she could call her professor and say, "Sorry I missed the second-most-important test of my life, but I was incarcerated for grand-theft auto and, oh, and I might have accidently assaulted an officer of the law with a peach-colored tractor."

Feeling helpless and out of options—no way was she going back inside to ask for a ride—Glory kicked the gate.

Still not satisfied, she hauled back her left boot and kicked the metal bars as hard as she could. The gate didn't even rattle, but managed to split the rubber, right up the duck's face and over the big toe.

"Stupid piece of shit!" she yelled as loud as she could, kicking it again.

A low masculine whistle made her stop midkick. "Assaulting an officer and now an innocent fence? I never took you for such a spitfire. Especially not in rubber ducky boots. Those come in steel-toe?"

Glory spun around, ready to show him just how painful her ducky boots could be, when she stopped. One look at Cal and everything inside of her went still and she felt like she was going to crumble right there.

Cal leaned back against the bumper of the sheriff's cruiser, one arm resting leisurely on the roof of the car, the other hung loosely from his belt loop, looking big and safe and bad-ass. He wore a MCGRAW'S CONSTRUCTION cap, a really warm-looking jacket, and that sexy grin, which always managed to make her heart do these silly little flips. The man looked so at home in his own skin it ticked her off even more.

"Apparently, it *may or may not* have pissed me off," Glory said, proud that her voice gave off the unaffected tone she'd mastered over the years.

Cal's smile died at her comment. His boots clicked on the pavement and he walked forward, not stopping until he was standing so close she could smell the rain on his skin. "I know you didn't steal Miss Kitty's tractor. Never for a second thought you did."

Glory felt her chest tighten and all she wanted to do was lean forward and disappear into his big, strong arms, just for a minute, to know what it was like to have someone to lean on. But she wasn't sure if he'd hold her back and she realized with a wrinkled nose and a sinking heart that if she could smell every ounce of yummy-macho-male on him then he could smell Mr. Ferguson's cows on her.

She stepped back and to the side, making him turn so he was standing upwind.

"Maybe you could have voiced that opinion a few minutes ago, while Jackson was twisting the rope for my public lynching."

Cal let out a tired sigh. "I was just trying to defuse the situation, remind everyone that this was all over some stupid tractor so we could get out of there."

"Really?" She said in a tone that translated into *bullshit*. "Because it seemed to me that you were reminding everyone that you are a bros-before-hoes kind of guy," Glory said, hating that her throat caught on the last few words.

She wasn't an idiot. She knew what everyone in town thought: that she had slept with an off-limits man—just like her mama. But the truth was, Glory and Damon had never made it past second base. Not that *that* made what she'd done any less wrong. He'd still been a teacher at her school, a judge in the pageant she was entered in, but he'd made Glory feel something that she'd never felt before—wanted.

Not in a sexual way; she'd never had a problem with that. She'd been fending off boys since she grew boobs in the sixth grade. But Damon had sought her out, taken an interest in her life and her dreams, told her how smart she was. Made her believe for the first time in her life that maybe she deserved what everyone else had.

As an adult looking back, Glory could see that he had taken advantage of a confused and lost girl. But at the time he'd made her feel as though she mattered, as though she wasn't just Julie-Marie's castoff, as though she wasn't a complete waste of space.

"Does it hurt?" Cal asked, reaching out to touch her wrists.

Shocked that Cal would try to touch her, since he'd clearly gone out of his way to avoid being near her over the years, she stepped back right before his fingers made contact.

Irritation tugged at his lips and he reached up to fiddle with the bill of his cap, cupping it in his palm and pulling it farther down on his head. The movement tugged his shirt up, giving her an unobstructed view of his flat stomach disappearing behind his button fly.

Oh, my...

She jerked her gaze up and off his more-than-impressive package, hoping it was raining too hard for him to notice her ogling. "It's fine."

Cal pushed up the bill of his hat, his intense blue eyes flickered with amusement and—*crap*! He'd noticed. "You sure, Boots? Because you're looking a little flushed there."

"Allergic reaction. Close proximity to assholes for extended periods of time tends to have that effect on me."

"So you're saying a ride to the hospital with me would only add to your discomfort."

It would, but not in the way he was implying.

"I don't need to go to the hospital, and—" She took in a deep breath and added, "You're not an asshole, Cal."

"That seemed painful for you to say."

Swallowing a big bite of humble pie, she looked him in the eye. "No, I mean it. I was so ticked I forgot to say thanks for coming down and bailing me out. I know you probably did it because Brett forced you to, but I appreciate it all the same. And you don't have to worry about me leaving town and costing you—"

"Five grand."

Glory gasped. "Five grand?"

There was no way she was leaving town, because there was no way she could afford to pay him back if she did. Then all of her earlier anger vanished, leaving behind a deep sense of gratitude. If he hadn't posted bail, she'd be calling Sugar County Jail her home until the sentencing. And based on how that went, maybe even longer.

"Judge Holden's a fair guy, Glory. You don't need to worry, Jackson was just trying to scare you," Cal said softly.

Glory looked at the shattered lights of the cruiser, the accordion hood, and she wasn't so sure.

"I'm not thinking of skipping town, if that's what you mean," she said. "But if it makes you feel any better, you can hold the keys to my car. It isn't worth five grand, but that way you know I can't leave."

"I don't need your keys, Glory, and I don't think you're a flight risk," Cal said, and the belief she heard in his voice made speaking hard.

"Okay, then. Thanks." She gave a silly little flap of the hand that she hoped came off like a wave and walked backward. Right into the gate.

Glory turned around and dropped her head to stare at her ruined boots. And just when she thought it couldn't get any worse, she felt a warm jacket slide over her shoulders. She opened her mouth to tell him that she was covered in shit and she would ruin his soft and fuzzy and incredible-smelling jacket, but instead a sob came out. Followed by another one and a mortifying snort. Until finally her entire body was shaking.

Large hands settled on her hips and slowly turned her until she was nestled in the most glorious chest she'd ever felt. Wanting to grab on but terrified of looking as desperate as she felt, Glory dug her fingers into the edges of the jacket, pulling it closed. She rested her cheek over his heart and tried to calm her breathing to match his steady beat.

And somewhere between his arms coming around her and feeling his lips press against the top of her head, Glory wondered if she would ever figure out how to become the kind of woman that good men, men like Cal, saw forever in.

Fall in Love with Forever Romance

LAST CHANCE FAMILY
BY HOPE RAMSAY

Mike Taggart may be a high roller in Las Vegas, but is he ready to take a gamble on love in Last Chance? Fans of Debbie Macomber, Robyn Carr, and Sherryl Woods will love this sassy and heartwarming story from *USA Today* bestselling author Hope Ramsay.

SUGAR'S TWICE
AS SWEET
BY MARINA ADAIR

Fans of Jill Shalvis, Rachel Gibson, and Carly Phillips will enjoy this sexy and sweet romance about a woman who's renovating her beloved grandmother's house—even though she doesn't know a nut from a bolt—and the bad boy who can't resist helping her...even as she steals his heart!

Fall in Love with Forever Romance

ALL FOR YOU
BY JESSICA SCOTT

Fans of JoAnn Ross and Brenda Novak will love this poignant and emotional military romance about a battle-scarred warrior who fears combat is the only escape from the demons that haunt him, and the woman determined to show him that the power of love can overcome anything.

DELIGHTFUL
BY ADRIANNE LEE

Pie shop manager Andrea Lovette always picks the bad boys, and no one is badder than TV producer Ice Erickksen. Andrea knows she needs to find a good family man, so why does this bad boy still seem like such a good idea? Fans of Robyn Carr and Sherryl Woods will eat this one up!

Fall in Love with Forever Romance

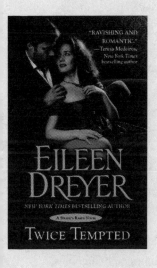

TWICE TEMPTED
BY EILEEN DREYER

As two sisters each discover love, *New York Times* bestselling author Eileen Dreyer delivers twice the fun in her newest of the Drake's Rakes Regency series, which will appeal to fans of Mary Balogh and Eloisa James.

A BRIDE FOR
THE SEASON
BY JENNIFER DELAMERE

Can a wallflower and a rake find happily ever after in each other's arms? Jennifer Delamere's Love's Grace trilogy comes to a stunning conclusion.

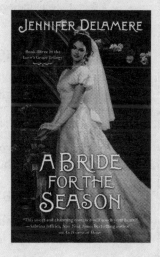

Find out more about Forever Romance!

Visit us at
www.hachettebookgroup.com/publishing_forever.aspx

Find us on Facebook
http://www.facebook.com/ForeverRomance

Follow us on Twitter
http://twitter.com/ForeverRomance

NEW AND UPCOMING TITLES

Each month we feature our new titles
and reader favorites.

CONTESTS AND GIVEAWAYS

We give away galleys, autographed copies,
and all kinds of exclusive items.

AUTHOR INFO

You'll find bios, articles, and links to personal websites
for all your favorite authors—and so much more.

GET SOCIAL

Connect with your favorite authors, editors, and
other Forever fans, and share what's important to you.

THE BUZZ

Sign up for our monthly romance newsletter,
and be the first to read all about it.